THE

LOVE

INTEREST

THE LOVE INTEREST

HELEN COMERFORD

BLOOMSBURY

LONDON OXFORD NEW YORK NEW DELHI SYDNEY

BLOOMSBURY YA
Bloomsbury Publishing Plc
50 Bedford Square, London WC1B 3DP, UK
29 Earlsfort Terrace, Dublin 2, Ireland

BLOOMSBURY, BLOOMSBURY YA and the Diana logo
are trademarks of Bloomsbury Publishing Plc

First published in Great Britain in 2024 by Bloomsbury Publishing Plc

A catalogue record for this book is available from the British Library

ISBN: PB: 978-1-5266-6758-8; eBook: 978-1-5266-6759-5;
ePDF: 978-1-5266-6760-1

2 4 6 8 10 9 7 5 3 1

Typeset by Westchester Publishing Services

Printed and bound in Great Britain by CPI Group (UK) Ltd, Croydon CR0 4YY

To find out more about our authors and books visit www.bloomsbury.com
and sign up for our newsletters

For the powerful women in my life,
especially my sister, Janine

HEROICS AND POWER AUTHORITY

POWERS

Because of the accelerated evolution of the planet (the EV),
there are more people with powers now than ever before.
We all know it is the law to register your power with the
Heroics and Power Authority. But sometimes people
need help to do the right thing.

Powers come in all shapes and sizes. They run in families.
If you see someone drain the lights from a room, they could
be a conduit, absorbing power like King Ron. If you see someone
fix a machine with a touch, they could be a technopath like
the Controller. If you see someone fly ... well, you get
the idea. Report their family today.

HELPING IS
HEROIC

In the wrong hands, powers
can be dangerous, even
weaker female ones.

Do your duty – report any
and all suspected powers
to the HPA. Registered
people will be helped,
tagged and protected.

EVOLVED
CREATURES

Be vigilant around nature. Keep
an eye out for EV creatures and
always remember:

BLUE

Blue eyes
Large body
Unusually aggressive
Evolved creature

To report suspected powers or EV disturbances

CALL 777

Help the HPA to Help You

CHAPTER 1

One day soon my town will need a hero. So it was written by the Diviner in the nineteenth century. And so it was also written by most of the shops in Nine Trees who have used the prophecy to decorate tea towels:

2024
In the sharp blue heat of truth
A hero will emerge
In the three of three of trees.
– The Diviner, 1880

'Look, they've got a new line of prophecy posters. What painting have they used?' I waggle a poster at my best friend, Joy. She tilts it to see past the bright lights of the Culture Complex foyer.

'*The Scream*, it's by Munch.' Joy scoops her brown hair

behind her ears. 'I think he painted it as a response to the Rocks Prophecy. You know, the one without a location, but with pelting rain and rumbling land ...'

'And slipping clay.' I hang the poster back in the little gift shop attached to the box office. 'I can see why he'd be stressed.' We drift into the line for cinema tickets. 'Did you see the £35 sticker? Who'd pay that much for a poster?'

'The tourists, Jenna Ray!' Joy grips my arm. 'Do you really need me to explain this to you?'

'N—'

'Imagine—' Joy lowers her voice, like she's presenting a horror podcast. 'You're on your way to the city, but hey, you're passing through pretty little doomed Nine Trees. Sure, a sexy new hero is going to turn up, but no one thinks waiting around for that to happen is a good idea. But! Maybe, you can risk stopping for a souvenir? You don't have time to shop around. You just want to grab a poster and get out before the disaster hits. Thirty-five pounds for a poster? Just buy it. You've already been here for too long and it'll be worth ten times more after Nine Trees has been wiped off the map.' She gives herself a shake. 'It's clever really. A disaster will strike this year and it's only spring. Imagine how much they'll be charging for souvenirs in November!'

'Oh, we'll all be dead by then.' I laugh and Joy laughs and then we both fall silent. I stare at some popcorn lying sadly on the floor and wince as someone steps on it.

'You girls seem worried.' A lady with grey curls joins the queue and smiles gently at us. 'Just because a new hero is coming doesn't mean there's going to be a huge disaster. I've seen them before, of course. I was a little girl when the power plant malfunctioned and King Ron first appeared.'

I nod politely and elbow Joy, who is rolling her eyes.

'But remember the Controller?' the lady continues. 'His emergence was simply—'

'Saving a cat that was stuck up a tree,' we chorus.

She nods, reaches into the pocket of her powder-pink duffel coat, hands me one of the council's *Carry On As Normal* pamphlets and wanders serenely away.

'Didn't you want to see a film?' Joy calls after her.

I flick the leaflet and decide against bringing up the other hero emergences, the ones with higher death tolls. 'I don't need this. My house is covered in them; Dad keeps bringing them home from work. You have it.' I drop the glossy paper into Joy's hands.

'Don't be rude.' She pushes it back.

We look at the pamphlet between us for a beat, then Joy jumps at me and tries to stuff it down the front of the oversized cardigan I borrowed from my sister. I bounce back, narrowly avoiding the man behind us. He tuts. Joy giggles.

'That lady wanted you to have it!' Joy thrusts it towards me.

'And I want *you* to have it.' I gently push her hands back. 'You're welcome.'

Joy opens the pamphlet and shakes her head in mock disbelief. 'You don't even want this lovely map of all the town's shelters?'

'No. I know where they are. They've been lit in neon since New Year's Eve.'

3

It's finally our turn at the ticket machine. My finger hovers over the screen. 'Did we want the seven o'clock showing of *All You Need Is Love: A Classic Love Story for the Modern Age*? Snappy title.'

Joy drapes herself mournfully across the machine and taps the seven o'clock option. 'Nick left for Portugal today.'

'Uh-huh.' I manage to catch both tickets as they shoot out of the machine.

'Portugal, Jenna. Portugal!'

I pass her a ticket and we wander towards the pick-and-mix stall.

'Is it even any safer in Portugal?' I love Joy, but I'm not sure I've got the energy to listen to Nick's holiday plans again. Maybe I can distract her with sweets?

'There was that whole thing with EV sharks along the coast, but the rustic mountain village Nick's mum chose to escape to will probably be extra safe.' She sighs, managing to infuse her breath with melancholy. 'Is it so wrong to want him and his lovely arms here, to die with me?'

I narrow my eyes at her. 'Shouldn't you want him to go on without you and live a long life filled with love and laughter?'

'Psssht. No.' Joy whacks my arm. 'I've got to wee.'

'I'll be here.'

Joy skips off towards the toilets and I perch on a polished metal bench on the outskirts of the cinema section and play with a curl of my Afro. Even though my feet are now glued to the tacky floor, the Culture Complex is my favourite place in Nine Trees.

It was built the same year as I was born and, for some reason, they decided it should look like a great big greenhouse. Ferns decorate the balcony that runs around the building; green tendrils droop down over signs for the cinema, the library behind me and the restaurant to my left. The front of the complex is made of hexagonal windows. A few wispy clouds drift through the bright spring-evening sky, but even inside the complex the air feels heavy, like there's a storm coming.

My breath catches as I exhale. Before anything bad can happen, I picture a boy with a dark blue swimming cap and a kind smile, water streaming off his strong shoulders as he lifts himself out of the water. Okorie Ogundipe. I don't want a boyfriend, but thinking about Okorie's humble smile when he inevitably wins his race is better than spiralling about our impending doom.

Focus on swimming; that's a more wholesome cure for panic. The feel of the water as I cut through it, the bubbles that stream past as I flip turn, the droplets of water on Okorie's chest after training. Feck. It's not OK to use him like this when I've never even had a proper conversation with him. I'm objectifying him, but he's keeping my heart steady and my lungs full, and it's not like he'll ever know.

'Your green cardigan is too big for you.' A small girl with red pigtails arrives at my lap, pursued by her horrified dad. 'It is pretty though, and I like the buttons because they have glitter on them.' She puts her hands on my knees and smiles up at me.

Frantically packing away the image of Okorie in his trunks, I blink and focus on the preschooler critiquing my style.

'Rosie! What did I tell you about touching strangers?' Her dad reaches for her and she dodges, her small hands still pinching the fabric of my jeans.

'It's OK.' I give her a closer look at one of the buttons. 'I'm glad you like it. It's the sparkly buttons that made me want to wear it.'

'Thank you.' The dad pushes his thick glasses up his nose.

'Green is my favourite colour.' Rosie leans on my lap and inserts her fingers into the baggy wool of the cardy.

'Rosie!' The dad drags Rosie off me. 'I'm so sorry!' He's gone crimson.

'You're pretty,' Rosie says as her dad pulls her away.

'Thank you!' I call after them.

Rosie is dragged through the foyer, past the central box office and towards the family restaurant. I chuckle as she breaks free and legs it for the ball pit. As Rosie's cry of triumph fades, a strange moment of quiet washes over the Culture Complex. There are still people in the busy foyer, but no one is talking. Perhaps they're thinking about the prophecy. I place my hands firmly on my lap to stop myself from fiddling with my fingers. The pink light filtering in through a passing cloud makes the golden-brown skin of my hands look almost silver, like I'm underwater.

'Ready to feel warm, fuzzy and like we'll never be able to love like they do in the movies?' Joy is back and clutching an enormous bucket of popcorn.

'Am I?!' I leap up to join her.

Walking into a cinema is one of my favourite things. We're

intentionally late, to miss the adverts, so it's dark when we push our way through the swing doors. It's gloriously disorientating, wandering up the sloped walkway into a cavern lit with images.

'Let me go on the aisle. I always need to pee,' Joy whispers, far too loud.

We settle in our seats and balance the popcorn on the armrest between us, ready to watch the romantic comedy. We thought it would be a good distraction, although I can already guess the plot:

Boy meets girl, they trade quirky banter and—

Oh look!

They have an unexpectedly deep connection.

   And oh wow!

   They share a life-affirming experience.

      But oh no!

      Something goes wrong and all hope is lost!

         Except it's not. By the end of the film they'll kiss in the rain

           or get married

             or something.

As the lead couple rescue a baby monkey together, my mind strays back to the prophecy. I picture a crack running up the middle of our cobbled high street, splitting the earth. A tree falls through the window of the bank and scatters its white blossoms over my trapped sister. I shake my head, but even Okorie won't displace the image of Dad, standing helpless at the council, as my town, my home, falls apart around him.

'Wait!' Joy shouts at the screen. 'Don't kiss your ex!'

My chair squeaks as I sink down and try to imagine the hero that the prophecy has foretold. He'll swoop in at the last moment and save the day. He'll be big, muscly, and have spectacular facial hair. It'll be like when King Ron appeared in the seventies; the hero will arrive and everyone I love will be fine.

'Well, obviously she saw them kissing. As if they'd all have the same dentist in LA. It's like a billion miles across.' Joy offers me some popcorn and then reaches over to stop my hands, which, I hadn't realised, had been going through a cycle of rubbing and clasping.

'Watch the film, Jenna,' she whispers. 'It'll help.'

I nod and put my head on Joy's shoulder to watch the leading lady cry over what could have been, and what definitely will be, by the end of the film.

'My bus is in two minutes,' Joy says as the credits roll and the lights fade up. Halfway into her coat she hesitates, even though we're at the end of the row and there are people waiting to get past.

'Don't worry, Ray. We'll be all right,' she says.

'Let's do something tomorrow,' I say confidently.

'Tomorrow.' She nods slightly too fast, hugs me, and legs it for her bus.

A band of pressure grows around my head as I make my way out of the cinema, and I pop into the bathroom to splash water on my face. The shock of the cold helps a bit, but the brown eyes gazing back at me from the mirror are still anxious.

Tomorrow, I'll wear my Afro in a side parting and borrow Megan's bronzer, which is the perfect colour to make my skin tone glow. Tomorrow I'll look powerful.

A deafening roll of thunder stops me as I step back into the foyer. Through the glass front of the complex, the dark sky is alive with flashes of light. Even though we're inside, my heart beats faster and I edge closer to the box office.

'A lightning storm.' An usher is waiting with a dustpan and brush. 'It's right on top of us.'

There's a loud buzz and the lights go out.

Gasps echo around the complex. As my eyes adjust to the soft glow of the emergency lighting, I can see the silhouettes of people moving; some heading to the automatic doors, others getting to their feet in the restaurant. There's another blinding flash and a crash of thunder which sounds like the complex has been hit by a tank.

'There's no way I'm going out there.' A man in a *King Ron* hoody leans on the box office next to me.

Has the complex just been hit by lightning? The alarm bells in my brain are jangling, but it's not like when I walk past a big group of people or speak in class. There's a pinch in the air irritating the back of my throat and making my eyes sting. I inhale deeply, hoping that I'm wrong, but the smell of smoke is unmistakeable.

CHAPTER 2

The fire alarm screeches into life, and I slip into a stream of people moving calmly towards the exits. Smoke tingles my nostrils and my eyes dart around the complex. I'm half expecting to see fire racing down the drooping ferns or bursting from the restaurant, but there's nothing. Just more and more people clogging up the foyer.

We're all trying to move towards the doors, but no one wants to go outside. How are there so many people here? No one has opened a fire exit yet and this press of bodies is growing tighter around me, pushing against my shoulders and back. Were all these people sitting on each other's laps in the cinema? I don't know if my heart is beating faster because I'm stuck in the growing pressure of this crowd or because I'm about to go out into a lightning storm.

My breath catches and then vanishes.

No.

Please not now.

'It's the EV. It's got to be,' a man leaning against my shoulder mutters. 'A crazy EV storm with the killer winds and super-charged lightning like the one that hit Salvador.'

Has an EV storm hit Nine Trees? My knuckles move in small circles, pressing into my chest. The crush is growing tighter around me, but all I can do is exhale and exhale again, hoping my lungs will fill. This can't happen now. We can't go out into an EV storm. We can't stay in the complex. I can't move. This breathlessness is how it started last time, when I knocked a pack of pasta with my bag and an aisle-full of people watched me trying to clean up the scattered fusilli. I can't have another panic attack. I can't hide in the loos here. There's a solid chance they're on fire.

I breathe out *two, three, four* as another flash illuminates the foyer and gasps ripple through the crowd. I exhale heavily again and focus on memories of the sea: the rise and fall of the waves, the push and pull of the tides, the storms I've watched pass over the horizon whilst I counted the forks of lightning from the safety of the beach. The pressure on my chest eases as the waves roll through my mind. The sea must be fierce tonight.

'Fire!'

My heart skips a beat, but I keep breathing.

'The library!'

11

I whip round to see a flickering orange light coming from the library. It's the books. The books are burning.

'*Please head to your closest exit. Help any women or children that you see.*'

The storm chooses that moment to illuminate the foyer again, but the shock of the crowd disappears under the screech of the alarm.

'Mother Earth,' I whisper, balling my hands into fists. If Joy was here, she'd make a joke or do something weird like pretend to be a game show host. '*Tonight on* How to Die: *Lightning storm or fire?!*' She'd probably do an American accent. '*Jenna Ray, the choice is yours ...*' I hope she didn't get caught out in this.

Sweat blurs my vision and the creeping smoke rubs out the detail of the foyer. I pull my T-shirt up around my mouth and breathe, sucking the air through the cotton, and step. Breathe and step. The crowd grows grey and faceless, but I'll still force myself to move as a part of it. Coughs cut through the air as the smoke thickens. I breathe and step.

'The fire is coming.' Someone behind me gasps and tries to squeeze past me, but I'm stuck too. There's nowhere for either of us to go, just a slow-moving wall of people. I won't have an attack. I suck in air faster and try not to imagine the rack of prophecy posters igniting.

'The fire is coming!'

A shoulder thuds into my back. I stagger and fall on to my knees, but I barely touch the sticky floor before I'm up again.

I'm coughing too now, hollowing out my lungs as if that will help me to fill them again.

People push past and stream out of the doors either side of the complex. I don't want to push back. I don't want to be the reason that someone else falls, but that means I find myself waiting at the centre of the front wall, at the end of both queues. Waiting patiently for my chance to live. It's weird that in all this smoke, noise and chaos, I can feel my hand shake as it holds my T-shirt over my mouth.

'The doors, they won't open!' a man in front of me shouts. Beneath the shriek of the alarm, I can hear him banging on the glass wall of the complex. There's so much smoke now that I can barely see, but I know from memory that this area doesn't have any exits.

My heart is beating hard enough to break. All my instincts are screaming at me to move, to run, that my path to the door is finally clear, but I hesitate.

The staff shouting directions at the exits are getting harder to hear, but how has this man missed the shining green lights of the fire exits?

'It's not a door!' I yell.

A gust of fresh air blows across my face as the last few people steam through the exits, and then it becomes unbearably hot. Staying in here is death. The flames reflect off the glass and makes it feel like we are surrounded.

'We need to go!' I scream at the man.

The alarm stops for a moment and even though my ears are ringing I catch the quiet sound of a child crying and choking. I wave my hands through the molten grey, searching for them. Their cries vanish beneath the alarm as it restarts. I can't find them.

This isn't real.

It must be a nightmare.

Please let this be a nightmare.

I wipe the sweat from my eyes and take another wheezing breath. I think everyone else might be out. Everyone except me, the banging man and the lost child.

I don't care if my body is drowning in its own terror; I can't leave without them. Staggering forward, I wave my hands through the thick smoke until they hit something soft and wet. I think I might have hit the kid in the face, but once I know where their small body is I take hold of their hand.

'Hey!' I shout, turning my attention to the man hammering on the glass. I try to grab him, but his panic has made him much stronger than me. I thump him on the back to get his attention.

'Hey!' I shove him ahead of me towards the watery slither of green in the distance and drag the child behind. I can't breathe, but we're almost there. The green is shining just ahead of us when the man spins round and shouts, 'Where is she?!'

He pushes past me, running back where we came from.

No! I think, but I don't have the breath left to say it. My free hand finds the bar on the fire exit. I open it and gulp in the sweet night air. The oxygen is dark and cold and feels as smooth as water as it rushes down my throat. I push the coughing child out on to the pavement and blink at her, trying to clear the smoke from my eyes. It's the little girl, Rosie.

I spin, hoping to see firefighters. Someone needs to go back in to get the man, her dad, but there's no one. There's no one else. A flash lights up the distant town. The storm has moved on, but everyone else must have rushed away from the huge metal frame of the glass Culture Complex. There are some people drifting through the car park, but there's no staff to be seen. The sirens howl on the other side of town. They're too far away. Everyone is too far away.

There's no one else.

Tears spring into my eyes. I'm his only chance. The only people who know that there's still someone inside are me and this small child.

What else can I do?

The cold air has done nothing to cool my red-hot panic, but I push Rosie towards the confusion of people in the car park, pull open the door and run back into the inferno.

It's so much worse. I don't know how it could have got so much worse in just a few seconds; it's dark, but so bright and hotter than anything I've ever known. I was wrong before; this is what death looks like. Sweat streams down my face and into my eyes. Every inch of me wants to run straight back out of that door, but I can't.

'Hey!' I shout, lurching forward with my arms out, hoping that I'll be able to feel the man because I can't see him, and I can't hear him this time either. I didn't know that fire could roar. I can't breathe. I fall to my knees. I'm not fast enough. I don't know why I thought I could do this.

'Get up, Jenna.' I push myself up and make it a couple of

15

steps before I'm back down on the floor. I need to find him, but there's no air. I can still see the green of the exit sign. I could still make it out, but I'm not leaving Rosie's dad in here to die.

'Hey.' I crawl forward. He's got to be here. He can't have got far. He might be right in front of me. Maybe we can both still go home. I reach out, but my fingers find nothing but smoke. My arms wobble and I collapse.

'Hey,' I whisper. I twist back to look for the exit, but the green is gone.

I always thought dying would make me sad, but I'm not. I'm angry. I'm angry at myself.

I can't save his life. I can't even save my own.

I'm choking.

My stinging eyes close.

Sweat rolls down my hot cheeks.

Everything is heavy.

Dad and Megan will be so
annoyed with me.

There's no more air.

There's just heat and the dark.

Fingers.

There are fingers gripping my cardy and pulling me up.

Hands.

A hand passes under my knees and another curls
around my shoulder.

Arms.

I'm in someone's arms.
I'm being held tight.
My joy is distant, but it's there.
I'm being rescued.

It's so hot higher up, but a moment later cool air surrounds me, rushes into my lungs and makes me cough. My eyes water as I prise them open. I can't make out much apart from the flames leaping from the Culture Complex.

'There's a man,' I croak.

'I'm on it,' the person holding me replies, and before I know what's happening, I am lying on the cold concrete of the car park and he's gone. My head is swimming, trying to make sense of the cool and the calm. Am I really OK?

A gust of wind blows my cardy against me and a violently coughing man is suddenly on the ground beside me.

'Daddy!'

17

I lurch up to see Rosie throw herself on her father. He's OK. I sag with relief and ease myself back on to the ground. My eyelids close, but fire still dances across my vision as I draw another deep, cool breath into my body. It must have rained during the film. The damp is soaking up through my clothes to soothe my baking back.

'Hi.' The energetic voice above me sounds more like someone at a party than a disaster. I force my eyes open to find the person who rescued me standing over me.

Tight, my sluggish brain comments. His black-and-red uniform is tight enough to show off every muscle he has.

Dimples. The young face gazing down at me has dark hair, dark eyes and dimples.

Kissable. His lips are pulled into a smile. They look soft.

Pose. His clenched fists are on his hips and the flames from the Culture Complex leap into the air behind him.

Mother Earth.

It's him.

I frantically blink away all thoughts of sculpted muscles and kissable lips.

I've just been rescued by the brand-new hero.

'I like your cardigan,' he says.

It's the hero! I've never been up close to a hero before, but it's not as intimidating as I'd have imagined. I wipe my streaming eyes. It's hard to tell from the ground, but he doesn't look like a huge and muscly super-strength type. He's slim, and he's young. He looks the same sort of age as me.

The hero rubs a shoe against his calf. His hands drift past

18

his thighs as if he's looking for pockets that aren't there and then he clasps them in front of him. We're all waiting for him to go and rescue someone else, but he's still staring at me. 'This is awesome, right? You're my number one.' He's smiling at me.

The words that he's saying sound like English, but nothing is making sense. Luckily my own personal hero, Rosie, has recovered enough to interrogate him.

'Are you a hero?' She edges closer to the boy. 'You don't look very old. But are you old? Are you thirty?' Rosie reaches for his utility belt and the hero is suddenly on the other side of me without seeming to move.

'Um, I'm not thirty. But I'm definitely an adult now.'

I blink and try to get my brain in gear. Did he just teleport? Or is he super-fast? That would make sense with how quickly he was able to find Rosie's dad. He seems nervous; his deep brown eyes keep flicking back to me as if he needs something from me. Does he need something from me? Should I be doing something other than lying here sweating?

'What's your name?' I manage.

'Well, they said I'd figure out my name on my first mission, so I guess I'm Ember,' he answers enthusiastically. He's British, but his voice has got a softness to it that I can't place.

The Culture Complex is blazing on the other side of the car park, but the sirens are getting closer, and there hasn't been a flash in a while. The storm is over and now we deal with the fallout. At least the distant chatter of the crowd is still subdued. They haven't noticed the hero yet.

19

The hero who is looking down at me with the weirdest expression.

Did my jeans burn off? I subtly glance down and exhale when I see all my clothes are still there. Why is he still looking at me?

'You think it's all right?' he asks.

'What?' I manage before another coughing fit consumes me.

'Ember,' he repeats when I've finished. 'Is it a good name?'

Rosie's dad shuffles closer to us.

'Thank you,' the dad manages.

'You're welcome, sir,' Ember replies.

Rosie comes over to me, and without saying a word sits down and leans on me.

'But seriously—' Ember starts. 'Wait, what's your name?'

'My name?' Why does he care what my name is?

'Tell him your name,' Rosie prompts.

'Jenna.'

'Jenna.' Ember nods as if he approves. 'How old are you?'

'Seventeen.' I clench my lips shut. That was a strange question. I don't want to give this hero any more of my personal details.

'Jenna.' He crouches beside me. 'What do you think of Ember as my hero name?'

Several responses surge towards my mouth, but *Why do you care what I think?* and *Shouldn't you be saving people?* are beaten by—

'It's not great, Ember.'

His face falls and I immediately feel guilty.

'Oh. I thought, you know, it's like fire but more, er, mystical.'

He waggles his fingers. There's a loud crack from the complex and the flames get even brighter, blazing almost white in the smoky sky.

'It's a terrible name for a hero, Ember,' Rosie's dad croaks.

'Oh.' Ember's forehead creases softly as he frowns at me. 'What do you think it should be?'

'Maybe Blaze?' It comes out before I've had a chance to think, and his eyes widen. Have I insulted him? Is Blaze actually an insult and I never realised?

'Blaze …' he says slowly.

'Sorry,' I start.

'Blaze!' He jumps up. 'It's perfect! And you thought of it! You of all people! Blaze! Hi, I'm Blaze. The Blaze? No, just Blaze. Hi.'

'Excuse me, Mr Blaze?' Rosie's dad says. 'It looks like the town is on fire?'

'It *is* on fire!' Blaze nods confidently. 'I am absolutely on that!'

He winks at me and then he steps into the air and shoots into the sky.

'Wow.' Rosie peers past my cardy.

My insides feel weird. Maybe it's because he winked at me. Why would a hero wink at me? Maybe it was a wink for everyone. Can winks be for everyone? And why did he just say *you of all people*? What did that mean? Maybe he's got me confused with someone else.

He disappears in the smoke rising from the high street. There's so much of it! I push myself up, and Rosie rises with me. I can't see how far the fire has spread. Has it got to our street? If this really is the prophecy, will there be any of Nine Trees left standing in the morning?

There's another crash from the complex and my head whips round to take in the shuddering building. 'I think we should move away from the—'

And then the Culture Complex explodes.

London Reels After Soft Prophecy

River Times, 25th June 1999

1999
A hero will emerge
West of the River Thames
Where life hangs in the balance
Amongst the oak leaves

The world is in turmoil today as London's Oak Leaves prophecy was revealed to refer to a tabby cat called Mr Onion. Mr Onion was rescued from the highest branches of his neighbourhood oak tree by a new hero, who has chosen the title the Controller.

The rescue itself was impressive. The Controller used his technopathic abilities to turn his gadget pack into a hoverboard. But his emergence leaves London authorities frustrated at the millions wasted on shelters and safety precautions.

'I know we should all be grateful to the Diviner,' said paramedic Gillian Cole, 46. 'But it's like this was her idea of a joke.'

The emergence has also left unanswered questions about the Controller and the direction his heroic path will take. With no humans rescued, there is no significant 'first' from his prophesised emergence – the person who often goes on to play a pivotal role in the hero's life as a friend, a sidekick, or even a Love Interest.

As Mr Onion was handed back to his owner, Victor Tim, 84, there were several quips about a possible octogenarian sidekick. However, with Mr Onion safely back in his basket, Victor Tim did not hesitate to dismiss the press and the world's newest hero.

There will no doubt be parties tonight on the streets of London as the city celebrates a deathless prophecy, but we are left wondering what course the Controller's future could take.

CHAPTER 3

An unfamiliar rattle invades the dark space between dreams and wakefulness. A trolley is out there somewhere. There are people too, passing in waves of chatter and sighs. Are they the sounds of a dream I've already forgotten? The waking world pulls me upwards, but Mum appears and holds out her hand.

'Want to keep dreaming, Jen-bear?' she asks. 'I've got something to show you.'

I nod. If I can be with her, I'd stay asleep forever.

'OK, baby.' The dark is lit by rays of sun and Mum steers me into our bright kitchen. She smooths out a set of blueprints on the dining table and the gem on her bracelet flashes green across her face. 'It's a smart bed. It can tell when the user needs something. See, here is a pad that measures your oxygen, and this sensor here will tell their doctor if they're stressed. I'm making it for hurt heroes.' The paper ripples as a breeze makes its way in through the open window. 'Just look.' Mum has her

24

hand on my back. She would always put her hand on my back when she showed me her work.

My throat is burning.

'Mum, I don't feel well.' I glance away from her work and towards our dripping tap.

With a rustle of paper, Mum gathers up her plans and walks out of the back door.

I don't try and call her back.

It never works.

I don't want to stay here, but I know waking up will bring a whole new type of pain. With a last drip from the tap, the dream fades, leaving nothing but a familiar pang of sadness. My throat is dry and, somehow, so are my lungs. My eyelids feel like they've been glued shut.

'She's waking up.' Megan's voice is hushed, which is odd. My sister has never been one for the gentle 'Good morning', preferring instead to shout 'Get up!' at me on her way to the bathroom. I inch my fingers across the bed, hoping to find my water bottle. My sheets feel wrong; they're stiff and they smell like soap.

'Jenna?' Dad says.

Megan and Dad swim into view as I manage to get my eyes open. They are sitting either side of me in plastic chairs. This feels strange until I realise that we're all in a tiny hospital room. The night before crashes back into my mind: the heat of the fire, Blaze, the explosion. Did I die?

Two doctors pass the closed door, talking loudly about stool samples. This is enough to convince me that I'm still alive.

'How are you?' Dad asks. He's sitting in front of the window. The sunlight streaming in makes me grasp at the memory of my dream, but it's already gone, so I focus my prickling eyes on Dad instead. He's dressed for work, with the top button of his neat pale blue shirt undone. He normally looks much younger than his age and shaves away any grey hairs that dare to grow on his smooth pale head. My chest aches as I notice a grey fuzz in the morning light. Today he looks every one of his forty-eight years. 'Jenna?' he says. 'How do you feel?'

It feels like I've been wiped out by a wave of molten sand, but telling Dad that might age him even more. I open my mouth to say something reassuring and realise I won't be able to do more than cough until I have some water.

'You should drink.' Megan presses the bed's remote and passes me a squidgy plastic cup as I slowly rise to a sitting position. The expression on her face is much softer than I'm used to. She's wearing a big red jumper over her leggings and her chunky box braids are tied back with one of her headwraps. I drain the cool water, feeling each refreshing particle as it's absorbed by my parched body, and look around the small white room.

'You got this cute little private room for some reason.' Megan follows my eye to a painting of Nine Trees's harbour that's hung next to the TV. 'Proper five-star treatment, although you were passed out for most of it. Nice little silver lining to the town burning down though.'

'Megan!' Dad looks appalled.

'An upgrade is an upgrade, Dad.'

If Megan is making jokes about the town burning down,

26

maybe there weren't too many casualties? My forehead creases and I feel something stuck just below my hairline. I gently touch the bandage, causing a small stab of pain. My arm hurts too; it's laced with cream-covered scratches. I remember the rush of heat and glass as the Culture Complex exploded.

'There was a little girl,' I say, and they wince. I can't blame them. It sounds like someone has replaced my vocal cords with sandpaper.

'I don't know if she's here, darling. But I do know that no one died last night, no one at all. We were all so lucky.' Dad reaches for me but drops his hand, like he's afraid to touch me.

I hold out my arms and he shuffles over to give me a hug. My dad is always gentle, but now he embraces me like I'm made of glass. Megan gets involved and holds us both far too hard.

'Ow!' I chuckle as they spring back.

Someone must sit on the remote control because the TV that had been silently playing the news in the corner pipes up.

'—was struck by lightning multiple times—' The polished news anchor, Linda Morden, coughs, and I reach for my water in sympathy. I can't imagine having cameras trained on me after a night like last night. 'Excuse me. It was a smoky night for a lot of us.' Linda looks down at her notes and continues. 'The severity of the storm has been attributed to the EV – the accelerated evolution of the Earth, that is causing an increasing number of weather events, powered people and animal attacks. Luckily our new hero, foretold by the Diviner, emerged to save the day.'

A picture of the boy who saved me fills the screen and I get a proper look at his dark flicky hair, deep brown eyes and dimples. He's smiling and the background is artfully out of focus. It's the type of photo you'd find in a magazine. He looks too perfect, it's like he's not a real person.

Dad frowns at the screen. 'How old is that kid?' He raises the remote to mute the story, but Megan bats his hand down as the hospital appears.

'*Sydney Jones is on the scene, coming to you live from Nine Trees Infirmary with the latest.*' The anchor smiles at the camera for a beat too long as we switch over to the reporter.

'*Thanks, Linda.*' Sydney appears, blocking the entrance to A&E and looking suitably serious in a designer raincoat.

'Those two hate each other,' Megan whispers. 'It's such good TV.'

Dad pointedly turns up the volume.

'*A cat. A listed pub. A cinema-cum-library-cum-restaurant. A bus full of innocent people. What do they have in common?*' Sydney leans slightly to the side as paramedics rush past. '*They were all rescued last night by a man—*'

'Boy,' Dad mutters.

'Shhh!' Megan says.

'*—sudden appearance meant the difference between life and a fiery death for many residents of Nine Trees.*'

'Blaze,' I croak. I still can't believe he wanted to call himself Ember.

Sydney cuts short her dramatic pause and clutches her ear. '*And we've got breaking news! Our source at the council has revealed that the name of this hero is Blaze! A truly fascinating choice of—*'

'*Thanks, Sydney.*' Linda is back, relegating Sydney to a corner of the screen, where she looks furious. Megan bursts out laughing as Linda continues. '*We can confirm that the name of our new hero is Blaze. There has been a lot of speculation over what the hero might call himself in the lead-up to the prophecy—*'

'You already knew his name?' Dad asks.

I nod, reluctant to use my voice.

'Did you meet him?'

Megan cuts in. 'We don't have to do this now. She can barely talk.'

'*And here to talk to about lightning striking last night –*' Linda gives a conspiratorial grin – '*is national treasure and head of the Heroics and Power Authority, our HPA, King Ron.*'

Linda beams as the screen switches to a double shot of her and her guest. King Ron, the heroes' hero. He looks impeccable, as always, with a precise side parting, neat white beard and blue pocket square poking out of his suit jacket. He is the reason people my age know what a pocket square is.

Even though the rest of the nation adores him, there's always the same sound in our house when King Ron comes on TV. It's a combination of Dad exhaling softly and Megan tutting as loud as she possibly can. It sounds like the brakes on a roller coaster. I'm not sure what's more annoying, King Ron's cheesy charm or my family's reaction to it.

They normally wheel him out to talk about prophecies or foreign affairs, and even though Dad is constantly muttering about the dodgy dealings of the HPA that the council have to

29

manage, it's weird to see King Ron on TV to talk about something that I was involved in.

'King Ron, it's a pleasure to have you with us.'

'It's a pleasure to be here, Linda.' He gazes at her above his steepled fingers. 'And I must say, Linda, despite the turmoil of the night you look as bewitching as ever.'

'Keep it together, Linda,' Megan mutters as the anchor giggles.

'Well, I … well, yes,' Linda manages. 'Yes. There's almost too much to talk to you about, King Ron. We will of course cover the news that the Nine Trees prophecy of the last Diviner has now passed, but let's start with the hot topic: Blaze. What can you tell us about him? Where is our new hero from?'

'I'm not at liberty to divulge too much. But, Linda, it's been over two decades since I hung up my cape to take over the running of our HPA, and of course our other hero, the Controller, has been missing for almost as long. It feels good to finally have another British hero.'

Linda looks so excited she might be about to vibrate off her chair. 'Another exclusive; our new hero, Blaze, is homegrown! Eyewitnesses have confirmed that he has the powers of super-speed and flight. Is he from one of the families we know produces powered individuals?'

'Shall I draw his family tree?' Ron chuckles. 'What can I say? One set of Blaze's grandparents are from a respected powered family in China. The other side of his family is British, with a smattering of powers through the generations. Blaze is a very special young man.'

There's a pause as Linda waits for him to continue, then her face crumples into a look of frustration mixed with adoration when she realises he's done. *'Is there nothing else you can tell us, King Ron?'*

'It's just Ron King now, I'm not a hero any more.' He gives her a wink and Megan mimes throwing up.

'I think this country will always see you as a hero,' Linda replies.

'Too kind, Linda.'

'I sent you a link to his last opinion piece in the *National*, didn't I?' Megan turns to me, eyes burning with her familiar righteous outrage. '*"The compassion of women. Why female powers are weaker."* Compassion? I'll tell him where he can shove my compassion. I honestly don't know how any woman can bear to speak to that patriarchal ball bag. You just keep repeating her name until she loves you, eh, Ron? Oh, Linda, Linda, Linda, Linda!"

'Shhh!' Dad snaps.

'I suppose what I can talk about are Blaze's heroics.' Ron leans towards the camera. *'At just eighteen, he is our youngest ever hero, but he still rescued twenty-eight people last night and the aid he gave to our valiant fire service saved even more homes and businesses. If you'll excuse the pun, Linda, the kid was on fire.'*

My family sighs.

'But maybe we should look at a different kind of spark.' Ron lingers over the word and Linda giggles obediently. *'Let's talk about—'*

Mother Earth.

I'm on TV.

A picture of me has appeared in a little square between Ron and Linda. It's my school photo from last year. I hate it. I'd decided to try liquid eyeliner for the first time, and it had smudged. Moments before a photo is not the best time to discover that tissue and water won't get that stuff off. My eyes look sort of smoky, which I'd been going for, but also quite red, like they're full of make-up.

This doesn't make sense.

Why is my picture on the screen? Does the hospital have a new feature where it shows each person their worst photo … on the news …?

'You're on TV!' Megan yells.

Dad fumbles with the remote and accidentally turns the volume up to full.

'… *Blaze rescued* …' Linda shouts.

I inhale too fast and choke on a lungful of air.

The TV is muted. 'Mother Earth!' Dad tries to turn the sound back on and changes the channel.

'Dad!' Megan snatches it off him and brings back Ron at a normal volume.

'… *the first person that Blaze rescued. He plucked her out of the flames of the burning Culture Complex.*'

'*Your Love Interest, Kate, wasn't she the first person that you rescued?*' Linda asks.

Ron nods. '*When I absorbed the power of that critical nuclear power plant, my Kate was the on-call technician, and I'll tell you, Linda, looking into the eyes of that first person you save is*

32

something special. Zhànshì pulled his Xiu out of a landslide at the start of his journey. The Sheriff first appeared to rescue his Nancy. I'm not saying that Jenna Ray from Nine Trees is Blaze's true love, but they're similar ages and, I'll tell you this, Linda, he can't stop talking about her.'

Dad's eyes are wide, mirroring my own shock. Blaze had said *'You're my number one'*. Evidently, what he meant was – *You're the first person I rescued, get ready for a whole world of madness.* He'd been acting strange. Was he trying desperately to fall in love with me whilst I lay sweating on the concrete?

'What is happening?' Megan whispers.

My heart is thudding so hard I'm worried it might break out of my chest and hit my sister in the face. This shouldn't be happening to me. Sporty, secretly anxious, not remotely interested in a relationship, Jenna Ray is not someone who people fancy. She's not available – I'm not available. No one gazes at me the way that Linda is gazing at Ron and it's never bothered me. I don't need to sneak off behind the maths block with a boy or have dramatic arguments in public. I've got better things to do. Like whatever I want because I'm single. And I like it that way.

I can't do this. I can't have all these people looking at me and talking about me. Why is this happening to me? Why am I on national TV?

'We've got Sydney Jones at the hospital. Perhaps we'll even be able to get Jenna Ray's side of the story. Until then, with the Nine Trees prophecy out of the way, we should all now be focusing on the search for the next Diviner—' Linda turns back to Ron and suddenly she's mouthing again.

Dad tosses the remote down. 'You were the first person he rescued?'

I shrug again. My throat aches. This is awful, so awful, and whatever I say next is going to set them both off. Dad is on the edge of a stress spiral and Megan has gone a strange shade of red.

They're staring at me.

I don't want to talk.

My voice is too weak to say what I want to say.

I open my mouth.

I close my mouth.

I cough.

'THIS!' Megan yells. **'This is exactly the problem with heroes, the HPA, and that chauvinist dinosaur, King knobbing Ron.'** She's off on a stellar rant. It's quite a lot louder than usual. **'The whole "first" thing is completely inappropriate too. It has such sexual connotations.'**

My cheeks heat as Megan shouts about sex and I glance at Dad. He's not listening to her. He's ranting too.

'... and I don't understand exactly who gave them permission to broadcast my daughter ...'

'... the last thing we need is something else reinforcing the belief

that this kind of interaction will some-how fundamentally change who a woman is …'

'… I understand that he saved her life and of course I'm grateful, but heroism shouldn't be transactional …'

'… part of this broken patriarchal system. How DARE they try to sweep my sister up in their knobbery …'

'… not them. Not the HPA. Not after everything that happened. This is not happening … You have no idea what they're capable of.'

'Did he even ask you?'

'Did you agree to any of this?'

It's gone quiet.

They're both looking at me again and it takes me a second to detangle their rage and find the questions they just asked.

I want to shout too, but my voice isn't working. 'No!' I manage.

'Of course!'

'This isn't happening!'

There's a knock on the door. 'Hi, Jenna, they said this was your room. It's Sydney Jones, *on the scene.*'

We all stare at the door. The handle wobbles, like Sydney's manicured hand is resting on the other side.

'Sydney Jones, from the Global News?'

I can't feel my heart any more, I think it's stopped.

'We want to hear all about your rescue, Jenna, in your own words.'

Even if I had a voice, I couldn't talk to her. If we invite her and the cameras in, the whole country is going to watch me have a panic attack.

'We all want to hear about your first impression of Blaze.'

Dad puts a hand on my shoulder, and I realise that I've been shaking my head.

'It's OK. I'll tell them to go away,' he says.

I nod.

'I'll tell them that you can't talk—'

I nod again.

'And that you've got no interest in being involved with this hero in any capacity.'

I nod decisively. It doesn't matter how tight he held me when he rescued me. I'm not interested. I don't want a relationship, especially one that will make me the heeled bait that's dangled off a cliff or the star of my own reality TV show.

I've spent a lifetime being trained to recognise what the HPA do to women. They chew them up and spit them out. I won't be a Love Interest. Not now, not ever. Blaze needs to find himself another girl.

CHAPTER 4

Jenna is grateful to Blaze for saving her life.
We all are.
But she has no interest in continuing a relationship,
in any capacity, with the hero.
She needs time to heal from this traumatic
experience.
Please give her, and our family, space.

Those words are everywhere.

They were on the news seconds after they'd come out of Dad's mouth, written between oversized quotation marks and set against a background of broken hearts. They were being analysed on the radio this morning before I managed to switch it off. And they are swirling round my head, mixing with the memory of smoke, and making my stomach churn as I walk towards town.

A few white petals drift past as I hop over a clogged-up drain and the words are there as I land.

Jenna is grateful to Blaze for saving her life ...

Of course I'm grateful, but every time I hear a DJ laughing about '*overprotective fathers!*' or a soft-voiced academic discussing how long it takes to heal from the trauma of almost dying in a fire, there's a part of me that wants to push Blaze off a pier.

I don't want to be Blaze's magical first.

I need everyone to stop talking about me.

I am not going to be a Love Interest.

This end of the high street seems quiet, but my heart still hammers as I step on to the cobbles. After sneaking out of the hospital with Dad and Megan last night, this is the first time I've been out in public. Megan wanted me to call in sick, but Mr George is trigger happy when it comes to firing staff and I'm saving for university.

Turns out I needn't have worried. Nine Trees town centre is normally a melee of bands, buskers and screaming kids, but today it's quiet. Particles of soot hang in the air, and beyond the hazard tape, there's a black trail of destruction where the fire raced from shop to shop.

... no interest in continuing a relationship, in any capacity ...

If everyone was excited about Blaze having a new *friend*, maybe I could have joined him for a milkshake, but I'm a girl. Being Blaze's friend was never an option. They want Jenna Ray, a Love Interest. They want to take my future and turn it into

39

something filled with danger, heroes, villains and, worst of all, cameras.

I crunch across the shattered window of Nine Cheese, the former jewel of the high street, which is now a burned-out husk. Perhaps the window was smashed by a wave of molten cheese. I wonder how Blaze would deal with that. Maybe he'd use his super-speed to catch it all in a fondue pot. It's OK, Nine Trees, Blaze is here, and he's got enough cheese for everyone …

As the high street curves up towards the Harbour Bridge, the sound of the waves grows to a comforting roar. The news had said that the harbourside fared better than the centre of town and, stepping on to the wide harbour path, I can see what that means. The businesses along here, the dainty sets of tables and chairs, the shops on the opposite side of the harbour, even the bunting, were untouched by the fire. They were all saved by Blaze.

Blaze.

Should I have immediately fallen in love with his perfect face? Am I the only girl in the world who would kind of hate the hero who rescued her? Maybe Blaze can blur off and rescue someone who's interested in talking to reporters and staring deeply into his eyes. I can become the first *first* who didn't matter, and everything can go back to normal.

A seagull screams at me from the railing overlooking the harbour and I automatically check its eyes. They're pale-yellow orbs with a black dot in the centre. It's just a normal, noisy seagull on the hunt for chips. I raise my eyebrows at it as I skirt the picnic benches that belong to Nine Teas Cafe.

The salt on the breeze makes my tongue tingle and I stop to

stare at the water. Even though it's cloudy, it's a beautiful day. Out at sea the peaks of the waves are fluffy white, and people are dotted along the piers and taking photos of the West Breakwater Lighthouse. Everyone is enjoying our new safety, like me. There's even someone wandering around the closed East Breakwater Lighthouse.

Everyone is fine.

Like me.

The prophecy has happened, and my family are safe. We've said clearly that I don't want to be a Love Interest. It doesn't matter that my arms still sting and there's a twist in my gut that won't go away. If I believe I am fine, I can be fine, just like everyone else.

Joy is unlocking the shop as I arrive and looks too cuddly in her puffy pink jacket.

'Hi!' I grab her in an attack hug.

'Jenna!' She breaks free and spins to grab my face. 'How are you?'

'I'm fine. I know I sound awful, but it doesn't hurt to talk any more. I can't believe you missed all of the—' I mime a lightning strike and make the sound of an explosion. 'I'm glad you got home safely.'

Lighthouse Souvenirs is a surprisingly big shop crammed full of gifts and postcards. It always smells a bit fishy because of the mussel stall next door. I scoot past Joy and flick the lights on. The bandage on my head looms at me from the mirror above the door.

Joy follows me through the shop to the tiny till area behind the fishing nets and switches on the radio.

'OK, enough about Diviner dread and our unknown future,' an enthusiastic voice shouts. 'Let's get on to Jenna Ray. We've had loads of you messaging in and lots of you thinking along the same lines as Terri from Cumbria, who says, "Of course Jenna isn't ready for a relationship after an experience like that. Everyone needs to step back and give her time to come to terms with her new life."'

Whack! I hit the radio off so hard I've probably broken it.

'Jenna—' Joy starts, but Joy 'Love Is Everything' Jusic's opinion on the whole Blaze thing is even less welcome than Terri from Cumbria's.

'I can't believe Mr George wanted to open today, I don't know what tourists he's expecting in Nine Trees or who else could possibly want to buy a fridge magnet, but good to get back to normal, isn't it?' I clear my throat. My words are claggy, like they're covered in soot. 'The pool didn't burn down, thank the skies. I was supposed to be training in open water today, but Megan said I should go somewhere with a lifeguard because my lungs are still recovering. I'll head over later. I can always hide under the water if people are being weird. So, we're reducing the prophecy merch today?'

'Jenna.' Joy's hand is over mine. 'Are you OK? Should you be here? You look pretty fragile.'

'I'm fine!' I say cheerfully.

She narrows her eyes at me. 'You almost died. That kind of trauma doesn't just go away.'

'I don't know what to tell you. I've recovered.' I grab the pricing gun and reduce her nose to 50p. 'Boop.'

42

'And what about this whole Blaze thing?' She peels the price tag off her face. 'That's intense. Being the first person he rescued makes it special, right? They're saying you could be his Love Interest.'

I shrug and wander towards the prophecy posters.

'Do you know they're calling you the mysterious Jenna Ray on the news?'

'Mmhnn?' My noise is the audio version of a shrug. Maybe I should have called in sick and spent a day hiding under the covers. That seems to be the only way that I can avoid talking about—

'So, what's Blaze like?'

'He's just some boy with powers and a perfect face.' My voice is dripping with emotion – hate, frustration, exhaustion, I don't know, but whatever it is it stops Joy's questions.

'Boop,' I mumble, reducing the range of posters which have the prophecy scrawled across them. So many destructive and inaccurate images—

Tidal Waves – I reduce that to £1.50

Asteroid – £1.50

Lightning –

I pull the poster from the display to show Joy. 'Wait, do you think this poster with lightning on it should actually increase in value, because that's what happened? Look at that fork there, it looks a lot like the one that struck the Culture Complex.'

Joy shakes her head at me, so I go back to pricing posters.

Earthquake – £1.50

Flock of pigeons with electric-blue eyes – £1.50

Fire.

43

Fire racing down the hanging ferns and dropping on to the box office. Flames looming and surrounding me as a child cries in the roaring dark. Smoke in my lungs, in my eyes, in my hair. My hands shake as I click £1.50 on to a flicker, and I decide to spend my morning tidying the soft toys instead. Everything is fine when you're stacking cuddly seals. Everything is fine.

'Hi, Jenna.'

The plastic bucket I was shelving clatters to the floor and adrenalin shoots through me. I know that voice.

It's Okorie.

Okorie with the fresh fade, soulful eyes and record-breaking front stroke. I'm still bending awkwardly to reach the shelves.

Maybe he hasn't seen me? No, he said my name, he's definitely seen me.

I should stand up. Should I stand up?

This is ridiculous. We swim together. Why am I so afraid to talk to him?

Maybe it isn't even him, maybe it's just a customer.

'Hi, Jenna, it's Okorie. Okorie from swimming? Are you stuck?'

'No.' I straighten and knock a stack of buckets off the shelf. They crash to the floor, making more noise than I knew cheap plastic could make.

Okorie Ogundipe is in our shop.

And he's fully clothed, which never happens in my imagination. He's wearing jeans, a comfortable-looking jumper, and there's an optimistic pair of sunglasses perched on his fade.

44

He looks as huggable as Joy, but in a different way. What's he doing here?

Okorie looks at the multicoloured mess on the floor and then back at me. 'Are you all right?'

'Me?' Why is my voice so high-pitched? 'Yes, this happens all the time.'

Joy slides into view behind him and mouths *'It's Okorie!'* at me, which might be the least helpful thing she's ever done.

'Were you looking for something?' I ask.

'Just, you know …' He reaches for something, so I step out of the way. His hand moves fluidly, back to his hair. 'I heard you worked here, and I wanted to see if you're OK after all the fire and the …' He waves a hand in a way that clearly means *being rescued and splashed all over the news*.

He's never said much more than *'Nice race, Ray'* to me before. I really hope I'm not blushing. I knew he was kind, but it's never been directed at me. It's almost too much to handle. I like being single, yes, but Okorie might be the one exception to my **Not Interested. Not Available** status. Maybe we could go for a hot chocolate, and he could dab whipped cream on my nose, like they did in that film, before leaning across the table and—

'Jenna?'

My eyes widen as I force myself back into the room. I can't remember what he asked me, but I take a guess. 'I'm fine, thanks.'

He nods thoughtfully and I breathe a small sigh of relief. I'm going to pay attention now. I focus on his lips. They look soft.

'We've been swimming together forever, Jenna.' He leans against the shelf. He's as graceful out of the water as he is in it.

'And I don't know why we've never really talked. I just felt like I should come and see you. It's silly.' He shakes his head.

'It's not,' I burst out. Now I am going red. 'It's not silly. It's nice. Thank you.'

'Maybe I was too shy and now you're at this crossroads and I thought, it's now or never, Okorie. Most people master the art of postponing the start – I read that somewhere. Anyway, hi.'

He's surprisingly poetic, but I don't know what he's talking about.

'I thought perhaps we could train together for that county meet.' His dark eyes are intense. 'Perhaps you could help me improve my form?'

Okorie 'The Champ' Ogundipe is asking me for help swimming?

'I've never seen anyone as at home in the water as you, Jenna.'

And complimenting me on my swimming?

'Perhaps we could get a juice after too.'

And thinking about rehydrating with me?

Joy is back and frantically mouthing *'That's a date'* at me.

This is actually happening! Okorie, the most beautiful boy on the swimming team, is ASKING ME OUT ON A DATE!

The words *'Yes, yes, yes please, yes'* are on the tip of my tongue when a shout floats in from the harbour.

'Is that Blaze?!'

Every muscle in my body freezes. Through our wide, open door, beyond the racks of sunglasses and sweets, a small boy is pointing up at the sky.

'No, it's just a bird,' his mum says.

'I thought it might be a plane,' adds Sue from the mussel stall.

'No! Look! It's Blaze. He's in his uniform and he's flying this way!' the boy cries.

'No …' This isn't happening. I drop down behind the shelves. Okorie looks down at me. He must think I'm weird, but right now that doesn't matter. I don't want Blaze to see me.

'You should go,' I whisper.

'Can I help?' he whispers back. 'Want me to get rid of him?'

Again, *yes please* settles on my lips, but I can't ask Okorie to step between me and a hero. I don't want him sucked into all of this. And anyway, I'm too much of a feminist to ask a boy to fight my battles for me. I'm just going to hide instead.

'It's OK.' I look up to his concerned frown and lovely eyes. 'You should go, but I'd like to meet you to train.'

'Really?' A gorgeous smile flashes across his face. He's got a cute little gap between his front teeth. 'OK, I'll get out of your hair. I'll message later?' He turns to go and hesitates. 'You deserve a life that lights you up, Jenna Ray. I read that somewhere.'

My insides glow pink. I've been fantasising about Okorie for so long, I forgot he was a real person. But here he is, right in front of me, and his mind is as beautiful as he is. 'Thank you,' I whisper.

'See you soon.' He heads swiftly out of the shop, leaving me on the sandy floor, and I breathe out slowly. Okorie has left my head spinning and I need to be sharp if Blaze manages to find me.

The excited chatter on the harbourside peaks and someone shouts, *'Can I get a selfie?'* The knot in my stomach is back and twisting. Blaze has landed.

'Hi, Blaze,' Joy says loudly. 'Did you want a fridge magnet?'

I crouch lower and look under the shelves to watch him rub one of his black boots against his calf.

'Um …' His feet shuffle. 'Jenna Ray works here, right? I wanted to check in.'

'She's not in today, she's recovering, poor thing.' It's lucky that Joy can act. 'Can I take a message?' There's a slap on the counter. 'Hey! If you're going to take pictures of us, come in and buy something. Prophecy posters are reduced to clear.'

'That's kind of you,' Blaze replies. I'm trying not to breathe too loudly. Does he have super-hearing too? 'Maybe I could leave a note and a get well soon gift? Does she like chocolate?'

'Yes.' Joy's voice is cautious.

'Or one of these jigsaws or—'

In the same moment that I realise he's coming my way, Joy shouts 'Wait!' and then he's there, looking down at me with a bewildered expression on his face.

I scramble up. 'I was just restocking the stuffed seals and now they're done.' I glance over at Joy.

'Oh! There you are, Jenna! I thought you were still sick, anyway I'm just going to— sorry, that's the phone. It's not the kind that rings.' She picks up the phone and shrugs at us. 'Hello, Lighthouse Souvenirs? Yes, we are having a sale …'

I wipe my hands on my jeans. He's standing right where Okorie was a few moments ago, but somehow feels much less real. I don't know what it is about him that is just too shiny. It's like he's a polished pop star.

Face to face, we're similar heights. Blaze's short dark hair is slightly wavy, and his brown eyes rest on my face for a moment before looking off somewhere behind me. He swings his arms, and my eyes are drawn to the red line of his suit that runs across his muscles. I blink quickly and focus back on his face.

He's staring at the ceiling.

Doesn't he know how to talk to girls?

Or maybe he doesn't want to be here? Perhaps that's it? But if he doesn't want to be here and I don't want him here, why doesn't he leave and stop ruining my life?

'How are you?' he asks.

'Fine.' My manners kick in. 'Thank you for saving me.' I look up at the ceiling too in case there's something interesting up there, but it's just a dusty lampshade.

'Your voice sounds awful.'

Perfect. He chased Okorie away and now he's insulting me.

'Thanks? Blaze, I appreciate you coming to visit and all, but—'

'Wait!' He's looking at his hands. 'Sorry. I'm just … we heard from your dad, but I wanted to come and ask you in person.' He clears his throat and briefly catches my eye before looking above my head again. 'I was astounded by your grace last night and by your beauty. Your eyes shone, even in the smoke of that burning building. Would you go on a date with me?'

My nose scrunches. I knew this could happen, but it still feels weird. Is this how Blaze speaks? He sounds like a young

49

King Ron. Joy slides into view behind him, phone still squeezed between her shoulder and her ear. I look hopefully at her for some guidance, but she just shrugs.

My eyes flick back to Blaze. 'No,' I say.

'Really?' Surprise makes his voice sound real again. 'It doesn't have to be a big thing, just one date? It would really help me out.'

'No.' Did I stutter?

'Is it because I left you by a building that exploded?' He looks at my forehead and then my bandaged arms. I thought he'd be hurt or angry about my rejection, but his eyes are full to the brim with guilt. And they're rising. His whole body is. Blaze is floating, inching up towards the ceiling. 'I was going to lead with that, but Ron said … I feel awful. I saw that explosion from the middle of town and came back, but you'd … I'm really sorry.' He's several inches above the ground now. 'There was so much going on and I thought you'd be OK, and it was my first day and you were my first rescue and you helped me find my name and I took you to the hospital, but only after a building exploded at you and now I'm here even though I knew you didn't want me to come.'

WHAT IS HAPPENING? Why is this hero brain-dumping on me? And how can he already have so much guilt? He's only been a hero for twelve hours. I've said no and I need him to leave me alone, but he's spiralling. This boy floating in front of me did save my life. Maybe I can be kind, like Okorie. I reach up and put a hand on his arm. He lands with a surprised bump.

'You saved my life, Blaze.' I blink away the memory of being held in his arms.

There's a flash from outside and I notice the growing crowd with their phones out. I pull him down so we're hidden by the shelves.

'And you're really OK?' he asks. Now that we're hidden behind a cluster of stuffed seals, Blaze finally seems comfortable enough for eye contact. His face isn't perfect after all. His nose is wonky. I take a good long look at it, as this will be the last time I see it up close.

'I'm fine,' I say.

He doesn't miss a beat. 'You know it's OK if you're not?'

I look away. I'm not going to tell him that last night I dreamed of the sticky floor of the Culture Complex bubbling and melting. Or that when I close my eyes, I can still see the flames. 'Don't be too hard on yourself. Like you said, it was your first day and you're the youngest ever hero and everything.' *Now please go away* doesn't quite make it on to the end of my sentence.

'I've been training since I was ten so that's no excuse.' The image of a ten-year-old Blaze standing alone in a cavernous gym stamps itself on to my brain.

'You've had powers since you were ten?' I ask.

'No, but I came from a powered family.' He swallows. 'I was a sure thing.' He shifts and glances up, like he's about to leave. That's good, but I can't let him go without putting an end to this 'first' business.

'Look, Blaze, this is it, OK? This has to be it. I know I was the first person you rescued and it's an honour and everything, but I don't want to be involved with the HPA. Or you, sorry.'

51

'Because of your dad?' Blaze stares into the glass eyes of a seal.

'Because of me.' My voice is coming out stronger than I expected. I deserve a life that lights me up, like Okorie said. 'You know that me just being your friend isn't an option. You know what the HPA want, what the media want, and it's not what I want. Can't you get a sidekick or something?'

Blaze waves off any thought of sidekicks; there's still hope lingering on his face. 'You'd be friends?'

I press my fingers into the floor to stop myself throwing my hands in the air. 'It isn't possible. I'm your first, I'm a girl, we're similar ages; there's only one thing the world wants me to be. If things were different, maybe we could be friends, but not like this.'

His brown eyes rest on mine for a long moment. 'I understand. This isn't what you want.'

Relief washes through me. 'You'll leave me alone?'

Blaze hesitates for a moment and then nods. His mouth is set and there's a pink tinge to his cheeks. For the first time I get the feeling I could like this boy, but that's irrelevant because I'm never going to see him again.

'Good luck with everything.' I stand and offer him my hand. 'Bye then.'

He jumps up and takes it. 'Bye, Jenna Ray.' He gives me a small smile and beams out at the cameras before blurring away.

The crowd is still lingering so Joy flips the sign from OPEN to CLOSED and shuts the door.

'Let's have a little break.' She bounds over to me. 'Start

talking, Ray. What did he say? How do you feel? ARE YOU OK? Because you actually look slightly better than you did earlier.'

'Do you know what, I feel better.' The first real smile of the day spreads across my face. 'Okorie asked me out. And me and Blaze talked. He understands me. There's no way they'll try and make me a Love Interest now.'

Blaze

@therealheroBlaze

Got to chat to #JennaRay today. Talked about the 🔥 rescue & being friends. Lucky to have met her. #grateful

COMMENTS **5.2k**   SHARES **10.7k**   LIKES **1m**

CHAPTER 5

Joy takes her role as the weekend manager of Lighthouse Souvenirs very seriously, so when heavy grey clouds roll across the sea and scare everyone indoors, she announces that it is no longer financially viable to stay open.

'You'll thank me when we're the last shop open on the harbourside.' Joy shrugs on her jacket. 'What are you doing now? I'm going to head to the station to welcome Nick back, want to come with me? We can talk about what might have been if you hadn't told a hero to fly away home?'

I've been around for other Joy and Nick reunions, and I have no desire to stand there awkwardly while they grope each other.

'No, I'll go and revise. Say hi for me.'

'I shall! I can't wait to see what he's brought back for me.'

A chip wrapper bounces past like a tumbleweed as we step out on to the deserted pavement. I stamp on it and put it in the bin. 'So much has happened in the few days Nick has been gone.'

Joy shakes her keys. 'And he said if I didn't die, he'd bring me something shiny.' Her phone rings. 'Hello, 455398?'

'Such a dweeb,' I mutter, and she sticks her tongue out at me. A couple of years ago Joy decided she would answer her phone by saying her phone number, like her nonna did, and that she only needed to use the last six digits because there's only one network that works in Nine Trees.

'Yes, I'm happy with my current plan.' Joy hangs up and rolls her eyes.

Whilst she locks up, I wander over to the railing and look at the slate-grey waves lapping against the boats below. Diving in now would be a welcome relief from the churning sky pressing down on us. I'm not surprised the harbourside has emptied.

'They're just normal clouds, aren't they?' Joy joins me at the railing. 'You don't think it could be another EV storm, do you? Like the lightning storm?'

I shake my head. 'I don't know. We only had the one prophecy though, right? So even if it is the EV, the Diviner didn't see it ripping our town apart.'

'Right. Except we've had her last disaster prophecy now.' Joy presses against the rail and dangles her arms out over the sea. 'The only prophecy left is the one about her successor, which is obviously useless. Not even the HPA know what's coming next.' She groans and sinks down to rest her head on her arms. 'I don't know. Maybe I'm just being weird, but it doesn't feel finished. What if her next prophecy was going to be about Nine Trees too, but she died before she could make it? Or maybe what happened last night wasn't even our prophecy? *The sharp blue heat of truth.* That could mean anything. Why did the stupid Diviner have to be so vague?'

The knot in my stomach twists. Maybe that's the same fear that Joy is feeling, but it's my turn to be brave.

'It's the right year though,' I say. 'It all lines up. There was a disaster and now we've got Blaze, just like she said.'

'Yeah.' Joy breathes out slowly as the lumps of cloud seem to grow above us. 'Imagine being the Diviner, all alone, watching people who haven't been born yet suffer and die. She must have been so lonely.'

The iconic image of the veiled figure in black pops into my head and I suppress a shudder. 'It won't be long until the next one is found. The Diviner's prophecy said it would be this year.'

'Yeah. Poor thing. Great for us, crap for her.' Joy gives herself a little shake. 'Let's go. No point being caught out in whatever is coming. Love you.' She gives my fingers a quick squeeze.

'Love you. Get home safe.'

Joy leaves first. Maybe there was something better I could have said to lift her out of her bleak mood, but she'll be distracted by Nick soon enough. I shake off the dread and jog up the steps to the cobbled high street, proving once and for all that my smart sportswear is appropriate for work, even if my *'clothes can do more than one thing argument'* doesn't work with Dad.

The rain starts as I jog past Nine Cheese, falling in drops so fat I could dodge them if I tried. Not that I would. Each splash of water makes my skin tingle, like a kiss from the sea. A lone rain-splattered van rumbles past as I huff down the empty high street. The council have been busy; the street is no longer crunchy with glass, and Nine Cheese's window is boarded over. Everything will be fixed soon.

My lungs burn as I sprint under the white blossoms, and I slow to a walk as I turn on to my street. A car passes carefully to avoid splashing me. The child in the back sees me and waves frantically. I wave back, confused; I must look like one of their friends. Our road is much busier than usual. Cars and vans are parked along the kerb and blocking in our neighbours.

Has there been another disaster? I walk faster, passing people milling around in raincoats. The closer I get to our house, the busier it becomes. I pick up the pace. Is our house on fire?

'No, she's not in. No one is,' a woman says on the phone as I pass. 'We'll just wait. That's what the other stations are doing. Her shop is shut and there's no swimming competitions or anything like that, so she won't be long.'

I stop dead.

Are all these people here for me?

'I know we need something to go alongside Blaze's statement,' the woman continues. 'We'll get her.'

My heart accelerates to a hundred miles per hour and I swallow back a mouthful of vomit.

They're waiting for me. Every camera-toting, coffee-drinking, shiny-haired one of them.

I slowly pull my hood over my damp Afro. I already feel dizzy. I can't have an attack here. No one has noticed me. Not the crowd of twenty-odd reporters crammed on to our front garden, not the people scattered around the street and not the people who I now realise are fiddling with their equipment in their camera vans.

I feel like a drop of blood in a shark tank.

Worried that any sudden movements might alert them to my presence, I turn slowly and walk, as casually as I can, back the way I came.

'She has to come back at some point,' a man lounging in an open van says. His colleague eating crisps in the front seat agrees and puts their feet on the dashboard.

'We can wait,' they reply.

I push my fist into my chest as my heart beats even faster. It was over. Blaze nodded; he understood. It was finished. What did he say to make all these people mob my house? What did he do?

My head is spinning and the walls of the alley judder either side of me as I find my way to our back garden. I let myself in as quietly as I can and spit a glob of vomit into our dead rose bush. I'm so dizzy all I want to do is fall to my hands and knees and wait until the ground becomes firm again, but I'm almost there. It's just a few quiet steps to our back door.

Squeak!

There's a bright red ball under my foot which must have been chucked over by next door. Wincing, I ease my foot off it.

Squeak!

'She's in the garden!'

I run the rest of the way to our back door, my hand

scrabbling around in my bag for my keys. From the corner of my eye, I see heads popping up above our fence.

'Jenna! Can you tell us what you and Blaze spoke about today?!'

I get one finger into my key ring and try to pull it out, but it catches on the lining. As the keys tumble back into my bag, all the air vanishes from my lungs.

'Jenna! Did you kiss when you hid from the cameras?!'

My fingers scrabble past hand cream, sunglasses and my phone charger. My sleeve catches on the zip. I manage to stab under a fingernail with my keys and tears spring to my eyes, but I finally have them.

'Jenna! Do you think that your mum leaving has stopped you wanting a relationship?'

No.

I can't think about her.

I can't do this. I'm going to throw up or faint. I can't breathe. My shaking hands grasp the right key and I almost sob with relief. I fall through the back door and slam it behind me.

They're still outside, shouting my name in a never-ending chorus.

'Jenna! Jenna! Jenna! Jenna! Jenna! Jenna! Jenna! Jenna! Jenna! Jenna! Jenna! Jenna! Jenna! Jenna! Jenna! Jenna! Jenna! Jenna! Jenna! Jenna!'

Tears stream down my face.

I can't breathe.

I can't let them see me like this.

My hip bashes off the wooden worktops as I race around the kitchen, drawing our pale-yellow curtains and yanking down the blinds that cover our glass back door. Finally hidden, I sink down with my back against our rattling fridge.

I need to *calm down!*

I have to calm down, but I'm so dizzy and every breath is hollow.

They're still there, I can hear them.

My heart is thudding.

I can't breathe.

I can't stop this.

There's a burst of noise as the front door opens and slams.

'Jenna?' Megan is a watery swirl of bags and jumper as she runs into the kitchen. There are thumps and rustles and then she's in front of me with her hands on my knees.

'Jenna, focus.' Her voice is calm. 'Focus on me and breathe out.'

I try and suck in air so I can do that, and it all catches again.

'No.' Megan's voice is still gentle. 'Don't try and breathe in, remember? Only breathe out. Breathe out and count to four.'

I force what little air I have left out.

'And breathe out, two, three, four.'

Somehow, some air has snuck in and I'm able to breathe out again with my sister.

'And breathe out. Whilst you breathe out, focus on the rain.'

The rain.

The pressure in my chest eases as beyond the kitchen and the shouts of the press, I find the rain thudding on the roof and

61

pattering on the windows. I breathe out, *two, three, four,* and picture the fat cool drops of liquid joining as they run down the glass of the kitchen window, roll across the brick and stream down the street to join the sea.

I breathe out and wipe my eyes. Megan is still kneeling by me, her hands on my knees.

'Any better?' she asks.

I nod.

'Stay there. Keep breathing out and counting. I'll make some camomile tea.'

She wipes a tear from my face and gets up to switch on the kettle. 'There are photos of you and that hero all over the news.' She slams two mugs on the counter. 'All he said was that you talked. But that's enough. He should know that's enough.'

My phone is vibrating non-stop in my pocket. I fish it out and the first message that pops up is from Joy.

Have you seen this?

She's sent me a screenshot of a social media post. The words swim in and out of focus.

Blaze @therealheroBlaze

Got to chat to #JennaRay today.

Talked about the 🔥 *rescue & being friends.*

Lucky to have met her.

#grateful

It's had over a million likes in the last hour.

Megan marches back over to me, slowly crushing a box of camomile tea. 'Put your phone away, Jen-bear. You don't want to read what they're saying online. He's using you. The HPA are using you. I won't let them do that to my sister. I'll destroy that boy first.'

The rain comes down harder outside, turning into a low rumble across our house. I don't need to read anything else that's been said online. I've seen enough. I asked him if he would leave me alone and he nodded. I told him that I couldn't be a part of all this and he understood. I almost liked him. I was kind to him and he lied to me.

How could he leave and immediately post this on social media? He's told the world that we're friends. Which means we have a relationship. The possibility of me being his Love Interest is now even more present than before. I push myself to my feet and, even though I still feel wobbly, the anger flowing through my veins is like fire. Saving my life does not give Blaze the right to tear it to pieces. I take the box of tea from my sister's hands. 'Don't worry, Megan. I'll destroy him myself.'

CHAPTER 6

How do you destroy a hero? And what does that even mean? My finger trails down the wood of the banister. It's not like I'm going to join that anarchist Villains group and start attacking the HPA. I don't want to hurt anyone, but I can't wake up every day with news reporters camped out on my front garden.

The post clatters on to the doormat as I pass. On top of the bills and Megan's satirical magazine is a golden envelope with my name on it.

'Tea?' Megan calls from the kitchen.

'Coffee?' I reply. Too loud. I'm being too loud. There's probably a reporter on our doorstep with a notebook wondering how they can spin this new information.

BREAKING! Jenna Ray asks for coffee in the morning. Here's Professor Bev Erage to tell us what that means …

I pause in the corridor, away from all the windows, and open the envelope. Is it from one of the reporters?

No.

It's from the HPA.

Jenna Ray

The Heroics and Power Authority cordially
invite you to the first annual

BLAZECON

Come and meet your new hero

Today (Sunday, 19th May) from 10 a.m.,
at the National Museum of Hero History

My fingers trace the black embossed BLAZECON before settling at the top of the card in the perfect position to rip the thing apart. I make a tiny tear and hesitate.

Last night I made a vow to destroy this boy, and this could be my only chance to do that before my life is completely dismantled. If I go to the convention, I could find him, tell him that I hate him and hope enough people overhear for it to become news. I could completely humiliate him. Blaze will become the first hero in history to be dumped publicly, and very loudly, by someone who isn't even his Love Interest.

The edges of my mouth twitch up as I imagine *those* headlines.

BREAKING! Jenna Ray tells Blaze that she hates him. Here are some powerful women to discuss why Blaze is terrible and why we should never bother Jenna Ray again ...

This convention is a gift. I carefully fold the card and slip it into the pocket of my hoody. I'm going to rip this thing up in front of him and throw the shiny pieces at his lying face.

'Toast?' Megan asks as I wander into the kitchen. I nod and she pops another round down. 'Dad's gone to the police. He wants to get a restraining order.'

'Against who?'

'Against everyone, especially the reporters outside and ESPECIALLY anyone to do with the HPA.' She yawns widely and dark bags scrunch under her eyes.

'They keep you up?' I jerk my head towards the circus outside.

She holds up a finger as she finishes yawning. 'No, I just had some weird dreams.' Megan passes me a mug shaped like an owl, which I take excitedly before looking back up at her. 'Wasn't there any coffee left?'

'Yes.' She pours a stream of thick brown liquid from the cafetiere into her thermos. 'But this coffee is for people who aren't pretending not to have anxiety.'

'I don't have anxiety,' I mutter, sitting at the kitchen table.

'See?' She tucks the thermos into her rucksack. 'My coffee. Did you see they're holding a festival of Blaze or something? I'd love to pop in and have a word with the little rat, but they were saying how exclusive it is on the radio. Just super-fans and

66

super-donors. Perhaps if I was funnelling money away from normal people and into the pocket of that stinking cesspool of an organisation, the HPA, I'd be able to go and punch Blaze in the nose in person.'

Megan's cheeks have gone pink, and her fingers are digging into the soft material of her satchel. She's probably about to break another bag. I didn't think she could get angrier at the patriarchy, but somehow, she's levelled up. Today, with Blaze, regular Jenna would probably only manage 'You're stupid and I hate you', before running out of things to say, but I'm going to channel my inner Megan.

'Patriarchal ball bag,' I murmur.

Megan glances at the front door. 'Are you going to be OK if I go to work? You'll just stay in and revise, right?'

I roll my eyes. 'Yes, Mum.'

'Don't you yes mum me! You almost died and now you're being stalked by a hero and the entirety of the British media.' She grabs my head and kisses the top of it. 'Just stay inside.'

'Get off.' As I wriggle free, the invitation jabs me in the stomach. 'I'll be fine.' I hate lying to my sister, but maybe I will be fine. I just need to make it through the reporters, to the city, and figure out what I can say that will make sure that Blaze never bothers me again. My stomach churns.

'Don't worry, Jen-bear, this will blow over.' Megan deftly unknots her headwrap. 'Here. You can wear this over the bandage.'

'Really?'

Megan never lends me her headwraps; she says I can't be

trusted with them. The one she's holding out is her favourite. It's silk and when you hold it taut you can see it's decorated with loads and loads of vulvas, painted on in swirling patterns, although bunched up and tied around her box braids you could never tell. Megan says it makes her feel powerful.

'Here we go.' Megan positions it carefully in my hair and ties it in a bow. 'Beautiful! Oh, and—'

She leans over to the pile of post by the kettle. 'This came yesterday. I ordered it to wear when I work with Hugh. Have I told you about Hugh?'

'The homophobe?'

'Yeah.' Megan rips open an envelope and pulls out a new scarf. She holds it so I can see the design.

'Is it two women kissing in the rain?' I reach out to touch a sequinned drop of water.

'Tasteful, isn't it?'

She knots it round her head and leans down next to me. 'Smile!' She holds up her phone and we take a headwrap selfie. With Megan's arm looped around my shoulder, some of the tension eases from my chest. This is what a hug from Mum used to feel like. Then Megan ruins it by giving me a big sloppy kiss on the cheek.

'You're actually dribbling on me!'

'Love you too.' She rolls away and picks up her bag. 'Be careful today, OK?'

'Yep. You too.' I jump up to get my toast. 'Bye.'

There is a burst of noise from the reporters as Megan opens the door. 'Calm down, I'm not Jenna! I know we're both brown.'

She slams the door and I picture her pushing past microphones, cameras and wading through a thousand questions about me. This mess is all my fault.

No.

It's Blaze's fault.

I rage eat six slices of toast coated in chocolate spread and try to figure how I'm going to get to BLAZECON. There's no way I could walk. The bus up the Safe Road only runs around once a fortnight. A taxi will cost everything I've saved for uni so far …

The sudden ringing of the doorbell makes me drop my last crust in surprise. Is it a reporter? They haven't rung the doorbell before. Is it Joy? She normally shouts through the letter box.

The piercing sound continues over and over. I don't want to answer it. There's no way someone ringing my doorbell is a good thing. My heart thuds in my ears as I creep over to our front door and try to sense who's on the other side. Whoever it is, they're not getting bored of ringing the bell. They might just be leaning on the button.

No postie has ever tried this hard to deliver a parcel. I can't open the door. All those looming faces, flashing cameras and shining microphones will cram through the doorway and swarm over our house.

'I'm not the press,' a bored voice yells. 'I'm your ride.'

It's a trick.

'This isn't a trick. I got rid of the garden party too.'

My hand shakes, but I open the door a crack, with the chain still on, and peek out. The person on our doorstep does look like a driver. They're wearing a tailored black suit and a cap with a shiny peak, with a white shirt that's unbuttoned low enough for me to see a silver they/them necklace glinting against their dark skin. They've got an almost cartoonish lock of black hair curled under their cap, glossy plum lips and eyes that scream *I've got places to be.*

'I promise, they're gone.' The driver motions at our garden.

I let the door swing fully open and see that our garden and driveway are gloriously empty. There are just a few takeaway coffee cups and discarded wrappers left strewn across the grass. I could swim a marathon in the relief that washes over me, but I don't have time. The next problem is already on my doorstep.

'Did Megan send you?' It's a long shot, but this driver, with their sharp eyes and funky hair, is exactly my sister's type.

They shake their head. 'Don't know a Megan. You're going to want to get changed.'

'Sorry, who are you then?'

The driver holds out a lanyard and my heart drops. This is what my dad would call an 'out of the frying pan' moment.

'This says you're the head of wardrobe at the HPA, Mia.'

'Whoops.' The lanyard is flipped. 'Better?'

The embossed, very official-looking pass now says DRIVER.

'I do all sorts. So, about this.' Mia motions to my sport leggings and hoody ensemble.

I cross my arms. 'What do you want?'

'I want you to get in my posh car and come to BLAZECON. It's a very exclusive invite. First event to celebrate the new hero. Anyone who's anyone, et cetera. That's your ride.' Mia jerks a thumb at a black car that looks like a cross between a limo and a tank. The wheels are enormous, it has extra windows in the middle and the silver statuette on the bumper is nothing I've ever seen before.

'Then what?' I ask. The silver wheels of the timo sparkle at me. I want to get to this convention, but what is Mia going to want in return? 'Will you push me onstage to say how much I love Blaze, the HPA and all the men who wear silly suits and save the day?'

'Ouch.' Mia raises a perfect eyebrow. 'And no. My job is to get you there. You'll just be a guest, free to wander round and play arcade games or, skies, I don't know, get a signed photo of King Ron … I've never been to one of these things.'

'But you want me to talk to the press …'

'I've been told there's no press allowed.'

No press?

Mia leans on my door frame. 'And no one is even allowed to take photos. There's an official photographer. No other images allowed.'

No camera phones.

This really is it. The perfect opportunity to see Blaze without making the news again.

'King Ron, the busload of primary school kids Blaze saved, the fire and ambulance services that Blaze helped,' Mia continues. 'Blaze himself. They're the event. Honestly, Jenna, you'll be one of the least interesting people there.'

This is perfect! Finally, the HPA are doing something that will help me end this. My family aren't going to like me accepting a ride from the HPA and they're really not going to like that

I'm going to BLAZECON, but this is too good an opportunity to miss.

'OK,' I say. 'I'm in.'

'Terrific.' Mia sounds like they couldn't care less. For some reason this makes me like them. 'Also.' Mia ceremoniously turns round the pass to read HEAD OF WARDROBE. 'I brought you a dress.'

A suit bag appears in front of me. 'And shoes.' They nudge open a box by my feet and a pair of strappy heels glare up at me.

My fingers reach up to brush Megan's headwrap knotted around my Afro. 'Do you know what, I think I'm fine.' I grab my keys off the back of the door. 'Let's go to BLAZECON.'

Mia is unruffled. 'Great.'

'But we need to make a stop first.'

'What. Is. THAT?!' Joy points at each of the car's extra windows. 'It looks like it was made by someone who learned what a car was supposed to look like from their butler.'

'I know. Will you pretty please come to BLAZECON with me?' I nod back at the car. 'You get to ride there in the timo.'

'Should I change?' Joy smooths down her perfect, dainty summer dress.

'*You* look fine,' Mia calls through the window.

'OK.' Joy tilts her head at me. 'And we're going to BLAZECON … why?'

'To tell Blaze to leave me alone forever.'

'Should you say that in front of …?' Joy jerks her thumb at Mia.

'I don't care what you say as long as you get in the car.' They flip on a pair of sunglasses and wind their window up.

Joy nods. 'Let me get my lip gloss.'

BLAZECON is in the city, which means a two-and-a-half-hour journey round the moor on the Safe Road or—

'Buckle your seat belts, kids. BLAZECON ETA forty-five minutes,' Mia calls from the front.

Using the black leather seat that runs the length of the car as a handrail, I wobble down the brightly lit interior, navigate the fragile-looking golden drinks cabinet, and make it to the front. The driver's section is separated from the luxurious back by a black barrier, but I can still perch on a seat and angle myself so I can see Mia's face. They look far too relaxed.

'Are you taking us along the Wild Road?' I ask.

'Of course. It's faster.'

Joy joins me. 'Getting from one end of this timo to the other is the most exercise I've done in weeks.' She hands me a glass bottle of apple juice. 'I found these though, in that gold cupboard.'

'Shouldn't we go on the Safe Road?' I push the bottle of apple juice into my hoody pocket. The EV has completely taken over the moorland that the Wild Road runs through. It doesn't just get the extreme weather and the blue-eyed psychotic animals; even the trees are dangerous there.

Every night there's a different story on the news – *Giant hailstones destroy vehicles on the Wild Road.* Or – *Drivers should be aware that blue-veined roots have broken through the tarmac at miles three, five, seven, twenty and thirty-two of the Wild Road.* Or – *In the wake of the Honeymooner tragedy, claw-resistant engines are now mandatory on the Wild Road, along with reinforced windows and wheels.* Almost no one from Nine Trees uses the Wild Road.

'Wait. Are you taking us on the Wild Road?!' Joy almost chokes on her juice. 'A boy at school knows someone who was attacked by EV squirrels along there.'

'Relax, OK?' Mia flicks the indicator, following a sign that says WILD ROAD accompanied by a load of warnings. 'The HPA use the Wild Road all the time. The rumours are vastly exaggerated to prevent traffic.'

Joy's eyes are enormous as she looks at me, but Mia sounds too bored to be lying.

Mia continues. 'There have only been five deaths this year—'

Joy coughs. 'It's May.'

'—and the EV threat level is only moderate for this area. This is an HPA vehicle, it can handle moderate.' As we cruise under the dark canopy of the trees, Mia pushes a button above their head. 'But, just in case, stealth mode.'

The interior of the car immediately goes dark and pale blue strip lighting flicks on above our heads. The windows mist and my worried-looking reflection appears in the dark panes. The car jolts and seems to get higher.

'Pumping the wheels,' Mia explains. 'Do you have your seat belts on?'

We bump over something that is probably an EV root and Joy and I hurriedly strap ourselves in.

'I'm not sure we should—' I start, but Mia holds up a hand.

74

'It's safer if you don't talk.'

'You *do* know about the squirrels, right?' Joy asks.

'They're one of the reasons we all need to quiet down.' Mia grips the wheel hard. Not so relaxed, then.

Joy leans back with a sigh that I recognise. It's her tried and tested *'guess we're all going to die then'* nonchalance. 'Well, if the trees close in and the animals attack, Jenna's boyfriend can always come and save us.'

I elbow her. 'Not my boyfriend.'

'Mia, will you still give us a ride back if she breaks up with him?'

There's a jolt and the seat belt cuts against my chest as one side of the car lifts and then crashes back down.

'Mother Earth,' I mutter.

'I'll be quiet,' Joy whispers.

'If you could,' Mia replies.

We fall into an uneasy silence.

We are on the Wild Road.

Since the Nine Trees prophecy was released to the public five years ago, it has been an inevitable danger hanging over Nine Trees; a constant for the families who refused to bow to the fear and leave. But the Wild Road, the looming tangle of dark trees on the edge of town, wasn't somewhere any of us needed to go. Ever.

ONE HUNDRED PER CENT AVOIDABLE DANGER; that's what the HPA are driving us through now.

This is all Blaze's fault. That stupid hero, with his stupid social media presence and his stupid face.

I don't want to sit here for forty-five minutes thinking about how much I hate him. My stomach tightens as I try to look beyond the reflection of my vulva headband. There are probably thousands of blue eyes blinking out there or gnarled roots twisting out of the darkness ready to wrap around our wheels, but all I can see is my worried face.

Joy elbows me and shows me the game she's playing on her phone. An EV deer with electric-blue eyes is trampling cottages and kicking hunters in the Highlands.

'Are you a hunter?' I whisper.

She snorts. 'No, I'm the deer.'

'Shhhh!'

I reach for my own phone and find it full of messages from friends, acquaintances and reporters who all want to know about Blaze. I push down the nausea in my chest. This is horrible, and all these people are draining my battery. I've only got thirty per cent left.

After what feels like an hour of dark, bumpy transit, we glide to a stop.

'Are we here?' Joy's voice seems incredibly loud.

'No.' Mia's whisper is tense. 'There's something out there. I can see it on our scanner. I don't know if it's one big thing or lots of little things, but we're just going to sit here quietly as it passes, OK?'

We nod and wait.

With the engine off, I can hear the wind rustling through the leaves and what sounds like a twig tap – tap – tapping the window, as if it's asking to be let in.

We wait.

Joy's hand edges into mine.

I don't look at our worried reflections.

I rehearse what I'll say to Blaze in my mind – *Hi, I think you're really manipulative and you might have saved me, but that doesn't mean you get to derail my life and upset my family. I wanted to make sure other people saw this conversation, Mr Social Media Hero, so this time you can't gloss over the fact that I want you to leave me alone. Here's your invitation back and stay out of my life.* And then, instead of tearing the invite up, I'll shove it in his mouth so he can't tell me any more lies. I nod. It's a solid plan, but the longer we wait on the Wild Road, the harder my heart beats.

We wait.

The branch taps.

I think I can hear the thump of giant footsteps, but it might be my imagination. What huge thing could be on the Wild Road with us? An EV deer, like in Joy's game? A pack of vicious blue-eyed squirrels ready to rip through our very expensive car? A hundred killer EV seagulls who will lift us up and fly us over Nine Trees to throw us off a cliff?

Maybe it would be good to have a hero with us at a time like this.

'That'll do,' Mia mutters. The car rolls forward and in what feels like no time at all, the lights flick on and the windows un-mist.

'We are out!' Mia honks the horn as we pass a sign welcoming us to the city.

From there it's a few suburban streets, one boring traffic jam and around twenty billboards for *Brooke's World Season 8* before we arrive outside the National Museum of Hero History. The elaborate white columns are decorated in bunting and banners, and surrounded by a swarm of excited people.

'Welcome to BLAZECON,' Mia announces.

CHAPTER 7

Mia points out the car park, indicating where they'll wait for us, and taps the steering wheel until we're out of the car.

'Have fun.' They sound like a bored parent at the pool.

I lean back in through the door. 'I'm going to tell your hero where he can stick this whole Love Interest thing.'

Mia gives me a thumbs up. 'You do you. I'll be over there.'

'This won't take long.' I slam the door and yank my hood up. People are pointing at the ridiculous vehicle we just got out of.

'Stealth mode,' I whisper to Joy.

'I don't think that's going to work,' she mutters.

My heartbeat thrums through me as we make our way up the wide, white stone steps of the museum. We skirt the fat base of one of the columns, which has PHOTOGRAPHY BANNED posters taped to it, and join the queue that stretches across the elaborate Grecian approach to a single wooden door.

'Well, now that door feels even more ridiculous than usual,'

Joy mutters. ' "How big do you want the front of the museum?" ' She slips into her *'I'm a stupid adult'* voice. ' "Oh, well, I'd like the steps to be a billion metres across and the columns to be a billion metres high so thousands of people can all wait there to get through one tiny door." '

'Uh-huh.' Searching for Blaze whilst keeping my face hidden is hard. I need to stay calm, but the atmosphere approaching the entrance is charged with excited screams, fluttering banners and fans brandishing their invitations. This is not the National Museum of Hero History that we've visited on school trips.

'Are you Jenna Ray?!' a woman in a BLAZE T-shirt shouts at me as she passes on the stairs.

'No, I just look like her,' I reply automatically.

'She gets that a lot,' Joy adds. 'We're going to see what freebies we can get.'

'Well, good luck.' The woman gives me a suspicious look before jostling past to get in line.

My heart sinks slowly into my trainers as the queue passes under a giant banner of Blaze's face. There's dramatic classical music blasting from speakers and small BLAZECON 2024 flags decorating the doorway. Why did I think this was a good idea? Not only am I surrounded by hero-worshippers and probably the entire British HPA, but there's got to be reporters here. Why did I believe Mia?

'Come on.' Joy threads her arm through mine. 'We'll get in, find Blaze, tell him off, and then have a go on the earthquake simulator. Maybe we can go to the King Ron Canteen and get the world's most expensive hot chocolate too.'

Stepping through the wooden door feels like it should be significant, but there's just more of a queue and the familiar glass-fronted reception desk. A man with a clipboard is checking people in.

'Name?' He doesn't look up.

'Jenna Ray,' I say as quietly as I can, holding out my invitation.

'Pardon?'

'Jenna Ray.'

'What, love?'

He finally looks up as I say, 'Jenna Ray!' just as there's a break in the music. Everyone in the immediate area turns to look at me, including the woman with the BLAZE T-shirt, who looks mortally offended.

'Plus one.' Joy flashes the invite that Mia gave her.

'In you go then, Jenna Ray.' The ticket man quirks his eyebrows at me. I'm too full of nerves to figure out what that's supposed to mean, so I mutter 'thanks' and grab a map of the convention.

Despite announcing myself to the foyer, I feel like I disappear the moment I step through into the crowds of the Great Court. This enormous room would have once been an outdoor space around the round central museum building, but now chatter and classical music crashes off a sweeping glass roof and bounces back down to the smooth marble floor. Stalls have been dotted around and a festival stage juts out in front of the central building.

'Maybe there are dressing rooms at the back or something?' I mutter.

'On it. Let's check the Meet Blaze stall en route in case it

81

really is that easy.' Joy grabs my hand, and we snake through the crowd between a stall full of photos of King Ron and the edge of the stage. Lights spin on the truss that frames the platform, and below a woman in black is adjusting some microphones. I really want to leave before the heroes, past and present, get up there to talk about how great they are.

'My name's Blaze and I have a massive face,' Joy murmurs as we pass the entrance to the west wing of the museum and the enormous banner of Blaze that hangs down in front of it. 'Ah, the Meet Blaze booth doesn't open until two thirty.'

'There's no way I'm staying that long.' I pull my hood a bit tighter.

We pass a stall with a poster display of the various bodies of King Ron's sidekick Prince #2, the Robot Sidekick. His unicycle iteration from the early nineties has always been my favourite. According to Dad, Prince #2 was even more popular than Ron before the sidekick's tragic demise. I slow down to look at an image of the shining android in a refugee camp giving people water. I bet Blaze wouldn't stick around to make sure the people he saved were OK in the aftermath. He'd probably be too busy posting on social media about how amazing his rescues were. I scan the hall and the ceiling for signs of him, and almost bump into a man doing the same.

'This was a bad idea,' I mutter to Joy.

'Come on, Ray. What else were you going to do with your day?'

'Swim?' I count off my options on my fingers. 'Go to the beach. Swim. I could have just stayed home and poked myself in the eye.'

'You said swimming twice.'

82

We come to stop under a tall poster displaying the Diviner's final prophecy.

> **2024**
> **The Diviner does not love**
> **She does not judge**
> **She does not lie**
> **Her role is to see.**

That prophecy has always made me shudder. No love, no control, and no glory, like the men the HPA make heroes. We don't even know what the Diviners looked like. What must it have been like to have nothing but the future?

'Interested?' A man wearing a museum waistcoat waves us closer to the Are You the Next Diviner? booth. 'Come and see if you're the one who has been foretold, the one who will write the next book of prophecies and show us how the heroes will save the world.' He waves his hands like he's telling a ghost story and then drops them when he sees the look on my face. 'It's just for fun.'

'We're all right, thanks.' I steer Joy away.

'Would you even tell them if you could see the future?' she asks.

'Let's just find Blaze and get out of here.' I hook Joy's arm and we weave around the top of the hall, towards the merchandise stall near the east wing of the museum. Maybe Blaze will be there, signing pictures of his face.

There are bubble guns, laser pens and other plastic hero stuff for sale on the merch table, but no Blaze.

'He's not here.' I do a last, pointless check of the ceiling. We've been round the whole court and there's no sign of the hero. Why did I think this would work? We should just go home before someone notices me and makes my situation even worse.

'Oh! Look!' Joy swings me round. 'A Love Interest stall. We should do some research.'

'Let's just go.'

She pretends not to hear me, and I am dragged past the tiny wooden door to freedom to a long table covered in a pink tablecloth, with various books, postcards and stickers for sale. A framed picture of Kate, King Ron's Love Interest, looking beautiful in black and white, is on a stand in the centre. Megan insists that the HPA like it when Love Interests die young, so they can stay pretty forever, just like Kate.

Her famous quote sits in cursive just below her pursed lips.

The perfect Love Interest is brave enough to support her man. And beautiful enough to brighten his darkest hour.

'I just threw up in my mouth,' I say into Joy's ear, and she laughs far too loudly. Today would be so much worse if I didn't have my best friend with me.

A gaggle of girls arrive and shoulder past us to fire questions at the staff member.

'How do we meet Blaze?'

'Do you know if he likes blondes?'

'That Jenna Ray girl, she's not actually his Love Interest, is she?'

'Um—' The staff member in the waistcoat shrugs. 'Maybe?' she says.

'No!' the girl closest to me bursts out. 'No. He's too good for her.'

'She looks really awkward and all muscly,' another adds.

I glance down at my arms. My muscles are defined. They're what make me so fast in the water, so I've always liked them.

'He should be with a girl like me,' a girl concludes, flicking her curly golden hair.

I take her in from beneath my hood. She'd look perfect in a frame with a cursive quote. I'm ready to slink away when Joy clears her throat. Oh no.

'Well, I heard that Jenna Ray is a champion swimmer and actually I also heard that she's really funny and also, not that it should matter, but she also, actually, has an excellent face and body.'

Everyone at the table turns to stare at Joy and I crouch a little to hide behind her.

Golden Curls looks Joy up and down with a slight sneer on her face. 'Mo-ther Earth. Do you know her?!' She smiles, suddenly giddy with excitement. 'Do you know Jenna Ray? Can we meet her?!'

Joy tilts her head. 'What is your deal?'

'This is Sydney Jones, *on the scene*, at BLAZECON, as the official press representative—'

My head whips round and there she is, Sydney Jones, in the flesh, metres away from me. The press is here! Mia lied! Mia's a liar!

'—where there's an exciting day ahead. King Ron and Blaze will make an appearance and there are rumours that some other persons of interest, including Jenna Ray, are in attendance. Let's talk to some of the Blaze fans.' Sydney beckons her camera over and targets Golden Curls. 'Would you like to tell us how your day has been so far?'

The Love Interest stall at BLAZECON is the last place I want Sydney Jones to find me. My survival instincts kick in and instead of dissolving into a nervous puddle, I grab Joy and make a speedy exit.

'—And I just met someone who knows Jenna Ray!' I hear Golden Curls telling Sydney as we melt into the crowd.

As soon as we're a safe distance away, we burst out laughing. With Joy's hand in mine, this is nothing like yesterday. Maybe I can deal with the press.

'You're ridiculous.' I tell Joy, wiping a tear from my eye.

'And you're muscly.' She grabs my arm. 'Grrrr!'

'Grrrr?!'

We stumble, giggling, into a huge round of applause in front of the central stage. A man in a bright-blue tuxedo motions for quiet.

'It certainly sounds like you're ready to welcome him on. Hero fans, it's King Ron!'

The crowd screams and claps so loud that my ears will be ringing for days. Being around this much energy is exhilarating, but I refuse to enjoy King Ron. His latest theory is that, with the exception of the loveless Diviner, female powers are naturally restricted to protect our fragile bodies and keep them safe for childbirth. Creating life is absolutely a superpower, I'd like to see King Ron carrying a child, but being told that's all my 'precious' body is for makes me want to tear down buildings.

'You're crushing my hand!' Joy shouts above the crowds.

'Sorry!'

Joy massages life back into her fingers as King Ron saunters on to the stage and waves to the crowd like we're his loyal subjects. He pauses in the centre of the stage to brush down his pinstripe suit. Joy gasps beside me as Ron flips backwards in a movement that shouldn't be possible for a man his age. He lands with one knee on the floor and sticks his arms out to use his conduit power to draw streams of white electricity from batteries set on the sides of the stage.

'He's going to do the Eliminator!' Joy whispers loudly.

'Surely he's too old for that?' a man behind us says.

Ron brings his shaking, glowing arms to his sides and throws a cheeky wink out to an older lady, who promptly faints. All concentration again, he claps his hands together above his head and a net of white lightning crackles up, spreading through the air above him.

'Ooooh!' Joy's eyes are as wide as saucers, but I narrow mine. Ron is a showman, always has been. He's pulling power from some preset battery and making his audience goggle at sheet lightning so they'll forget all about his behaviour towards women.

With a grunt he merges the power into a single bolt and sends it surging up into the truss frame. There's a BANG and confetti showers on to the stage.

'This is EPIC! I didn't even see the piñata up there!' Joy shouts at me above the cheers.

I hadn't seen it either. We weren't supposed to. We were just supposed to be looking at him, like always.

King Ron grabs a microphone and saunters to the front. 'Good afternoon.' He waits as the crowd screams and claps. 'Are you having a nice time?' More screaming and clapping. 'I wanted to say hello. All right? How do you do? To you, our fan clubs, our supporters, our old friends and our new friends.' He looks directly at me and my insides freeze. 'Welcome to BLAZECON. I'm going to answer a few questions for you lovely lot. Ask whatever you like. You know me, I'm just an old man who loves to reminisce. But don't you worry, I won't keep you too long. I know you all are really here to see Blaze!'

The crowd shout back a mixture of *noooo* and *Blaaaaaze!*

I shuffle back, taking Joy with me, so King Ron can't pick me out of the crowd again.

'Stick with me for—' King Ron looks over at the host, who holds up all his fingers. 'Ten minutes and then it'll be time for the man of the hour to light up the stage! Now, I know I sound like a broken record, but I'm going to kick off with a call for the Diviner. Young lady, we know you're out there. We need your sight so our heroes can fight. The other day, I was thinking about the similarities between being the Diviner and mother-hood. Care, guidance, nurture—'

The crowd has grown around us, and it takes too long to escape King Ron's nauseating demand for the Diviner. By the time we find some open air, we're near the entrance again.

'Do you think King Ron can still do a flying kick?' Joy asks as we stop, facing the front door.

Any fun I'd been having at BLAZECON evaporated the moment that King Ron picked me out of the crowd. 'I just want to find Blaze, give him my message, and get home. I'm done, Joy.'

'What message?' a familiar voice asks. My jaw clenches and I turn to find Blaze, wearing a puffy black jacket over his hero suit and a baseball cap as a disguise. His face lights up when he sees me. He thinks he's won.

'Hi, Jenna! I didn't know you were coming. I was going to ask if you wanted to go for an iced latte or a Frappuccino, as friends of course ...'

'You!' His face falls as I stomp over. I stop so close that our noses are almost touching.

'What's wrong?' His perfect brow creases.

'I told you that I didn't want to be a Love Interest, *your* Love Interest.' He smells like rain. I take a hasty step back.

'I—' He looks confused.

I plough on, not ready for him to apologise. 'In the gift shop. You agreed that it was over, and then you posted about me –' I take a breath and force myself to lower my voice – 'and every reporter in the country turned up on my doorstep.'

'They did?'

'Yes, Blaze, I've been trapped in my house.'

'I would have— You could have called, and I would have—'

'How?! I don't have your number, Mr Hero. We've interacted twice and it has upended my life. No one else seems to understand that we don't actually know each other!'

I glare at him, and he stares back, his brown eyes suddenly hard.

'Look, I don't know why you're upset with me.' He holds his hands up. 'I never said you were my Love Interest.'

My mouth drops open. The boy from the gift shop would have apologised or started to hover, but that's not what's happening now. He's defending himself. I'm not going to be able to take my apology and storm off victorious. This is a fight. I'm in a fight, with Blaze, at BLAZECON.

'But you didn't say that I wasn't!' I clench my fists.

'I don't control the media.' He crosses his arms. People at the back of King Ron's crowd are turning round to watch us, but I'm too angry to stop.

'You control your mouth!'

'Go on, Jenna,' Joy mutters behind me.

'Oh, Jenna and Blaze are fighting!' someone nearby says. 'Enemies to lovers. It's an enemies to lovers thing!'

'No!' I snap at the small audience we've drawn. 'It's not an enemies to lovers thing! It's not anything.'

'Fine!' Blaze's cheeks flush pink. 'It's not anything.'

My hand is round the invitation. This is it, this is when I throw it at his face or force it into his mouth and tell him how finished this is. But he gets there first.

'You're not my Love Interest.' His voice is sharp. 'I am not interested.'

'Finally! Neither am I!' I shout back.

'I adore enemies to lovers!' another voice says. 'Oh, what's that?'

Something bounces off trainers, strappy sandals and bags filled with merch and rolls to a stop by my feet. It looks a lot like a grenade.

CHAPTER 8

Blaze moves first. One second, he is looking at me, the next he is on the floor grasping at where the grenade had been. The small metal ball with blinking purple lights shoots up above the heads of the crowd. King Ron is still chatting onstage, but people are turning to watch as Blaze launches himself at the flitting grenade.

'Look! It's Blaze!' someone shouts.

'Is this part of the show?' Joy murmurs.

'Um—' I trail off as the blinking purple gets faster. Blaze is a blur as he chases it, occasionally pausing long enough with his fingers stretched out for me to see the panic on his face. This isn't part of the show. This shouldn't be happening.

'Ladies and gentlemen.' King Ron must have seen what was happening from the stage. His voice booms across the court. 'Please make your way to the exits.'

'Skies,' Joy mutters, grabbing my arm. 'Come on.'

'Out!' Security run towards us. 'Everyone out!'

Joy disappears in the flood of people and, despite my desire to get to safety too, I turn back towards Blaze. The crowd flows past me, towards the exit, as Blaze chases the grenade above the stage. My eyes ache as I watch, afraid to blink. What happens if he catches it? Is he going to end up like The Pacifier, killed flying a bomb away from civilians? Is it high enough not to hurt the remaining crowd? Am I wasting my chance to get away?

The purple lights stop blinking—

WHITE

—erupts from the grenade and I'm too slow to throw my arm up to cover my eyes. My back hits something hard and the air is forced out of my lungs.

WHITE. My vision is white.

Why am I on the floor?

Where am I?

I can't see.

My heart is thundering and the only other thing I can hear is a high-pitched whine. It's like the white clouding my vision is screaming at me. I blink desperately.

BLAZECON. My mind tries to restart. I was in the Great Court of the museum watching Blaze and the grenade. I must still be there. My head is spinning, and panic is rising in my chest. I squeeze my eyes open and closed, willing my sight to come back.

After a thousand years of white it finally fades. My relief is short-lived as someone swims into focus above me. Blaze?

No.

It's someone wearing a bright blue boiler suit and a helmet with an opaque mirrored visor.

A Villain.

My arms are too wobbly to push myself up. How am I helpless on the floor, again? Am I cycling through the various dangers you can experience at ankle height? First fire, now the fecking Villains. We've all seen the footage of them doing battle with the heroes. They're men with unregistered, dangerous powers and they will do anything, and go through anyone, to hurt the HPA.

The Villain crouches and reaches for my face.

'Leave me alone!' My voice sounds like it's coming from the other side of a vacuum.

The Villain pauses and his shoulders fall in a way that looks like he's considering me. There's another blinding flash and I blink my eyes clear to see the Villain jerk upright, his limbs straightening unnaturally. He crashes to the ground, revealing King Ron standing on the stage looking at me and slowly lowering his hands. I've just been saved from a Villain by a power bolt from the leader of the HPA.

Security pile on to the felled Villain and drag him away. I stagger up and away from them all, almost tripping over a woman pushing herself to her feet too. King Ron is still in the centre of the stage, and now he's scanning the Great Court.

Blaze.

He must be looking for Blaze.

A lot of people hadn't made it to the exits when the flash

bang went off and they are scattered across the marble floor of the court, slowly stirring. There's no sign of Blaze amongst the fallen bodies. I can't see Joy either. But at least there's no blood. No one looks badly injured, just shocked. They are grimacing, crying and helping each other up. It's almost a relief I can't hear properly. The National Museum of Hero History must sound like a war zone.

'Blaze.'

The voice is just audible over the ringing, but it echoes like a loud speaker.

'Blaze. Tell the world how you got your powers.'

Where *is* Blaze?

Most people are back on their feet now and the crowd push past me towards the door, but I'm rooted to the spot.

Is Blaze dead?

I play back the moment where that grenade spewed white across the court. I think I saw which direction Blaze was flung in the split second before my sight went.

'More grenades!' someone screams. The surge towards the exit becomes more powerful as people push each other to reach that wooden door. Three new silver balls are circling the stage, firing darts at King Ron and his security team. They're not grenades. They're mini gun robots, which isn't necessarily better.

It's still not safe to stay, but I slip through the dazed crowd towards the west wing of the museum, where a huge BLAZECON banner lies crumpled on the ground.

'PLEASE HEAD TO YOUR CLOSEST EXIT AND HELP ANY WOMEN AND CHILDREN,' the tannoy shouts at us.

It's happening again. I should be leaving but I'm going deeper into danger. People stagger past, holding each other, heading for the exit, and I know I should join them, but I'm focused on the cloth bundle in front of the entrance to the west wing.

It's got to be Blaze.

Why isn't he moving?

Why hasn't anyone else helped him?

Did he hit his head on the wall, or break something when he fell? My insides feel like acid. What if he died and the last thing he did was argue with me?

I hold my breath as I reach the bundle and fall to my knees to gingerly tug the material away. His black, puffy jacket appears first, and then his face. A bright pink burn is scorched on to his cheek and his eyes are open, unblinking.

'No,' I whisper. His eyes flick up to find mine and I'm so relieved I could burst. 'Are you OK? Can you sit up?'

The silky material pools around us as I get him free of the banner. He's unstable, but immediately tries to stand, so I grab his hand to help. His palm is hot in mine. Am I holding it too tight? It's strange to have all this relief pooling with the anger and hatred from earlier. It's like oil sitting on the top of water. It shouldn't feel good to help Blaze, but it does.

King Ron and the security team are all busy with darts, and I can't take my hand back yet. Blaze is swaying; I think he's in shock.

'You should go to the hospital.'

Blaze gives me an odd look, but before he can reply a shadow falls over us.

'Found him!'

Above us, on a hoverboard, is another Villain in a blue boiler suit and helmet. His helmet tilts towards me. 'You should go, Jenna Ray.' He points at Blaze. His voice is distorted, but he sounds like he's enjoying himself. 'But not you. We want to talk to you.'

Is this the moment when Blaze gets a nemesis? Like King Ron and Diamond Joe, or the Controller and – wait, did the Controller not have a nemesis either? I don't have time for this. I should be running; the last thing I need is to be stuck in the middle of a super-powered fight, but Blaze is just holding my hand, staring up at the boiler-suited Villain, and still swaying. Maybe he has a concussion?

'Let's go somewhere a bit more private.' Boiler Suit flicks another grenade into his hand. Blaze still doesn't react. My free fingers curl around the apple juice in my pocket and, using all my strength, I fling the small bottle at Boiler Suit. It bounces harmlessly off his chest. His helmet points in my direction. 'Um, ow?!'

In a flash of black, Boiler Suit is knocked off his board.

He falls.

He stops.

He rises back to his feet.

He casually adjusts his sleeves.

My forehead furrows as I try to make sense of what I just witnessed. Boiler Suit should have crashed head first into the ground in front of me, but the impact never came. He stopped a few inches off the ground and rose back to his feet to land a few metres away. It didn't look like he was flying, like Blaze, but like he'd been picked up by a huge hand. Do the Villains have an invisible giant on their team?!

Boiler Suit swings his helmet towards the hero that hit him. The man in black has landed in a crouch, one palm on the floor, one arm in the air: the perfect hero landing pose. His black balaclava obstructs everything but a glint of grey eyes.

'The Secret Ninja!' I whisper. I'm fizzing with adrenalin but can't help being a little impressed. The Secret Ninja is one of the HPA's more elusive heroes. He doesn't do press. He doesn't have a social media account. No one knows anything about him, except that he can fight.

Blaze is still hurt, he must be, but he drops my hand and strides towards Boiler Suit. 'What do you want?'

'A chat, Blazey-boy, that's all. Perhaps you could get rid of him? No one likes a third wheel.' Boiler Suit jerks his thumb towards the Secret Ninja, who springs into action and launches a flying kick at him. Boiler Suit dodges jerkily; it still looks like he's being manoeuvred rather than moving under his own power. The Secret Ninja rolls to a stop right next to me.

This is really happening: a multi-hero face-off which I am far too close to. I stagger back. I know how this goes. I've seen footage of the heroes in action. First there's banter, then hand to hand, then suddenly there are buildings collapsing or some poor woman in a deadly situation. I back slowly towards the exit. Blaze is alive and the Secret Ninja is now up to a tally of two flying kicks. I've almost been grabbed by the Villains once already, I don't need to stick around and be collateral damage.

Boiler Suit regains his balance and puts a hand on his hip. 'It's been a while, hasn't it, Mr Ninja. I brought you a gift.' He snaps his fingers.

For a moment, nothing happens, and I'm about to turn and run when a blue flicker catches my eye. A silver ball with flashing blue lights has appeared above the Secret Ninja.

'Look out!' I throw my arms up to protect myself from another blast, but this one doesn't explode. It fires a weighted silver net at the Secret Ninja, who drops like a stone. Mother Earth, if the Secret Ninja is down, do I need to stay? I've already thrown my only juice bottle at this bad guy, I'm not sure what my next move would be.

Another silver ball appears beside Boiler Suit. This one has red blinking lights, and it fires a flurry of darts at Blaze. The last thing I need is to get hit by one of those things. I put another few metres between myself and the action, before slowing again to check on Blaze. He is a smudge of black as he dodges the darts. Then he's in front of Boiler Suit landing a punch. I almost cheer as the Villain goes flying.

The invisible giant is back. Boiler Suit stops mid-air by the Greatest Battles stall. His helmet lolls like he's ashamed or asleep. I think Blaze might have knocked him out. The hoverboard races to meet Boiler Suit and he is dumped on to it. There's a clack as his helmet hits the hoverboard and his arm drops to hang limply off the side. Definitely unconscious. Blaze is winning! The hoverboard shoots across the court and Blaze blurs after it.

That's it. It's time for me to get out of here. I leap over

forgotten bags and broken hero merch and race towards the door. The marble floor and glass ceiling of the Great Court echo with the sounds of a hero battle. The whoosh of a hoverboard. The zap of King Ron's power. The clatter of the net as the Secret Ninja frees himself. The screams of the crowd. There are even sirens drifting in through the crowded exit. I am deep in the action. If my family could see me now, they'd lose it; even I'm angry at myself. Why didn't I just run with everyone else?

As I pass the front of the stage, another blinding flash makes me stagger and stop to shake away the dots dancing in my eyes. I can't stay here. Darts are raining down on the stage and King Ron is drawing power from the rig to shoot blasts of white energy at the silver balls. The Secret Ninja is with him, spinning a mic stand and using it like a sword to take out the darts.

This is bad. This many heroes and Villains in one place means something super-dramatic is about to happen. The thuds of action echo under the stage as I pick my way past. Some other non-hero types are watching from beside the exit, ready to dash out if it gets too serious. They are safety. I'll become part of the crowd, make my way to the door, grab Joy, go home and never get involved in this nonsense ever again.

There's a whoosh behind me and I drop to the ground as the hoverboard flies over my head, pursued by Blaze. Boiler Suit's arm is still hanging limply as the board dodges the hero. If Boiler Suit is unconscious and security have taken the other, captured, Villain away, then why are those balls still coming? How is there still so much chaos happening?

100

I don't care.

I shouldn't care.

But it doesn't make sense.

All the heroes are so busy fighting, they haven't stopped to think. Imagining an invisible giant was ridiculous, but there's definitely someone else here. I rock on my toes. There's a clear path to safety ahead of me. I just need to climb over a broken stall, and it is a short run to the exit. I can escape this madness, but there's someone orchestrating all of this and I know where I'd be if I was in charge of this mayhem. I can't stop myself. I look up.

On the truss up above the stage, there's a cluster of speakers and, behind them, another figure in a blue boiler suit and helmet crouches. He moves his hands like a magician and, down below, the hoverboard changes direction, evading Blaze. I feel the hot flush of something that might be pride at figuring it out.

There was never a giant.

There was a telekinetic.

Not bad for a teenage girl from Nine Trees.

Feck. The telekinetic has frozen with his helmet angled down towards me.

He's seen me.

He leaps up, raises his arms and one of the glass panes in the sweeping roof of the Great Court lifts.

'Blaze, up there!' I shout.

Blaze looks up and sees the new boiler-suited figure, but in the split second he is distracted, a net from one of the silver balls drops on to him and he crashes down from mid-air on to the stage. There goes my pride. All I am is a distraction. Finally free of Blaze, the hoverboard and unconscious Villain shoots up and out through the gap in the ceiling.

Two bad guys are down, one's captured and one's unconscious. The net clatters on to the stage as the Secret Ninja frees Blaze and a moment later, Blaze is back in the air and speeding towards the final Villain. The telekinetic floats towards his escape, but Blaze arrives in front of him, blocking the way.

High above me, the two of them are in a stand-off. The telekinetic is floating with his hands angled towards the ground, and Blaze, still in the air, has his hands on his hips. Are they talking? Is Blaze using his highly trained hero voice to tell the Villain to give up now and come in quietly?

I've done my bit and I don't need to stay and watch Blaze finish up. I climb over the fallen stall and my foot snags in its tattered pink tablecloth. 'Feck!' I wriggle free of the Love Interest display and leap over the shattered picture of Kate, but instead of landing back on the marble floor, my feet hang in the air. There's pressure under my arms, around my waist and pushing at my feet. I'm being held up. This must be how my dolls used to feel.

'Let her go!' Blaze's distant voice is full of fury.

I am twisted slowly round to face the stage. The telekinetic's hand is stretched out towards me and Blaze is up there next to him. I can tell from all the way down here he has no idea what to do next. Feck. I try to flail my limbs and break the telekinetic's hold, but I can't move. I should have escaped. I should have left Blaze to it and then maybe it wouldn't be me taking the part of woman in mortal danger.

The telekinetic flicks his fingers and I drift slowly up above the stage. Too far above King Ron and the Secret Ninja for them to help me. Too high for anyone to do anything other than watch. I can't imagine what I must look like drifting slowly above the mess of BLAZECON, in my leggings and hoody. I almost laugh as I float higher. Perhaps this is only fair. Everyone else seems to be flying. Gravity feels like a plug sucking at me, desperate to drag me back to the marble ground, but the telekinetic holds me tight.

There's nothing to grab, no way to stop myself, and I'm so high now I wouldn't want to break free, even if I could. Blaze locks eyes with me and I want to shout—

'SEE! This is what happens when you lie on social media!'

But if I open my mouth I'm going to throw up, so I glare at him instead.

Blaze's frown is determined as he turns to shout something at the telekinetic, leaving me dangling in mid-air without even his eyes to tether me.

I hate him.

I hate all of them.

I hate myself for staying to help.

I'm going to come back as a ghost and haunt them. I'm going to steal Blaze's socks and his keys and the lids off all his skincare products. I'm shaking. Maybe it's laughter. Who knew floating by the ceiling of the National Museum of Hero History would be this funny?

The telekinetic tilts his head at me. I want to look into his eyes and see what he's planning. His helmet is in the way, but it turns out the telekinetic can communicate fine without facial expressions. He gives me a wave that turns my insides to ice.

An almighty shove hits me in the back and then everything is a blur; the sun shining through the roof, the screams bouncing up from the floor. The telekinetic is no longer holding me. It's just me, flying, about to crash into a wall or plummet down to meet the polished marble floor.

I'm in mid-air and slowing down.

'Feck, feck, feck.'

My stomach rises to my mouth as gravity takes me and I hurtle down towards the broken stalls of the Great Court. There's nothing I can do. For the second time in a week, I'm about to die. Not the roaring fire this time, but the empty air and the cold hard earth.

'Ooof!' Blaze says as I land in his arms, and we drop another few metres together.

'Sorry,' I manage. My heart is thudding in my ears.

Blaze shifts the arm that he's hooked under my legs and holds my torso tight with the other as he regains control. 'I've got you.'

It feels odd to be in his arms again. An uncomfortable heat is being generated in my core. I don't know if it's hate or relief. As my arm moves automatically around his shoulders, my hand brushes the soft skin on the back of his neck. Above his sore-looking burn, his cheeks flush pink and he won't meet my eye.

There's no sign of the telekinetic. He must have got away when Blaze saved me. Maybe Blaze is angry – more angry – with me, but, beneath the terror of the last few minutes, I'm still angry with him, even if he did just save me. Being held by Blaze is confusing.

We land in front of the stage to a smattering of applause from the die-hard fans who are wandering back into the court. Blaze lets me down and I take a wobbly step away from him. He shakes out his arms. 'Feck.'

'All right, I'm not that heavy,' I say.

'Everyone is heavy when they're falling,' he snaps.

'Technically, this was your fault—' Someone bumps into me.

'This is Sydney Jones, on the scene, and I'm here with Jenna Ray, who, as you will have just seen, was heroically rescued by Blaze.' Sydney grins at me and a camera is thrust towards my face. 'Jenna, how did it feel to be snatched away from certain death by Blaze, again?'

I look at Blaze for help, but he just gives me a little smile. 'Gotta go.' And then he's gone, flying up and out of the gap in the roof.

I look back at Sydney. 'I—'

I what?

I'm going to throw up on you?

I'm going to curl up in the foetal position?

I'm going to have a panic attack on live TV?

'Yes, Jenna?' Sydney says.

'Ms Jones.' King Ron jumps nimbly from the stage to land between me and the camera. 'I think we should let Jenna go and recover. That was quite an ordeal for her.' Behind his back he motions for me to escape, but the floor isn't solid any more. King Ron continues regardless. 'I, however, have a plea for information. We have been attacked by the Villains in the most cynical way. They waited for a celebration of lives saved and crises averted and then put hundreds of innocent people at risk. If anyone knows someone who has been acting suspiciously or spouting anti-HPA nonsense, we need to know. We do the right thing; that's what the HPA do. And we need you, the public—'

A hand grips my arm and yanks me away.

'Joy?' I stumble after her. My heart is hammering and the BLAZECON banners and white columns are spinning and blurring together. Someone has put the classical music back on; it sounds like a violin is screaming at me.

'Joy.' I find her hand. 'Are you OK?'

'I'm not the one walking like a drunk person. Come on, it's not far.' Joy grips my hand and pulls me forward.

We pass through the columns, go down the wide white stairs and I'm helped into the timo.

'So,' Mia says as the car pulls away. 'How did it go?'

CHAPTER 9

The timo is silent as it passes the now-familiar press circus outside the museum.

'They've just started arriving,' Mia tells us. 'I'd say you two got out in the nick of time.'

The windows are tinted, but I still slide lower in my seat. Getting out in time is not how I'd describe what just happened. Why did I stay in that mess? The backs of my legs where Blaze caught me must be slightly bruised; it feels like I'm still in his arms.

'Anyway,' Mia continues. 'I thought we could take the Safe Road back to Nine Trees. It'll give you time to decompress.'

'Decompression is probably a good idea,' Joy says. I'm not going to look up. I can feel her eyes on me and I don't know if I'm ready to talk yet. 'Do you need some juice, Ray? Or something else sweet?'

'There'll be some cereal bars back there somewhere,' Mia calls over the clicking of the indicator.

'Aw. You do care.' Joy rummages through the drinks cabinet and a moment later a cranberry-and-raisin cereal bar is slid into my hand. My stomach gurgles. I didn't realise I was hungry. I take a tangy mouthful that's so big no one will expect me to speak, and look up at Joy's worried face.

'So.' Mia catches my eye in the rear-view mirror. 'What happened in there?'

My mouth is full, so my answer stays safely in my brain. Talking about it will make it all too real. *What happened in there? Well, I should have run, multiple times. Instead, I stayed and got attacked by the Villains, almost died and got rescued by Blaze, again. Yes, the Villains were there, and the Secret Ninja, and Sydney fecking Jones.*

I shrug and slump back in my seat.

'Are you OK?' Joy slides closer to me.

I nod and take another big mouthful. The words *'Not really. I think that I've just made everything much worse'* stay safe behind the cereal bar.

'What did you see, Joy?' Mia asks.

'Well.' Joy closes her eyes to compose herself. 'Imagine this.'

I roll my eyes. Here we go.

'Jenna and Blaze are having a little chat and Jenna is absolutely schooling the kid.'

I swallow. 'I don't know if that's what happened.'

'Are you telling this story, or am I?' Joy lifts her eyebrows at me.

'Fine.' I wave her on.

'So, Jenna has basically got Blaze in tears and then a grenade rolls in. And to his credit, Blaze dries his eyes and tries to catch it. He misses and gets blasted across the court. Don't worry, he's fine. And Jenna is all, *"I hurt his feelings, I should probably see if he's dead now."* He's not, he's fine, like I said, so Jenna helps him up and basically fights a Villain for him. She threw a juice bottle at the bad guy.'

'You threw a juice bottle at a Villain?' Mia sounds impressed and I can't help but smile.

'So that fight moves on.' Joy is on the edge of her seat now, using her hands to act bits out. 'Blaze is like POW and the Secret Ninja turns up and is like BOFF and the Villain is like ARGH and flies away on his hovering skateboard—'

'Hoverboard,' I supply.

'Yes, hoverboard. And then Jenna is like, *"Hey, heroes, the main bad guy is actually up there?!"* And the heroes are like, *"Oh boy! We're really stoopid! Thanks for figuring out everything, Jenna,"* but the main bad guy floats Jenna up and flings her across the court and Blaze finally does something useful and catches her.'

'A Villain threw you across the Great Court of the museum?' Mia is open-mouthed.

'Yeah.' Somehow, Joy's retelling is making my heart feel lighter.

'And then Sydney Jones pops up and Blaze leaves Jenna in front of a camera and, I'm afraid, that's why Blaze is a ball bag.' Joy clasps her hands. 'Thank you.'

My loud laugh surprises everyone, including me.

'He's not a bad guy, really,' Mia says. 'He's sweet.'

My smile evaporates and I adjust my headwrap using the window. We're out of the city already and the moor rolls past, a strange mix of perma-brown and new buds in the drizzle. Fingers crossed we're all done talking. I don't need to hear the HPA line on how great Blaze is.

'If one acts like a ball bag …' Joy shrugs.

'It sounds like,' Mia says, 'Jenna found Blaze when he needed her and helped him to save the day. That's classic Love Interest behaviour.'

'More like hero behaviour. Jenna did more good in there than those other "heroes".' Joy looks at me proudly. I want to tell her that nothing like that will ever happen again, but I don't have the energy. I direct my attention to the row of crooked black trees with unnatural blue flowers that we're passing.

'What do you know about the Secret Ninja, Mia?' Joy asks.

I look back at them. The Secret Ninja is an enigma. He just appeared one day in the early noughties. No prophecy, no emergence, no sidekick, no Love Interest, just a man in black doing heroic things.

Mia shrugs. 'No one knows anything except that he helps the HPA sometimes. I've never got to dress him. He always wears that drab black thing. Do you remember Ron's outfit from the eighties? Blue spandex, red belt and boots? Now that's how to dress a hero.'

'What about the Villains?' Joy isn't finished pumping Mia for information. 'The press only ever says that they're evil. What is their deal?'

'I don't know what to tell you.' Mia adjusts the mirror to look at us both. 'The Villains hate the HPA, but they don't normally attack in such a public way. Their outfits are slightly better than the Ninja's, but still lacking imagination. Blue boiler suits? Why?'

'But why do they keep attacking the HPA?' Joy ticks the classic bad-guy motives off on her fingers. 'Rule the world? Ill-fated attempt to save the world? Control of resources?'

'Avenge a loved one?' I add.

'Good one,' Joy says. 'Revenge?'

'Money?'

Joy moves on to her second hand. 'Timeless feud?'

'Greed in general?' I tap her finger.

'Misinterpreting a prophecy?'

'Oh, nice!' I say. 'Like that guy in the nineties who hijacked a cruise ship in the Caribbean because he thought the prophecy said it would hit an iceberg?'

'Ill-fated love story?'

I roll my eyes. 'You're an addict.'

'Could you two stop?' Mia cuts in. 'Apparently, it's Blaze. There's something about Blaze that has got them riled up.'

I remember that first voice cutting through the shock of the explosion.

'Blaze. Tell the world how you got your powers.'

'Blaze's powers turned up when he was a teenager, right?' I lean past the headrest. 'Like all the other heroes?'

'Of course,' Mia replies.

'Then what's so interesting about him?'

'You tell me.' There's a click and rock music fills the timo. 'ETA two hours.'

'That's one way to end a conversation,' Joy says quietly.

I give her a half-smile and lie down on the long seat. My phone is dead, and I don't want to think about Blaze any more, or anything really. I close my eyes, picture the waves sparkling in the sun and pretend to nap for the rest of the journey.

It starts to rain between Joy's house and mine. Mia walks me to my front door with an umbrella.

'I'm sure Blaze would be very upset with me if I didn't see you home,' Mia says.

'I'm sure he wouldn't.' My keys jangle as I fish them out of my pocket, but the front door is yanked open from the inside before I can use them. Megan is silhouetted in the corridor, like a vengeful shadow. Dad skids to a stop behind her. The umbrella sheltering me disappears.

'Uh-huh.' Mia trips down our drive. 'There we are, safe and sound. I don't do terrifying, so ... Nice to meet you, Jenna, Jenna's family.' Mia's door slams. I'm tempted to follow. I could fling myself into the back and scream, *Just drive!* That would be one way to postpone the yelling. But I force myself to stay put, leaning slightly away from my furious family as the tyres of the timo screech away.

'Hi.' My voice wavers. I've never felt nervous at my own front door before.

Megan grabs me and crushes the air out of me, then Dad muscles in and holds me so tight I think that they decided to teach me a lesson by hugging me to death. Then he lets me go and it begins.

'*What were you thinking?!*'

Dad's voice isn't quite a shout, but it doesn't need to be. '*Why were you at that convention?!*'

'**When you said you were going to be fine today, I didn't think that meant you were off to try and get murdered!**' Megan adds.

'*If there's a disaster, you run, you hide. What were you doing in the thick of it?!*'

'**I saw the way that boy left you with Sydney on the news. I'm going to destroy him.**'

'*You're grounded. You're grounded forever. Apparently, that's the only way to keep you safe.*'

'**WHAT WERE YOU THINKING?!**' they both yell, and the rain falls harder, like it's on their side.

'Could we go inside?' I hate this. I hate that I've scared them, and I don't want to make them angrier, but passers-by are slowing down to watch. I don't think I can deal with a *Jenna Ray chewed out by her family* SPECIAL on the news.

Dad pulls me in and slams the door behind us. I rush into

113

the kitchen and wedge myself into the corner of the dining table that sits under the stairs, hoping that they might be done shouting and I can make myself some toast.

Our kitchen is yellow. I remember helping Mum choose the orangey tiles that sit above the wooden worktops. As we painted the walls pale yellow, she told me this was our sunniest room. But the yellow doesn't always work. In the days after Mum left, the room felt like it had a fever. Now, in the lamplit gloomy afternoon, it feels like it's about to catch fire.

Megan follows me in and automatically goes to the kettle, but Dad isn't finished.

'The HPA are bad news in every conceivable way. All they care about are their heroes, money and power. They won't look after you; they don't treat women well. Your mother hated working there. The things she told me. The things I've heard about them since.' He slides into the seat across from me. 'I don't want you involved with them.'

My insides harden. He's done it. He's played the M card: *Your mum was an engineer with the HPA. Then she left and broke our hearts. Therefore, you should accept everything I say without question because we both know that an actual conversation about her causes me to withdraw for hours, if not days.*

I manage to keep my voice calm. 'I don't *want* to be involved with them. I went to the convention to tell Blaze to leave me alone.'

'And how did that work out?' Megan sets out the mugs.

'You can't engage, Jen-bear,' Dad says. 'The only way to

114

make this go away is to cut off all communication. You do not want to be a Love Interest. Look what happened to Kate.'

'She died,' Megan calls over the rumble of the kettle. 'King Ron let her fall off that bridge, and how old was she? Twenty-five? Twenty-six?'

'And it's not just Love Interests who get chewed up and spat out by the HPA.' Dad reaches for my hand, but I yank it away. 'Best friends, family members, plucky reporters, genius scientists, people who are just in the wrong place at the wrong time. If you're not the main character in the story that the HPA tells, then you're expendable.'

'Even the Diviner was just a servant to those testosterone-fuelled dick holes,' Megan adds.

Keeping a lid on my frustration is getting harder. Why won't they hear me? 'I know all this. I don't want to be a Love Interest. Not even a little bit. I'm not interested in Blaze.'

'The Love Interest's stories never end well, sweetheart. Like I said, women are not treated well by the HPA.' Dad is doing that thing where he talks to me as if I'm ten.

'Are you even listening to me?' I leap up and knock my head off the underside of the staircase. 'Ow! I don't want this. I don't want him.'

'And that's why you went to see him? I'm not sure you should be allowed to make the plans.' Megan places a mug in front of me. 'Sit down, Jen-bear. We're just worried.'

I slump back down in my chair, rubbing my head. 'Just stop telling me things I already know. I shouldn't have gone. I made a mistake. I don't know how to deal with all this hero stuff.

I KNOW.' I breathe out. I need to stop shouting at the people that I love. 'Today was awful. Could we just watch TV?'

'No,' they both say far too fast, and I know that there's footage of me being hurled around and rescued by Blaze on every channel.

'No,' Dad says. 'And the only way I'm going to be able to sleep tonight is if I know that you are never going to see that boy again. Can you promise me that, Jenna?'

Blaze's smile as he left me with Sydney Jones flashes through my mind and I stop myself from snarling. 'I am never going to see that selfish, manipulative, immature hero again. And if he turns up, I'll send him packing or kick him in the balls. OK?'

Megan hits me on the back. 'That's my girl!'

Dad looks at me for a long moment before hitting a hand off the table. 'OK! This is now a Blaze-Free Zone and you can both help me make gyros for dinner.'

Megan and I both nod. 'On it!'

All the tension seeps away as the music goes on and my family start bustling round the kitchen. This house, my family and my head are now all a Blaze-Free Zone.

There's no mention of the hero when Megan bangs on my door in the morning or when Dad rushes in to say bye on his way to work. But school, school on the first day it's reopened after Blaze heroically saved the town and ruined my life, school will be different. People will stare at me. They'll ask me questions. It doesn't matter what I want; this whole day is going to be about Blaze. I pause as I pack my bag. My knuckles have gone white as I grip my swimming stuff.

'You don't have to go.' Megan is at my door, her small work satchel dangling from the crook of her elbow.

'If he changes my life then he wins.' I shove my swimming gear in on top of my psychology textbook.

Megan swoops in and kisses me on the head. 'You call me if it gets too much.'

I nod.

'Because I hate my job.'

I nod again.

'And I get paid a fraction of what my useless male colleagues earn. Honestly, I'd leave work to rescue a lost paper bag. A sister in peril is an A-plus excuse.'

I smile. 'I see.'

'Seriously, even if you get a bit bored, I'll be there. Out of my way, capitalist puppets!' She tramps across my dark blue rug, pretending to shove people on her way out of my room. 'My sister needs me!'

Megan yells bye on her way out of the door and I'm left dreading facing a whole school of Blaze questions. I'm still going to go, and I won't call my big sister for help, but I will wear the headwrap she left on my bag.

CHAPTER 10

The sun is low and blinding as I reach what remains of the Culture Complex. This is not the way to school. I could have turned left out of my house and been at school in five minutes, but as I took off the last of my bandages this morning, I knew I needed to come here. To crunch across the glass in the car park where I was deposited by Blaze. To see what's left of the complex, black and jagged in the morning light. Maybe I just needed to remind myself of what I survived. What I can survive.

The roof fell in when the complex exploded, and beyond the struts and fallen beams, there are blackened hints of what used to be the interior. Part of the circular box office is still there and a section of cinema screen is somehow still standing. It's hard to see in the bright sunlight, but the light reflecting up out of the crumbling black looks almost blue.

My eyes travel away from the main section to the chunks of

fallen balcony that are scattered around the complex, looking like intensely dangerous slides. My throat aches as I remember the books that balcony used to hold. They all became smoke and ash.

There's a crunch from behind me and I turn to see a girl with a blonde pixie cut trekking across the car park towards me. She looks like she's on her way back from a night out: high-heeled boots, tight jeans and a short leather jacket. I grit my teeth. She's probably a Blaze mega-fan.

'Hi,' she says as she reaches me.

'Hi?'

'I'm Emily—'

'Hey!' A man in high-vis is rushing towards us. 'Hey! You can't be here.' He arrives breathless and motions to a sign that says RESTRICTED AREA BY ORDER OF THE HPA.

'Sorry.' I hadn't even noticed the sign, but at least I don't need to engage with Emily the Blaze fan now. I turn to go, before spinning back round. 'Sorry, why?'

'Why aren't you allowed in a burned-out building?' The man raises his eyebrows at me.

'No, why aren't I allowed to look at it?'

'It's a good question,' Emily adds.

The man shrugs. 'It's a HPA thing. They do this wherever there's been significant EV activity.'

'So, this got hit by an EV fork of lightning and now the HPA have cordoned it off?' I ask.

'Exactly that. There can be residual energy from EV events like the lightning storm. It's not safe for people to be around.

So …' He motions to the grey trousers, white blouse and blazer of my school uniform. 'You've got somewhere to be, I think?'

His patronising tone makes me grit my teeth, but snapping *'I just wanted to look quietly at the place where I almost died'* isn't going to improve either of our days, so I adjust my bag and speed walk back through the car park before Mr High-Vis or Emily the Blaze mega-fan can say anything else annoying. I hadn't paid attention to the signs on my way in, but they are everywhere.

RESTRICTED ACCESS

OFF LIMITS TO PUBLIC

DANGER OF EV EXPOSURE AND DEATH

Places like the Wild Road are deemed unsafe because of EV animals and plants all the time, but I've never heard of places being cordoned off because of residual EV energy before. The energy left by the EV storm must be intense. It's incredible that I survived. That our town mostly survived.

All thoughts of the restrictions around the Culture Complex fade as I cross the river and the school looms ahead of me. This will be fine. It's school. School is something I'm good at, as long as I don't have to speak in a group of more than five people.

I let out a long breath as I pass through the school gates.

                           '—there she is!'

I can ignore the whispers coming from the gaggle of younger girls by the vending machine.

              'Jenna Ray—'

And the rugby boys by the picnic tables.

                    'I didn't know she went here!'

And a pair of cleaners coming out of the English block.

And all the other groups I can't bring myself to look at as I hurry past our red-brick assembly hall towards the ugly concrete science block. I clench my fists. Once I'm with my year twelve form group I'll be safe. It's not far to our lab and I can't turn back now; I'd have to pass all those people again.

The whispers get worse as I make it through the rotating door that always jams and into the flaking corridor of the science block. The crowds of students are denser here.

        '—thrown across the museum!'

Why am I doing this?

                 '—first person he rescued—'

Blaze won't even know if I went to school or not.

I can't win this.

        '—Love Interest!'

I can only lose.

'Hi, Jenna!' An arm is slipped through mine and my heart beats even faster. It isn't Joy. 'Are you coming to training later?'

Okorie grins down at me.

               '—going out with Okorie Ogundipe too?!'

'Y-yes,' I manage. Now floaty butterflies are bouncing around with my anxiety. He's so hot, I think I might vomit.

'Good weekend?' he asks with a twinkle and I burst out laughing.

'Like you don't know,' I say.

'It looked dramatic, for sure, but I guess my favourite part of all the stories was about you turning Blaze down.'

'Do they actually say that?' My heart lifts a tiny bit. 'I haven't been watching the news.'

'Well, this morning's headline was BLAZE AND LOVE INTEREST STILL AT ODDS, and I can read between the lines.' His smile makes my knees turn to water.

'That's good.' I try to lean on the wall, but it's too far away so I just kind of sway.

'It must have been intense.' Okorie gently pushes me upright. 'Maybe we can chat about it at swimming later? You promised me tips, remember?'

'It's a date,' I say.

Wait.

What did I just say?

Am I going red?

I'm going red.

He just wanted to chat to a fellow swimmer and now I've made it awkward.

Okorie laughs. 'All right, it's a date. Most people master the art of postponing the start, but not you, Jenna Ray.'

The emergency loudspeakers let out a high-pitched squeal that makes everyone wince.

'PLEASE REPORT TO THE ASSEMBLY HALL.'

My heart gives a hard thud. 'I might skip this.' There will be far too many people in that hall.

'ATTENDANCE IS MANDATORY!' The speaker is so loud I can almost see wiggly lines coming out of it.

'Guess we're going to assembly then,' I say, and keep my eyes on Okorie as people stream back into the corridor.

He places a hand on my arm. 'We can stand near the door.'

Sneaking in at the last minute and standing near the door works like a dream. I find a place where I can just see the backs of blazers and a tiny section of the stage. There's no sign of Joy, but I can feel Okorie's heat next to me. I roll my shoulders and flash him a smile. Should you be able to feel someone else's body heat through your school uniform?

In the burble of conversation, I catch the odd talk of *fire* and *Blaze*, which is to be expected the first day back after the Nine Trees prophecy finally hit. But no one is looking at me, so perhaps I've got time to flirt with Okorie. Not that I'm good at flirting.

'I didn't ask how your weekend was,' I say. Is that flirting? Or is it just small talk?

Okorie doesn't seem to mind. 'Less exciting than yours. Put my little sister's hair in cornrows. Helped my dad with the boat.' He waggles a hand still stained with yellow paint at me. 'Went to the beach with a book.'

Something inside me melts at the thought of Okorie doing his little sister's hair. And what was he reading on the beach?

My imaginary perfect weekend now ends with me lazing in the sand with Okorie as the sun goes down.

'You're staring, Jenna.'

'Oh!' I flick my eyes away from him and back towards the stage.

Okorie leans close to whisper in my ear. 'I didn't mind.'

'Welcome back!' Ms Paul breezes on to the stage and the hall immediately falls silent. She may have grey curls and rosy red cheeks, but you do not upset Ms Paul. 'We did it.' She gazes around the room, her eyes fierce. I don't know whether what we all did was good or bad. 'My dear school, we survived!'

The hall bursts into applause and I join in. She's right. No one would have bet on every student, every member of staff and every brick of the school remaining intact after the prophecy hit. The whoops and cheers of everyone here are something to be grateful for.

'The storm could have at least taken out the maths block,' someone in front mutters.

'And now we look ahead.' Ms Paul strides forward. 'We look at our prophecy-free future and all the possibilities that it can hold. Apprenticeships, university; we can finally get the funds to give our tired little school a makeover.' This gets another cheer. 'But at the same time, we need to maintain our vigilance over the EV and the other threats to our society. We need to do our bit for the HPA—'

My teeth clench.

'—for our new hero, Blaze—'

People have turned their attention away from Ms Paul and

are scanning the hall. They're looking for me. Is this what's going to happen every time someone says his name?

'And each other,' Ms Paul concludes.

'—she's by the door.'

My chest squeezes like a vice as an ocean of heads turn towards me. Even Okorie is looking at me. My chest tightens. I can't stay here.

Ms Paul coughs loudly. 'And that includes looking after pupils singled out by heroes and the HPA. EYES UP HERE!' Her voice is so sharp even I glance up at the stage, before using the opportunity to slip through the door and into the empty corridor.

Ms Paul's voice echoes after me, talking about respect and litter, as I walk with steady steps away from the hall.

I'm not leaving.

I just need a quick break.

Blaze hasn't won.

I will get my life back on track.

My chest is tight, but I'm not having an attack. Not yet.

'I'll just go and sit on the wall outside the school for a few minutes until I'm back to normal,' I tell myself. 'That's what I'll do.'

My feet take me down the winding path from the assembly hall to the school gates and I pause for a moment, looking for a sunny patch where I can sit.

'Hi.' The Blaze mega-fan with the blonde pixie cut, Emily, stands up from the only sunny spot on the wall.

'Jenna!' Okorie rushes up to the school gates. 'Are you all right?'

Feck. My cheeks are burning. I must have looked so weak running away from assembly, but Okorie is the last person I want to know about my panic attacks.

'You know, I just …' I wave a hand and decide to try the one thing that boys never ask follow-up questions about. 'Got my period.'

Okorie looks at me for a beat and then laughs. 'Really?'

'No.' His laugh is so warm, it makes me smile. 'I needed to get away from everyone.'

'Fair enough. Come on then.' He swings his backpack over an arm. 'Where are we going?'

My mouth falls open and I glance around for the Emily girl, but she's gone. That's good. I don't want there to be any witnesses to me bunking off school with a boy. I bite my lip. 'Have you been to Hidden Beach?'

Hidden Beach takes about half an hour to get to from school, but with Okorie chatting about his sister and her new obsession with seals, the walk flies by. The clouds roll in, but it doesn't matter. In what feels like no time, we're at Lighthouse Hill, the deceptively steep grassy slope topped by our town's third lighthouse.

'Dogs are land seals now, otters are thin seals, whales are mega seals. I made her seal-shaped pancakes. The world becomes a magical place when you see it through a prism of seals.'

We bound up the wooden steps and skirt a few puffing tourists. There's a tour group gathered by the wide white base of the lighthouse. It's much beefier than the slim brick lighthouses that guard the harbour. I pick a route round the hilltop that keeps us as far from them as possible.

I've never skipped school before. I'm not certain if it's guilt over missing classes, fear of being looked at, or proximity to Okorie that's making my heart hammer. But when I make my way to the cliff edge, all my muscles unclench as I gaze down at the endless grey waves.

Okorie exhales gently beside me. 'It's like a foam roller for the mind.'

'Yeah.' None of my other friends understand the sea, but Okorie seems to. As soon as I see it, I feel safe. I feel free.

'There's evidence the Diviner wrote her second book of prophecies in this very lighthouse,' the guide shouts.

I snort. The tour guides of Nine Trees have found 'evidence' for a lot of things.

'And did you know that King Ron himself was conceived in the lighthouse too?' I say, leaning into Okorie.

'Really?' He laughs. 'How are you so knowledgeable?'

I tap my head. 'It's my superpower.'

The grass-covered slope facing the town becomes a craggy cliff face as it curves round the coast. The salt tang of the wind settles on my lips as we follow the path along the edge. Below are the rocks that hide my favourite place in the world. My heart is beating faster again, but it's definitely not an attack this time. It's the excitement I always feel when I'm heading towards the sea for a swim. My whole body is buzzing, warming itself up for the dive in.

At the top of the route to Hidden Beach, I tighten my

rucksack so it fits snugly between my shoulders and turn to Okorie. 'You've done this before?'

He nods, pulling his bag tighter too. 'I promise I won't die.'

I grin. 'You know just what a girl wants to hear.' I can almost hear Joy in my head cheering: *You're doing it, Jenna, you're flirting.*

To the untrained eye, the path to Hidden Beach looks like certain death; a sheer, sometimes crumbling route that winds down the cliffside with only tufts of purple flowers to grab on to. It's not actually that bad, unless it's raining, or has rained in the past week – then it's super dangerous. The bonus is that no tourist would ever know that there is the most beautiful beach in the world at the bottom. Even the locals who do know prefer Town Beach, with its toilets and car park. Hidden Beach, a small and perfect stretch of sand surrounded by boulders, sits on the edge of Nine Trees like the secret cherry on a cake.

The sun breaks through the clouds, shining shafts of yellow on the brown rock as I pick my way slowly towards the beach. Halfway down, I grip the rock shaped like a pepper grinder and Okorie slides to a stop next to me to enjoy the view of the cove below. At some point the EV will take Hidden Beach away from me; EV animals or plants will take up residence, or an EV weather event will smash this cove to pieces. One day the British coastline will become as wild and dangerous as the Dunes of France, but today it looks empty of any wildlife, even gulls.

'I should get my family to come here more.' Okorie dumps his bag as we reach the sand. 'We're swimming, right?'

'Right.' I head to my normal boulder and search through my bag for my costume. 'No peeking.'

'No problem.' Okorie is already in his trunks. My cheeks flush red, but he's running towards the waves. It's like one of my fantasies, but it's happening. I fumble with my towel and take a million years to get changed.

Normally I wear a wetsuit – Megan did some research on sea temperatures and ganged up with Dad against me – but today I only have my indoor kit. I grin. The shock of cold water will be exactly what I need to keep my head around Okorie. I pull on my swimming cap and goggles and sprint into the sea as fast as my outfit will allow.

The grey May sea is still cold enough to feel like needles as it touches each part of my body, but that passes in a sharp moment and I am left with the delicious coolness that leaves no space for fear, anxiety or Blaze. The waves lift and hold me as I settle into an easy front crawl heading out to the opening of the cove.

'What took you so long?' Okorie stops to tread water as I reach him. 'I'm already on my fifth lap across the cove.'

'Then you're too tired for a race?' I ask. We rise and fall with a rolling wave and Okorie's smile widens.

'Please. I'm only just warm.'

'To the boulder?' I point at a rock jutting out of the sea about twenty metres away.

'OK, a sprint! Front crawl?' Okorie asks.

'No.'

'Breaststroke?'

'No.'

'Backstroke?!'

'No.'

'Don't tell me you want to do butterfly.' Okorie's eyebrows meet above his goggles.

'No.'

'What then, Jenna Ray?! Do you want me to fly?'

My mind bats away any thoughts of Blaze with ease. There's no space for him here. My fantasy is somehow coming true. I'm swimming with Okorie Ogundipe and for as long as that lasts, I only want it to be me, him and the waves.

'The stroke I choose is … doggy-paddle,' I say.

'No way am I—'

'Go!' I set off doing the fastest doggy-paddle I can manage. Okorie laughs and a moment later there's a huge amount of splashing behind me. There's a reason we're not taught doggy-paddle in school. Twenty metres seems to take an age, but as I place a hand on the rough rock, Okorie is still splashing behind me.

He arrives at the rock, breathing hard. 'How are you not exhausted?'

I grin and shrug. 'Years of practise?'

'Power to you. Train hard, win easy. After that, front crawl must be a breeze. Rematch, with an actual stroke?'

I roll my eyes. 'Fine.'

Okorie nods. 'Front crawl to the beach. GO!'

He dives under the water.

'Cheater!' I yell, and dive in too.

Okorie wins that race, I win the next, and we swap swimming tips in the waves. Okorie moves his hands to my shoulders to adjust my form and I smile underwater. The craziness of the weekend has been washed away and this might be the best morning of my life. I didn't realise I had a type, but now I know what it is. If I'm going to fall for a person, they need to be kind and have a record-breaking front crawl.

'OK. I am cold!' Okorie lets me go and strides out towards the beach.

'Aw, come on.' I stand and the water swirls around my waist. 'We can race again?'

'You're a machine, Jenna.' Okorie pulls off his swim cap and goggles. 'I'm sorry, I'm done.'

'Fine!' I fall back into the water and sit submerged, letting the sea sap away my urge to lure Okorie back in. The push and pull of the waves also eases my desire to grab him and tumble on to the sand together. Bubbles race past my face and I break the surface, standing to take off my cap and goggles. No luring. No grabbing. No tumbling. Our moment in the sea is over, but I'm OK.

'Are you going back to school?' I crunch up the sand to meet Okorie by his bag. How is he already half dressed?

Okorie nods, pulling on his shoes. 'I've got a mock exam after lunch. You coming?'

—*she's by the door.*

The memory of all those eyes from the assembly hall makes me shudder. I glance back at the sea. 'No. I've got free periods after lunch anyway. I might just stay here.'

'OK. Well.' He pulls on his bag. 'This was … Thanks for the swimming lesson.'

'Anytime.' My grin freezes as Okorie steps closer to me.

'You really are special, Jenna. You'll get through this,' he murmurs. His words are warming me up from the inside and even though I'm still in my dripping costume, his hands are back on my shoulders.

'Thank you.' I don't know what else to say, but this was never really a conversation. I lean into him, tilting my head up, and he drops his lips towards mine.

'Hi! Jenna!'

We break apart. I don't want to acknowledge this new person. I want to close the distance between me and Okorie and finally kiss him, but he's looking over at them, so I look too.

Feck. It's Emily, and she's waving.

Okorie shakes his head, smiling. 'I'll – er – I'll leave you with your friend.' He leans in and gives me a peck on the cheek. 'To be continued?'

'To be continued,' I repeat, too stunned to tell him to stay or that Emily is not my friend.

'Later, Ray.' Okorie jogs along the beach and climbs back up the cliffside.

'He's almost as fast as Blaze, isn't he?' Emily is suddenly beside me, watching him go.

'What do you want?!' I turn to her with a snarl. 'Why are you following me?!' *Why did you just stop me from kissing the boy of my dreams*, I want to add, but stop myself.

She holds up a finger. 'Just a sec.'

Okorie reaches the top of the cliff and turns back to give me a wave, and then he's gone.

'OK.' Emily turns back to me with a bright smile. 'Hi, I'm Emily and I'm the liaison for the Villains. You're going to want to put some clothes on.'

Baby Blaze has been REJECTED! Is he really MAN ENOUGH to be our hero?

By Sarah Popkin for H-Mail Online

4302 shares

In these crazy times, with prophesies, Villains, and nature ready to tear you to pieces if you dare to step off the path, we turn to the heralded HPA for sanity.

The heroes! Tall, certain and full of testosterone … until now. What is happening to our brand-new baby hero? Yes, he's got the face and, I'm allowed to say (just), the body. He's got the uniform, he's got the name, he's got the dramatic emergence, but, guys, where oh where is his LOVE INTEREST?!

He pulls a small-town girl out of a fire and this JENNA RAY doesn't want anything to do with him. Why? I ask. WHY? There's nothing more interesting going on in that dull little teen's life, so what is wrong with Blaze?

Was it the way he saved her? The way he spoke to her? Does our new baby hero not understand how to talk to women? And if he can't do something as basic as develop a relationship with his first rescue, how can he be trusted to do anything else?

I don't want to say it, but everyone else is ... Has our country ended up with another dud like the Controller? Is this lost little boy really the hero that we so desperately need?

I guess we'll just have to wait and see ...

135

CHAPTER 11

Emily, the liaison for the Villains, is smirking at me. It's not a full smile; I'm sure she knows that would make me sprint straight back into the sea. It's a smirk, and it's feeding the anger growing in my core. My fists are clenched, but it's not OK to shove this girl even if she does have the most annoying facial expression I've ever seen.

'Gosh. Jenna Ray! I honestly did not think I'd be able to make this happen.' Emily perches on the boulder by my stuff. 'Ew! Is this seaweed?!' She flings a dark purple leaf off the rock and settles back down again. 'First, you're arguing with security guards, and then you're hiding in school, then you're running away from school, then you're very busy frolicking with some boy that isn't Blaze. What would your mother say?' She raises her eyebrows at me.

Can I punch her? A violent response could be an appropriate reaction to a Villain liaison. I could say I was terrified. No one would ever need to know my motivation was her interrupting an almost kiss and then mentioning my mum. I should probably be terrified. My heart sped up when Okorie was in front of me and it's still beating hard now. Maybe punching her and running away is exactly what I should do? The Villains are the last people who I want to get involved with.

'Please.' Emily motions to my clothes. 'I promise I won't peek.'

My lip curls up. Is she mocking my attempt to flirt? Was she hiding behind a rock the whole time? When it comes to fight or flight, I've never been so firmly in the fight camp.

'What do you want?' I snatch my tracksuit trousers from my bag and pull them on.

'The Villains have a proposition for you.' She shakes out my pink post-swim fleece and tries to pass it to me. 'Here you go.'

I glare at the fleece until she puts it gently back on my sandy pile of stuff.

'Why, exactly, would I want to listen to your group of anarchist nutjobs.' I grab my fleece and wriggle into it. The split second I can't see Emily, I expect her to jab me with a tranquilliser or throw a net over me, but as I pull my head out, she's still sitting on the boulder, waiting.

'Is a little bit of anarchy all that bad? You're not a fan of the current system, are you?' She leans towards me. 'Lots of girls would have jumped at the chance to become a Love Interest, but not you.'

'Not wanting to get involved with the HPA and wanting to join the Villains are two very different things.' Now there's sand from my fleece trickling down the inside of my swimming costume. Everything about this interaction is uncomfortable. 'Did you happen to see me getting thrown across a museum by the Villains yesterday? Because it was all over the news.'

Emily's smirk somehow turns sympathetic, and it makes me want to shove her even more. 'Let's not waste time debating who threw who across what, eh?' she says. 'The world is broken. Anyone who isn't a man is considered less than. Just look at the Diviner. The most powerful human on the planet was little more than a servant because of her gender. I do enjoy the HPA simultaneously telling women that they're weak whilst demanding the new Diviner reveal herself to save us all, but don't you get tired of being underestimated?'

'WHAT DO YOU WANT?!' My shout surprises both of us.

Emily pauses for a split second before continuing like I hadn't opened my mouth. 'The Villains feel, Jenna, that they have a unique opportunity to expose the HPA and make the public see the evil at the heart of their organisation.'

'So?' Don't the Villains always think this?

'So, Jenna—'

'Repeating my name won't make me like you.'

'For the sake of a world being slowly broken by those in power, will you help the Villains?'

She's '*for the sake of the worlding*' me. It's classic hero speak. There are so many speeches from great men and their dastardly foes that include that phrase. The Villains might want to change the world, but they're using the same tired language as everyone else. I'm not in the mood for this. *Maybe* I'd be more open to saving the world if I'd just had an incredible kiss with Okorie.

My stomach growls, in tune with my mood. My brain has now registered all the swimming and I need a snack.

'No,' I say. 'I will not help the Villains. I'm going home.'

Emily breathes out slowly, like she's getting frustrated with me. Good. I hook my bag with my foot and scoop even more sand over my belongings as I drag it towards me. If Emily had some kind of weapon, surely she would have used it by now. And she's a liaison, so does she just talk? That's all she's done so far. Even still, I don't take my eyes off her as I cram my bag closed.

'What if the Villains had something that you wanted?' Emily asks.

'Bye, Emily.' I walk up the beach and Emily doesn't follow. Was it that easy? Did I just need to walk away from her? I'm at the base of the cliff when Emily shouts after me.

'This is Sima Ray's bracelet.'

Everything inside me turns to ice and my hand freezes on a rough brown rock. A short scramble and I'll be back on Lighthouse Hill. A quick walk and I'll be home. But I can't. Emily has just said my mum's name.

Why is she bringing her up?

I don't want to think about her.

Does she know my mum?

'Why do you …' My voice wavers as I turn back to see Emily holding up a gold bracelet. I recognise it. Even from here. A thick gold band with a flat green gem that used to sit on Mum's wrist and sparkle light up her fingers. She only ever took it off for bath time and to do the washing-up. I can picture it clearly sitting on the cistern of the toilet as she played with me, laughing as she poured soapy water from a toy watering can over my head.

'This is your mum's, right?' Emily crunches across the sand towards me. 'When's the last time you saw her?' she asks. 'When's the last time you spoke to her?'

When I was seven, Emily. She made my teddy bounce across my bed to kiss me on the nose. She told me that I was special, and she loved me, and when I woke up, she was gone. Her clothes, her creams, all her things had disappeared with her, but I knew she was coming back. I knew it for years. I knew she was coming back until the day I knew I'd never see her again.

'The Villains can take you to her.' Emily places the bracelet in my hand. It's solid and heavy, but it used to be so much bigger. 'They're not asking you to join the Villains. They just want one small thing from you and then they can set up a meeting between you and your mum.'

'How do they know where she is?' The gold is smooth under my thumb. No one knows where Mum is. She disappeared completely, from our home, from Nine Trees, from every thought and conversation our family could remove her from. When I was young, I dreamed of an offer like this, but do I still want it now? And why should I trust a group that, just yesterday, attacked me in a museum?

'Sima Ray left it with the Villains.' Emily takes my hand and I'm too numb to stop her slipping the bracelet on to my wrist. 'They've made some changes to it. Some polish, a tracker, a microchip under the gem that will gather information from any nearby HPA computers or kit.'

'What are you doing?' I snatch my hand back. The bracelet slips to sit just below my wrist. My skin might be lighter, but this is just what it looked like when Mum wore it.

'They're not asking for much. Wear this bracelet around Blaze for a few hours and it will hack his hero suit. They just need information to find something. No one is going to get hurt.' I shake my head, but she doesn't stop. 'It will be easy. They're already calling you his Love Interest; he'll jump at the chance to spend time with you. Do that and they'll take you to her.'

Do I want to see my mum again? Every atom of the anger that's grown over the last ten years screams '*NO!*' But will I regret it if I don't take this chance? A wave crashes on to the beach, but I can't hold on to the sound of the sea. My mind is in free fall. This could be my only chance to see her. But what if this is my last chance to get my life back? Blaze won't come anywhere near me after BLAZECON, so the attention of the media will have to fade soon. Do I really want to risk it all for the hope that the Villains will take me to my mum?

Okorie flashes through my brain. What will he think if I agree to date Blaze after almost kissing him?

'No.' My voice is quiet, and Emily decides to ignore it.

'The plan is simple and you're already in the perfect place. The Villains have been tracking some EV creatures who—'

'I said no, Emily.'

She scrunches her nose. 'You probably need time to think about it. It's a big decision.' A boat speeds into the cove; there's a helmeted Villain at the wheel.

'Is that the telekinetic?'

Emily glances over at the boat. 'Yes. That's him. I'll tell you what, Jenna Ray, I'll leave you here to think things through and, in –' she looks at her watch – 'around three minutes some EV creatures are going to show up.'

'What?' I spin, trying to take in the sky, the sea and the cliff all at once. 'How do you know that?'

'It's not hard to read the EV when you understand it.' Emily backs down the beach. 'Don't worry, the Villains will call the HPA and tell them you're here. There's only one boy who can get here fast enough to save you after all.'

I try to follow, but I can't move; my muscles are locked in place at the foot of the cliff. 'Tell the telekinetic to let me go!'

Emily shakes her head. 'This will be your chance to agree to a date with Blaze. It'll be a lovely quiet rescue. No cameras. Nice and intimate.' She winks. 'I bet you're happy I interrupted that kiss now.'

'You can't leave me here with EV creatures!'

'Oh, you'll be fine.' Emily strides down the beach and gives the telekinetic a thumbs up. 'We'll see you soon,' she calls over her shoulder as the telekinetic lifts her up and floats her over to the boat.

The hold on me eases and vanishes. 'Hey!' I sprint down the beach after her, but the boat is already speeding away. Feck. She said there were EV creatures on the way. What is coming? A shark that can swim up sand? A puffin with the taste for blood? A seal with razor-sharp teeth? I need to get off this beach. There's a bunker under the lighthouse; if I can make it there, I should be OK.

A few metres from the cliffside, a pigeon lands on a rock in front of me. I'm about to rush past when the bird looks up.

I've never seen an EV creature up close, but I know what to look for. We all do. BLUE.

Blue eyes

Large body

Unusually aggressive

Evolved creature

The hairs on my arms rise. It's got the scrawny look of a pigeon that would normally be pecking at chips around the harbour, but it's much bigger, closer to the size of a seagull, and its eyes are electric blue.

It tilts its head at me and pecks the rock. There's a sound like the snap of a bone and cracks race across the boulder. The pigeon looks up at me again.

Perhaps Emily and the Villains were just tracking this one bird? Although one large, super-strong pigeon is more than enough to end my life. Mother Earth! How am I in mortal danger *again*? Is reoccurring acute peril my toxic trait? Or is it something that you can catch, like a verruca? Keeping my eyes on the bird, I edge back towards the water as slowly as I can.

It will be fine.

I will be fine.

I can save myself this time. I'll get back into the water and swim round to Town Beach and tell the authorities that there are EV pigeons on Hidden Beach. I'll show the world that I don't need saving on a daily basis. I'll show the Villains they can't use psychotic birds to manipulate me.

Another pigeon lands and gazes at me with electric-blue eyes. Followed by several more. They perch on the rocks and on the cliffside. Hidden Beach twinkles with the blue eyes of this flock of killers.

'I'm going.' My hands are out in what I hope is a peaceful gesture for pigeons. 'Just give me a few more seconds.'

'Jenna.' I, and the pigeons, all look at Blaze as he lands on the beach beside me. They tilt their heads at him. 'I'm going to pick you up and we'll fly away, nice and fast,' he says out of the corner of his mouth.

'I think that flying is a bad idea.' My voice is calm, even though my heart is racing. More birds circle the beach and the ones closest to us are ruffling their feathers. 'I think we should go for a little swim.'

Blaze goes tense beside me. 'I can out-fly them.'

He's going to get me killed. By pigeons. 'Are you sure about that?' The pigeons must hear the hint of panic in my voice. The rustling on the beach reaches a crescendo, punctuated by high-pitched *coooos* and head tilts, and then it's like something snaps and they're in the air. Coming together to rise up as a deadly grey feathered mass.

'Blaze!' I yell, but his arms are already looped around my waist. A moment later we're in the air, hurtling above the waves.

'They're fast!' Blaze shouts. The birds are keeping up. Grey feathered bodies swoop at us and Blaze spins us away. 'They're not going to be able to keep this pace for long.'

A blue eye draws level with me, before Blaze twists us again. 'They don't need to. We have to go under!' I yell.

'Really?'

Why is he fighting this? 'Really!'

He stops above the waves.

'Deep breath!' I shout as we drop into the water.

Blaze tries to stop just below the surface, but I drag him down with me and hold him there a couple of metres deep. Seconds later the surface is frothing as what looks like hundreds of beaks peck at the waves. Blaze's eyes are closed, and his face is scrunched up. He looks terrified.

He's losing his air too. Big bubbles of oxygen slip past his lips and race to the surface. At this rate he'll drown before the birds get bored and *they're pigeons*, so unless they've got an evolved attention span, we only need to wait for a few seconds. I take his face in my hands and my lips find his. I force my air into him and he immediately relaxes. I push his lips closed as I pull away to make sure he doesn't inhale a lungful of water.

The surface calms as one by one the birds give up. I tap Blaze's arm and we kick our way to the surface together, breaking into the cool air just as my lungs start to burn.

'Are they gone?' Blaze rubs the seawater out of his eyes.

'Yes.' I keep one hand on the floundering hero as the flock of EV pigeons wings away across the water.

'Thank the skies.' Blaze stops kicking his legs and a moment later he's hovering above the surface. 'I'm not a fan of the water. Thank you for helping me, for, um—'

'Sharing my air,' I say quickly, before he gets the wrong idea.

'Yes. That.' He frowns at me. 'That shouldn't have worked.'

'And yet here you are, free of beak holes.' It's odd treading water and having a conversation with someone above you.

'I don't want to argue.' He shakes himself. 'Do you think we can talk? I can fly us somewhere quiet?'

My finger slides under my mum's bracelet. It would be so easy to slip it off now and let it settle at the bottom of the sea. I could get rid of the bracelet, say no to Blaze and swim back to Nine Trees a free woman.

'Or I can give you a lift back to land?' Blaze floats up out of the reach of a passing wave. 'I can't leave you all the way out here.'

Despite Emily's generous thirty seconds of thinking time between giving me the Villain's offer and calling Blaze, I need to buy myself some more time to make a decision.

'OK.' I rise with a wave and shunt away the memory of swimming with Okorie. 'Let's talk.'

CHAPTER 12

The East Breakwater lighthouse is my idea. It's still closed for repairs, so no one sees us as we fly up from the sea and land on the grey concrete of the pier. I always liked this slim brick lighthouse, and the shipwreck museum they managed to squeeze into the small room at the base, but it's been shut for years. I hop on to the sea wall and sit with my legs dangling over the crashing waves. More sea spray isn't going to hurt; my tracksuit and fleece are already soaked through.

Blaze radios the HPA and then sits carefully next to me, leaving a wide gap between us. 'The birds are already approaching the Channel. The French HPA and their hero, Vitesse, are standing by. He'll be ready if the flock gets beyond the Dunes. Now they know what's coming they'll be able to stop those birds attacking anyone else.'

'That's good.' I kick my legs.

'Jenna— Skies!' He shuffles back a little as a particularly

strong wave crashes off the sea wall below us. 'Sorry.' He clears his throat. 'Jenna, I'm in trouble and you're my only hope.'

I stop myself from rolling my eyes. How have I been '*for the sake of the worlded*' and '*you're my only hoped*' in the space of ten minutes? 'At least it's a better start than your speech in the gift shop,' I mutter.

Blaze runs a hand through his hair. 'Urgh. I'm sorry. All that stuff about grace, beauty and shining eyes. It's what Ron said to Kate. He told me … and I thought …' Blaze is staring at his knees. Despite his fancy red-and-black uniform, he looks like a lost teenage boy. 'I'm sorry. I'm sorry about so many things, too many things, but I've got a plan to make things right between us. I know how to make all the press attention and HPA stuff stop for you.'

He meets my eyes. 'Go on one date with me and I can give you your old life back. That's what you want, isn't it?' A patch of sunlight catches his dark hair as he edges closer. 'To be able to go back to swimming and studying and just being a normal teen in Nine Trees? One date and you'll never have to see me again.'

'Just one date?' My fingers find Mum's bracelet and twist it around my wrist. This could be enough to satisfy the Villains too. Maybe I can have it all? I can get my regular life back and find a way to see Mum?

Blaze only wants one date out of me.

The image of Mum chatting to Dad and Megan at the breakfast table clogs up my brain. It's a silly thing to picture. Mum left for a reason, she probably doesn't want to come back, but …

Just one date and I'd get to see her again.

All the Villains want me to do is wear their bracelet around Blaze. I'm already doing that. If I just leave it round my wrist for this date, surely that would be enough. And maybe Mum does want to come home? We'd go back to watching random sports on TV or walking down to the beach together. She'll be on my side, and we can tease Dad and Megan. She wouldn't tuck me in any more, obviously, but I could still say goodnight and feel her arms around me.

I'm already suffering from acute reoccurring peril. How much more damage can one date do? The skin on my wrist tingles. Skies. I need to stop twisting this bracelet before I give myself a rash.

'I know you don't trust me or like me, but give me five minutes to explain,' Blaze says. I blink at him. My mind is such a mess of hope and guilt, I'd forgotten he was here. 'If the answer is still no, I'll take you home and leave you alone.' He puts his hand on his heart. 'No thoughtless posts on social media, no dropping by to see you at work, no contact ever again. I promise.'

It's Blaze that the Villains are obsessed with. That's what Mia said. What if they were lying about not hurting anyone? What might they do to this boy if I help them? Is it terrible that concern for Blaze is dwarfed by the hope that I might see Mum again? Maybe not. Blaze has been awful to me. And he's a hero. He can take care of himself.

'I'm listening.'

A wave crashes against the sea wall and spray splatters us. Blaze looks like he wants to fly away, but he stays seated. 'Do you know about the Controller?' he asks.

'Yes. the Controller was included in the mandatory Hero Education we had every Monday morning from years seven to eleven. So, yes. I know about him.'

'Right.' He rocks gently as he talks. 'I'll just do a tiny bit of context, but I'll be fast. The Controller saved a cat. That was his first. Ha ha hilarious, the Controller's emergence was a cat rescue. But the thing about firsts is they set up the hero for the rest of their career. Where is the Controller now?'

'No one knows.'

'Exactly! He was a joke. He still is a joke. He was an insanely powerful technopath, but no one cared that he fixed the millennium bug or saved that care home. He rescued a cat first and that's what defined him. That's why he disappeared.'

'Are you saying that I'm a cat?'

Blaze's brown eyes shine at me. 'I'm saying that you rejected me.'

The clouds choose that moment to part, and a ray of sunlight illuminates his worried face. He barely needs it; his skin is already a touch golden and the burn on his cheek has pretty much faded. His mouth was made for smiling, but his pink lips are set in a sad line.

He's beautiful.

Objectively.

Objectively, Blaze is beautiful.

And I rejected him.

And I had every right to.

'Me not wanting to be a part of the whole HPA thing is not going to ruin you,' I say, but my voice is quiet. This is exactly what I wanted to happen when I went to confront him at BLAZECON.

'It shouldn't, but it's already happening. They're saying I'm too immature for a Love Interest, too young to know what I'm doing, too green to be trusted.' He's looking at his hands. 'This isn't your fault, or your problem. I do know that, even though I've acted like a jerk. But, Jenna, if I'm not a hero, I'm not anything. I've made so many difficult choices; I gave up everything for this life. I can do so much good, but heroes get dropped. I don't want to disappear like the Controller. One date with you would make it all go away.'

His dark eyelashes flutter. He's on edge, watching the waves, waiting for one that's too big. Maybe he can't swim? I could help him. I could show Blaze how to love the water. I shake off the thought. One date. If I'm doing this, that's all there's going to be.

'After our date, there's an American singer whose people have been in touch. Sam with a female symbol. She wants to date me. She's pretty desperate to be my Love Interest, apparently. So, I thought, if you and I go on one date and –' he does air quotes – ' "*figure out that we're friends*", then I won't be a reject and you'll just be someone who dated a hero once. It's not what they want, but it's better than nothing. The Jenna Ray chapter of my story will have a satisfying ending.'

His soft brown eyes meet mine, so I snap mine closed to think this all through. It's a simple plan; he comes out looking desirable, I come out looking boring.

But what if he's lying? What if we go on one date and he

posts that it's the start of something special? Or what if we go on one date and I get murdered by some random bad guy? So far, every time that I'm with Blaze, I almost die.

But what if this is the only way I'll ever get to see my mum again?

'Sam with a female symbol,' I mumble. I know Sam ♀, she's Joy's favourite. Every single one of her songs is about love.

'Jenna.' Blaze's warm fingers find mine. 'I swear it will all work out.'

My eyes flick open. 'I'll do it.'

His smile is dazzling. He looks like he wants to lean forward and kiss me, and, for a split second, a tiny part of me thinks that might be quite nice. I pull my hands out of his.

'When is the date?'

'How about today?'

Better to get it over with. 'Fine.'

He looks back at his hands. 'I don't want to trick you or take you anywhere you don't want to go. So, I should tell you more about the event.'

I raise my eyebrows. 'It's an event?'

'It's a hero wedding.'

Mother Earth, a hero wedding. Easily the most dramatic and dangerous type of hero event. The last hero wedding in Japan left a crater in the centre of Tokyo. There's always some bad guy waiting to take his revenge or make a point, or just make a mess.

'Red Stripe is marrying his Love Interest, Brooke,' Blaze continues. 'They're having a soirée at his hideaway. Very small. Very tasteful. Lots of security.'

'Couldn't we just go for that iced latte?'

He shakes his head. 'If only. This is the date that will fix everything. It's public, but we're not the focus. We just need to go to the reception for half an hour. We'll go early; no one will attack before the cake's cut. I'll look after you.'

This is a bad idea.

'Then you'll never have to see me again,' he says.

This is such a bad idea.

'And you'll never have to even think about hero stuff again.'

Both of these things will also be true if I die.

'Do I have time to go and get changed?' I motion to my soaking-wet tracky bottoms and am swamped with guilt as I think of home. I'm breaking my promise to Dad. This is exactly what he was afraid of.

Blaze leaps up gracefully. 'Maybe it's better just to go. We can get clothes there.' He's concealing his relief better than I thought he would.

'Can I leave a message for my family?' I swing myself round to face him and the lighthouse. 'They're going to be worried.'

They're going to be furious. Dad will ground me for the rest of my life and Megan will probably go on a one-woman mission to dismantle the HPA.

Blaze fishes a phone out of a hidden pocket. 'Press here and speak into this and we'll make sure that your dad gets the message.'

It seems just like a normal phone. I walk around the lighthouse and lean against the thick bricks of the base. What can I say to Dad and Megan to make what is happening OK? I can't

153

tell them about Mum. There's no way they'd want me involved with the heroes or the Villains. And what if I fail? They'd be so disappointed. And what if the HPA listen in or even decide to release it to the press?

I breathe out and press the button. 'Hi, it's me. I'm fine. There was a thing and some EV pigeons, but Blaze came for me and I'm completely safe. We're actually going to swing by a thing now. Blaze thinks it'll help convince everyone to leave me alone, so that's nice. Um. So, don't worry. I'll be back soon.'

Blaze is tapping something into his wrist piece as I head back over to him. 'If I go really fast, we can be at Red Stripe's hideaway in fifteen minutes.' He holds out his arms. 'Can I pick you up?'

'Thanks for asking.' I nod and a moment later I'm back in his arms. 'Why doesn't it feel like I'm going fast when I fly with you?' I loop my arm around his shoulders. This is different. We're not on the same side, but at least we're on the same page now. I feel more comfortable held against him. Too comfortable. My mind strays to his eyelashes, which are long, dark and very close to mine. He still smells like rain.

'I generate a sort of field around me.' He takes a step and we're in the air again, hurtling up out of Nine Trees and across the sea. 'It's the same reason I can carry you for so long. You've got less gravity when you're flying with me.'

'I knew it!'

He chuckles. 'Really? Have you been reading up on me?'

'No. I just have a lot of first-hand experience. Ah.' I crane my neck to see how far we've gone.

'What's wrong?'

'Nothing,' I say.

We're rocketing away from Nine Trees, across the open water. Somewhere far behind us is my bag with my school uniform, my keys and my phone. I should have asked if we could make a pit stop at Hidden Beach. I guess there's no turning back now.

CHAPTER 13

What I know about Red Stripe could fit on a Post-it. He's a good-looking all-American boy who emerged about a decade ago during the San Francisco earthquake and, of course, immediately met his Love Interest, Brooke.

As we shoot over the waves, my first guess is Red Stripe chose some sunny island for his hideaway, but it's not long before we're approaching vast mountains. Tree-covered slopes shade the dark turquoise water below and we shoot past a waterfall crashing from one of the peaks. We must be heading north; the temperature steadily drops, and a few patches of snow are still dotted about.

Fjord. We're flying above a fjord. I've always wanted to swim here. I've got a picture on my wall that looks just like this.

'We're in Norway?' I ask.

'Red Stripe's got family from here,' Blaze replies. 'Are you cold?' He reaches round me to push a button on his chest and glorious warmth immediately soaks through my wet fleece.

'You've got a heater in your suit?' It's all I can do to stop myself snuggling into him.

'Comes as standard.' Blaze sounds smug.

'Mother Earth, what is that?!' All thoughts of Blaze's heat vanish as I see a building protruding from one of the mountains. The glass monstrosity looks like the love child of a multistorey car park and a cruise ship.

'That's the hideaway, I guess.' Blaze slows as we approach. 'It looks like it should be in California.'

'I thought it was going to be a cave with a waterfall entrance. How can this be a hideaway? He's built himself a hotel.'

I count five levels of wide, blue-windowed luxury, topped with a lively deck and pool, before we touch down on the drive. There are insanely expensive cars parked up along one edge and a helicopter sat in the centre.

'Who drove here?' I ask as I drip seawater up the polished marble stairs.

'Who knows, Jenna? It's one of the great mysteries of the hero world.' Blaze presses the doorbell and the door is immediately yanked open.

'Stop! Would you look at you two?!'

A tiny woman with a headset grins as she ushers us through the door into Red Stripe's ridiculously large, mostly glass hideaway. Inside, our feet echo on the grey tiled floor and the distant sound of the reception thrums through the high ceilings. Will Blaze be able to buy something as ridiculous as this one day?

'I LOVE a natural Afro.' The tiny woman leads us deeper into the house. 'It's bouncy. It's curly. It's soft.' She stops abruptly and reaches for my hair. 'It's natural! You don't mind, do you?'

I sidestep into Blaze. Megan always told me the only people who were allowed to touch my hair are hairdressers and people I want to kiss. 'I'd rather you didn't.'

The tiny woman pulls her hand back immediately. 'Ah! Sorry, babe. Strong boundaries.' She nods rapidly at me. 'Gotta respect that.'

'Did Mia call ahead?' Blaze politely ignores the fact I am now standing on his foot.

'Of course.' The tiny woman beckons, and we pass through a round room with a central sculpture of a man in a cape, and a frame that just says *REFLECT*. We're back in another corridor a moment later. We must have already walked the length of my house a couple of times and I haven't seen a room that you can sit down in yet. I roll my neck. All my muscles are tensing up. I can't believe I'm about to step willingly into the world of the heroes.

'You're not the only ones to turn up to Red Stripe and Brooke's big day without outfits.' The tiny woman leads us down a set of gravity-defying black metal steps sticking out of the white wall. As I carefully descend, I'm glad I'm with a boy who can fly. 'Tempo came straight from a forest fire in the Amazon and one of the other heroes just rescued his Love Interest from a beach swamped with EV creatures!'

'I think that's us,' Blaze says, shooting me a look as we step down into an airy basement. I raise my eyebrows. I didn't realise that this was a thing we do now, share looks.

She smacks her hand off her forehead. 'A-doi! Of course it's you, Beige.'

'Blaze.' He really is very polite.

'Oh wow! Sorry! So many heroes, so little time. Do you know our firm clothes half the stars in Hollywood too?'

'That's nice.' The hint of sarcasm in his voice seems extra British right now. 'It's good to be busy.'

I stop myself from laughing. It would be rude, and I really don't want Blaze to know that I find him funny. I can't do anything to make him think this could be more than a one-time thing.

'And here we are!' The tiny woman points to a door that lights up as we look at it. This house does not work like any other house I've been in. 'Go on in, the dresser is expecting you. I've got to head back up.' She taps her earpiece. 'Apparently one of the Love Interests has shown up wearing a white dress! Horror!'

She disappears so fast she could have teleported. We both stand and look at the door for a moment. For some reason talking to that woman has left me feeling like I've got motion sickness, and the person waiting behind the door is probably even worse. Standing quietly in the basement feels like the most peaceful option.

'Shall we?' Blaze finally asks.

I sigh. 'After you, Beige.'

It just slips out.

I didn't mean to tease him.

Pet names and in-jokes are not allowed.

He laughs. 'I don't hate it.'

I stare at him for a beat too long as I wrack my brain for a comeback that isn't cruel or flirty, then I give up and I step past him to rap on the door.

The door swings open and we're hit with a blast of rock music. 'Come in!'

The endless wine cellar stretches into the dark, but the front few metres have been turned into a plush dressing room. A fluffy white carpet is penned in by rails of designer suits and dresses. There doesn't seem to be anyone around, then Mia pops up from behind a shelf of enormous hats.

'Hello again.' Mia's voice sounds amused and still a bit bored, even though they have a tape measure around their neck and a pencil slotted into the side of their over-large black quiff. Mia's no longer wearing a black suit; now they're in a short red military jacket, with golden lapels. To my surprise, seeing Mia makes me feel slightly less sick.

'Mia, you're here!' Blaze blurs over and gives them a big hug.

'All right, put me down! We get it, you're strong.' Mia bats at his suit until he gently puts them back on their feet. 'Of course I'm here. They draft in extra hands for hero weddings, and when I heard the one and only Jenna Ray needed a dress I made sure it was my shift in the cellar.' Mia winks at me, and I roll my eyes.

'I forgot that you know each other.' Blaze looks between us.

'All right, baby hero, here you go.' Mia tosses a small silver parcel at him and the smell of chilli and cheese wafts past. My stomach gurgles. 'Why don't you wait outside? You're keeping your hero costume on, so just brush off some of that sea salt, eh?'

'Do you want some?' Blaze holds his burrito out towards me and my stomach grumbles again.

'No, thank you.' I turn back to Mia and watch from the corner of my eye as he slinks out of the room.

'Brrrr.' Mia pretends to shiver. 'You're a convincing ice queen.'

'Are you going to dress me or just insult me?'

'I can't do both?' Mia kicks a shoebox over. 'Shoes.'

Don't be heels.

Please don't be heels.

I cautiously lift off the top of the box with my toe. A pair of smart, dark green, flat shoes are nestled in paper.

'They're not heels!'

Mia's mouth quirks. 'No. I've tried to dress you before, remember? When you went to the hero convention and ended up on TV in your PJs?'

'I was wearing leggings.'

'So.' Mia holds out a suit bag. 'I picked out this. Why don't I put you in it? Don't look until it's on and we can do a big reveal.'

'For Blaze?' I ask, the motion sickness creeping back in.

'For you. Let's make the next twenty minutes all about you.' For the first time, Mia sounds sincere. 'Can I put some make-up on you? I think we only need the barest of basics; a touch of pink for the lips, a smudge of gold on the eyes.'

I nod, a little excited despite myself. This is a step up from sneaking into Megan's box of powders, glitters and gels. I've always wanted to have my make-up done by a professional.

'Great.' Mia is all business and before I know what's happening, I'm out of my clothes and in a fluffy dressing gown. Moments later, I'm in a chair with eyeliner coming at me.

There are no mirrors, just the dusty shine of old bottles and the gentle hum of the air conditioning. My eyes are lined, and Mia gently brushes a powder over the lids and across my cheekbones, and the front of my 'fro is curled and clipped. I'm then instructed to stand and not to look as Mia guides me over to a puddle of material on the ground.

'Don't you dare look, Jenna Ray!'

I gaze obediently at the sloped ceiling as Mia guides my arms into the dress and does up the buttons that run up the back. Mia is different when they're in wardrobe. They're humming along with the music and their eyebrows are perma-puckered below their quiff. You can tell how much they care. I roll my neck again.

'Don't look!'

'I'm not!'

I don't want to look. I can't imagine what Mia is putting me in. It'll probably be something ultra revealing, but designed to dangle artfully when a bad guy holds me off the side of a skyscraper. Classic Love Interest attire.

'Right.' Mia takes my hand and guides me across the room. The dress swishes just below my knees, which is reassuring. It feels like it's made of soft, silky cotton.

'Step into your shoes for me.' They direct my feet into the green flats, which are surprisingly light.

There's the sound of something being dragged across the carpet, and Mia is back next to me.

'OK.' Mia sounds nervous. I'm nervous. My heart is pounding in my chest. 'You can look.'

I blink as I look down from the brick ceiling to find a full-length mirror in front of me. And there I am.

Green.

The dress is forest green. It has a tasteful scoop top, short sleeves that fit comfortably on my shoulders and a waist that tapers in before the material erupts into a full, knee-length skirt.

'Wait!' Mia clips a wide silver belt around my middle. It has an antique clasp with a wave pattern and a pearl at its centre. 'OK.' She breathes out. 'How much do you hate it?'

The front of my Afro is pinned up and to one side with a hairpiece made of a fan of peacock feathers, and the make-up makes my face look soft and glittery.

'It's really nice, Mia,' I say quietly, and grimace as they punch the air. I wish I hated it. Enjoying any of this will lead to disaster.

'I knew it. Mix classic with retro, add some mystery, remove the heels and you've got Jenna Ray's style.'

'This is a one-time thing,' I tell Mia as they shimmy into a victory dance.

'Whatever you say, Jenna Ray, I know how to style you now. I cracked you.'

Mia cracked me.

I didn't think I had a style, beyond sporty or stolen from Megan, but I love everything about the outfit Mia assembled. I look like myself, but formal enough to go to a wedding. It also won't draw anyone's eye. The calming green feels almost like camouflage. Mia cracked me.

'No need for another layer to keep you warm. Brooke planned the wedding, Red Stripe picked the location, which is why they're having a pool party at the top of a Norwegian mountain. They must have spent a fortune on heaters. Can we take this bracelet off?' Mia taps my wrist. 'I've got some other options here.'

'Jenna!' Blaze bursts in and stops when he sees me. His face goes blank. I thought that I'd looked OK, but he seems upset.

'Knocking rules still apply up here on the mountain, Baby H,' Mia snaps.

'Sorry,' Blaze mumbles. 'It's just the first dance is about to start. That's the best time for us to be photographed.' He turns to me. 'You look – er – fine. Are you ready?'

'Yep.' I look fine? I don't dare look at Mia; after all their hard work, I look amazing. At least Blaze is making it easy for me to keep hating him.

'Let's get this over with,' I say. 'Thank you, Mia.'

'You're welcome.' Mia sees us to the door. 'Look after each other, OK?'

'Yes, boss,' Blaze replies and Mia hits him over the top of the head.

'How many times?! Don't boss me, Baby H.'

'Sorry, boss.' Blaze blurs past before they can get him again and waits by the steps.

'Try and enjoy yourself,' Mia says as I step past.

There's no way that will happen. 'Bye, Mia.'

'See you soon.' Mia winks at me and closes the door. Is winking taught by the HPA? There's no other part of life where people wink as much as they do there. Maybe King Ron sets quotas? I rub the goosebumps rising on my arms. Mia might be a lot, but leaving wardrobe is like stepping on to a frozen lake.

Blaze is hovering just above the bottom step, looking like he doesn't know what to say.

'Shall we?' I offer him my arm.

'Let's.' He's all business as he loops his arm through mine, and we make our way back up into the house and to a blue glass-fronted elevator. 'I've scouted ahead. If we go through the games room, we can join the party without anyone noticing us.'

'Sounds good.' I'm glad Blaze isn't holding my hand; my palms are sweating.

My heart beats faster as the elevator pings open on the top floor. We step out into a sunny room with a pool table, a darts board and an arcade shooting game. These make sense, I suppose. Red Stripe can fire molten missiles from his hands, he'd want to keep his aim in peak condition. Chatter and the dull thud of a bassline grow louder as we head towards a set of sliding glass doors.

What am I doing? Out there will be heroes, Love Interests, cameras, danger and, maybe, a way to find my mum. I grit my teeth.

'OK?' Blaze asks with his hand on the door.

I nod. 'Do it.'

CHAPTER 14

The door slides open and a wave of heat and thumping music slams into me. The mountain must be behind us; from where we are there's nothing but people and sky. The only other wedding I've been to was my aunt's at City Hall, and it was nothing like this. It shouldn't be this warm out here. It's like we've wandered into a nightclub on the sun.

Blaze steers me past the heaters, through the glamorous groups and over to the first pool I haven't immediately wanted to jump into. There are heroes from across the globe dotted around the deck in their hero outfits; Tempo in his silver suit and cape, the bulky figure of the invincible Shān, who must be really uncomfortable in his brown leather outfit, even King Ron, who has swapped his three-piece suit for smart dark blue trousers and a white shirt rolled up at the elbows.

At least Blaze was right about us being the least interesting people here. We pass a denim-clad country singer, whose name

166

I can't remember, and girls I recognise from Joy's magazines in bikinis and sarongs, holding fluorescent cocktails. Maybe Sam ♀, Blaze's wannabe Love Interest, is here somewhere? Although Blaze doesn't seem like he's looking for anyone. Perhaps we can hang out by the buffet, find some more burritos, get our picture taken and then blur off back to Nine Trees.

'Jenna Ray!' The shout comes from a large man with an orangey tan and a bleached blond comb-over. He's close enough to come over and say hello, but I can tell by the curl of his lip that's not what he wants. 'Look who it is!'

The celebrities in our vicinity turn to look and the name Jenna Ray ripples through the mass of people. My chest aches. I didn't think they'd care about us.

'Blaze finally got the girl!' someone else shouts, and every-one bursts into applause.

They're all watching us. I thought they'd be like the tiny woman with the headset and not even know our names, but they're devouring me with their eyes. They've decided what's going on between us and they're predicting the rest of my life as they smile at me. Danger. Cameras. Constant attention.

'Aw! Look at them!'

Eyes and smiles. Canapés and cocktails. Heat and noise. There's no way out of this crush, nowhere for me to run.

'They're so cute together!'

All my air vanishes.

Not now.

Please not now.

I can't have an attack in front of all these people.

167

Blaze smiles and waves as we move deeper into the crowd.

I can't breathe. I can't even try. I plaster a smile on my face. I can't let them see me choking and gasping for air. The colours of the costumes, bikinis and tiny hats blur together, and I blink back the tears. I can't let them see me cry.

'*Who are you wearing, Jenna?*'

I'm surrounded.

My lungs feel like they're in a vacuum. I need to cough or choke or fall to my knees and suck in air until they work again, but there are so many eyes.

'*Didn't you just get thrown across a museum? How was that?!*'

Blaze's arm tightens on mine. I can't get away from him or any of the people staring at me. He whispers something, but I can't hear it above the thundering of my heart.

'Almost there,' he says again. 'Just going to get some water,' he calls with a cheerful wave.

And we're back inside the cool and the dark.

I can't breathe.

Blaze pulls me through a huge pool house and into a dark corner. Tears are rolling down my face. I need to get away from him, from everyone.

'Here.' He pushes me gently on to a step. 'Breathe, OK? No one can see you here.'

My head is spinning.

I try to suck in some air, but it doesn't work.

'Do you want me to go?'

He's a watery mess in front of me. I shake my head; I don't want him to see me like this, but I don't want to be alone either.

I don't know what to do.

I can't breathe.

I can't breathe.

I can't—

'Hey.' Blaze's hands are either side of my face. 'Just focus on inhaling.'

I'm still shaking my head.

'You can. Breathe with me. I'm breathing in.'

I can't do it.

'And out.'

I force the last of my air out.

'Good,' Blaze says. 'I'm breathing in.'

I remember Megan telling me to concentrate on my exhales.

'And out.'

I've got enough air to breathe out properly.

'Breathe in.'

Air floods my system.

'And out.'

Tears are still rolling down my cheeks. I didn't even consider that all the attention I got on a date with Blaze might do this. Stupid. How was I so stupid?

'Breathe in.' Blaze's voice goes sharp. 'Don't think about anything but breathing.'

I breathe in.

'And out.'

We keep breathing together until my lungs are full.

Blaze's cool fingers leave my face and a moment later a bunch of tissues are placed in my lap. He sits next to me on the

169

step, close enough that our knees touch and, for the first time, I don't want to shove him away.

The tissue practically dissolves as I wipe away the traces of my panic. My eyes must be red. I can't look at Blaze. He's probably wondering how long he needs to wait here before he goes out to join his hero friends. Maybe this is how he was supposed to meet Sam ♀. Am I going to wreck that too? I set my eyes on the small slice of mountain I can see beyond the main house.

'How are you feeling?' His hand is on my back. No. His hand is *rubbing* my back, moving in circles across the light material of my dress. 'Is this OK? My mum used to do this when I was upset or sick. It always helped. Back rubs and flat lemonade solved pretty much everything.'

The back rubs do help. My heart is no longer trying to break out of my chest.

'Thank you,' I mumble. 'Do you think they saw?'

'No.'

I finally turn to him. 'Really?'

'You were smiling.' He looks different. His mouth is creased with worry and a tuft of dark hair is sticking out at an angle.

'How did you know something was wrong?' I ask.

'Well, you weren't breathing.' He shrugs. 'And I used to have panic attacks too.'

It should be harder to believe that this confident, super-powered boy had panic attacks, but he understood what was happening, and he's still here now, rubbing my back.

He's not who I thought he was.

I can't start liking him now; there's too much at stake.

The pool house spins around me as I wobble to my feet, but before I can escape, Blaze gently guides me back down on to the step.

'Why don't you give yourself a minute?'

'Because—'

Because you're still next to me.

Because I just want to do enough to find my mum and get out without getting to know you.

Because my body has betrayed me again and feels safe next to yours.

'Wait.' Blaze blurs off and returns a moment later with a bottle of water. 'It's sparkling. It's the only type they had. I don't think any bubble-free liquid is allowed at this party.' He opens it for me, and I take it with a shaking hand. 'Take small sips.' He drags over a wicker chair that looks more expensive than our family car and places it beside the step. 'Is it the attention that's the trigger?'

There's no point denying it, so I nod and busy myself with the water. The sip I take is more air than liquid, but I immediately start feeling better. What happens now? In all the world only two people know about my panic attacks: my sister and this hero. He's staring at me, but when I catch his eye, he looks up at the tinted glass ceiling.

'You don't need to be embarrassed.' Sometimes Blaze sounds polished, like a TV character. This is not one of those times. 'Um. Lots of people have to deal with stuff like this.' He clasps his hands. 'Not that it's not horrible. I mean, I know it's horrible. Not that I'm comparing my experience to yours. But maybe it was similar—' He floats up from his seat. 'No. I mean, what I'm trying to say is—'

Are the words this floating boy is looking for going to be awkward, profound, or perhaps another apology? I'm too tired to move, so I take another sip of water and wait to see what's about to happen.

'What I'm trying to say is, oh—' He realises he's floating and lands with a bump. 'They're not fun.'

I snort. 'They're not.'

'Being paraded around in front of people, being with me, it's …' His brown eyes hold mine. I can see him trying to process it all; it's like he's been cracked open. Worry and guilt shine along the lines of his shoulders. Mother Earth. He's going to do the heroic thing and call it all off to protect me. As I lean on my lap, the bracelet presses into my leg, just above my knee. I've come this far. I need to do enough to see my mum.

'It's a one-time thing.' I lean closer to him. 'I can do it.'

He blinks at me. 'Really?'

'Yes. If you help me, Blaze.'

TICK

Blaze jumps up.

TICK

The sound is coming from everywhere, like we're standing in the centre of Big Ben. I stand slowly and look out at the party.

BOOM!

A column of water explodes from the pool. I guess my hour and a bit of safety is over, back to the mortal peril. Blaze is already on the deck, catching swimmers as they fall. I could go

172

back to my hidden step and sip sparkling water until this is done, but what if I can do some good out there?

I rush over to the sliding doors and hesitate. A hero – Tempo, I think – has frozen the plume of water and the swimmers close to the blast hang in mid-air. Another flying hero helps Blaze pluck them out of the air. The lack of clothing makes everything feel more chaotic than BLAZECON. One of the catering carts was knocked over in the madness and a rainbow of liquid is spreading across the pale tiles.

I slide the door open. I should go out. I know first aid.

'Stay there!' Blaze blurs past and a moment later he's back in the thick of it.

'Ow!' A girl in a white bikini and sarong sits shakily up next to the pool house.

'Are you OK?' I slip through the door to crouch next to her.

'Yeah.' She scrapes her wet blonde hair out of her eyes. 'This was always going to happen. Honestly, why would anyone marry a hero?'

'I've got no idea.' My voice trails off as I recognise her. She was on every billboard on the way to BLAZECON advertising *Brooke's World Season 8*. It's Brooke, Red Stripe's Love Interest; the bride.

TICK

'Crap!' Brooke wobbles up and I grab her arm to steady her.

TICK

'Come on,' I say. 'Let's go in there—'

BOOM!

This time, an explosion of colours fills the air. I cover my

173

face, but nothing hits us. The screams of terror turn slowly to murmurs of confusion. Was that just a firework?

'Red Stripe!' a deep voice calls from the hideaway's roof. 'I have her, like I was always supposed to, like I would have if you hadn't got in the way.' A man in a black cape stands above us. He has one arm looped around Brooke's waist. She is being dangled off the roof, with the craggy rocks of the mountainside as a dramatic backdrop. Feck. I should have got her inside before this guy pulled his *'look over there whilst I snatch the girl'* move.

'It should have been me waiting at the end of the aisle!' the man in the cape wails. 'It should have been me!'

I don't know if I'm the only person who sees Brooke roll her eyes.

'You let her go, Bravo!' Red Stripe leaps forward, his golden hair and beautiful beard shining in the sun. He rips open his wedding shirt to reveal his red hero suit.

'Never!' cries Bravo.

'It's time to go, Bravo.' To everyone's surprise, another man steps in front of Red Stripe. It's the man with the orangey tan and a bleached blond comb-over who outed us earlier. 'I've got this.'

'Trevor, no—' starts Red Stripe, but Trevor grabs the ice-cream cart and lifts it above his head with one hand.

There's a collective gasp from the party guests; evidently no one expected this Trevor to have super-strength. The cart wobbles in his hand, like he doesn't quite have control, like he doesn't really know what he's doing.

He can't be HPA. Is that why I don't recognise him?

A slow trickle of sauce runs down Trevor's arm. My brain flicks through all the heroes I've seen on TV again. This large, orangey man definitely isn't one of them, but he has super-strength. The HPA doesn't have a favourite power, but if they did, it would be hyper-macho super-strength. Perhaps he's so highly trained that he can just make it look like he doesn't know what he's doing?

No! I know who this guy is! He's that American billionaire businessman who is constantly under investigation for doing terrible things to his workers, or the economy, or pretty much anyone who isn't a wealthy white man. He's definitely not a hero or part of the HPA. Why didn't any of the news reports on him ever mention that he has powers?

Trevor shifts and the ice-cream cart wobbles. He can't throw it without hitting Brooke. Bravo knows that, which is why he's smiling. Trevor must see that too. He sways again and steadies himself. He's not going to risk hurting someone, let alone killing the bride on her wedding day, is he?

Brooke screams, 'No!' at the same time as I shout, 'Blaze!'

Trevor launches the cart towards Bravo and Brooke. As it arcs towards the roof in a spray of sauce and sprinkles, Blaze blurs ahead and snatches Brooke out of the way. The cart hits Bravo and he crashes out of sight, landing on the other side of the house.

'Don't let him get away!' cries Red Stripe, and a horde of heroes charge through the house. Their steps echo as they disappear down the stairs. I hope none of them get lost in there.

'Yeah!' shouts Trevor, arms in the air like he just scored a goal. He reaches into his blazer and pulls out a pistol. 'Yeah!' He fires a shot above his head and several people drop to the floor.

Blaze lands next to me with Brooke in his arms.

'Thank you,' she says as he sets her down.

'No problem.' He falls silent as Trevor bounds up to us.

'What a team! He may be young, but he's quick!' He holds up his hand for Blaze to high five.

'About that,' Blaze starts.

Brooke steps forward. 'Allow me.'

'You're welcome, darlin',' Trevor drawls.

Brooke nods, considering him carefully, and then punches him in the face.

CHAPTER 15

'How did they get this photo so fast?' I ask. The screen of Blaze's phone shows a photo of Trevor holding his broken nose and us trying not to laugh. 'Is it bad that I kind of like it?'

'No.' Blaze grins at me. 'A paparazzo must have snuck in, I guess.' We're on a bench by the glass-walled edge of the deck, just close enough to a heater and with an uninterrupted view of the dark fjord below. The last rays of the setting sun give Blaze's face a pink hue.

Trevor stormed out and his helicopter took off before Red Stripe got back from his fruitless Bravo hunt. That was probably when we should have left too, but Brooke insisted we eat some waffles, and then the wedding cake was cut. After Bravo, it was like the party reset. No one seemed interested in talking to me or about me or talking at all; everyone wanted to dance. When Brooke danced round to find me, I couldn't stop myself from joining her. Watching her laugh and sip champagne with her knuckles red from punching Trevor Donaldson has given me a new respect for Love Interests. Maybe I'll even watch her show.

Blaze disappeared during the dancing, and I finally found him here, watching the sky above the mountains shift from yellow to pink to red as the sun set somewhere behind them. He's found the perfect place. Our knees touch as I look at his phone. It's odd how comfortable I feel sitting next to him. What a difference a disastrous hero wedding makes.

'I bet Trevor is going to love this.' I yawn. My eyes are heavy, but it can't be that late; the sun has only just set.

'Yeah. He's not a man that likes being laughed at.' Blaze stretches out his legs. 'Are you cold?'

No, I'm not cold, but for some reason I say, 'A bit.'

He shuffles closer and puts his arm around my shoulders. I should pull away, but he's so warm and my eyelids are starting to droop.

'I think it worked, Jenna.'

'It did?' My words are slowing down. They are harder to find.

'Listen to this. "… and Blaze not only saved the day, but it seems he's finally found some common ground with his first rescue, Jenna Ray. Things are turning round for the world's youngest hero …"'

'That's good,' I murmur.

The cool air making it past the heaters carries the fjord with it, I can taste it as it settles on my lips. The thumping music seems to be fading into the background.

My head is on his shoulder.

'I'll give it a day or two and then organise a date with Sam ♀.'

'OK.'

The pull of sleep is delicious.

'Thank you, Jenna. Thank you for helping me.'

'Mm-kay,' I mumble as my wrist settles between our legs, with the bracelet against his hero outfit. 'It's OK.' The dark washes over me.

'She's here!'

My covers have wrapped themselves around me like seaweed and it takes me a moment to struggle free. My eyes and limbs feel heavy with sleep, but Megan is at my bedroom door with her eyes blazing.

'When did you get back?! I fell asleep in the living room waiting for you!'

'Er …' The last thing I remember was dozing with my head on Blaze's shoulder. Did he sneak into our house and put me to bed? Skies! Did I leave anything embarrassing out in my room? I whip my head round. There's no underwear out, just my wetsuit thrown over my desk, which is OK.

Dad rushes past Megan. 'Are you all right?'

I nod and in an instant his fear turns into something else. He gets angry at the news, at the HPA, at the world in general, but he barely ever gets angry at me. Right now, he's furious. Which is unfair, because this all started because of some EV pigeons.

'I'm fine. There were EV birds on Hidden Beach, but I'm fine.' I sit up and the covers fall to reveal my green party dress. Dad inhales sharply. 'I can explain.'

'We got your message.' Megan is often angry with me, so

her tone is familiar. 'And we saw that photo of you with him. You looked like you were having a *lovely* time.'

Dad holds up a hand. 'Why don't you tell us what happened. Start at the beginning when you ran away from school and put yourself in danger.'

My duvet scrunches as I pull it up to my chin. 'I couldn't stay. Everyone was looking at me and talking about me.' It sounds pathetic, but both of their faces soften for a moment. 'I just needed to think and then there were the birds and you know the rest.' I yawn. 'Could we maybe talk later?'

They glance at each other, and I yawn again for effect. Maybe they'll reschedule their fury for later to let me get some more sleep, then I can get my story straight. I can't tell them about the deal with the Villains. They'd never let me risk myself to try and find Mum, and if I tell them and fail, they'll be heartbroken all over again.

'If the attention was so bad, why did you go to the wedding with Blaze?' Megan sits on the end of my bed.

'He said that if I went on one date with him, he'd be able to spin it so the press left me alone.'

The silence as they process this is intense. Maybe this half-truth will be enough?

Megan slowly puts her head in her hands. 'Mother Earth, you're so stupid.'

Dad comes over to the bed too. 'But you promised.' His voice is soft, but the guilt hits me like a tidal wave. He shakes his head like he can't quite understand what has happened. 'You can't trust them. I told you that you can't trust them.

Staying away was the only way to stay safe, the only way …' He blinks rapidly like his brain has rebooted. 'If you take the smallest step on to the Love Interest's path, they'll shove you down it so fast you won't have time to realise what you've lost.'

'But it'll work.' They think I'm an idiot. It's better than them knowing the truth, but it still hurts. My eyes sting; I think I've got make-up in them. 'Blaze is going to start dating a singer from America. It's all arranged.'

'I told you not to—' Dad rubs his temple. 'You can't trust them.' He steps out of my room before rushing back in. 'House arrest.'

'What?' I scramble out of bed and immediately regret it as my family see my dress in all its glory. Megan whistles softly under her breath.

'You're not to leave this house.' I've never heard Dad's voice this cold before. 'I'm going to tell school that you're sick. Joy can drop your schoolwork round. If this hero says it's over, fine. For the next week the only place Jenna Ray exists is in this house.'

'I can't go out for a whole week?!' I clench my fists.

'Don't, Jenna,' Megan mutters.

'You can't keep me in the house for a week! It wasn't my fault!'

'Did he force you to go to that wedding?' Megan asks.

It would be so easy to lie. I could blame it all on Blaze and they'd feel sorry for me, maybe Dad wouldn't even ground me. This is all mostly Blaze's fault anyway, but for some reason the thought of saying it makes me feel queasy.

I sigh. 'No. I agreed to his plan. I thought it would work.'

Dad's face goes blank and then he turns on his heel. 'Two weeks,' he calls over his shoulder as he marches out of my room.

'Just—' Megan looks my dress up and down. 'Just don't make this worse.'

Two weeks?!

I'm not allowed to leave the house for two weeks?!

He can't be serious. I go to follow him but pause with my hand on the white gloss of the door frame. The mood he's in, he could ban me from leaving the house for a whole month. I step round Megan and flop back on to my bed.

What am I supposed to do about swimming?

Wait, what am I going to do about Mum?!

Feck! The bracelet! I shove my hand under the covers before Megan can notice it.

'So—' Megan smooths down her work shirt.

Dad rushes back in. 'Phone.'

I look at him blankly.

'Give me your phone.' He holds out his hand.

'Er …' The spot on my bedside table where my phone sits and flashes at me is empty. 'I think it's still on the beach.'

Dad's eyebrows lower even further, but going to a wedding with a hero is something he can punish me for; leaving my bag whilst I escape the EV is not. He storms out again.

'Hidden Beach?' Megan asks.

'Yeah. My bag is there, and my uniform.'

'I'll see if it's still there.' Megan leans down and grabs me in a tight hug. 'You're so stupid.' She leaves too.

I leap up and slam my door behind them. None of this is

182

fair! I didn't ask to be trapped in a burning building or have a hero stalk me. I didn't ask for any of this. It's been less than a week since Blaze pulled me out of that fire and everything is a mess. I wrench my covers open and leap back into bed. If they think I'm too stupid to leave the house, then I'll just stay here, under my quilt, for the next two weeks.

They'll feel so guilty when they see Mum walking up our driveway and I can tell them then that everything I did was to bring her home. There's no way they'll call me stupid then. My eyes are heavy and the anger in my chest is being dampened by exhaustion. They'll understand when I bring Mum back. They'll see that all of this was worth it.

Waking up for a second time in the most expensive dress I've ever worn is surreal. The only light in my room is the soft glow from the street lamp outside my window. The house is quiet and there's a chill in the air. I must have slept the entire day.

My stomach gurgles loudly as I roll out of bed. There's no clock in my room and my phone is still MIA, but it feels late enough for me to use the kitchen without having to endure more of Dad and Megan's anger.

The expensive green fabric pools by my feet as I slip out of the dress and pull on tracksuit bottoms and a hoody. How are you even supposed to wash a dress like this? Perhaps the designer dress crowd just wear them once and then burn them, so they're never seen in the same outfit twice. I pull on some socks, feeling light-headed. The wedding waffles feel like they were weeks ago.

The clock in the hall flashes 23.45 as I pad through the dark, trying to breathe quietly. Everything sounds loud enough to wake my sleeping family. The rumbling of my stomach. The creak of the stairs. The rattle of our fridge. The pop of my toast launching out of the toaster.

A few rounds of toast with a generous amount of salted butter and mushroom pâté and I'm finally full. I finger Mum's bracelet as I finish off my oat milk.

'What happens next, then?' I whisper to the gold band.

It vibrates.

I hold it up to my ear. 'Hello?'

It vibrates again.

Is this how the Villains are going to communicate? Do I need to learn Morse code?

'What am I supposed to do?' I whisper.

The bracelet shudders and goes still. Sitting in our dark kitchen with a stomach full of toast is not my preferred situation for problem solving. I wonder what Joy would make of this. She'd probably turn out to be a master code cracker and head off in her floaty dress to save the day. Weirdly, I wish Blaze was here. He'd help me if he could, even though I'm betraying him.

I shake my head. I'm not betraying him. I'm exploring options that might lead to my mum.

The bracelet yanks my wrist up so fast I'm forced to my feet.

'Wait …' It slides up my wrist and presses hard against my hand. 'Ow!' I close my hand, so it slips off and it hovers in front of me for a moment, like it's giving me time to realise that I'm

184

about to lose my only way to find Mum. 'Wait,' I whisper again, but it zips out of the room towards the front door.

'Crap.' I leap after it and catch it before it tries to smash through a window. Hanging on to it with all my weight, I slip my feet into my trainers, grab my keys, and manage to get out of the door quietly.

The bracelet pulls me down the dark street like a puppy. The pavement glistens orange under the street lamps and the air is fresh. It must have rained whilst I was asleep. My keys jangle in my pocket as I fall into a jog heading away from home and back into danger. Mum's bracelet is leading me like a guide from my past and a flicker of hope burns in my chest. Maybe it's taking me to see her.

My heart beats faster as the bracelet guides me down on to the river path and past school. The dark trunks of the local wood loom ahead and I swallow a shiver. I haven't seen another person since I left the house. Fear sneaks up my spine as I draw closer to the trees and the deep shadows between them. What if the Villains were never going to take me to Mum? What if they just want the bracelet and information on Blaze and, once they have what they want, they murder me and chuck my body in the river?

The bracelet tugs me towards the metal gate into the wood.

Or maybe they're hoping there's a handy EV creature in there that will devour Jenna Ray, that girl who was almost a Love Interest. Then they can come and pick the bracelet out of the pile of my bones.

Or maybe Mum is in these dark trees waiting for me. The

gate squeals as I let myself in. It's getting harder to convince myself that I don't care if I see her. Perhaps her hair has started to go grey, like Dad's. My trainers stick in the mud as I walk down the dirt path, past trees that seem ghostly in the starless night. It'll be worth it when Mum holds out her arms and says, 'Hello, Jen-bear. You've got big.'

'Hello, Jenna.'

My heart jumps into my mouth as Emily appears from behind a grey trunk. The shock is quickly washed away by disappointment as the bracelet loses momentum and my arm drops. It's not taking me to Mum then.

'How have you been?' Emily flicks a dim torch at me.

'Where's my mum?' I rub some life back into my arm.

'Great. Good small talk.' Emily leans on a trunk and springs back up. 'Ew, it's wet. The Villains have a message for you. Wait— It wasn't just wet, it was slimy? Ugh, trees!' Emily shakes the back of her jacket. 'Let's talk about the great work you've been doing.'

'OK. I risked everything to wear this near Blaze for a few hours, like they asked.' I slide the bracelet off. 'Here. Take me to see my mum.'

'Ah, no, afraid not.' Emily pushes the bracelet gently back towards me. 'They thought this would hack Blaze's suit, but the bracelet – what were that nerd's words? – the bracelet performed suboptimally and we need to revert to an analogue approach.'

My stomach drops. 'What does that mean?'

'Well, there are two strands. Strand one, they need you to get the bracelet near the internal HPA computers. They need you to get into the base.' An owl hoots somewhere above us. What

186

do they mean get into the base? 'Strand two,' Emily continues, 'they need you to do some good old-fashioned spying. You're going to have to spend a lot more time with the hero.'

My shuddering inhale makes it sound like I'm going to burst into tears. Blaze and I had a sort of happy ending. He's moving on, he'll date Sam ♀ and everyone will stop judging him. More importantly, I'm moving on and I still have a chance to salvage things with my family. 'I can't. I can't do that. I did my bit. Just tell me where my mum is.'

'That's the thing.' Emily places her hand on my arm. 'When the Villains said they were looking for something, they actually meant someone.'

'No,' I whisper, but Emily's words are heading my way like a meteorite.

'The Villains don't know where your mum is, but the HPA do. They are holding her captive, and the Villains need your help to find out where.'

CHAPTER 16

'What do you mean the HPA are holding my mum captive?'

Mum had gone. Mum had disappeared. But in all these years, even when the Villains offered to help me find her, I never thought Mum might be in trouble. I'd jealously imagined her living somewhere else, in some beautiful cottage with a small garden full of roses, thinking how much easier life is on her own. In these fantasies sometimes she'd even had a whole new family with another daughter who was better than me in every way.

'The Villains didn't tell me much.' Emily tries to brush the tree slime off her jacket. 'But they know the HPA have your mum and she's in trouble. She needs you, Jenna.'

Why did the HPA take Mum? Is it because she used to work for them? My heart is racing. None of this makes sense. 'How do the Villains know her? Why does the HPA have her? Tell me what's going on.'

Emily shrugs. 'I wish I could. I'm just the messenger. All I know is you're the only one who can help the Villains find her.'

Wait.

If Megan were here, she'd be calling me an idiot for believing everything that this girl says without a shred of proof. The Villains could have spent a couple of hours looking into our family and found out that my mum had walked out on us. They could have seen her bracelet in a photo and found a replica. It's the perfect way to control the girl who would be a Love Interest.

I didn't have time to say this on the beach, but I do now. 'Prove it.'

'Prove that your mum is missing?'

'Prove that the Villains know her. That the Villains would want to help her.'

'Took you long enough.' Emily fishes a tablet out of her bag and the screen lights up the grey trunks of the wood. Something above us rustles and flaps away. 'Here.'

The image is so bright it only comes into focus after I blink the spots from my eyes. It's Mum, but she's older than I remember. She's grinning up at the camera with a mechanical project spread out below her.

I grit my teeth. 'This doesn't prove anything.'

Her hair is starting to go grey, but her smile is the same.

'Look what she's making.' Emily tips the screen as if I can't already see every excruciating detail; the happiness in her eyes squeezes my heart like a vice. Her fingers are primed over a long silver object that's a couple of feet wide.

'Recognise it?' Emily asks.

I dip my head to look closer. There are wires, metal panels and tiny screws; it could be anything. I straighten to tell Emily that this isn't good enough and then I see it. Mum is working on one of the Villain's hoverboards. Next to her is a familiar-looking Black man with thick-rimmed glasses and mini dreadlocks sticking up from the top of his head. I think I might recognise him, but my mind is too busy devouring this new image of my mum.

'She was helping them,' I say.

Is this why she left us?

'Apparently, she is amazing with electronics. Not a technopath, but a bit of a genius when it comes to inventing tech.'

I knew Mum was an engineer back when I didn't know what an engineer was. It's really her. She was helping the Villains.

'Why? Why was she helping them?'

'We all have our reasons.' Emily slides the tablet back into the bag. 'The Villains aren't evil. They're a counterbalance. An alternative. There's a huge network of people who oppose the HPA; people who aren't willing to be tagged and constantly monitored. People who think that we shouldn't be fighting the EV, we should be trying to understand it. I'd be lying if I said you were the Villain's first choice for this mission, Jenna Ray.'

Rude. I open my mouth to tell her that, but she's still speaking rapidly.

'If there was another way, the Villains would find it, but you are already halfway into the HPA. You're the one who will be able to find the information in time.'

'What do you mean *in time*?' I demand.

Emily continues, but her voice is shaky. 'There was another

190

person who helped the Villains; she was caught by the HPA too. The HPA released her eventually, but she wasn't the same. They'd taken everything.'

My heart squeezes again. 'I don't understand.'

'I saw her. Pari.' Emily's voice thickens with emotion. 'She's a shell. Whatever the HPA did to her, they left her empty.'

'What do you mean empty?' My voice rises in panic. 'What does that mean?'

'Empty, just empty.' It's like Emily's too traumatised by what she saw to put it into words. 'There's nothing of the old Pari left. She doesn't speak, she doesn't move; she'll eat, but only when someone feeds her. Her spark is gone. She's empty.'

Empty. The word hangs in the cool air and freezes me to my core.

'You think the HPA are going to do that to my mum?' I whisper.

'Yes. If you don't find her, and soon, that's exactly what's going to happen to her.' Emily swings her bag up, suddenly back to her old cocky self. 'So, what are you going to do, Jenna Ray? Suck it up and help rescue your mum, or go back to bed and leave her to her fate?'

I don't know if I want to cry or swear at her. I think I might hate Emily.

It's too dark to read Emily's face, but she sucks in air in a way that tells me I'm not going to like what's coming next. 'You understand that gaining access to the HPA and enough freedom to search the place means you need to do more than just go on a few more dates with Blaze, right?'

Everything inside me that was frozen in terror for my mum starts to crack under the weight of this new fear for myself. My life, my friends, my family, any hope of a real romance with Okorie; it's all slipping away.

'You'll need to get close to King Ron and even closer to Blaze.'

This is a nightmare.

'To save your mum, you're going to have to become a Love Interest for real.'

The moon breaks through the clouds and shafts of silver light up the trees. It feels almost like we're underwater. Blaze's kind face floats through my head. The boy from the wedding didn't seem evil. Can I really spy on him? And does Mum deserve my help? She walked out on us to live a life of danger helping the Villains. She chose them and left us behind. I haven't heard from her in ten years; not a letter, not a birthday card, nothing. Am I really going to destroy my life to help her?

I know what I'm going to say before my words ring out into the dark wood.

'I'll do it,' I say. 'I'll become his Love Interest.'

'Beans, oat milk, porridge, bread. Are you writing this down?' Megan hits the steering wheel. 'Earth to Jenna.'

'Beans, oat milk, porridge, bread,' I repeat, tapping something on to the notepad on my phone without looking down. My sandy bag had been waiting for me in the corridor this morning. I'm surprised I didn't trip over it last night when the bracelet was dragging me out the house to the woods.

A sleepless few hours staring at my dark ceiling wasn't

enough to process my decision, and the low-lying terror of being too slow to save Mum is a shard of ice in my chest, but at least I'm doing something now.

Since the Villains can use the bracelet to track my movements, I told them that I would get to a public place, so they could do something vaguely threatening to attract Blaze. Pouring away the last of the milk at 2 a.m. felt horrible, but when we weren't able to make tea this morning, Megan enlisted my help for the big shop.

Our supermarket is a perfect confusing maze of aisles. It should be easy to make sure Megan is nowhere near the Villains or Blaze. Blaze can 'rescue' me and I'll have my chance to talk to him. How do you offer to become a Love Interest? I don't think a Love Interest has had to search out the hero to consent to their role before; normally it just happens.

Sam ♀ comes on the radio. I guess she has people to do this sort of thing for her.

'*Love is a battleground—*'

'No.' Megan hits the radio off and yawns.

'Still not sleeping properly?' I ask.

'Not really.' Megan rubs her face. 'I keep dreaming about a lighthouse. Probably means I'm worried about money or something. OK, dinner tonight. Maybe we could get some plant mince for a chilli—'

Nine Trees Harbour flashes by, lit by the warm spring sun, as we drive across the bridge. There are tourists out on the piers and boats coming in with their catch. It's peak Nine Trees, like the town wants to illuminate the life I'm about to lose.

'—cake?' Megan's still talking.

'Yes.' Across the river, the school has students milling around by the gates. Will I ever even get to go back there?

'So, we'll get fruit cake?'

'What?' I shuffle round in my seat. 'No! We're not getting fruit cake.'

'You were a million miles away, little sister.'

I make a non-committal noise and pick at my jeans.

'What's going on in that head of yours?' she asks.

I panic. 'I was thinking about Mum.'

'Oh.' The car judders over a speed bump as we enter the busy car park. 'What about her?'

Megan makes the word 'her' sound like she's talking about a war criminal. When we talk about Mum, Dad disappears, but Megan always defaults to fury.

'Nothing,' I say quickly. 'I just think about her sometimes.'

Megan snorts. 'I don't. Who needs that woman?' She swings into a parking space. 'I promised Dad we'd be in and out in half an hour.' She cracks her fingers. 'Let's do this.'

Megan has always made the big shop fun, but I'm not in the mood for this right now. I'm too busy playing with my fingers and scanning the car park for the Villains. Maybe there was another way to get Blaze's attention. Maybe I could have just juggled chainsaws or swum with sharks.

The automatic doors swoosh open, and we step into the bright world of bags, bargains and generic tinkly music.

'Grab a trolley, Jen-bear. I'm going to the veg aisle.'

We pause in the broken flow of customers as she waits to

see if I'll take the bait. I'm not going to. I need to ditch her. I don't have the time or energy to play this stupid old game with my sister.

She edges towards the veg aisle, holding my eye, and her mouth turns up into a slight smile as she puts her game face on. I'm not going to play, but my feet are itching to go, and my fingertips are tingling.

'Go.' She spins and power walks towards the lettuce.

'Crap!' My body makes the decision for me and I leg it over to the trolleys. It's silly, but we play this game every time we shop. It doesn't even have a name. It's just a race to see what will happen first. Will I reach Megan with the trolley, or will she overload her arms and start dropping onions? Leaving Megan hanging would be the ultimate betrayal and it's probably too early to sneak away unnoticed.

'Sorry, excuse me.'

I swerve past a parent and toddler. I haven't lost this game in a long time.

'Jenna!' Joy steps in front of me. She's in her school uniform and holding a basket.

'Joy!' For a split second I think about skipping round her so I can still win, but I haven't seen my best friend in what feels like a lifetime and maybe she can run interference with Megan. 'It's so good to see you.' I reach for her, and she opens her arms for a hug, but I grab her hand instead. 'Come on!' I snatch a trolley and steer them both towards the vegetables, arriving just in time to catch Megan's armful of food.

'Hi, Joy!' Megan picks a radish off her jumper.

'I can't believe you two still do this.' Joy glares at me. 'What happened, Ray? You ran out of school and the next time I see you, you're on the news at a hero wedding?'

'You two catch up whilst I shop,' Megan says. 'But stay close. Need to add anything to the list? Tampons?'

'No. I started using that cup you bought me.'

Megan gives me a thumbs up and wheels the trolley off towards the buzzing lights of the cheese counter, intentionally ramming a *Do you need a strong man to help you load your car?* display.

'I've got a cup too now. I thought it got lost up there once, but there's not actually anywhere for it to go.' Joy taps the vague area of her womb. 'Okorie asked after you yesterday afternoon. He wanted to know if I'd heard from you. Then the wedding hit the news.'

Okorie must have read that I went straight from swimming with him to being Blaze's wedding date. It would have popped up on his phone. *Ping! Betrayal Alert. Jenna and Blaze a couple.* I swallow hard.

Joy narrows her eyes at me. 'Start talking.'

Sometime soon the Villains are going to turn up, followed closely by Blaze. Should I just tell her that? Maybe I should tell her to get her shopping and get out of here in case things get complicated. Or I could ask her to distract Megan whilst I head back to the car park?

Joy leans past me to grab some apples. 'Are you in love with the hero?'

'What?!' My mouth drops open.

'It's the only thing that makes this all make sense.' Joy selects apples five and six for her basket. 'I'm making a crumble. The only possible reason for you to U-turn and go to a hero wedding is that you're in love with him.'

It doesn't matter that I'm now picturing Blaze putting his arm around me on the top of the mountain. I'm not in love with him. It would be like falling in love with a mermaid. Actually, it would be worse. At least there are no reporters under the waves. I will never be in love with someone from the HPA.

'How can you think that?'

'You were laughing with him in that photo.' Joy's face creases with confusion. 'If it's not that, then what happened?'

'Of course you skip straight to love.' I march off after Megan to give myself a moment away from Joy 'Love Is Everything' Jusic to think.

'Jenna!' Joy's voice is urgent, but I don't turn round. Maybe I can tell her what's really going on. If she keeps it to herself, she should be safe enough?

'Jenna!' Joy cries. I spin round to find her surrounded by floating silver orbs. It's the Villain's tech. My mum's tech. An orb floats down in front of my face. Crap. I should run now, I don't want Joy and Megan getting pulled into this.

BING BONG. **'This is a customer announcement.'** The voice coming over the tannoy is all wrong. It sounds too excited. **'You are all now hostages of the Villains. You may finish your shopping, but you won't be allowed to leave until we get what we want. Relax, pull up some garden furniture, open an overpriced fizzy drink and don't pay for it. It can be**

your compensation from the broken system for this morning's trauma. If you attempt to leave you will be incapacitated. We won't lock the toilets either. Have a nice day.'

The silver orbs zoom up and zip over to the front entrance. When I told the Villains to do something vaguely threatening, I thought one of them would just stroll past in a boiler suit, but they've locked down a supermarket full of people. This is my fault. The squeak of trolleys and quiet chat of shoppers fades away and the supermarket falls silent. It's like everyone is taking a breath and deciding how to react.

All at once the sound returns. Shouts rise up from the nearby aisles.

'*Come here!*'

'*Call the HPA!*'

'*Grab the jam and let's get out of here!*'

'Do you think they know you're here?' Joy rushes over to me. 'We need to hide you.'

I need to tell her that this isn't real, that she doesn't need to be scared.

'Actually—'

'Jenna!' Megan and her trolley arrive back with a clatter. She's filled it with massive multipacks of crisps. 'Get in!'

I point at the trolley.

'Yes!' Megan shoves the crisps to one side. 'Get in and we'll find a way out.'

'No, it's OK.' There's a short pause whilst everyone, including me, waits to hear how it's OK. I click my fingers. 'We should split up! They'll never find us if we split up.'

Megan holds my gaze. 'Get in the trolley, Jenna.' She might as well be wearing a sign that says *ULTRA-PROTECTIVE MODE ACTIVATED*. There's no way she's going to let me out of her sight. I turn and consider running, but I'd have to go through Joy.

'What are you waiting for?' Joy asks. 'Get in.'

This is bad. The supermarket is full of terrified shoppers who I've put into harm's way. The Villains are not above risking innocent people to get what they want, I learned that at BLAZECON.

My sister is scared too, but not for herself. She's scared for me.

Joy grabs one of the brightly coloured packs. 'Come on, Ray!'

My insides twist into a knot. They're determined to protect me, but I need to get away from them. 'Let's just lie low. They'll get what they want and leave. They don't even know that I'm here.'

BING BONG.

In the second before the voice comes back I close my eyes. I know exactly what it's going to say.

'Could Jenna Ray please come to the customer service counter, that's Jenna Ray to the customer service counter.'

CHAPTER 17

Megan pulls me towards the trolley. 'Get in.'

My options are getting into a trolley full of salty snacks or telling my sister the truth. The multipacks crunch and rustle as I hop in. 'Just find somewhere to hide,' I say. 'I think those orbs will be covering every exit.' I'll stay in the trolley for now and then find an opportunity to get clear of them.

Joy dumps a multipack on my head.

'Let's see how well the Villains know our big supermarket. Did they date one of the girls from the pharmacy? I don't think so. There's a door next to the pharmacy counter that leads to the staff area.' Megan's voice is artificially light. She gives the trolley a shove. 'Oof! You're heavy!'

'You're not supposed to say that to teenage girls. And why do you know about this secret door, Megan?' Joy's cheery voice adds to the guilt crushing my insides.

'No comment,' Megan replies.

They're so calm; they're trying to hide how scared they are for me. I didn't want this to happen. I didn't want them pulled into this thing with the Villains. The trolley moves faster and Joy huffs. 'Oh wow. How do you weigh so much? You're tiny.'

'I'm not,' I mumble from my den of crisps.

'I think she's dense, like a star.' Megan's voice gets closer. 'Stay still, there are orbs everywhere.'

Have the Villains already rung the HPA hotline and asked for Blaze? How long have I got to get away from Megan and Joy? And why did they leave the awful tinkly music on? The Villains have more of a grungy drum-and-bass vibe.

The tin aisle flashes past in jagged segments framed by salt and vinegar and cheese and onion.

Beans.

Beans.

Beans.

Beans.

Chickpeas.

Orb.

'Run!' Megan yells, and the trolley picks up speed.

'There's nowhere for you to go,' I shout. They're going to hurt themselves trying to save me. 'Let me out!' I fling the multipacks off me.

'No! Stay hidden!' Joy shouts.

A stream of orbs surrounds us and shoppers flatten themselves against the tins as we race past. We're rapidly running out of aisle and the trolley is still picking up speed. The cold dead eyes of the fish laid out in ice stare at us as we race towards them.

'The fish counter!' I yell.

'Turn!' Megan and Joy dig in their heels and we swing round, missing the fish counter by centimetres. A pyramid of bread looms up out of nowhere.

'The buns!' Joy screams.

I cover my head as the trolley barrels into the display and soft packs of bread rain down on me.

'Come on.' Megan drags me out of the bread rolls and helps me out of the trolley. There are rolls scattered across the bakery section and the orbs are in the air circling us. Are these orbs armed? Would the Villains go as far as injuring Megan or Joy to make this look realistic?

'Stop running. We just need Jenna Ray.' The voice comes from all around us as the orbs zoom past. It sounds frustrated.

'You're not taking her!' Megan steps in front of me and a pack of orbs swirl into a blob above her head.

'Move.' An orb hovers in front of Megan's face.

She curls her lip. 'Make me.'

'No!' I push past Megan before they can hurt her. 'No. I'll go with them.'

'Jenna!' Megan grabs my hand and I shake her off roughly.

'Stop! Stop trying to protect me! You're not Mum!' Her mouth drops open. Shock, fear and hurt race across her face; I can barely stand to look at her. 'Just stay here.'

'Ray—' Joy reaches for me.

'You too.' I step out of reach. 'I don't— I don't need you to save me.' I glance at Megan, who looks like she's frozen solid. 'Come on then,' I snap at an orb, which spins and floats off towards the front of the store.

'Wait—' Megan cries, and there's a whoosh as a wall of orbs floats between us.

I turn and head towards the entrance. An orb drops down to fly next to my head. 'Don't you dare hurt them,' I say.

'We're not going to hurt anyone, Jenna.' The voice is a whisper. 'We're just doing our bit to make you a Love Interest. You're in mortal peril, so Blaze will come and save you. That's how every single interaction you've had so far has gone, and this was your idea, remember?'

'I saved him once.' Hidden shoppers are peering past the produce into our aisle, so I keep my voice low. 'You've made a mess.' At least I'm away from Megan and Joy now.

'*You've* made a mess,' the voice snaps back. 'All we did was close some doors.'

'Don't argue with her. How does that help?' a faint voice drifts out of the orb.

'Is that Emily?' I ask.

'Let her go and release the hostages!' Blaze lands on the customer service counter and my heart gives a strange thump. Even though he's kitted out in his hero uniform, his hair is less perfect than usual and there's a smudge of toothpaste above his lip. Was he having a lie-in?

'Finally,' the orb mutters.

'Are you OK?' Blaze fixes his brown eyes on me and the guilt in my stomach intensifies.

Using him feels wrong. Putting Megan, Joy and all these other shoppers in danger is wrong. Feck. Is helping the Villains the wrong thing to do?

BING BONG.

Blaze whips his head round. 'Show yourselves, Villains!'

'This is a customer announcement; Blaze, the hero, is currently at the customer service counter and would like to tell everyone exactly how he got his powers.'

'This again?' Blaze laughs. 'Stop playing games and tell me what you want.'

'Just the truth, Blaze. We'll give you to the count of three and then something bad will happen to someone you care about.'

'What?!' Orbs zoom into place around me. 'What are you doing?' Injuring me was not part of the plan.

'One.'

A small hatch opens in the orb directly in front of me, and I go cold. They're going to shoot me. Why did I think I could trust them? Even if my mum was helping them, they're anarchists.

Blaze steps up into the air and scans above the aisles. 'Where are you?'

'You won't find us. You don't need to. All we want is the truth, hero. How did you get your powers? Two.'

Maybe the Villains are just going to kill me and find another way to rescue Mum. They don't like me; I know that much. Maybe I was only ever a disposable pawn to them. The orbs wobble and red lights blink around me. I can't run, there are too many of them. I could almost laugh. I'm about to get murdered by tech that my mum made.

'Three.'

I scrunch my eyes closed. There's a hiss of air, but nothing pierces my skin. Arms hold me and a body is pressed close against mine. My feet are off the ground, so I'm going to guess it's Blaze.

My eyes fly open. We're speeding towards a jagged hole in the roof. This must have been how Blaze got in.

'Wait,' I gasp as we shoot through the hole and into the bright sky. 'My sister—'

'I can't,' mutters Blaze, and we fall for a split second before he regains control.

'Blaze, what's wrong?'

He doesn't answer, but flies across the town. This is not the fast, smooth flying that I've got used to. Blaze is holding on to me like we're hugging, and he loses altitude as we fly over the hospital.

'Look out for the clock tower!' I hadn't realised quite how safe I was on the ground in the supermarket.

We dip again as we fly over the river. A van races along below us, swerving round buses and pedestrians to keep up. I don't recognise it. Did Megan steal a vehicle to follow me? My bracelet vibrates around my wrist, and someone waves frantically at me from the front seat. It must be the Villains following us. The person in the front is miming something, but I have no idea what they're trying to tell me.

'Where are we go—' My heart ends up in my mouth as we drop again and almost hit the bunting strung across the harbour bridge.

'The base.' Blaze's voice is slurred.

'Mother Earth.' He must have been hit by a drugged dart. I spread my fingers out, searching across his broad back, and find the dart immediately. 'You were shot!' I yank it out.

'OW!' Blaze blinks at me.

'Is that better?' We rocket above the harbour. The square clock tower of the council looms on the other side of the water. The HPA base is underneath the council buildings. We're almost there.

'I think so.' He swings me into his arms. 'But I should get back to the …'

His eyes glaze over, and we stop and hang in mid-air above the harbour. A siren screams somewhere in the distance and people are shouting and pointing from the old-fashioned tourist boat below us.

'Blaze?' I whisper urgently.

His face goes slack, and his eyes drop closed.

'Blaze!'

He lets me go.

Falling.

We're both falling.

Or we're both still and the world is flying upwards.

Screams echo around the harbour. Not mine. I'm not screaming. Not Blaze's. He's not awake. The air screeches too as the wooden deck of the tourist boat hurtles towards us. I really am going to die this time. I grab Blaze's hand. He's going to die too and it's all my fault.

We shoot past the crow's nest.

The last thing I said to Megan was that I didn't need her.

I close my eyes.

We stop.

'Blaze.' I wrench my eyes open, expecting to see him awake and in control, but we stopped a metre from death and his head is lolling. I raise my voice. 'Blaze!' Is he doing this unconsciously?

No. I know this feeling of being held. It's different to whatever it is Blaze does. We've been saved by the same Villain who flung me across the museum and froze me on the beach. And he still has us. I crane my head around; is their van here? Is the telekinetic up in the sky somewhere on a hoverboard that my mum made?

'Jenna Ray?' A tour guide dressed like a pirate creeps over. 'Are you al—'

My head jolts as we shoot sideways and suddenly, where the wooden planks of the ship's deck had been, there is the murky water of the harbour.

'Don't!' I yell as the force holding us disappears.

I manage to shift my body and enter the water in a dive, but Blaze crashes in next to me and sinks past in a stream of bubbles. My body finally relaxes after what feels like hours of stress and uncertainty, and I swim down after him.

What is that Villain's deal?! Couldn't he have just put us gently down on that boat?

Blaze's suit has no spare material to hold, so I grab him under the arms and pull him towards the surface. Leaving us where we were would have been easier. Why flick us away from the boat and into this filthy water? He must really hate Blaze and me. When I find out who that telekinetic Villain is, I'm going to tip a bucket of harbour water over his head.

There's chaos as I break the surface and pull Blaze up with me. Both sides of the harbour are edged with people and blue lights are flashing from the bridge.

'They're here!'
'She saved him!'
'BLAZE IS DEAD!'

'This way, Jenna.' The pirate beckons me back towards his ship. I pull Blaze over to his wide wooden ladder, and the pirate and his mate help me get Blaze on to the ship. His breathing is OK. I guess I just need to get him somewhere quiet until the drugs wear off.

'This is Sydney Jones, on the scene, at Nine Trees Harbour ...' I go cold. Sydney Jones appears on the harbourside next to the ship. 'Where Blaze has just fallen out of the sky, but was pulled out of the water by his Love Interest, Jenna Ray. Jenna, can you tell us what happened? Is Blaze dead? Why did he fall out of the sky? What happened at the supermarket?'

'Er.' Emily didn't have any words of wisdom about Sydney fecking Jones. My heart is racing and I'm dripping harbour water on an unconscious hero. Maybe I should throw Blaze back into the water and jump in after him.

'Sydney!' The crowd parts and King Ron appears, kitted out in a bulletproof vest. 'We don't have time to talk. We need to get these two young people back to the base. Blaze is not dead, but he does need medical attention.'

Men wearing black combat gear swarm on to the deck and

Blaze is on a stretcher being carried to a waiting HPA van a moment later.

'Miss?' One of them offers me a gloved hand and I follow him past a pouting Sydney Jones. I climb up into the dark van and manage not to tread on the stretcher or Blaze. Numbness spreads through me as I sit next to a soldier in full combat gear.

They are taking me to the base.

Don't panic.

The difficult bit is over, and no one got hurt but Blaze. I swallow down the guilt and stop myself from fiddling with the bracelet.

This is what I signed up for.

This is what the Villains wanted to happen, what I wanted to happen.

This is how I save my mum.

Ron leaps in gracefully behind me. 'Let's get back to the base, Miss Ray; we've got a lot to talk about.'

CHAPTER 18

The HPA's main British base has always been just below the surface of Nine Trees, and when our prophecy went public five years ago, choosing a sleepy seaside town as a HPA location suddenly made a lot more sense. The HPA only release prophecies five years ahead of their date, but they must have known since the nineteenth century that Nine Trees was going to host some kind of disaster.

Once, a long time ago, when I was supposed to be waiting in the council's canteen for Dad to finish work, I'd tried to find my way into the base to see some heroes. I found silver HPA doors shining in the dark wood council corridors, but they'd had eye scanners on them. I hadn't been brave enough to try.

Now young Jenna's dream of spying on the base is about to come true. I wipe my palms on my damp jeans and try not to shiver as I bump up and down on the hard bench of the van. King Ron is opposite me and another four soldiers have crammed in around Blaze's stretcher. The van jerks and breaks roughly again, and I imagine the horde of people in the road all heading down to the harbour to see if Blaze is dead.

It's surreal sitting quietly across from King Ron. His hands are clasped over his black combats. He's different under the dim internal lights of the van. His eyes are creased with worry, and he hasn't looked away from Blaze's unconscious face. There's no pun on the tip of his tongue, no charming smile. This is the first time I've seen King Ron look small.

'They drugged him.' My voice is too loud in the silent van.

Ron's eyes flick up to meet mine. 'Yes. We know. His suit monitors his vitals.'

'That's good.' He's still staring at me. Does he want me to say something else? 'It was nice of Blaze to come and rescue me.'

Ron nods slowly, his eyes still on mine, like he's trying to scan my retinas for all my secrets. If I look away, I'll look like the guilty spy that I am, so I hold his gaze and stop myself breathing a sigh of relief when the van finishes the short journey to the base. The doors swing open to reveal an underground car park and I wait until the men are off and Blaze is unloaded before jumping down myself.

'Scan her and then bring her to my office.' Ron turns on his heel and marches through a set of glass sliding doors.

He doesn't trust me, and he shouldn't.

'This way, miss.' Two soldiers accompany me through the echoing car park.

I glance back at Blaze on his stretcher and then we're

through the sliding doors and in a concrete area that looks a bit like airport security. The walls are bunker grey and in the centre of the room is a console and a booth that reminds me of a shower cubicle. My insides clench; they're going to scan me and my Villain bracelet. I'm not sure I fully embraced what being the 'woman on the inside' of the HPA would mean. I was prepared to do whatever it took to help Mum in theory, but now I have to follow through.

'Step into the scanner, please, miss.' A soldier motions to the cubicle, and the other one sits at the console.

Back in the wood, Emily had flicked the band around my wrist and asked if it was still comfortable. *'Keep this on at all times so we can find you. Don't stress about the HPA, they'll never notice it.'* She'd snorted when I asked how she could be so sure. *'Because the Villains' tech is better than theirs.'*

'Arms up and over your head.'

I put my arms above my head and my wet jumper sticks to my wrist above the bracelet. Not that that will help if their scanner is good enough to pick it up. My heart is thumping against my ribcage. The soldier at the console taps a button.

A blue light flashes past my face and back again.

'There's something there, sir.'

I try to keep my face calm, but my palms are prickling with sweat. What do the HPA do to spies?

'Scan her again.'

The blue light flashes past and the soldiers step back from the console. One has a hand on his pocket. Does he have a weapon in there?

'W-what's going on?' My arms are still in the air. I don't know what else I can do to make myself look like less of a threat.

'Miss.' The senior soldier steps over. 'Please lower your arms and roll up your sleeves.'

They found the bracelet. Of course, they found the bracelet. Why did I trust Emily? They're going to take the bracelet and make me disappear, just like Mum. I lower my arms and push up my sleeves.

'Now, please reach into your pockets, slowly, and bring out what's there.'

My head spins with relief as I reach into my pockets and pull out £3.50 in change. 'I'm sorry, I didn't realise I had to take my money out.'

A silver tray is held out. The money clatters on to the tray and the sound echoes around the silent reception.

'And your bracelet.' I give them what I hope is a breezy grin as I slide the bracelet off and add it to the tray.

'Anything else in your pockets?'

I pat myself down and find a damp tissue and a curl of seaweed, which I also put on the tray. Maybe, after I've passed the scan, someone will offer me a towel.

The blue light flashes past again.

'Clear,' the soldier at the console calls.

'Here's your guest pass.' The other hands me a lanyard. Jenna Ray is officially a GUEST of the HPA. 'Would you like your seaweed and tissue back?'

'No, thank you.' I pick up my change and return the bracelet back to its place. 'Any chance I could have a shower?'

The seaweed and damp tissue are chucked in the bin, and I am led into a brushed grey concrete corridor.

'Is the council above us?' I ask.

The soldier looks up. 'Not quite. I think we're under the council gardens, or maybe the car park.'

The concrete wall becomes a window and I peer down at a dimly lit gym. The dark grey mats stretch away into the darkness with no sign of a back wall. It's enormous. This must be where Blaze trains. His unconscious face flits through my mind. It's my fault he got hurt. I hope he's OK.

'That's the training studio.' The soldier has warmed up to his role of tour guide. 'The hospital, wardrobe, and all the accommodation, where we're going, is also on this level. Next level up is ops, offices and the canteen. Then it's the council.'

We leave the training studio behind and my fingers trail along the smooth concrete. 'And is it all grey?'

'Oh yeah!' the soldier replies happily. 'The walls, the floor … we've got some art in the reception areas upstairs, that's pretty much all grey too.'

The HPA base really has committed to grey as a theme. The soldier hands me a light grey tracksuit and shows me into a predictably bland guest room where I can shower. As the hot water washes away the grime of the harbour, I can't stop myself thinking about Blaze. Did he grow up alone in a grey room like this? Train in that cavernous grey gym? Was he here, living under our feet like a secret super-powered mole for years before the prophecy hit? Maybe I can postpone my trip to Ron's office even more by going to check on him.

214

A new soldier is leaning on the wall outside my room when I emerge. He hands me a bag for my wet clothes.

'Can I see Blaze?'

'Ron first.' The soldier sets off and I rush after him, trying to settle the butterflies bouncing around my stomach.

'What's he like, Ron?'

'He's a hero,' the soldier replies, like that's all anyone would need to know. Maybe the last soldier got reassigned because they were too chatty.

We walk up a winding metal staircase in silence and arrive in another corridor that stretches into the distance. Level -1. This is where the offices are, I remind myself. We pass a door that says *SURVEILLANCE*, another that says *DEFENCE*, and a third called *LOGISTICS*. They are the rooms that Emily said could have information. Get some alone time in one of those rooms and the bracelet can have another go at hacking the system, whilst I search for a breakdown of the risks the prisoners pose, CCTV feeds of the cells, or even receipts for the prisoners' loo roll. Something in these rooms will lead me to Mum.

We must be properly under the council when we finally arrive at a dark wood door. It's the first thing on this base that hasn't been concrete or metal. I breathe out. Ron doesn't trust me, and if I'm going to be a Love Interest, that needs to change. My bracelet rests on the base of my thumb, and there's a sour taste in my mouth.

The soldier knocks smartly on the door.

'Enter!'

He takes my bag of clothes and holds the door open for me. I step through into an office that can only be Ron's.

There's so much history.

And so much … Ron.

The long, thin room is panelled in dark wood, and, at the far end, Ron is sitting behind a heavy wooden desk in a wing-backed green leather chair. Dominating the wall behind him is a massive pop art print of his face. Ten young Rons wink at me in different colour combinations, whilst the man himself stares at me like he's trying to read my mind. I'd laugh if I wasn't concentrating so hard on not shaking.

The red-patterned rug stretches in front of me and his desk seems to be getting further away. I can't look nervous, but I can't overcompensate and look too confident. Mother Earth, I think I've forgotten how to walk.

'Take a seat.' Ron motions to a wooden chair as I finally reach his desk. I pick up a cushion decorated with an embroidered crown and the initials *KR* and sit down with it on my lap.

'Miss Ray, I don't believe we've ever formally met. I'm Ron King.'

'I know.' I dig my fingers into the cushion and breathe out.

'You seem nervous.' Ron leans towards me.

'The best lies,' Emily had told me between complaining about tree slime, *'contain grains of truth. They are simple and believable.'*

'I am nervous.' I force a small smile on to my face. 'Today I've been held hostage, flown under the influence and dumped in the harbour and now I'm sitting in King Ron's office, when all I thought I was going to do was the big shop.'

Ron relaxes back. 'And what happened in the supermarket?'

216

'The Villains locked us down.' I grip the cushion harder. A couple of minutes of advice from Emily really wasn't enough to prepare me for an interrogation. 'I was hiding, but I was afraid they'd hurt my sister, so I gave myself up.'

'And how long were you alone with the Villains?'

'I don't know. They weren't really there. There were these orbs shouting instructions and then Blaze arrived.'

'Have they said anything else to you?'

'That you were evil.'

Ron doesn't miss a beat. 'Did you believe them?'

'They took me hostage and drugged Blaze. No, I don't believe them.'

'You're anxious around the press.'

I blink. 'Yes.'

'And didn't have any desire to be involved in the hero business.'

'No.'

'But you keep on cropping up, Miss Ray.'

'Yes.'

'And you agreed to go to the wedding with our boy.'

'Yes.'

'Why?'

'Because I like him.'

'Why?'

'Because he's beautiful.'

Ron tilts his head at me. I hope the surprise I feel isn't showing on my face. That wasn't a grain of truth; that was the whole truth, and I don't know where it came from.

'Go on,' he says.

My heart is racing again. The words forming on my lips are what I need to say to win over Ron, but I wasn't prepared for them to be true. 'He's beautiful inside. He has a kind, brave heart. Even when we hated each other we still rescued each other.' I shrug. 'We're connected. I don't know if I believe in fate, but I know the universe keeps pushing us together.'

My words fade and my brain tries to catch up.

'*We're connected.*'

Maybe that's true. Maybe that's been true since the moment he saved me from the flames. Dad's face pops up in my mind and then Megan's, but I push the angst away. I can't think about them now. There's no room here for doubt.

'I don't know how much longer I can fight it. Even if I was reluctant at first, I'm Blaze's Love Interest already and it's time for me to embrace that.'

My words settle on the dark wood of Ron's desk as he gazes at me. 'Ha!' He slaps his desk. A smile lights up his face and he looks almost as young as his pop art portrait. 'The world wanted it. Blaze wanted it and it seems you've finally come round. You had us worried for a while there, Miss Ray.' He claps his hands, excited as a puppy. 'What a Love Interest you'll be: young, athletic, terrified of the press, of course, but that's something we can work on. What a love story.'

I've barely said anything, but it's enough for King Ron to believe I'm ready to dedicate my life to the HPA. This is what I needed to happen, so why do I feel nauseous?

'What an adventure. You and Blaze are going to ignite the hearts of the nation.' Ron has got what he wants, and his charm is back on at full. He beams at me, and I have to stamp down the little voice in my head that says, *'Maybe he's not so bad!'*

'Can I see Blaze?'

Ron's smile gets even wider. 'Yes, of course, love.' He hits a button on his desk and the soldier opens the door. 'Take Miss Ray to see her hero, will you?'

'Thanks.' I jump up.

'No, thank you, Miss Ray, and good show pulling our boy out of the water.' Ron follows me to the door. 'Welcome to the team, Jenna.'

'Thank you.' I manage another smile and the soldier leads me off down a grey corridor.

'We're connected.'

The whole world has been telling me that I'm connected to this hero, and I didn't want to believe them, but I'm eager to see him now and make sure he's OK. The HPA are holding my mum hostage somewhere and he might be involved, but I still need to replace the image of his head lolling above the deck of the ship with one of him smiling at me. What is happening to me?

'Hi.' Blaze sits up as the soldier waves me into the ward. There's a row of beds with advanced-looking pads and sensors, and Blaze is in the one closest to the wall. He's dressed in a grey tracksuit too.

'Hi.' I perch on his bed and the ward door swings shut with a bang, leaving us alone. 'We match.'

'Yeah. Same outfit …' Blaze sucks his teeth. 'Awkward.' He takes a sip of water and I chuckle. Was he always funny?

219

'So awkward. How are you feeling?' I pull my legs up to sit cross-legged in the space at the end of his bed.

'Like I was drugged, fell out the sky and had to be dragged out of Nine Trees harbour?' He mirrors me, crossing his legs under a blanket. Once again, his eyes are full of guilt. 'It's happening again. I'm putting you in danger and then apologising and it's not OK.'

It's time to roll the dice. I breathe out. 'And it's going to keep happening, no matter what we do, no matter who else you date. It's put my family in danger, my friends in danger.' I want to catch his eye, but he's looking at his hands. 'So, I think that I should officially become your Love Interest.'

CHAPTER 19

'You want to be my Love Interest? But you said—' Blaze floats off the bed. 'Wait.' The blanket lifts, hiding the space underneath him, so it looks like he's being floated by a magician. 'Not again. Down, go down!' The blanket drops as he drifts up above my head, waggling his arms. 'Down! Mother Earth!'

'Blaze?'

He sighs heavily and twists so he's lying flat, looking down at me from the ceiling. 'Yes, Jenna?'

'Can you get down?'

'Um.' He makes a pushing motion with his arms. 'No. Not right now. Sometimes my power malfunctions.'

'Oh.' I lean back against the bedstand so I can see him properly. 'Need me to get Ron?'

'No!' Blaze's head bumps off the ceiling. 'No. Last time this happened he laughed at me for a solid fifteen minutes and then sent me on a meditation retreat. I am in control; you just took me by surprise.'

'Sorry.' Chatting to Blaze whilst he's lying on the ceiling would be hilarious, if he didn't look so annoyed. 'I'm sure stuff like this happens to heroes all the time.'

Blaze snorts. 'I doubt it. It's so embarrassing.'

'It's natural.'

He goes pale. Is he about to throw up on me? Have I managed to upset him even more? 'Should I go?'

'No.' He plants his feet on the tiles and stands, so his upside-down face ends up next to mine. 'No, please stay. We should talk.' Blaze is still pale, but he looks happier now that he's rooted to the ceiling.

'Isn't all your blood rushing to your head?'

'No. It's my whole gravity thing. I mean, obviously it's broken, but it still works well enough to stop me getting a headrush.' He brushes some hair from his eyes, and it falls up, away from his face. I don't think I'll ever get used to this.

'You were dead set against being my Love Interest.' Blaze is wide-eyed. 'What changed?'

This partnership can't be too serious. It can't go too deep. As soon as we've rescued Mum, I'm going to find a way to end it. So, there's no way I'm repeating what I said in Ron's office.

'I want to be safe again.' I almost cringe as the hope in his eyes freezes. 'If I was your Love Interest, then the HPA would protect me, my family and my friends, wouldn't they?'

'Yeah.' His hand is in his hair again. 'Of course. But you'll become more of a target.'

222

'I already am a target. I've had run-ins with the Villains. It's impossible to go back to school and Sydney Jones is everywhere. Everywhere!' My voice is rising. Turns out there's not much acting involved in this conversation. 'I was trying to protect my old life, but it's already gone. I need help to deal with this new world. And I like you, Blaze.' The old Jenna would be blushing, but I keep my voice confident. 'I think I can help you and you can protect me.'

He wobbles violently. 'You like me?'

'You're fine,' I say quickly, and his face drops again. 'I think we could be friends and give the world what they want. If that's what you want ... Have you started seeing Sam ♀, the pop star?'

Blaze looks away and I bite my lip. I never thought he might say no, but perhaps he doesn't want a fake Love Interest who just wants to be friends. Maybe Sam ♀ will turn out to be the real deal. Or maybe he wants to go and find a person who could truly love him.

'I haven't met the pop star yet.' He pushes down with his hands and flips in the air to land on the floor beside me. 'So let me get this straight. You'll tell the world you're my Love Interest, do interviews, go to events, become a public figure. In return the HPA will train you to deal with the press and everything else that comes with the role. We'll protect you and your family. But, in reality, you and I will only ever be friends?'

His brown eyes are hard. Maybe he's about to kick me out, but all I can do is nod.

Blaze holds out his hand. 'You've got yourself a deal.'

*

223

Rain hammers down on me as I trudge from the HPA car to our front door. This is going to be terrible. I betrayed Dad, upset Megan, ran off with a hero and agreed to become his Love Interest. I need to go in and tell my family fast, like pulling off a plaster. There will be shouting, ranting and tears, possibly mine, but Dad and Megan will understand, eventually.

Our front door is unlocked, and I click it closed behind me, trying to figure out what I'm walking in to. The lights are on, and the house is warm but silent. Perhaps they're both in bed already. I check in with my body. My heart is beating slightly fast, I feel a little nauseous, but I also feel strong. I've made a choice and I can deal with the consequences. I can do this. 'Hello?'

Dad pops his head into the corridor. 'Hi, Jenna, could you come into the living room, please.' He's gone again before I can read his facial expression, but his voice is unsettlingly calm.

'OK.' I kick my trainers off and go into the living room. Joy is perched on a sofa, looking uncomfortable, next to Megan, who glares at me as I shuffle in. In the centre of the room my old cuddly T. rex dinosaur sits on a side table.

'Take a seat.' Dad motions to the armchair and I sit down obediently. What is going on? Dad picks up the dinosaur. 'This is the talking dinosaur. You may only speak when you are holding the dinosaur.'

I grip the arms of the chair. 'But—'

Dad holds up the dinosaur. I close my mouth.

'This is an intervention,' he continues. 'We are worried about you. You need to sit still and hear this before your infatuation with the hero ruins your life, or worse, ends it.'

'What?! I'm not infatuated with him!'

Dad holds up the dinosaur. 'You can't see it, but we can. You'll listen to each of us because your decisions affect all of us. We'll tell you what the next steps are, and we'll tell you what the consequences will be if you don't follow them.'

My heart beats faster. Consequences? They don't even know I'm a Love Interest yet. I knew there were going to be consequences, but I didn't think they'd be presented at a meeting that includes my best friend. This is humiliating.

'Joy.' Dad hands the dinosaur to Joy, who takes it slowly.

She clears her throat. 'I'm sorry, Ray, but I've seen you run into danger, willingly, on two separate occasions because that's where the hero would be.' She glances at Dad, who gives her an encouraging nod. 'This whole thing also drove you away from school. When's the last time you did any schoolwork? Our year twelve exams are coming up. And when's the last time you saw your friends?'

'I was grounded!' I burst out.

Joy looks away and hands the dinosaur to Megan, who absently plays with its tiny arms. I clamp my mouth shut.

'Stop! Stop trying to protect me! You're not Mum!' My words from the supermarket echo around my head. *'I don't need you to save me.'* She looked so hurt. This whole intervention was probably her idea so she can shout at me. If she shouts, I'll give as good as I get. She's not the only one who's angry.

Megan catches and holds my gaze for a moment. The bags under her eyes have got even darker; I don't think I've ever seen her look this tired. She blinks and hands the dinosaur to Dad.

'You don't want to speak, darling?' He sits down next to her.

She shakes her head. Her eyes are shining in a strange way. Guilt explodes inside me. Is she crying? Megan never cries.

'I can say it for you then.' Dad fixes me with a stare. 'Jenna, you acted irresponsibly when you went to the convention, when you agreed to go to the hero wedding, and today when you went off with the Villains instead of staying hidden. You not only put yourself in danger, but you put those around you in danger too. Megan and Joy could have been hurt, or worse. Your actions bring the attention of the Villains, the HPA and the press to everyone in this room. You need to stop.'

I hold out my hand for the talking dinosaur. I need to tell them that I'm officially a Love Interest. If they're already this upset with me, they might as well know that too.

'I'm not finished.' Dad's voice is icy. 'The only reason we can see for you to keep interacting with this hero is that you enjoy it.'

My mouth drops open.

'That you're addicted to it.' Dad's fingers are tight around the talking dinosaur. 'We need you to give this hero up for the sake of your family, your friends and your own life, Jenna.'

It's like being knocked down by a wave. They think I'm selfish. 'Please.' I reach for the dinosaur again, but Dad shakes his head.

'Joy has an aunt in the Highlands who you can go and stay with until this settles down.'

'What?!' I'm on my feet. They want to send me away? We didn't ever consider leaving for the prophecy. 'Nine Trees is my home.' My fingernails bite into my palms as I ball my hands into fists. I can't remember ever being this angry with Dad.

226

'And it will be again, when it's safe for you to come back,' Dad says. 'When there's no chance that this entanglement with the hero could become permanent.'

'You're too late!' I shout. 'This is all too late. I've agreed to be his Love Interest!'

They all stare at me, dumbstruck, and in the silence all I can hear is my thumping heart. This isn't how I wanted to tell them.

Megan snatches the talking dinosaur off Dad. 'They forced you.'

I shake my head. 'This is the best way to protect you all.'

Joy grabs the dinosaur. 'Do you love him?'

'No!'

Dad gets up and walks past as if he's in a daze.

'Dad?' I follow him to the stairs. 'Dad, it was the right thing to do, I promise.'

He pauses halfway up and turns to fix me with eyes that are completely devoid of emotion. 'Do you know what, Jenna? You do what you want, and the rest of us will just have to deal with it.'

The front door slams behind me and through the window, I catch a glimpse of Megan's blurry figure disappearing into the rain. The stairs creak as Dad pads up and into his room. Should I go after Megan or go and bang on Dad's door? All I want to do is scream at them that I'm not selfish and that they don't listen. But if they did stop to listen to me, I can't even tell them the truth.

I wander back into the living room to find Joy still sitting there. She lobs the dinosaur at my head. 'Jenna Ray, start talking.'

CHAPTER 20

'But where has your mum been all this time?'

The rain sounds like machine guns hitting the bus shelter. Joy's bus has been five minutes away for about twenty minutes now, but it's given me time to tell my best friend everything. From Emily cornering me on Hidden Beach, right up to me telling Blaze that I want to be his Love Interest. The only thing I left out was the *'We're connected'* revelation, as it would melt Joy 'Love Is Everything' Jusic's head.

'I don't know where she's been.' The street is dark and empty, but I can't help checking to make sure no one has snuck up behind us to listen in. 'All I saw was that one photo.'

'I never understood how she could have left you all. You always seemed so happy, but it almost makes sense if she left to fight. What is it Emily said the Villains were?'

'A counterbalance.'

Joy swings her feet thoughtfully. 'This is a mess. Either your mum's evil or your new boyfriend is.'

'He's not my boyfriend!' I snap. 'And I'm not sure the Villains are the bad guys. Mum helped them and the reason Dad is freaking out is because he's convinced the HPA are evil, and if the Villains are the counterbalance ... Emily said the Villains wanted to understand the EV instead of fighting it, and something about that felt right.' Five minutes flashes red above us. 'I don't know! I don't think Blaze is evil either. Maybe he doesn't know everything that's going on?'

'And you're certain you don't love him?'

'Joy!'

She lifts her hands. 'I'm just asking. These are big decisions and maybe they would have been made easier by the fact that you fancy him?'

'I don't fancy him!'

'Whatever you say.' Her feet swing above the dark concrete. 'This is dangerous.'

'All I'm going to do is play the part until I've found out where the HPA are holding Mum, then the Villains can rescue her and I can fix whatever is left of my life. It's simple.' I sound much more confident than I feel.

'Shame about Okorie.'

Another load of guilt and sadness joins the churn in my gut. I told him I wasn't interested in Blaze and we had a magical moment on the beach. Now I've committed myself publicly to another boy. Okorie had been so kind and so very hot. His feelings are just another consequence I'll have to deal with.

I don't get to fall in love and find my mum. I just can't have both of those things.

'Yeah.' My voice is flat. 'It's a shame.'

'I'm sorry.' She squeezes my hand. 'Well, it's not like I can go back in time and tell you not to do this, so …' Joy leans back against the shelter and springs forward. 'Feck! There's a leak.'

'You shouldn't know any of this.' I brush the rainwater off her head. 'It's not safe. You can't tell anyone, OK?'

'Come on, Ray, who would I tell?'

'Nick.' I count them off on my fingers. 'Your mum, your dad, any number of people at school, you could accidentally say something in front of King Ron or Sydney Jones …'

'Ouch.' Joy clutches her heart. 'I can keep a secret. I never told you that Nick is convinced that the Secret Ninja is a robot.'

Mother Earth, what have I done? 'I just don't want you to get hurt.'

'Come on! I'm kidding. Nick tells anyone who'll listen his theories about the Secret Ninja. He's on about ten different forums.' She loops an arm around me. 'You can trust me. I'm glad you told me; this is a lot.'

'Yeah.' I lean my head on hers.

'Your dad and Megan, they'll come round.'

I picture Megan's shining eyes. 'As long as it all works.'

'Even if it doesn't, they're family.' There's a distant rumble and Joy hops up. 'Is that the bus?' Two small headlamps shine through the rain at the bottom of the street. 'That's the bus.' Joy turns back to me. 'Are you coming to school tomorrow?'

'No, I'm training at the HPA.'

Joy leaps back as the bus arrives in a spray of water.

The door swings open and the driver leans out. 'Sorry, girls! Did I get you?'

We shake our heads.

'They'll all ask me what's going on.' Joy steps up on to the steamy bus and I give her a quick hug.

'That's easy,' I say in her ear. 'Just tell them I'm a Love Interest.'

'Becoming a Love Interest doesn't happen overnight.' Ron is at his desk, holding a steaming mug with his face on it. I am being smiled at twice. 'You'll do three full weeks of basic training and then we'll start fitting the extra training and duties around day-to-day life.'

I nod. Three solid weeks with the HPA. That's good. They'll teach me how to get kidnapped and look wide-eyed at the cameras and I'll use my downtime to search for my mum.

Ron raises his eyebrows at my reaction. 'I know you have school, but I've already discussed this with your head teacher, and you've got a leave of absence granted we provide a tutor and you take your year twelve exams. Exams—' Ron snorts. 'We can train you to pass those.'

I nod again. Exams are something for future Jenna to worry about.

'Jenna, it's OK to be nervous.' Ron's mug is set down on a coaster. It's still smiling at me but the man himself is now frowning. 'This is a big, exciting moment for a young woman.'

My heart thumps loudly in my chest and I stop myself before I nod again. I'm playing this wrong. I'd wanted to come in and blast through this training, but a poker face isn't going to work with Ron; he's surprisingly empathetic. I open the door to a tiny bit of my anxiety.

'Sorry if I seem robotic.' I rub my hands. 'I don't know if I'm excited or terrified, but I know this is where I need to be.'

Ron leans back, looking at me thoughtfully, and then claps his hands. 'That's the spirit! And don't worry, Jenna. You don't need to be cool, calm and collected at all times, you're not the hero. We'll get you there, together. We're all a team here at the HPA.'

I grin and nod again. This is going to be much harder than I thought. For a chauvinist dinosaur, Ron is worryingly observant. And he's surprisingly kind, in his own weird way. I'm going to need to be cool, calm and collected enough as a spy to act like an anxiety-ridden Love Interest.

'Right. There's just one rule for you as a Love Interest and if you can remember this, you'll be fine.' Ron holds up a finger. 'If you're in any kind of trouble, call Blaze. Don't call our general number, call 778 instead and say, "Jenna for Blaze."'

I yank my notepad out of my bag.

'Call 778 and say, "Jenna for Blaze,"' Ron repeats slowly, and I make a show of writing it down. 'Doesn't matter what the trouble is: press, Villains, natural disaster, EV pigeons … If Blaze can't come we'll send our soldiers. Now, I have an online talk about my old sidekick, Prince #2, so I'm going to send you off to do some media with Mia.'

On cue, the door to Ron's office bangs open. 'Big R.' Mia cocks a finger at him. 'And little LI? If I'd put money on you being here, I'd have won big.'

I roll my eyes.

'Better the devil you know, eh?' Ron says. 'Have a good day, Miss Ray.'

'OK.' Mia leads me down a grey corridor. Today Mia's hair is in an elaborate braided plait that bounces on the back of their oversized white shirt. Their trousers are dark red velvet, but for Mia the outfit is positively understated. 'Media training is going to be the big one for you, because you're a scaredy-cat.'

'I'm not a scaredy-cat, I get anxious. Those are two different things.' I clamp my mouth shut. I just admitted to getting anxious, again, first with Blaze, now with Mia. Is there something about being a spy that lowers my inhibitions?

'Good, Jenna!' Mia turns to me with a smile. 'That kind of thing is perfect. Young, relatable, aware of your mental health. Keep saying stuff like that.'

'But it's true.'

'Even better.' Mia swipes us on to a bright, mirrored lift.

'Are you qualified to teach me media? I thought you were the head of wardrobe or the driver.'

Mia giving me side-eye is visible in every surface.

'Fine.' I glance at my reflection too. I'd waited until Dad and Megan had left for the day before rushing into the shower and throwing on my clothes. I decided that dark jeans and Megan's fluffy pink jumper were the perfect things to wear for my first day as a Love Interest. Maybe Megan will realise I've got it and come and shout at me. At least then she'll be talking to me.

The lift doors ping open. 'Here we go.' Mia steps out. 'Welcome to wardrobe.'

Wardrobe at the HPA base is nothing like Mia's little area in the Norwegian wine cellar. It is vast and surprisingly light for a room with no windows. Long racks of clothing line either side of the room, with two more levels of garments elevated above them, like a tall, wide staircase of cloth.

'At the bottom, we've got Ron's suits.' Mia pads up a wooden staircase to the next level. 'And at the top.' Mia waves their hand towards the predominantly red and black top level. 'We've got all the clothes for Baby H. I mean, Blaze.'

I chuckle. 'Baby H is fine.'

'On the other side, I've got some options for you and clothes for our guests.' Mia waggles their foot towards the racks. It's too far to see anything other than the colours, but there's a lot of green. 'But we're not here for wardrobe!' Mia jumps down. 'Come to my teaching area.'

At the far end of the room, tables covered in tape measures and scraps of material have been pushed to the side and a grey plastic chair sits on a round purple rug.

'Take a seat.'

I perch on the chair and wait patiently as Mia drags a large potted palm in front of me.

'OK.' They wipe their hands on their oversized shirt. 'This is Sydney Jones.'

'This is a pot plant.'

Mia tilts their head. 'Ah, I'm sorry, I didn't get the memo you had no imagination.'

'Fine! It's Sydney Jones.' The thick green leaves are still wobbling from being moved. It's a beautiful plant. If only Sydney Jones really was a silent, swaying palm.

'Now.' Mia circles me. 'When you talk to the press, you need to be prepared. Don't look at me, look at Sydney. You need to be on brand. You need to use the right tone of voice and you need to be in control. DON'T look at me. Look at Sydney.'

I flick my head back towards the plant.

'Now smile.'

I lift the sides of my mouth.

'Now smile like you understand what a smile is.'

'Mother Earth,' I mutter, and plaster a huge smile across my face.

'Good, now reduce that to fifty per cent. Twenty-five per cent. Ten per cent.'

Every muscle in my face tenses as I obey.

'Good!' Mia claps their hands. 'That is your press smile. Non-committal and effortless. Remember that smile.'

My mouth has only the slightest upturn and my eyes are about to crinkle, but I know I will never be able to make this exact face again.

'Next.' Mia appears behind the palm. 'Repeat after me – no comment.'

I push my hands under my lap. 'No comment.'

'Again.'

'No comment.'

'With the smile.'

I can't remember the smile! 'No comment?'

'You look like you've committed a crime. Again.'

I adjust my face so my mouth has a slight upturn and my eyes are just about to crinkle. 'No comment.'

Mia nods. 'Getting there.'

By the time there's a knock on wardrobe's door, I'm exhausted and fostering a new hatred for potted plants.

'How is our new recruit?' Ron marches over to us.

'See for yourself.' Mia motions to me and my body tenses.

'This is Sydney Jones, on the scene.' Ron focuses his attention on me. He doesn't make any attempt to change his voice, but he doesn't have to. Those words are enough to make my heart race. 'I've got Jenna Ray on camera, in a burgled jewellery store with her hands full of diamond necklaces. Jenna Ray, what are you doing here and what did you do with all the jewels?'

I force my ten per cent smile on to my face. 'No comment.'

Ron steps closer. 'But, Miss Ray, you've obviously just broken into a jewellery store. What do you have to say for yourself?'

Mia lifts their eyebrows at me.

I clear my throat. 'The situation is too complex for me to go into at present. The HPA will release a statement in due course.'

'Miss Ray.' Ron lowers his voice. 'You're live on TV. The nation is watching. Everyone is looking at you. Surely you want to defend yourself.'

My throat has gone dry, but I force the words out. 'At this time, I am unable to comment. I'm sorry, but I need to go. The HPA will release a statement in due course.'

Ron rocks on his heels. Is he regretting agreeing to train me? Can he see how uncomfortable this all makes me? He gives

Mia a curt nod. 'Good.' He turns back to me. 'A good start, Miss Ray. That will be enough to keep you out of trouble at least. Come with me, I've got some lunchtime reading for you.'

'Thanks,' I mutter at Mia on our way past.

'Keep practising your smile,' Mia replies. I don't respond and as we reach the door they shout after me, 'Keep practising your smile, Jenna Ray, I'm not joking. I want you smiling in your sleep.'

The door closes, shutting Mia's shouts in wardrobe, and I follow Ron back to the lift.

'Kate, my Love Interest, didn't like the attention at first.' He motions me into the lift. 'But, after a couple of years, she was giving me tips.'

'She was pretty amazing.' A slideshow of Queen Kate's glamourous photos race through my head, ending with the tragic shot of the body bag under the bridge.

'Everyone is nervous, Miss Ray.' His voice is softer, like he's remembering her too. 'Everyone is nervous, but over time you learn how to adapt.'

The mirrored doors slide closed. Ron looks immaculate, as always, in a dark blue three-piece suit with a pink tie, and whatever hint of sadness he was feeling has been banished from his face. *Everyone is nervous.* I can't believe that front flipping, constantly winking, casually chauvinist, eminently charming King Ron is ever nervous, but I've never looked at him as a person before. The doors thankfully ping open before I decide that I like Ron.

'Here we are.' Ron shows me into an empty canteen. He points out where I can get chips, beans and other beige foods, before leading me to a table with a stack of history books.

'Legacy.' He taps the books. 'I'll be taking you for those sessions and tomorrow our first one will be on The Sheriff's Nancy, a classic Love Interest from the Wild West. I want to know how the two met and what their life together was like. I don't need reams of details. You're a Love Interest, not a historian, but get an idea of how Nancy lived her life. Have some lunch, start reading and your next teacher will be along in an hour or so.'

He strides off between the tables before I can ask whether people in the hero business get proper breaks. 'I guess not,' I mumble in the empty canteen. I slip my jumper off, put it on one of the other chairs and slide it under the table, and then go and get myself some chips.

My eyelids are drooping as I reread the first sentence of **Case Study 2: The Sheriff's Nancy** for the fifteenth time. Chips might have been a bad choice.

Matthew Coombe was an eyewitness to The Sheriff's emergence, 16th April 1892, Buzzards Gorge, California.

He was interviewed for the HPA 12th November 1904.

Interviewer: Could you please tell us about the moment The Sheriff met his wife to be? We'd appreciate it if you could keep this brief and to the point.

Matthew Coombe: Well, sure. She always wore a yellow ribbon in her hair. That's what I remember about Nancy. That and her love for Jim, o' course. You call him The

238

Sheriff, but he introduced himself to me as Jim and that's how I'll always think of him.

Jim saved Nancy on his first day as a hero. His emergence. Isn't that the way? Heroes goin' and fallin' in love with the first girl they save. It's fate or destiny or some such. Somethin' drawin' one soul to another, like a horse to water.

The day they met I was groomin' my horse which I'd called Jacob after my brother. Jacob had died in the mines. A lot of the 49ers died in the mines. Me and Jacob …

A hand slams down on the table next to my head. 'Jenna!'

'I'm awake!' There's a tear as I lurch up. 'Crap.' The page I was reading is now pasted to my face with dribble. I gently detach it and tuck it back into the book, very aware that Blaze is waiting for me. When I finally look up at him, he's got a knuckle in his mouth and is making a show of not laughing at me.

He's wearing thick-rimmed square glasses.

Mother Earth. I can't stop staring at them. Somehow, they make his already beautiful face even more attractive. Feck! My defences are non-existent when I've just been woken up.

'Still waking up?' Blaze rolls up the sleeves of his grey tracksuit. 'Want to hit snooze for a minute or two?'

Although that would probably help me deal with this glasses bombshell, I shake my head and bite back a yawn. 'What's happening now?'

He flips my book shut. 'Now, I teach you how to fight.'

CHAPTER 21

'Learning to fight was the last thing I expected to do today.' My feet bounce as I cross the wide grey mat to join Blaze. Whilst I was getting changed into a new grey tracksuit, Blaze has laid out boxing gloves and pads and, to my disappointment, taken off his glasses. 'I thought I'd be considered too precious and fragile by the HPA to be able to defend myself.'

'Yeah, well, the HPA have some antiquated views about women. I knew you'd want to be able to look after yourself and Ron thought I was making up reasons to get close to you, so …' Blaze blushes and looks at the ceiling.

'Thank you.' I bite my lip. Finding out Blaze is a feminist is almost too much to deal with.

'I thought, maybe you and me could do some good. You could be an amazing role model,' he continues, looking back at me. 'You're strong, and independent, and you stood up to the Villains.'

Now I'm blushing. A role model? I hadn't even considered that I could do some good from within the HPA, but Blaze already had. First the glasses, now this. Day one of not getting closer to him is not going well.

'Anyway.' Blaze gives me a smile that I've never seen before. It's slightly evil. 'Drop and give me five.'

'Five what?'

'Push-ups.'

'Five push-ups?! Weren't we doing fighting?'

'Before we "do fighting", you need to be warm. Do you want me to make it ten?'

'What? No.' I drop on to the ground. 'There!'

'That's one,' Blaze says from above me.

'Are you just going to stand there and watch?'

'Fine.' Blaze drops to the mat and does a push-up. 'My instructors would have had you running laps by now.' He does another one and makes it look effortless. My face feels warm, which must be from the exercise.

'Lucky you're soft then.' I do another three before lowering myself on to the lovely soft ground. 'Five.'

'Don't swimmers have to be able to count?'

'Someone does it for us.' I roll up. 'What next?'

'Burpees.'

Burpees. Lunges. Squats. We do all the exercises together and the heat running through my body feels amazing. It's been too long since my last swim. It's fun doing this with Blaze too. His dark hair is a mess from jumping and he's got a wide grin across his face. It's like he's someone else.

'You're cheating, again!' I cry, mid-lunge, as Blaze's feet stop touching the floor.

He lands and holds up a finger. 'One, I don't know what you mean. Two, I'm the instructor here, any more false accusations and I'll make you run laps.'

'Not sure you understand what a false accusation is,' I mutter as I finish up my lunges.

'Right!' Blaze chucks a pair of boxing gloves at me. 'Your acronym is R.H.S.F. That's the order of responses for all Love Interests.' He holds up two pads. 'Run. Hide. Shout. Fight. I added the last one for you. You already know how to run, how to hide and how to call for help, so show me your punches. Right hand first.'

I punch the pad gently.

'Great. Perfect,' Blaze says.

'Really?'

'Yeah. You got rid of the tickle I had in my thumb. Punch me properly.'

'I'm not sure I like this new, funny Blaze.' I punch slightly harder.

'Bad time to figure that out, Love Interest. Keep your elbow tucked in.'

I tuck my elbow in and give him everything I've got.

'Yes, Jenna! Show me your left.'

Sweat has pooled in the bottom of the gloves by the time Blaze announces we're moving on. 'You're a natural, but punching won't be helpful for a while. So, I'll show you how to escape a hold if someone grabs you. Then you can …'

'Run, hide and call you.' I feel like a parrot. The HPA teach things by drilling them into your brain. Three weeks of this will turn me into a zombie. 'Let's go then. Escaping holds.' I hide a grin as I chuck the gloves down next to the pads.

Blaze blurs and a split second later he's behind me with his arms looped around my waist. 'This is a bear hold.' He has picked me up so many times, but for some reason having his arms tight against my waist feels different. All the heat from the exercise has gone straight back to my face. 'Try and escape.'

'I don't want to hurt you.'

'You won't.' I can hear the smile in his voice.

'All right then.'

Two summers ago, Joy decided that the prophecy might be about gangs or Vikings and that we should learn some self-defence. She wouldn't hear me when I suggested that the gangs would probably have weapons and that Vikings no longer exist, so we spent every Tuesday for a month learning to protect ourselves with an epic lady called Fiona. Fiona started with the bear hold too.

I bend at the waist and throw an elbow back towards Blaze's face. His grip loosens and I spin to try and hit him with another elbow. He lets go to dodge and staggers back. I go for the groin kick.

'Whoa!' he yells. I freeze with my foot below his groin. Blaze is in the air, just out of range. I slowly lower my leg. 'Yep. That's how to do it.' He lands.

'Sorry, you didn't ask if I already knew. Did I get you?'

'It's OK, that first elbow glanced my nose but—' He dabs his nostril, and his finger comes away red. 'Oh.'

'Crap!' There are no tissues in the studio. 'Where are the toilets?'

'It's OK.' Blaze blurs away and is back a moment later with a toilet roll. 'Argh! I forgot that running makes nose bleeds worse.' A few drops of bright red fall on to his grey jumper.

'No!' I grab the tissue and make a wad for him. 'Just sit down for a bit.'

In the corner of the room there's a cupboard with a first aid box, spare key card and some other miscellaneous stuff, including just the thing I was looking for.

'Here we go.' I place a wire bin in front of him and hand him a tampon, before joining him cross-legged in the middle of the mat.

'Oh.' He holds the tampon up with a look of panic in his eyes. 'How does it work?'

'You're a hero, Blaze, I'm sure you can figure it out.'

The tampon is turned over and over in Blaze's fingers until I take pity on him and unwrap it.

'Just pop that curved end up your nostril.'

He takes it and when he turns back to me there's a tampon and its white string hanging out of his nose. I clench my lips to stop myself laughing.

'You should cool down.' He sounds cross, but he's smiling too. First, he was funny and now he's all soft and vulnerable. If I'd told Joy I already felt a connection to Blaze, maybe she would have warned me spending more time with him would make me feel odd inside. My heart is sort of warm, but my insides are also full of uncertainty and guilt. Lots and lots of guilt.

'Sorry I gave you a nosebleed.' I lie back on the mat.

'I've had worse.' Blaze joins me. 'My mum dropped a plate on my head when I was little. And, when I was nine, my youngest brother stepped in front of my bike and I swerved to avoid him and ended up going face first into a parked car. Those stitches were still in when Ron arrived to make me part of the HPA. Oh, and there was this bad guy in Portugal who shot a boulder at me.'

'Do you miss them?'

'The boulder guy?'

I nudge his arm with my fist. 'No, your family.'

'Oh. Yeah. But I made a choice. It doesn't matter if I miss my dad's lo mein or my mum's pancakes or my stupid little brothers asking me questions about everything. Saying yes to the HPA was the right thing to do, and this is the life that came with it.'

His words settle between us as we look up at the distant ceiling. His voice is light, but if I say the wrong thing now, I'll close this little window into Blaze's past. Maybe that's what I should want to happen. Maybe I should steer us back to lighter things, but learning about him is addictive.

'How many brothers do you have?' I ask.

'Two.' I can hear the smile in his voice. 'They were six and four when I joined the HPA.'

I turn my head so I can see his face. 'When's the last time you saw them?'

He closes his eyes. 'Before.'

The word settles between us like a big nostalgic puddle. *Before.* His little brothers are from a life before Blaze came to the HPA, before his powers manifested, and before he became a hero and had to deal with all the pressure that comes with that. My brain is yelling at my hands to reach out and take his, but I stop myself.

'Why don't we go and see them?'

'What do you mean?' He looks over at me.

I shuffle closer to him. 'Well, you can fly pretty much anywhere in under half an hour. Why don't we pop round?'

'Pop round?' Blaze sounds as if I've suggested we fly to the moon. 'I'm not allowed.'

'Why not?' Am I doing this because I want him to be happy? I'm just going to assume I'm curious about his parents. Maybe they've got powers too. 'Where do they live?'

'Too far from here. I had to cut ties. It's safer for everyone if there's just one person I care about. That's only one person to protect. I shouldn't even be talking about them.'

I know that voice. It's the parrot voice I was using earlier. The HPA has spent years telling Blaze he's only allowed to love one person. I swallow down even more guilt. 'Thing is, you're also super-fast. You can go anywhere you want, and no one would know. We could pretend we're going on a date and, you know, blur over to see your family. I can write to them?'

Blaze's lips part, like he's surprised that I care. 'Jenna, honestly, it's OK. I'm happy here, I've got Ron. He's my family now. I know he's a lot, but he taught me everything I know. And now, I guess, I've got you too.'

The door to the studio bangs open.

'Well, what happened here?' Ron strides in.

'Jenna won, sir.' Blaze jumps up.

'Evidently.' Ron stops in front of us, so I push myself up too. My arms throb. Blaze was right, I should have cooled down. 'The world needs Blaze, I'm afraid, Miss Ray, so I think you're done for the day. Head on out through security.' Ron claps Blaze on the shoulder. 'Clean yourself up, eh, son? Maybe lose the tampon?'

'Yes, sir.'

Ron strides off and we follow. As we reach the door Blaze grabs my hand and gives it a squeeze.

'You're a badass, Jenna Ray.'

'And you're more.' The words slip out of my mouth, and I feel my cheeks heat as they land between us. 'You're more than I thought you were.'

Blaze gives me a slightly confused smile. 'OK, cryptic. I'll see you tomorrow?'

I smile back, ignoring the light flutter in my stomach. 'Tomorrow.'

He jogs off after Ron and I'm left alone outside the training studio. Security is one short, safe, grey corridor away. But I can't go home yet, Megan's pink fluffy jumper is still up in the canteen – it's time for my real work to begin.

SURVEILLANCE

DEFENCE

LOGISTICS

My roundabout route to the canteen can include all three.

This is just a wander with intel potential. There's no need for my heart to pound in my chest, but it still does as I jog up to Level -1.

SURVEILLANCE is my first stop. A clamour of voices echoes as I approach and I don't need to look inside to know that the room is full to the brim with soldiers. I slow down as I pass the open door, hoping that I might see something useful, but an image of several EV squirrels covers their huge screen. Surveillance is out. I'm not sure I'll ever be able to casually wander into there. I wipe my sweating palms on my tracksuit. This is more than wearing a bracelet whilst I chat to a boy. This is actively spying on the HPA, and I have no idea what I'm doing.

DEFENCE is a nonstarter too. The open door shows two guards building a huge tower of cards in front of a bank of screens too small for me to see. The chips from earlier still sit heavy in my stomach. I hope I don't throw up – that would definitely draw attention to me. I should have demanded spy training from the Villains. Perhaps Mia can teach me how to look innocent. Smile at five per cent. Eyes wide. Eyebrows scrunched in a way that says, sorry, I'm just a silly Love Interest who forgot her pretty pink jumper.

The door to *LOGISTICS* is closed.

No voices float out. There're no visual clues on the door's flat grey surface. There's no way to know if there's anyone in there. My heart beats even harder and I breathe out through my teeth as I approach it. On the other side of that door there could be an empty room and a vacant computer, ready to tell me everything I want to know.

I need to go in, but what if there are soldiers, with weapons, on the other side of the door?

What if there aren't?

'Come on, Jenna,' I whisper.

I didn't ruin my life and come to the HPA to flirt with Blaze and learn to smile. I need to find my mum before it's too late. This room could have all the answers that I need. My mouth tastes of metal as I reach for the door handle.

'Miss Ray?'

I spin round. Ron is walking down the corridor towards me, with a slight frown on his face and the pink jumper draped over his arm.

'I was looking for that!' I slap a big, relieved grin on my face. 'Is this not the canteen?'

'No.' Ron hands over the jumper. 'It's logistics.' He reaches past me and pushes open the door. A room full of soldiers jump to attention. 'Say hello to Jenna Ray, everybody.'

They obediently call out greetings and I take in the myriad computers and flashing lights, before Ron closes the door.

'The canteen is right at the end of the corridor.' His voice is kind, rather than suspicious. Thank goodness he thinks that women are stupid. 'Shall I show you out?'

'No. I'm pretty sure I can find my way this time.' I add an embarrassed giggle for effect.

'Down the corridor, down the stairs and follow the signs to security,' Ron says. 'If you get lost, just knock on any of these doors. All our offices will always have someone in there who can help you. Good evening, Miss Ray.'

He turns on his heel and marches back towards his office. I keep the silly smile on my face as I head back towards security. Was Ron watching me that whole time? I clutch Megan's jumper as a chill zips through me. *Our offices will always have someone in.* Maybe Ron doesn't trust me after all.

CHAPTER 22

Day three of training is a lot like days one and two. I smile with Mia, try not to enjoy sparring with Blaze and end up back in Ron's office.

'Whirlpools.' Ron leans back in his chair with his eyes closed, which is his preferred way to lecture. I haven't given him another reason to suspect I'm anything more than a Love Interest with a poor sense of direction, and he seems to have relaxed around me. 'Whirlpools are everywhere. I have been stuck in two of them and I actively avoid the water.'

Today's lesson is on 'things that can kill you and how to avoid them'. I write WHIRLPOOLS down and underline it.

'Didn't Prince #2 pull you out of one?' I ask.

'Ah yes. My old friend. That's a good story for a Love Interest. First you need to know about the pirates.' Ron holds up his hands. His eyes are still closed. I lean forward, like I'm hanging on his every word, and scan his desk. 'Now, these weren't old

251

pirates with cutlasses and eye patches, they were new pirates with semi-automatics, who like to overrun cruise ships.' Piled neatly on the dark wood are notes on an upcoming event, a document that says BLAZE – UNIFORM UPDATES and several receipts, but nothing that looks useful.

'I was fighting perhaps twenty of them. I'd used the Eliminator and I was running low on energy and that's when one of them appears and POW! kicks me over the edge and straight into a whirlpool. Awful things, whirlpools. Fast, damp, and so disorientating that that would have been the end of me if it hadn't been for Prince #2.' He opens his eyes to check I'm listening, and I diligently write PIRATES in my notepad.

'My old sidekick had just had a flight upgrade and was able to swoop down and pluck me out before I drowned. Fresh from my dip, I took out the remaining pirates and returned the ship safely to shore. So, Miss Ray, what's the lesson here?'

I glance at my notebook. The lesson was probably that Ron once defeated twenty pirates, but I don't think that's the answer he's looking for. 'Teamwork?' I try.

'Exactly, Miss Ray.' Ron gives me an approving smile. 'I defeated the bad guys, but if it wasn't for Prince #2, I'd have been sucked into the ocean floor. I miss those days. I miss my old friend. That's the hero life though. There's always a price for saving the world. He was the first fully designed, man-made sidekick, did you know that? An incredible work of engineering. He was the friend I needed after Kate …' Ron's smile fades for a moment before coming back stronger. 'Prince #2 was one of a kind. And you might ask why I didn't get another made after he was destroyed—'

It was because the AI chip that gave him his personality was lost, but Ron doesn't pause to see if I already know the answer.

'The scientists developed this tiny chip, you see. It allowed him to grow a personality, like an acorn that sprouts an oak. He became his own man.'

His tone is wrong. I blink as my brain detangles that last sentence. Prince #2 *became his own man* and I would have expected admiration from Ron, but there was a hint of anger in his voice instead. Maybe I imagined it. The softness of his smile and the crinkles around his eyes make him look like he's enjoying a moment of nostalgia.

'Once the chip was gone, Prince #2 was gone too.' Ron checks his *King Ron* mug and sighs when he sees that he's out of coffee. 'Powers. You can write that down too.'

'Powers?'

'Untrained, unregistered people with powers. There are more now than ever before and they are dangerous. There's a woman out there with the power to see the future and she is refusing to come forward. It's a wasted resource. Imagine the good all those powers could do if they were given to men trained to use them in the correct way.' Ron gazes into the distance, like he's not talking to me any more, but trying to convince the nation. 'We could defeat the EV. We could protect everyone. We could make the world safe again.'

My face feels hot. First the mansplaining, now this. People's powers are natural. The EV might be doing a lot of damage, but it's also given humans these incredible abilities. Taking a power from someone would be like taking their hand, and it's not men like him who he's talking about. It's the unregistered: the absent Diviner; the women and other non-male genders who barely ever register their powers with the HPA, because why would they? According to Ron and the whole fecking HPA their powers are weak and only men can become heroes. Megan would have argued him down and loved every second, but I'm a spy, so I just clench my fists under the desk and nod.

'There are so many powers now, Miss Ray. It's almost too much for the HPA to handle.'

A soldier raps on Ron's door. 'Thirty minutes to take-off, sir.'

'Ah yes.' Ron dismisses him and turns to me. 'Almost too much for us to handle, but we're still handling it just fine.' I return his reassuring smile. There's a sour taste in my mouth. I need a mint.

'Now, I think you're ready for an outing,' Ron announces. 'Would you like to accompany Blaze and me to a donor's event? It's at one of our other UK bases of operations.'

I manage to stop my eyes lighting up. Access to another HPA base will give me a new opportunity to get lost around potentially useful offices.

'What will we be doing?' I channel some of my nervous energy into the question.

'Nothing scary,' Ron replies. 'You have my word.'

'OK.' I set my lips and try to make my nod look brave.

Ron smiles fondly at me. 'You really do remind me of Kate sometimes.'

*

No one responds to my text saying that I'll be home late. My phone is still clutched in my hand as the helicopter takes off, just in case Dad or Megan stop hating me long enough to check in.

'Have you been in a chopper before?' Blaze's voice comes through the headset above the whir of the blades. He's sitting next to me looking too handsome in a tailored black suit. The glasses are back too. I need him to only wear his hero outfit, I've got used to that. Every time he changes into something different, I notice another part of his body. This time it's his hands, with his graceful fingers and his knuckles still slightly bruised from his last battle, sitting clasped on his smart black trousers. 'Jenna?' He's looking at me.

'No. It's not my preferred way of flying.' I grin, and he grins back. I blink and look out at the rapidly disappearing ground.

I NEED TO STOP FLIRTING.

Why has my brain decided that *now* is the right time to find my flirting groove? Is it the handsome hero who I also happen to be spying on? Who I've sworn to not make a connection with? Flirting with Blaze is not part of the plan. I will not fall for this boy.

The sun hangs over the turquoise sea as the helicopter swings round to head towards the city. My heart beats a little faster as we fly over the forest and follow the Wild Road. I suppose it's safe to be this far above that dark, twisting road of death. Unless those pigeons with super-strength make a comeback. I smooth down my dress, a full-skirted, dark green choice from Mia, that we accessorised with extremely heavy, dangly earrings.

'They're not real diamonds,' Mia had said as I put them on. 'But they're still too expensive for you to take off and lose. And you're determined not to take that bracelet off? Fine. It doesn't go with the earrings, but fine. Show me your press smile.'

In what feels like no time at all, we're racing across the city, only slowing to circle the columns of the National Museum of Hero History.

'Your other base is at the museum?!' I twist in my seat to see the sweeping roof of the Great Court. Last time I was here, I fought with Blaze and was flung about like a rag doll by the Villains. Now I'm working with both of them.

'Most of our labs are here. New hero tech and the like.' Ron lifts a briefcase on to his lap as the helicopter starts its descent. 'I've always enjoyed the symmetry. Progress and history. Two sides of the same coin.'

The helicopter crunches down and Blaze is out and offering me his hand a moment later. It's too noisy to say thank you, but my fingers curl around his as I step down. My dress flaps wildly around my legs as Blaze leads me out from under the spinning blades.

The white outer wall of the museum towers above us and we follow Ron along a gravel path and down some steps to a small metal door.

'Have you got your key card, son?' Ron asks. 'Mine's at the bottom of my briefcase.'

Blaze pulls out a key card and presses it against the door's black security panel. The blinking lights turn from red to green and the door swings open with a beep. I'm ready for more endless grey corridors, but instead am greeted with plush red carpet and diamond-patterned wallpaper. The under-museum feels more like an old hotel than a military base.

'Downstairs is less fancy,' Blaze whispers.

Ron opens the first golden door that we come to and ushers us into a small room with a mirrored wall and a table with three chairs. 'Quick briefing, kids.'

I go straight to a chair and sit, ready to listen, but when I look up, Ron and Blaze are side by side in front of the mirror.

'What's the event?' I ask.

Ron artfully moves a strand of his grey hair to join the correct side of his parting. 'One moment, Miss Ray.' He turns to fix Blaze's hair too and Blaze bats him off in a gesture that makes my insides clench. I can't forget that Ron is more than just Blaze's boss. He's his family.

'It's fine,' Blaze says, before remembering himself. 'Sir.'

'I still think a quiff would go down well with the public.' Ron motions to the space where Blaze's quiff could one day be.

'Noooo …' Blaze blurs behind me. 'Back me up, Jenna. No one wants to see a hero with a quiff.'

'History proves you wrong, son.'

'Maybe you should just cut it all off?' I suggest sweetly, and they look at me, outraged.

'Right.' Ron runs his hand through his hair again, as if he's trying to reassure himself it's still there. 'This is an easy one. We need you to do the rounds at a reception ahead of a donor presentation. Don't worry, you don't need to come to the presentation itself.' He swings a chair round and straddles it.

'The HPA have power, Jenna, but these people have money – money that we could do a lot of good with.'

'I understand.' I'll smile at rich people until I'm able to slip away and have a look round.

'Good girl.' Ron is up again and motioning for us to follow him. 'You can come back to this room whilst the presentation is on. No need to be nervous. Blaze will show you the ropes.'

Several red-carpeted corridors and two plush sets of stairs later and we're approaching the sound of chatter and classical music. I've managed to keep my bearings, but we haven't passed anywhere that looks useful. Blaze mentioned a lower level – perhaps that's where I need to look? But first I need to smile and chat and be a charming Love Interest. My insides squeeze. I'll be OK this time. This won't be anything like the wedding.

My heartbeat is fine.

My breathing is OK.

I'm not going to have an attack.

'You'll smash this.' Blaze slips his arm through mine and lowers his voice. 'You don't need to worry, unless intensely boring events trigger you too?'

I chuckle and squeeze his arm. One day soon I'll stop letting him make me feel safe, but right now, I need him.

'Here we are.' Ron pushes open a golden door.

This space must normally be for conferences, but today the wide room is packed with milling people. A string quartet plays something slow and sophisticated on a small stage in front of floor-to-ceiling windows that look out over the dark Great Court. Waiters circulate with tiny versions of normal food on silver platters. The people drifting past in expensive suits and cocktail dresses don't give us more than a cursory glance.

Ron waves at someone and marches off, leaving us alone at the edge of this whirlpool of privilege.

'Welcome to the money, Jenna,' Blaze whispers in my ear. Our cheeks touch. I lurch upright.

Time moves slowly at a fancy reception, but Mia has drilled me on small talk, and I am able to hold my own.

'Where did you travel from tonight?'

'How was the weather there?'

'Yes, it is worrying that we haven't found the next Diviner, but the HPA won't rest until she's on the team.'

A parade of people from different countries, with different accents, but who are all from this strange, moneyed world, drift over, stay for a few minutes and leave with their very own 'I talked to Blaze and Jenna' story.

A man with a Russian accent and deep frown lines has just left when Blaze freezes next to me. 'Wait! Is that who I think it is?'

'Oooh! The waiter? Yes it is.' A tray with tiny quiches floats past and I nab one. 'Mmmm!' The quiche has sun-dried tomatoes in it. It is exactly the right mix of tangy and creamy. 'You should try these.' I nab another one before the tray is out of reach. No one is really interested in me and there's loads of food; this is the type of party I could get used to.

Blaze's cool fingers turn my face away from the quiches. 'Jenna, look.'

'No …' I mumble round a mouthful of quiche. Orangey tan,

bleached blond comb-over, but this time wearing a dark grey suit, Trevor Donaldson glares at us with a look of barely concealed fury on his face. 'What's his problem?'

'Haven't you been on social media?'

'No. Not since we met.' I nab a tiny portion of cheese and crackers. 'Why would you miniaturise cheese and crackers? They're already pretty small.'

'He's coming over!' Blaze grabs my hand as it reaches for another cracker. 'Come on!' He pulls me through the murmuring crowd towards the champagne fountain.

'What's going on?' I look back over my shoulder. Trevor Donaldson is weaving through the crowd after us.

'Remember that photo of us laughing at him?' Blaze beams at someone wearing a mayoral chain. 'Hi, yes, lovely to see you, this is Jenna, please excuse us.'

'Excuse us,' I repeat as Blaze drags me on.

'Well, that photo went viral and – Premier! Always a pleasure! I hope the landslide clean-up is going well. We're just looking for someone.' Blaze spins me past someone wearing a French flag pinned to their lapel. 'The photo went viral and he became a meme, and men like that don't like becoming memes.'

There's a crash behind us and I look back to see Trevor stepping past an apologising waiter and a fallen tray of champagne flutes.

'He called me out on social media and he was such a –' Blaze pauses to censor himself – 'knob at the wedding that I responded and it became a bit of a thing.'

I groan, imagining the hashtags that must have accompanied this.

#BlazeVsDonaldson

#DonaldsonBurned

#BlazingRow

'I don't know if he was passed over by the HPA in the States or what else is happening in his head, but he really wants to take me down. If he wasn't a billionaire, that would make him a villain! He just won't leave it. What was his last post? *Looking forward to seeing this flighty little hero in person again. Let's see who the real man is #ready #DonaldsonVsBlaze.*'

'Oh boy.' I glance into the adjoining presentation room, where a long table has a number of metallic blue boxes set neatly in front of each seat. We duck past the stage and, as if sensing our urgency, the quartet strike up a faster tune. 'What did Ron say?'

'He said, *"There's no such thing as bad publicity, son."* And then he ruffled my hair.' Blaze whips his head round. 'Wait, I can't see Donaldson.'

I spin round too. The string quartet are reaching a crescendo as the partygoers nibble canapés and chat, but there's no sign of Trevor.

Ron strides up to us and claps Blaze on the back. 'How is the small talk going?'

'Yes. Very good, thank you.' I grab a mini apple pie off a passing tray and pop it into my mouth, still scanning the area. This should probably be my last canapé; I'm feeling uncomfortably full.

'Jenna's nailing it.' Blaze is hovering.

'Righto.' Ron looks between us. 'What's going on here?'

Before either of us can answer, fingernails dig into my wrist and I'm yanked backwards. Pain shoots up my arm. I still have an apple pie in my mouth, so shouting isn't an option, but my body spent so long throwing punches this week, it does what feels natural. I pull my arm down, turn and punch Trevor Donaldson in the face.

CHAPTER 23

Trevor staggers back with a cry, releasing me. A couple of people pause, champagne en route to their lips, and turn gracefully away as if they've decided that a Love Interest punching a billionaire is too complicated to have noticed.

'Not again, eh, Trevor?' Ron steps smoothly in front of a furious-looking Blaze. 'These Love Interests. I'll be having some stern words with Miss Ray. Come on, I need your help in the other room.' He puts an arm around a spluttering Trevor and steers him away from us, turning to wink at me behind Trevor's back. For the first time ever, I enjoy one of King Ron's winks.

The apple pie is still on my tongue and my knuckles throb: did I do more damage to Trevor or my hand?

Blaze is next to me. 'Are you o—'

'Jenna Ray!'

I know that voice. I spin to find Sydney Jones with her

hands on her hips and a look of triumph on her face. The room suddenly seems too hot and too loud. Everything inside me clenches and I choke down the pie in my mouth.

'Finally.' She smiles. 'We can—'

The apple pie comes back up and I projectile vomit on to her spangly silver dress.

The string quartet finish with a flourish and a portly man, with his fingers hooked in the pockets of his waistcoat, steps in front of the stage. 'We'd like to invite you into the adjoining room for the presentation.'

My face burns as Sydney Jones looks down at the chewed-up pie on her dress.

'Ew!' she whispers at me, brushing it off. 'Ew! Ew! I know you're nervous, but my camera girl has already left. Mother Earth, is this carrot?'

'Sorry,' I mumble, trying to keep my mouth closed in case all the crackers and quiches are on their way back up too.

She looks up at me. 'Well, they said I had to leave when the presentation started. Why don't you walk me out? Give me a quote or two, you owe me that.'

'Here.' Blaze hands Sydney some napkins. 'I just need to borrow Jenna.' His hand is in mine again, pulling me away from her and through the crowd. The money drifts around us and towards the presentation room like a shoal of dark, glittering fish, and we're soon alone at the edge of the conference room.

He's not saying anything, and I can't bear to look at him. He's probably completely disgusted.

A toilet sign glitters ahead. I drop Blaze's hand to rush in to find an array of complimentary toiletries, including mouth-wash. By the time I rejoin him in the quiet corridor I'm feeling better, although my cheeks are still red. I thought him witnessing my panic attack was the most embarrassing thing that could happen between us.

'This way.' His voice sounds odd. He swipes us into a lift with his key card and I manage to get in without making eye contact.

The mirrored doors slide slowly closed to show him tilting his head my way. I sigh and finally look at him. He's crying. He's laughing silently, so hard that tears are rolling down his cheeks.

'Mother Earth!' he gasps. 'You just punched Trevor Donaldson and threw up on Sydney Jones.' He wipes his eyes. 'Those were the best thirty seconds of my life.'

I whack his arm, but I'm so relieved that I've not grossed him out that I laugh too. 'That was mortifying.'

He laughs harder. 'This is Sydney Jones, on the scene, BLEURGH!!!' Blaze recreates my projectile vomit and I lose it. 'Oh, hi, Trevor Donaldson, BLEURGH!!!'

'Stop it!' I haven't laughed this hard in a long time.

'Jenna, we've got the Queen of Sweden coming over, could you look after her? *Sure thing!* BLEURGH!!!'

The lift pings open and we stagger out on to a red-carpeted corridor, both in tears.

'Skies!' Blaze collapses on me and his tears roll down my shoulder. 'OK. OK, sorry, we've got maybe forty-five minutes, what shall we do?'

He lifts his head so his slightly damp face is next to mine.

'Um.' My heart is racing.

Mother Earth, I want to kiss him.

I want to brush that stray hair from his forehead and press my lips against his.

I want his arms around me.

And he's looking at me like that's what he wants too.

My hand trails up his shoulder to the base of his neck.

'Jenna,' he says quietly.

The lift pings closed behind us, making me jump. I step swiftly away from him. 'Yes. Forty-five minutes. How about a tour?' I smooth down my dress and try to ignore the sweet burn happening in my core.

'A tour.' Watching Blaze muster enthusiasm for this is almost funny. Did he really want to kiss me? 'A tour,' he repeats with more life in his voice. 'Sure thing. The museum? It'll be creepy …'

'How about the base?'

His face lights up. 'Yeah! We can go and see the gadgets!' He steps back into the lift. 'Don't tell Ron about this, OK?'

'Yes, sir.'

He hums happily as the lift takes us to the lower levels. He's not acting like a hero with something to hide. The more I get to know Blaze, the more certain I am that he doesn't know the HPA are holding innocent people against their will. And the more I want to pin him against the lift wall and kiss him until we're breathless.

We step out into a corridor identical to the brushed concrete of the HPA base.

'We don't need to go down there.' Blaze tilts his head to the left. 'All the good stuff is this way.'

I glance over my shoulder at the low glow emanating from that corridor and follow Blaze into a lab. Maybe my mum used to come here for work. There are several long white workstations covered in papers and coils of wire.

'This is where they make all the hero kit.' Blaze gestures to the lab, in full tour guide mode. 'I think they even upgraded Prince #2 to full android down here.'

'You've never fancied a robot sidekick?' I raise my eyebrows at him, and he rolls his eyes at me.

'Sidekicks are so retro and having a robot was Ron's thing. Plus, sidekicks are always younger than the hero; what am I going to do, recruit a twelve-year-old? That's not safe. Oh!' He bounces between the lab desks to pick up something that looks like an elephant ear. 'This is an ultrasonic radar that lets you see through steel. Oh! And this is their latest grappling hook. The engineers talked me through the equations they use for this. I can show you?'

I twist the bracelet round my wrist. Maybe it'll be able to access something down here. 'No thank you, but it's a very kind offer, you big nerd.' A flicker draws my eye to a booth in the corner of the room which glows like it contains several screens. I suck in a slow breath. I need to see what's in there.

'Yeah, I'm a nerd. Why wouldn't you be?' Blaze pushes up his glasses and leaps over to the next gadget. His enthusiasm is adorable. 'This is the Night Night button.' He points at something that looks like a library stamp. 'It shoots a little bolt of energy that knocks someone out for thirty seconds.'

My heart drops. 'Thirty seconds?'

'Yeah. Just push the button and you can get away. It's also great if you want someone uninjured to interrogate.'

Just like that I have a plan and I hate it.

I wander over to stand next to him. Too close to him. I can feel his heat. I push down all my conflicted emotions and move even closer, so we're touching. He goes rigid beside me.

'Maybe I should get one of these?' I reach round him and gently pick it up. 'I don't like the idea of hurting anyone.' I step away from him.

'No lasting damage. I can ask for you.' He bites his lip. 'You should probably put that down.'

'Oh, yes, sorry. Whoops!' I fumble and fire the Night Night button at my foot. My eyes squeeze shut. There's a thud and I open my eyes to see Blaze out cold on the floor. He intercepted the bolt, just like the dart at the supermarket. I knew that he'd try and protect me. Blaze doesn't make good split-second decisions when it comes to me.

The guilt is a vortex in my chest, but I ignore it and race over to the booth. A bank of CCTV camera feeds shine up at me. The first inhabited room has a man in a HPA tracksuit sitting on the floor. The label at the bottom of his shot reads:

CELL 540. Cpl Brown. Power: None.

Threat level: N/A disciplinary

The next has a man lying on a bed staring, unblinking at the ceiling.

CELL 543. Miguel Rodriguez. Power: (EX) Strength (unregistered)

Threat level: Nil

The only other inhabited cell has a woman pacing between her bed and toilet. A Black woman with her natural curly hair cut short and her arms swinging like she wants to break through a wall. A woman I'd know anywhere.

'Mum,' I mutter.

There was a part of me that didn't believe the HPA had her. That didn't believe I would ever find her. I drink in her every movement. She's so small that the details of her face are blurred pixels, but she doesn't look hurt. I could stare at her tiny face forever, but my thirty seconds must almost be up. I lean in closer to read the minute label at the bottom of her screen.

CELL 546. Anonymous VILLAIN. Power: Unknown (unregistered)

Threat level: High

I freeze.

Mum wasn't just helping the Villains. She *was* a Villain.

What is it we've been taught? *The Villains are men with unregistered, dangerous powers who will do anything and go through anyone, to hurt the HPA.*

Guess the news was only half right about that. I choke back a hysterical giggle. Megan will be over the moon that women are represented in the Villains.

No.

Wait.

When I came round from that flashbang at BLAZECON, there was a Villain crouched next to me, reaching out for me.

It couldn't have been Mum.

It feels like the grey floor is disappearing from under my feet.

It can't be my fault she got caught.

But that happened right before the Villains approached me to help them. Mum. She'd been right next to me and I'd had no idea. A Villain was dragged away by the HPA and all of two days later the Villains tell me that the HPA are holding my mum. How had I not put two and two together?

Blaze groans and I walk swiftly back to his side.

'Blaze! I'm so sorry! You should have just let it hit me.' I help a shaky Blaze to his feet, still apologising, and he waves it off.

'I'm fine. It's good to know what the weapons I use do, I guess.'

My stomach lurches.

The screen had said power unknown.

Power unknown.

My mum has a power.

All the Villains have unregistered powers.

I've never felt like I am falling whilst standing still before. It's like I am falling through a dark chasm that leads to the ocean bed. The pressure on me is unbearable.

Mum is a Villain. Mum has powers. Mum is here.

Blaze touches my face gently. 'You've gone pale. Honestly, I'm OK.' He wraps his arms around me. 'Don't be too hard on yourself, we've all done things we regret.'

It feels like my body could give up and melt in his arms, but I can't let it.

Mum is a Villain. Mum has powers. Mum is here.

We walk back to the mirrored room in silence. He must think that I'm beating myself up about accidentally shooting him, but that thought has barely registered in the grey water churn that is my mind.

'I'm feeling a little dizzy.' It's the truth. My head is spinning as I slide into one of the chairs.

Mum is a Villain. Mum has powers. Mum is here.

'Hold tight.' I barely register Blaze's face next to mine. 'I'll get you something sweet.'

There's a gust of wind and I'm alone, looking at my distraught face in the wide mirrored wall. Why didn't the Villains tell me that Mum was one of them, that she had powers? The other woman, Pari, must have been a Villain too. Emily said they emptied her out. What does that mean?

A cool dread settles in my stomach as the pieces fall into place. Down here there is a man who looks like a zombie, with a note saying (EX) Strength on his camera feed. Upstairs, billionaire Trevor Donaldson is strutting around with his brand-new power of super-strength. They emptied that prisoner of his unregistered powers and poured it into Trevor. Just like Pari; she was a Villain and must have had a power too. She was emptied out and left for the Villains to find.

The HPA is stealing people's powers and leaving them broken.

I suck in a shuddering breath.

I won't let them do that to my mum.

I'm going to get her out of here.

CHAPTER 24

The HPA have my mum.

Lying in bed, replaying her tiny form pacing around that cell like I've got my own private CCTV feed, is going to drive me mad. I can't talk to Blaze about this for obvious reasons. I can't talk to Dad or Megan, who are still avoiding me. Most frustratingly, I can't get hold of the Villains because of the completely one-sided relationship we've got. I flick the bracelet; it hasn't buzzed or flown off or done anything except hang off my wrist looking pretty.

There's only one person I can talk to, and it happens to be her birthday. There's no HPA training on a Sunday, so I pull on jeans and a hoody and sneak out of the house.

May in Nine Trees would seem like an OK time to plan an outdoor event, but Joy's annual birthday beach bonfire is cursed. Not that that's ever stopped Joy. When the weather rolls in and causes ships to anchor and every sane person to take cover, Joy's birthday beach bonfire still goes ahead in the Town Beach sand dunes. On her thirteenth birthday there was a torrential downpour, and our shaky gazebo dumped a small lake on us. When Joy turned fifteen there were such strong winds that our pile of bags caught fire. Last year, Megan insisted I take burn-heal cream and an emergency whistle. Joy's birthday beach bonfire is as certain, and as volatile, as the sea.

The sun is shining and Nine Trees's high street is bustling as I swerve between shoppers and tourists. A group of kids shout as I pass and my grip tightens on my freshly bought potato salad, but they're not shouting at a Love Interest. They're shouting at a seagull that's just made off with one of their chips.

No one notices me. Everyone is focused on the ice-cream van or the busker with dark hair and a voice like the swell of the ocean.

He's singing about lips,

hands

legs

everything tangling.

The worry dims for a moment as I relive having Blaze's arms around me and his lips a breath away from mine. I speed up, going red. What is wrong with me? How can I be thinking about him when Mum is in trouble?

'Jenna!' Joy rushes over as I make my way to the top of the designated dune. 'I missed you! You look great! Are those new shoes?'

All other thoughts are obliterated by the relief of seeing my best friend. 'Happy birthday!' I pick her up and spin her around.

'Do you have security now?' she asks as I put her down.

'No.' I follow her gaze down the empty sandbank behind me. 'Why?'

'Nothing. I thought I saw … It doesn't matter. More importantly, how are you?' She whacks me on the arm.

'Well—' I hesitate. I was desperate to talk to Joy, to share my problem, but what will that achieve other than ruining her birthday?

'Jenna?' Joy is watching me.

'Ready for a birthday bonfire!' I slap a big smile on my face.

'You've got the day off?'

I nod. 'Has Mr George replaced me at the shop yet?'

She shakes her head. 'I think he's hoping you'll come back and he'll have an actual tourist attraction serving customers at the till.'

'Right.' I shudder. I can't think of anything worse than being trapped behind a till as tourist after tourist comes up and asks, 'Are you Jenna Ray?' I hold my leg up so Joy can get a closer look at my new cherry-red boots. 'And yes, they are new shoes. Mia isn't so bad once you get to know them.'

Joy beams at my shoes and then at me. 'Happy to hear that. Come on then. Let's leave the heroes at the top of the dune. Today your job is to have fun! Let me know if anyone is weird and we'll chuck them in the sea.' A sweep of her arm takes in our stretch of beach, from the fine dry sand of our slope to the wet golden ridges that line the way to the water.

'Sure thing, boss.' Even though the tide is out, and the distant waves are peaking foamy white, my hands tingle. I don't have anyone I can talk to, but a swim might help.

Joy skids down the dune to the pile of driftwood and broken crates that's being assembled. Sand trickles into my boots as I follow, managing to stay upright as the sand gently gives way beneath me.

'Jenna!' Our friends, classmates, Nick and some other people from the year above all fall silent and look over. Even though I've spent almost every day with these people for over a decade, my heart still skips a beat.

'What did I say?!' Joy yells. 'Don't be weird!'

'Sorry,' people mumble, and return to their conversations.

'Thank you.' I pop my bag down in the pile. 'Am I on picnic logistics?'

'No, you just have fun.' Joy is already storming off on another mission. 'Nick! Did you get the speaker working?!'

'Cool.' I swing my arms and look around for a group to join. Everyone is adding to the bonfire, fussing over the food, or laughing about something, probably from school. I've never felt out of place in this group of people before. Coming was a bad idea; maybe I can sneak away?

'Hi, Jenna.' Okorie strolls over. 'We've missed you at swimming.'

'Yeah.' My cheeks are heating. The last time I saw Okorie we almost kissed, but now all I feel when I look at him is guilt. He's everything I should want: kind, safe, swimming obsessed. I should want to kiss him, not Blaze.

He digs his trainer into the sand. 'You're really with him then, aren't you?'

No, I want to say. *He's part of an organisation that are*

*holding my mum captive. But it's more confusing than that
because you're perfect for me and I've sworn not to feel anything for Blaze, but seeing you is making me realise how much
I like him.*

I poke the toe of my boot into the sand too, but it doesn't
help. 'It's not really like that.'

'It's OK. I had years to ask you out, I guess I missed my
chance.' Okorie's lips quirk. 'It was magic though, that morning.
It was living.'

'It was.' It was living. Poetic Okorie has summed up my
choice in three words. He is normal, safe, happy, life. Blaze, the
mission to find my mum, the HPA, they're the opposite, but
there's no way back to Okorie now. 'It was magic. Can we still
be friends?'

'You got it.'

My mouth is open to ask how he is, but Okorie wanders off.
I guess that's fair. He helped me and I rejected him. He came
over to be kind, but I can't expect him to stay. I drop into the
sand and sit on the edge of all the fun. Why did I come here?
Did I really need to top my guilt up? Grains of sand prick under
my nails as I push my hands into the dune. Being on the
outskirts of my old life isn't helping my spiralling mind. No one
else comes over. I guess they're all afraid of being weird.

Sand rolls past as someone skids down the dune behind me.

'Wotcha.' Emily slides down to sit next to me. She looks
bizarre on a beach in her black oversized raincoat. 'Once again,
you're welcome for me interrupting that kiss.'

My jaw clenches as I bite back an insult. 'I need to talk to you, to them.' I try to keep my voice down. 'I didn't know how to contact you.'

'OK, calm down, Love Interest.'

'Don't tell me to calm down.' The relief and frustration of seeing her has brought tears to my eyes. I rub them away with the back of my hand.

She pushes a finger into the top of her boot. 'Urgh. I've got sand in my boots. Why would anyone choose to hang out here?'

'I've found my mum.'

'Good.' Emily's voice is infuriatingly calm.

'She's underneath the National Museum of Hero History.'

'Right, great.' Emily falls silent and looks back up the dune. What has distracted her? Apparently, she hates nature, so it's probably not the tiny birds pecking at the pink flowers that dot the dune, or the cries of the seagulls passing over us.

'Emily,' I say urgently. 'She's in cell 546. You need a key card to get in.'

'M'kay, cool, lovely, the Villains have issues with carded doors, can't go into it now, so they'll need you to steal a key card, then they can get your mum out.' She's still not looking at me. She stands slowly. 'Great job and all that.'

'I'm not finished.' I stand with her and lower my voice. 'The Villains didn't tell me everything. They didn't tell me that Mum is one of them, that she was captured at BLAZECON, that she has powers.'

'But now you know so, congratulations.' Emily waggles her fingers. How can she be so unbearable when she's not even giving our conversation her full attention? 'Well, feck.' She flips her wide hood up. 'You are being watched.'

'What? Oh.' The Secret Ninja stands at the top of the dune, silhouetted against a bright blue sky. 'Maybe he doesn't know who you are?'

'Protect your cover,' Emily hisses, grabbing my arm.

'Protect my friends,' I hiss back.

'Fine. Move!' She shoves me and we skirt the edge of the party towards a stretch of long, flat beach. 'Keep moving.' She pushes me again and I stagger, almost tripping over a rock.

'Ow!'

'You don't know me, Love Interest,' she replies. 'Act scared.'

The Secret Ninja keeps pace with us, walking along the top of the dune. I don't need to act scared. A member of the HPA has seen me talking to a Villain.

'Jenna? Are you all right?' Joy calls from the bonfire.

'All good,' I lie.

'Jenna? What's going on?' Okorie shouts.

'I'll be back in a minute,' I yell.

'Jenna? Is that the Secret Ninja?' someone else cries.

I'm not going to answer that. I don't want to look over and see the whole party watching open-mouthed as I'm held between a person in black and the Secret Ninja. Emily stops when we're a good distance away.

'I don't want any trouble.' She steps away from me.

Slowly, the Secret Ninja puts out his hands and shrugs.

The assembled watchers gasp as he launches himself at Emily, speeding towards her in a flying kick. She dodges and he rolls to land ready for his next attack. I should help. Maybe I can stop this hero attacking a girl who's been talked into being a go-between for the Villains. Although she's holding her own. Did the Villains teach her how to fight?

'Honestly. Could we—' Emily leaps over the Ninja's sweeping kick. 'Just—' She staggers back to avoid an uppercut. 'Not?' He lands a kick in her stomach that sends her crashing into the sand next to me.

She lies there motionless. I should help her – that would blow my cover, but she's a helpless girl who has just been kicked across a beach by a hero.

Emily shifts in the sand. 'Guess now is a good time for you to see that women are much more powerful than they want us to think we are,' she says quietly. 'Sorry about BLAZECON.' Emily rises slowly to her feet and brushes the sand off her black coat. She cricks her neck before fixing her gaze on the Ninja. 'Remember when I asked nicely?'

The Ninja rolls up his sleeves and runs at her. I want to tell her to move, dodge, run, but she stands there, waiting until he's centimetres away. Then she raises a hand.

The Secret Ninja freezes mid-stride, a look of fury in his cold grey eyes.

'No.' I shake my head.

This doesn't make sense.

No.

This makes perfect sense.

Emily is telekinetic.

Emily is *the* telekinetic.

279

She's a Villain.

She has powers.

She's a woman and she might have some of the strongest powers I've ever seen.

After all the talk of dangerous men, are any of the Villains actually male?

Heat rushes to my cheeks and my fear is drowned by red-hot fury.

It was Emily who froze me on the beach and left me at the mercy of the EV pigeons.

Emily dumped me in the harbour.

Emily flung me across the museum!

'No!' I swallow back all the names I want to call this lying snake and remember what she said about protecting my cover. 'Let him go!' I cry, but what I really mean is, *You're a liar!*

The Ninja twitches. He must be using all his strength to try and break free, but Emily is holding him without breaking a sweat. She lifts her hand and the Secret Ninja rises.

'Stop!' I yell.

She flicks her spare hand at me. I'm buffeted backwards and I skid to a painful stop. Same side or not, I want to get up and fling myself at her, but I'm frozen in the sand.

'Bye bye, baby.' Emily flicks her fingers and the Secret Ninja shoots away across the sea.

'You'll kill him!' I know the HPA are evil, but the Villains will be no better than them if they become murderers. The Secret Ninja is little more than a speck when Emily relents, and I see him drop into the waves.

The pressure on me disappears and I leap up. 'What did you do?!' I pull off my boots, ready to run in and save him. Emily puts a hand on my shoulder.

'Relax, hero.' She points up as a helicopter races over our heads in the direction of the Secret Ninja. 'They're not going to let him drown. He'll be fine. Wet, but fine.'

'You—' I start with a snarl, but she gives me a little smile.

'Cover, Love Interest,' she says quietly, before raising her voice for the benefit of my friends. 'I'd better go before your boyfriend arrives. You're a fool if you think you can trust them. A fool.'

She flicks her fingers and I fall back, landing hard on my bum.

'Why?!' I yell at her, but she launches herself into the air and away.

'Jenna!' Joy reaches me first. 'Are you OK?'

'That guy was telekinetic!' Okorie arrives next and helps me to my feet. 'Is it the same one from the museum?'

'Yes.' My teeth are gritted.

Emily has been playing me for a fool.

She's a Villain.

She has unregistered powers, just like Mum.

'Come and sit down.' Joy takes my hand. 'Have some cake.'

I hesitate. I don't know if I can have cake at a time like this.

'Can you fix it now?' Okorie asks.

'What?' I turn to him.

He tilts his head at me. 'This life and death problem taking over your mind. Is there anything you can do about it right now?'

I blink. To save my mum, I need to steal a key card, but I can't do that until I'm back on the HPA base tomorrow.

'No.' I sigh. I'll never stop being surprised at how insightful Okorie is.

'Then cake,' he says.

'Cake!' Joy repeats, and leaps off to cut it.

'Cake,' I murmur. 'Okorie, I really am sorry about everything.'

'Me too, but I don't need to be another thing for you to worry about, Jenna. This just wasn't our time.' He gives me a sweet smile and wanders back to his friends.

'Jenna.' Nick sidles up to me, shocking me out of my melancholy. 'You've been up close to the Ninja a couple of times. Come on, tell me, he's definitely a robot, right? Maybe you can help me get some proof—'

'Nick!' Joy loops her arms around her boyfriend's waist. 'Stop with your crazy theories. Jenna needs some sugar.'

Now that everyone has seen how crap being a Love Interest is first-hand, they're no longer weird. I am checked over, brought cake and juice, and even told some funny stories from school.

There's a smile on my face as the bonfire is lit and everyone sings a massively out-of-tune version of 'Happy Birthday', but my mind is going at a thousand miles an hour.

Tomorrow, I will risk everything to steal a key card from the HPA, but for now, there's cake.

CHAPTER 25

'Oof!' My brain is focused on the various places the HPA could have key cards, rather than the route between my bedroom and the bathroom, and I run straight into Megan in the corridor. 'Sorry.'

She staggers back, not looking at me, and reaches for her door.

'Megan, wait.'

Her face is pale and drenched with sweat. 'This isn't a good time.'

'Are you sick?' I reach for her, and she jerks back. 'Can I get you anything? Soup? Do you need soup?'

'I don't need soup,' she says, almost to herself. 'I don't need soup. I just need sleep. Real sleep.'

I shake my head. 'You look awful. I'll get Dad.' His door is open, he must already be at work, but I can call him.

'Don't,' she snaps. 'Don't do anything. That's what I need. I need you not to do anything.'

'Maybe we should go to the hospital?'

'No, no, no hospital. I've got water. I've got painkillers. It's a fever and the lighthouse. Always the fecking lighthouse. If I don't feel better later, we can tell Dad then, OK?' Her smile is slightly frantic as she backs into her room. 'There's a storm coming tomorrow. Don't get caught out in it. I don't need soup. Don't worry, Jen-bear.' She slams the door in my face.

That's the first time I've spoken to my sister in days, and she looks like she's dying. I want to barge in and look after her, but she doesn't want me to. After what I said to her, I'm not sure I even have the right to.

I throw on my HPA training tracksuit and a moment later I'm back outside Megan's door, tugging my sleeve over Mum's bracelet.

I'm going in.

I don't care what she says, I'm going to take her to the doctor's.

'Megan?' The door creaks quietly as I swing it open and peer in.

Megan is out cold, lying with one arm dangling off the edge of the bed. She said she needed sleep, and she does already look a little bit better. I back out of her room and gently close her door. I'll check on her again later.

A familiar rush of heat, followed immediately by guilt, flows through me when I see Blaze waiting for me at Security. He's also wearing a grey tracksuit and looks beautiful, even though he's frowning.

'Good morning.' I step into the security booth and lift my

arms to be scanned. It's a good thing this machine doesn't report back on emotions like a lie detector. My heart is already racing. I'd probably set off every alarm in the building.

'Jenna.' He nods at me formally. 'I'll walk with you to media training.'

I smile at the duty soldier as I pick up my guest pass. Why is Blaze being weird? He can't know that I intentionally shot him with the Night Night button at the museum, can he? Did he find out about Okorie? No, Okorie is just my friend, that's clear from last night, and I'm allowed to talk to other boys, aren't I?

'How lovely.' I put on a posh voice. I sound like Joy when she mucks about with accents. 'What's up?' I ask, managing to sound more like myself as we set off on the long walk to wardrobe.

'What happened yesterday?'

Feck. Of course he'd have found out about the bonfire kerfuffle. 'Oh! There was a thing with the Villains, but the Secret Ninja was there.'

'Why didn't you call me?' His voice is so much cooler than I'm used to. 'It's Rule Number One for Love Interests. It's the only rule you have.'

'But it was all sorted. I didn't think I should disturb—'

He swings round in front of me and stops. 'I can't protect you if you don't call me for help.'

Something about his serious brown eyes and soft golden skin sets off my internal spiral again.

A rush of heat.

A rush of guilt.

I want to kiss him, and I hate myself for it.

'It was OK though,' I manage. 'And it was your day off, so I just thought—'

'I'm a hero, Jenna, I don't get days off!' He breathes out and lowers his voice. 'Ron thinks they're trying to turn you.'

My heart stops. 'What?'

'What did the Villains want?'

'To tell me that the HPA are evil and so are you.' I watch for his reaction, but he gives nothing away. The stone-faced boy from BLAZECON is back.

'Did you believe them?'

Blood roars in my ears, but somehow, I hold his gaze. 'What possible reason would I have to believe them?' A tiny bit of Blaze's usual light creeps back into his eyes as I continue. 'They threw me across the museum.' My scowl comes naturally. 'They shot a drugged dart at me. I don't think you're evil, Blaze, but I know that they are.'

His shoulders sag and he almost looks like he's going to cry.

'Sorry.' I reach out for his arm. 'Sorry I didn't call you.'

He lets me touch him, but his face freezes over again. 'Ron will want to talk to you when he's back tomorrow.'

'OK—'

'I don't understand you, Jenna. I can't pre-empt anything with you. You rush into danger like …' He trails off, his brown eyes still piercing me.

'Like a what?'

'Like an idiot. You say you want to be safe, but that's not how you act. How am I supposed to protect you if you won't let me? How am I supposed to trust you if you break the most basic rule?'

286

My mouth drops open. I can't find a reply. In the eyes of the HPA so far I've got lost looking for the canteen, accidentally knocked out Blaze and failed to call in a Villain attack. These are not the actions of a Love Interest on the top of her game, but hearing Blaze call me an idiot is still like a punch to the gut.

'Just go to media. I'll see you later.' Blaze turns on his heel and walks away.

What the feck?!

Is he upset because I didn't call him crying when some super-powered people had a fight near me? It's not like it's the first time that's happened. This isn't fair, but calling Blaze back to argue with him would definitely be mission drift. I'm now on borrowed time with the HPA. Technically it's fine, they haven't caught me yet. My mum's life hangs in the balance, the boy I like calling me a name isn't the headline here.

'Trouble in paradise?' Mia calls as I storm into the training area.

'No,' I snap.

'Well, regardless, I've got just the thing to cheer you up.' Mia drags over a second potted plant and goes back for a third. 'Press conferences!'

The only key card in wardrobe was on Mia's lanyard around their neck. The canteen also doesn't happen to have spare cards lying around. I relive my every moment at the HPA as I eat a plate of chips and beans. Security is always manned. Taking anything from King Ron's office is like begging to get caught … A chip falls off my fork on its way to my mouth.

The training studio.

What feels like years ago, I went into the messy cupboard in the corner of the studio and found Blaze a tampon for his bleeding nose. There was a key card in there. I rise as casually as I can and deposit my half-eaten meal on the side. I have fifteen minutes until training with Blaze; perhaps it's still there. Perhaps I'll be able to get the card I need to rescue Mum right now.

I power walk along the corridor and down the stairs, trying not to look suspicious. Why does everything in this stupid base have to be so far away? I push through the swinging training-room doors with ten minutes to go until our session. Blaze is already there, sitting cross-legged in the middle of the room. His eyes are closed. I glance over at the cupboard.

'Hi, Jenna.' Blaze is looking at me.

'Hi. Still upset with me?'

He gets up. 'Let's just run your drills and then you can go.'

That's a yes, then, on him being upset. How much worse will this be if he finds out that the Villains have already turned me? That I am a spy and he should have never trusted me?

His voice is flat as we run through my punching and kicking drills and he calls it a day after half an hour. Being around Blaze without his passion is confusing. I can't get out of the training studio fast enough.

My meander towards security slows to a snail's pace as I pass along the windowed corridor that looks down on the training studio. I watch for Blaze to leave out of the corner of my eye, hoping he doesn't decide to stay and train. Luckily, he throws the pads into a basket in the corner and storms out before I run out of window.

This is my chance. I make a show of patting my pockets and add an exasperated sigh, for any CCTV cameras, before turning to jog back down to the studio. The doors swing open to reveal the wide, empty space. There's no one around and no approaching footsteps; the only sound is the gentle hum of the air conditioning. Terrified that the card will be gone, or there will be a sign that just says THIS WAS A TRAP, I go straight to the cupboard and wrench it open. Tucked in a corner, under a new layer of creased paper, is the key card.

My fingers curl around it and I shove it into my pocket. I turn, expecting to see King Ron with his arms crossed or a squad of soldiers rushing in, but the studio is still empty. I've done it. I walk quickly towards the door. I got the key card and I'm going to get away with it.

'Jenna?' Blaze pushes through the doors and I freeze. 'What are you doing back here?'

Emily's words come back to me. *The best lies contain grains of truth* … There's only one truth that can save me.

'I was upset about before and I wanted to talk to you. I wanted to apologise.' I close the distance between us. 'But more than that, I wanted to kiss you. Would that be OK with you?'

Blaze blinks. 'I—'

We lock eyes and the same intense heat that I felt in the museum, at the HPA donor event, washes over me.

'You really want to kiss me?' His fingers come to rest gently on my cheek and I am burning. Every inch of me is desperate to hold him.

'Yes.' My voice sounds like it's coming from a long way away.

The most brilliant smile spreads across Blaze's face and he tilts his head towards mine.

Our lips meet.

His lips are soft for someone so strong.

I thought the yearning inside me would calm when my body got what it wanted, but instead the heat is growing and tearing through me like a rip tide. His hands drift down to rest on my waist, but mine need to explore. My fingers move up his arms and I enjoy the swell of his muscles as he pulls me closer.

Touching him is perfect.

I could kiss Blaze forever.

His wrist piece beeps.

We ignore it.

The tips of my fingers trace a line over his tense shoulders and up his neck before losing themselves in the soft strands of his hair. Blaze groans and holds me tighter, somehow finding his way under my jumper without letting me go. His palms touch the skin of my lower back and the gentle pressure of his fingers sends sparks racing through me. My insides are molten. I didn't know that desire could burn.

His wrist piece beeps again.

We've surrendered to our bodies, but mine is still making demands: discover him, pull him closer, tangle into him. I don't know how long I wanted this, and I wasn't sure he wanted this at all, but any uncertainty is gone. Kissing him, falling deeper into him, is as natural as air. Gripping him feels like floating, even though I'm tethered to him. This feels so right, I could kiss him forever.

'Blaze! Sorry, Blaze, sir!' The voice comes from below us.

I draw my head back from Blaze's just in time for it to bump off something. 'Ow!'

'Crap!' Blaze hugs me closer as we realise that we've floated off the ground, right up to the ceiling.

'Sir, there's an ongoing earthquake in Japan. Magnitude eight,' a soldier calls from below us. 'The Japanese HPA have requested all available heroes.'

'Right, yes, sorry, yes. Thank you, I'm on it.' Blaze lands us, but the ground feels more like water under my feet.

'Go.' I'm still flushed and desperate to have his arms around me again, but I'm not going to stop him saving lives.

'Right, yes. Tomorrow?' His passion is back, lighting him up from the inside.

'Tomorrow.'

He gives me a peck on the lips and blurs away.

A rush of heat.

A rush of guilt.

A rush of sadness that I shouldn't feel.

Tomorrow.

Tomorrow my mum will be free and my reason for staying close to Blaze will be gone.

Tomorrow everything is going to change.

CHAPTER 26

It's raining as I walk up the steps from HPA Security. The fat drops sink through my jumper and on to my skin, making me tingle. Or perhaps that's the memory of the kiss. I give myself a shake to try and dislodge the feel of his arms around me.

I've kissed people before, but it didn't feel like that. I didn't understand Blaze's passion until now.

Hot.

Strong.

Tender.

I could have kissed Blaze forever.

It will never happen again, but I don't have time to get upset. And why would I get upset about not being able to kiss some boy again? It's not important. I touch my lips; I can still feel him there. It's not important.

As I climb up the steps to the harbour bridge, a figure in an oversized black raincoat blocks my way.

'Did you get it?' Emily asks.

'Yes.'

'Good. Hand it over.'

My fingers curl around the card in my pocket. 'No.'

'What do you mean "no"? Give me the card so I can get out of this horrendous rain.'

'I don't need to give it to you. I'm coming with you.'

I can't see Emily's face under her hood, but I don't need to.

'Feck!' she splutters.

For once I'm exasperating her as much as she exasperates me.

'No,' she says.

'Good luck getting in without it,' I reply.

'I can take it off you.'

She's probably the most powerful person I know, but I manage to keep my voice cool. 'I'll make a fuss, and I happen to be a Love Interest, near a HPA base.'

'Jenna, be reasonable.'

'I am.' I tighten my grip on the card. 'My mum's life is on the line, and I don't trust you or any of the other Villains. I'm coming with you.'

It's odd not being able to see the expression on her shadowed face as she looks down at me.

'Feck,' she finally says. 'Just come on then.'

I follow her up the stairs.

'Wait.' She slides behind me. 'If anyone asks, I've got a weapon pointed at you. See that silver van? Go to the back and get in.'

My hand almost slips off the slick handle, but I get the van

293

open and clamber in. The inside is a weird mix of shabby and techy. Underneath the silver benches that run up either side of the van are metal drawers with key-coded locks, and four hoverboards are strapped to the walls. There's also a couple of worn red blankets bundled in the corner.

A Black man with mini dreadlocks and large thick-rimmed glasses, turns in the driver's seat to look at me. 'Well, feck.'

'Just drive, Femi.' Emily climbs in and slams the door behind her.

'You were in the picture with my mum.' I wobble up the van as Femi indicates and pulls out.

'Why is she here, Emily?' Femi calls back.

'She's holding the key card hostage, Femi.' Emily imitates his voice.

'Didn't you threaten her, *Emily*?'

'It didn't work, *Femi*.'

Turns out the terrifying Villains squabble like children.

'Mother Earth. Pass me your phone, Love Interest.' Femi holds out his hand and I pass him my mobile. He holds it for a second and then chucks it back to me.

'There. Now your phone thinks you're at home.'

I turn my phone over in my hands. 'But you didn't do anything.'

'If you say so.' Femi indicates again and the van swings on to the Safe Road to the city. 'We were just going to nip in and get Sima. Now I have to tell my secret to some lovestruck teen.'

Sima. These Villains say my mum's name the same way I say Joy's. They're more than teammates, they're friends.

'You don't have to tell me anything,' I say. A technopath has a terrible time as a hero and disappears. Flash forward a couple of decades and there's an anti-HPA organisation with amazing tech and an intensely grumpy leader who can trick my phone with a touch. 'You're the Controller.'

Femi lets out an exasperated sigh.

Emily gets up to join us at the front. 'Yes, he was the Controller, until a combination of the media and the HPA drove him to madness.'

'I'm not mad!'

'Then tell it yourself!'

'It's not OK to call me mad!'

'Stop!' I hold up my hands. 'How am I the most mature person here?'

Femi kisses his teeth. 'This is why we need your mum. She's the nice one.'

Silence falls and I sit down on a bench with my back against the vibrating edge of the van. What am I doing? I could give these two powered people the key card, go home and wait for them to tell me that Mum is safe. She's their friend, they're not going to do anything to mess up her rescue.

Instead, I hold the key to her release. Me, Jenna *I got myself trapped in a burning building and flung across a museum and chased by EV pigeons'* Ray. If I'm caught now, that's it. No more school, no more breakfasts with Dad and Megan, no more Blaze, no reunion with Mum. I could wreck this for everyone, especially Mum. I was a terrible Love Interest and a worse spy. Why do I think I'll make a good Villain?

I should tell them to stop, hand over the key card and walk home.

So why won't I?

Because I need to make sure that Mum is safe and that's all there is to it.

'Can't you do this without a key card?' The thought is out of my mouth before it's properly formed in my head.

Emily sighs. 'You'd think so, but the HPA aren't completely incompetent. They know the Controller is involved with the Villains. Their doors are Femi-proof.'

'So far,' Femi adds from the driver's seat and flicks on the radio.

The reporters on the radio burble about the storm that will hit Nine Trees tomorrow and my eyes drift to the opposite wall. I hadn't noticed them at first, but the dull light inside the van is just enough to see a series of scrawls covering the walls that look like equations.

> Ceiling en
> Flash-bomb — blue + red orbs + purple — other H
> * B confes *
> S/F=point. E=backup
> Tech — 2 x HB — 10 blue — 10 red — 10 purple
> Check netting

'Look familiar?'

I roll my head to look at Emily. She's trying to shake some life back into her damp blonde hood-hair.

296

'We do our thinking in this van. That was your mum's. If I could go back in time I'd add "brackets, distracting daughter" to that one.'

I snort. 'It's hardly my fault that she got caught.'

'And yet, here you are.'

My eyes flick back to * β confes *.

'Why did you attack BLAZECON?' I ask.

Emily leans forward to look at Femi, but he stays resolutely focused on the road. She sighs and looks back at me. 'How much do you like Blaze?'

My heart thuds uncomfortably. 'He's fine.'

'Because you must have heard the HPA weren't all kittens and sunbeams, and then you found out that they were stealing powers.'

We bump over a crack in the road.

'What's your point?'

'The HPA track down powered people; apart from inadvertently making the EV worse, it's what they do. But we didn't know that the non-hero powered population were in trouble until Blaze.' I scrunch my eyes up, confused, so Emily continues. 'Pari, our friend, was captured. We searched for her for months, but by the time we found her, she was sleeping under a bridge in the city. She was empty; unable to communicate, unable to focus, and her powers were gone. Less than a year later, Blaze appeared on the scene.'

The chill starts where my shoulders touch the metal of the van, and sweeps through me. 'Emily, what were Pari's powers?'

'She had super-speed and she could fly.'

I close my eyes.

I can still feel his lips on mine.

His arms holding me as we floated up towards the ceiling.

I can still hear his laugh as he pretended to throw up in that lift.

All this time I'd hung on to the hope that Blaze was one of the good guys. Blaze told me that Ron took him from his family before he developed powers because he was a sure thing. He wasn't. He never got powers of his own, so he stole someone else's and left her broken and wandering the streets.

There's pain like a shard of ice being knocked through my chest. I think my heart might be breaking.

'Are you crying?' Emily whispers next to me. 'Femi! She's crying! What do I do?'

'I don't know,' Femi calls from the front. 'Pat her arm or something.'

A tentative hand is laid on my upper arm. 'There, there,' Emily coos, like I'm a baby.

I shrug her off and wipe my eyes. The ice is still there, but there's something stronger growing in my chest. Something I haven't felt since BLAZECON. My sadness, guilt and fear have been shunted away. My rage is back. I'm not going to cry for Blaze. I'm going to stop the HPA before they can hurt someone else the way they hurt Pari. I'm going to save my mum.

I turn back to Emily. 'What's the plan?'

The Villains' getaway van parks in an alley round the back of the museum. When it's finally late enough for us to implement the plan, I chuck my phone into one of their drawers and hop out of the van. The Villains have opted for midnight-blue boiler suits tonight. Mia would find some way to make these pop, maybe they'd add silver piping. I guess after tonight I'll never need to see Mia again. The thought is surprisingly upsetting. I stretch my cramped muscles and adjust the boiler suit so it sits properly over my hips.

Femi comes round with the helmet that every Villain wears when they're on a mission and places it over my head. I expect everything to go dark, but instead the mirrored sheen seems to make things clearer. Emily had said it was safe to whisper with these on. 'Thank you,' I say.

Femi pulls his own on. 'Fits?' His voice comes through my earpiece.

I give him a thumbs up and Femi turns his attention to the belt of orbs around his waist. The little purple light flashing on one of them takes me straight back to BLAZECON. Femi adds the red flashing dart orbs and blue flashing net orbs to his collection. I'm glad I'm on his side, this time.

My new Villain boots are tight over the bridges of my feet, so I duck down to adjust the laces. These boots have *SIMA* written on the tongue. Turns out, I am the same size as Mum.

'Key card?' Emily whispers.

I nod, the plastic card hot against my hand in my glove. I'm not showing it to them until the last possible moment. There's still a chance Emily will take it off me and leave me locked in the van.

'Let's do this,' Emily says.

My body fizzes with adrenalin as we pick our way through an alley crowded with industrial bins and creep into the shadows at the back of the museum. The helmet is uncomfortable, it's squished my hair and is digging into my shoulders, but this isn't the time to complain.

'Up and over, on to the helipad, like we talked about.' Emily lifts her arms and Femi floats up and out of sight. My feet leave the ground shortly after and she floats up with me. I catch a glimpse of the flickering lights of the city and then we're over the wall. My feet crunch down on to the gravel path.

The helipad, where Blaze helped me down from the helicopter, is in front of us and beyond the side of the museum looms, huge and white. The glass roof of the Great Court is also just visible, swooping up beyond the wall.

'Motion detectors.' Emily nods up at the blinking squares spaced out around the helipad's courtyard.

'I'll scatter our signals.' Femi types something into his wrist console.

The Villains both look at me. I panic for a split second before I remember the plan. I'm the one who's been here before. I need to show them down to the lab.

'This way,' I say confidently.

The crunch of our feet on the gravel path is intensely loud, but neither Villain seems worried. We skirt the helipad, staying in the shadows as much as possible, and I find my way back to the door that Ron had led us to.

It is the moment of truth for the key card. A cascade of doubts tumble through my mind as I pull my glove off. What

300

if it's out of date, or deactivated, or I accidentally picked up someone's library card? I'm glad the Villains can't see my face as I hold the card up to the door's black scanner. The flashing red lights turn green, and the door opens with a beep. I let out a breath I hadn't realised I was holding.

An uneventful trip in the lift brings us to the lab and cell level. A distant alarm wails as we rush towards the lab.

'Do they know we're here?' I gasp.

'I reckon so.' Femi stops by a wall panel covered in blinking lights and laughs. My mouth falls open. This is the first time he's sounded happy. 'Finally. I needed a challenge.' He cracks his knuckles.

'See if you can stop them without disabling all the lights this time.' Emily's voice is light too. I'm about to dissolve into a nervous puddle and these two are bantering like friends at a beach party.

'I thought HPA tech was Femi-proof?' I say.

'Not when I'm on the inside.' Femi lifts his hand to the panel. 'Let's send our image via every camera, eh? Very good and I think some malfunctioning motion detectors will keep the guards busy for a bit. Let's make them think we've arrived with an army.' Femi's second hand comes to rest on the panel. 'You don't recognise the guards any more, love. Any time you see them, kick up a fuss, eh?' More alarms join the wail outside. The whole museum must be going off. 'Good girl.'

'You're so creepy when you talk to machines.' Emily taps a pile of metallic-blue boxes on the lab's table on her way past. 'They've got a few of these, haven't they?'

'I've got the schematics.' Femi falls in behind me as we head down the corridor.

'Was Jenna right about the cells being down here?' Emily asks.

'Yup. The floor plans indicate the cells are straight ahead.'

A tiny bubble of pride grows in my chest. I got the key card. I bought the Villains to the right place. We're going to rescue Mum and I helped make it happen. The pride drains away as we approach the dim lights at the end of the corridor and my heart thumps even harder. The tightness in my chest isn't because we're raiding a HPA base, but because I'm about to see my mum for the first time in ten years. What will she look like? What will I say? Should I hug her?

We turn a corner to find a series of dimly lit cells with glass doors. The first is filled with those metallic-blue boxes and after that we pass empty cell after empty cell. The soldier on a disciplinary must be back on duty because cell 540 is vacant, and even cell 543 where Miguel Rodriguez, the lifeless man whose power was stolen for Trevor Donaldson, is uninhabited now. Nerves spark through me, will Mum still be here? It's only been two days since I saw her on the monitor in cell 546, but was I too slow?

Cell 545 is empty.

Cell 546 …

Standing, with her hands on her hips and her shoes on, is my mum.

She grins at the Villains. 'It took you long enough.'

CHAPTER 27

I want to hug her. I want to scream at her. There are tears running down my face.

'Who's the new recruit?' Mum nods at me and grabs a grey jumper. The HPA even dress their prisoners in grey.

She doesn't recognise me. Of course she doesn't recognise me. I'm dressed like a Villain. I can't get my hands under the helmet to wipe my face. The tears are pooling under my chin. When she was tiny and pixellated on the screen, I knew exactly who she was, but in the flesh I barely recognise her. There are lines around her eyes. Her hair used to be longer and curly, now it's grey and clipped with an undercut shaved in.

'Later, yeah?' Femi finds the control panel. 'Let's get you out first.'

The cell door swings open, Mum steps out and I manage not to gasp. I'm taller than her.

A light flashes on the control panel by the door.

'Uh-oh.' As Femi rushes over to it, an alarm screeches through the building. 'We've got company.'

My heart stops. This was fine when it was a covert rescue, but it's turning into a fight. How am I supposed to take on armed guards? My breath fogs up my helmet. What am I supposed to do?

Mum turns to me. 'What are your powers?'

'No powers.' Femi pushes past us. 'Just stay back, OK, new girl?'

'I'll look after her,' Mum says.

The irony is almost too much to take.

'Don't talk much, do you?' Mum is still staring at me.

I shake my head.

'Do I know you?' she asks.

I don't answer and follow Femi back along the corridor, past the cells.

'Wait!' Mum runs into the cell that's being used as storage for the metallic-blue boxes and grabs one. 'OK.'

Using the schematics on his wrist console, Femi leads us up a set of stairs and back to the red carpets and diamond-patterned walls of the upper level. The metal door we came through glints ahead, lit by a red flashing light.

'Guards outside?' Emily puffs as she sprints towards it.

'Yup,' Femi replies.

Mum grabs me to slow me down as, without stopping, Emily holds out her hand. The steel hinges of the door shudder and fall silently on to the carpet.

'Let's go!' Emily cries as the steel door floats up, turns on to its edge and shoots out into the night.

From the courtyard beyond, there are screams and thuds, but no gunfire, and by the time we reach the helipad the remaining guards are scrambling to their feet.

Femi is too fast for them; with two taps of his wrist console, he sends his orbs up and each remaining guard goes down with a dart in their neck.

'Come on, HPA!' Emily yells. 'Is that all you've got?!'

Next to me, Mum sighs.

'Let's get moving.' Femi sprints across the helipad and we race after him.

As we reach the high outer wall, the moon appears from behind a cloud and bathes our breathless party in silver. Emily turns to us. She's a black shadow against the shining wall as she raises her arms to float us up and over. 'Now—'

Emily vanishes.

I blink, trying to process what I just saw. She was there, there was a blur, and she was gone.

Oh no.

Blaze appears on the top of the wall. He's got Emily; her arms are twisted behind her. 'Lay down your weapons. I'm not going to ask again.' There's a blur and Emily is face down in front of us with her hands cuffed behind her back.

'I don't think so.' Femi sends his orbs after Blaze, but Blaze is already gone. He dodges a flurry of darts and cuffs Mum too. With Emily out of the game we've already lost. He's too fast. We'll never get past him.

There's only one thing that will distract him.

'Blaze!' I yell.

He freezes, halfway through restraining Femi, and whips round to look for me. 'Jenna?'

A dart hits him in the chest, then another. He wobbles, still looking for me. 'Jenna?' For someone so fast, he falls so slowly. He sways, his legs buckle, and he falls to his knees. 'Where are you?' he slurs before slipping gently on to his side.

I rush over to him. 'Blaze!' His eyes are still partially open. He lifts his hand and places it on my shoulder. His touch still tingles, even through a Villain's boiler suit. Blaze's eyes close and his arm falls back by his side. He looks so pale in the moonlight. Femi kneels beside us.

'Is he dead?' I ask, dreading the answer.

'No, just knocked out.'

I shouldn't feel almost faint with relief to hear that he will be OK.

Femi places a hand on Blaze's suit and there are some soft clicks behind us.

'That little feck.' Emily joins us, rubbing her wrists. 'We should just kill him.'

'No!' The word is out of my mouth before I can control myself.

'No,' Mum echoes quietly. 'We don't kill people, Emily. You know that.' She's staring at me. She heard my voice. She heard Blaze say my name. She knows who I am. 'We need to move.'

It's strangely peaceful in the seconds it takes for Emily to float me over the wall. This must be what an out-of-body experience feels like. You drift above all your problems. Mum knows who I am. Blaze knows who I am. Everything I dreaded has happened. What else is left for me to fear?

As I land between the industrial bins, the sound of shouting back in the courtyard and arguing in front of me switch back on. The alarm from the museum and sirens from everywhere else are bouncing off the thin alley and for a moment my brain can't figure out what happens next.

'Come on.' Mum grabs my arm and drags me along with the other Villains until I shake her off.

'I don't need your help,' I snap.

Femi and Emily reach the van first and jump into the front, so me and Mum hurl ourselves into the back. Their helmets are passed back and I expect Femi to speed away from the scene, but instead he backs out of the alley slowly and sets off at a steady pace towards the Safe Road.

Mum sits across from me. She opens and closes her mouth a couple of times and then holds up a finger.

'My youngest daughter is sitting across from me, isn't she?'

None of us answer her.

'OK then.' Her voice is terrifyingly calm. 'I've got something to do now, quickly, because I think I'm about to have a meltdown. This is a battery.' She holds up the metallic-blue box. 'It can store a person's power.'

'What?!' Emily twists to look.

'These things have a story so strong I could almost hear it from my cell.' Mum's eyes are closed. 'Tell me your story, little battery.' Her fingertips shimmer where they touch the battery. This is it. This is her power. Does she listen to objects? 'It was

307

created with hundreds of others and handled by people with ambition. They're connected somehow. They'll focus the pull and then be filled, soon. All of them. All at once.'

'The HPA have a way to steal people's powers,' Emily says. 'That's what happened to Pari.'

'It's for a person.' Mum's voice sounds like it's getting further away. 'Someone who moves power from one place to another.'

'Ron,' I say. 'That's what he does. That's all he does. He's a conduit.'

'Sima, come back,' Emily calls from the front.

'It's like a web. All connected.' Mum's words are even fainter. 'Made by the EV. Protected by the EV. The power understands. All of them will contain the EV. All of them will be filled at once.'

'Sima!' Emily shouts.

'What's happening?' I scramble over to Mum.

'Wake her up. Now.' For the first time, Emily sounds terrified. 'It's her power; she can read the history of an object, and of the objects that make up that object. If she uses her power for too long her mind can get stuck in all the stories that the thing contains.'

I grab the battery, but Mum is holding it fast. 'Wake up!' Her face stays peacefully blank. 'Come on!' Did I come all this way to lose my mum to a battery? 'Mum!' I yell.

Her eyes snap open and she drops the battery like it's burning her.

'Mum, are you all right?' I reach up to take my helmet off.

'Wait,' she says urgently. 'Wait. I can't see you yet. We need to figure this out before I can get emotional. OK.' She rubs her fingers. 'OK. We think Ron is going to use these batteries to steal powers?'

'They must help him target powers and then, of course, they'll help him store them.' Femi is surprisingly excited for someone suggesting something so terrible. A battery that seeks out and stores people's powers. The thought makes my stomach churn.

'But he doesn't have anyone else to drain,' Emily says. 'Sima was the only prisoner and she's legged it.'

'It doesn't matter.' Mum glances at the battery. 'He doesn't need to know who the powered person is, he could just go to a crowded place. What's the percentage of powered people now?'

'0.001 per cent of the population.' Femi clicks on the indicator. 'It was always that, although it could be more now. Everything else influenced by the EV has increased.'

'One in a thousand?' I ask.

'One in a hundred thousand people, or more.' Mum is still not looking at me. The reason Mum left is playing out before my eyes. She put her work with the Villains above her family. 'Ron could go to a big football match and find at least one of us. After they took me at BLAZECON, he came to see me in the cells. That man sensed I had a power immediately. Didn't remember me from six years of work in his organisation, but knew I had a power. I hadn't realised how lucky I was that he never bothered to acknowledge the female engineers.'

There was cell after cell full of these blue boxes. 'It would take him years to fill all those batteries,' I say. 'Did you say they would all get filled at once?'

'Jenna is right.' Femi slows the van to a crawl and I pop my head up to see we're in a dark car park. 'He's the only conduit and there's a limit on what one person can do.'

'Unless he has access to more energy,' Mum adds.

'You think Ron has found a way to supercharge his conduit power?' Femi backs into a space and kills the engine. 'If he's powerful enough, he won't need to know where people like us are – he can just stand in a room and pull, and their powers will come to him.'

'Like a psychotic hoover.' Emily leans over the headrest. 'How could he amplify himself?'

'I've heard of people using residual EV energy to boost their powers,' Mum says.

Femi twists to face us. 'The EV gave us powers, so energy left over from an EV event can boost them.'

I look between them and my stomach twists again. My mum, Emily and the Controller, bouncing ideas off each other whilst I sit here in my helmet. My jealousy feels like it could take over and shut off my ability to think, so I try to shake it off. Right now, I need to be more like Mum. There's something big and bad coming, and the Villains are trying to stop it.

'This power grab would take an intense amount of concentrated energy,' Femi murmurs.

The burned Culture Complex, covered in signs, flashes through my mind.

'Would an EV lightning bolt leave residual energy?' I am ignored.

'Even energy from the EV might not be enough. Do we have time to do the maths?' Mum looks between them. 'We don't have time to do the maths. But Ron can pull energy from anywhere, so if there was a peak in natural energy, he could use that too. Let's do the maths.' Mum grabs a marker and scrawls on the dim wall of the van.

Residual EV energy + Natural energy = X (available energy)
X = Battery operation + Ron's potential reach

Femi slams his hand off the steering wheel. 'I've told him so many times that the EV cannot be abused. His whole approach is wrong. It has its own defence system. It *is* its own defence system. People with powers, we're all linked to the EV, an attack on them will have consequences. If he manages this, the EV response at the scene could be catastrophic, the place he operates from could be completely destroyed.'

Mum rubs out an old plan to write:

X = Power of EV response?

She pauses, her marker still on the side of the van. 'Femi, do you think this could be what the Nine Trees prophecy was referring to? The Sharp Blue Heat of Truth. Could the Diviner be telling us it's finally our chance to expose Ron?'

Femi is almost vibrating in the front seat. 'You're right, this could be it. The EV has given us a warning through the Diviner; we can stop this!'

'So that's an A for enthusiasm.' Emily places her hand on Femi's arm. 'What's the next step?'

'Maths.' Mum circles Ron's Potential Reach. 'These batteries won't take a huge amount of energy to operate, and we already know that Ron can move power from place to place using his own energy, which is—'

'Humans produce around a hundred watts,' Femi supplies.

'So, we need to get an idea of X.' Mum draws a neat square around X. 'We need to know how much energy Ron has to draw on, so we know how far he'll be able to draw powers from, and what the force of the EV reaction could be.'

'How much energy could be left by a bolt of EV lightning?' I try again.

'A typical bolt could be over a gigawatt, that's a billion watts.' Femi answers without hesitating. How many numbers does he have in his head? 'So, an EV bolt will be, ah, much more. The amount of energy left behind would be enormous.'

'And a storm could be another energy source?' I bite my lip, dreading the answer. This is all leading to Nine Trees being in mortal peril, again.

'Oh yes, definitely, most storms have a massive amount of electrical potential, and then there's the kinetic energy of the wind ...' Femi trails off and all three Villains turn to stare at me.

'Why did you ask that?' Mum's voice is careful.

Physics was never my strong point and Mum's maths is making my head hurt, but even I understand the more energy Ron has access to, the more dangerous his conduit power and those batteries will be. 'The HPA have cordoned off the Culture Complex, where the EV lightning bolt struck, because of residual energy, and there's a storm forecast to hit Nine Trees tomorrow.'

There's silence as they digest my words, then Emily tuts loudly, 'Guess we don't need a calculation to know that Nine Trees is screwed.'

'He could drain every powered person in the country, us included,' Femi says.

I barely hear them. Mum has made her way back to me and is kneeling next to me. 'Take it off.'

I want to refuse, but this moment is inevitable. I pull the helmet off and shake my Afro free. Now I understand why Mum needed me to keep the helmet on. Removing the barrier and seeing her older, heart-achingly familiar face reignites all my emotions. Before I can decide whether I'm going to scream at her or burst into tears, her arms are around me.

'Brilliant.' Her voice shudders. She's crying and holding me tight. I can't stop myself, I hold her back. 'My brilliant daughter.'

There's love in my chest. Love and rage and sadness. 'I don't forgive you for leaving us,' I say into her shoulder. The tears are rolling down my face now too.

'I wouldn't expect you to,' she replies, holding me like she used to all those years ago. I could stay in her arms forever, but too soon she draws back. 'OK, now how do we deal with Ron?'

We jump apart as a loudspeaker squeals, **'THIS IS THE HPA. YOU ARE SURROUNDED. EXIT YOUR VEHICLE WITH YOUR HANDS UP.'**

CHAPTER 28

'**N**ope!' Femi yells, and the engine is back on an instant later.

'**WE REPEAT**,' the loudspeaker booms, '**YOU ARE SURROUNDED.**'

'Pass us those helmets, will you? And stick yours back on.' Emily is incredibly calm – no, not just calm, she's smiling. What's the name for someone who enjoys being in mortal peril?

We sling them their helmets and Mum picks up mine. She blinks rapidly as she holds it and then sticks it on to my head.

'Got anything for this, F?' Mum yanks another helmet out of a drawer and pulls it on. It looks odd above her grey HPA tracksuit.

'I might,' Femi responds cheekily. He presses a button on his console and, a moment later, screams and explosions echo from around the van. 'Let's go then.'

He puts his foot down and we hurtle past men leaping out

of a burning HPA jeep and screech out of the car park. Me and Mum hang on to the headrests of the front seats, watching as Femi swerves down an empty residential road.

'Anyone on our tail?' Emily asks.

'No,' Femi says. 'How did they find us?'

'We need to check for trackers.' Mum digs into another drawer and pulls out a scanner.

'Check the Love Interest,' Emily calls back.

'Me?' I stay as still as I can as Mum runs the scanner over me.

'We need to talk about this whole Love Interest thing too,' she says.

The brakes squeal and we stagger against the side of the van as Femi hurtles round a corner and on to a road lined with warehouses.

'Yes, now seems like the perfect time for that conversation,' I say.

The scanner beeps as Mum holds it up to my shoulder, to the spot where Blaze touched me when he was lying on the ground outside the museum. 'Found it.'

It turns out Blaze is just as deceitful as I am.

'Feck,' I mutter.

'FECK!' Femi cries.

The Secret Ninja is in the middle of the road in front of us.

'FECK!' Emily screams.

We hit him.

We hit the Secret Ninja and I can almost feel the front of the van crunching. Femi is still swearing, but he doesn't stop the van.

'Did you kill him?' I lean into the front.

'No!' Mum yells.

The sound of tearing metal fills the air and the Secret Ninja's hand appears through the van's floor. It grabs Mum's ankle.

'Oh!' Her eyes immediately close and the skin on her ankle shimmers. Have her powers activated?

'Emily!' I yell.

'Off you go!' Emily reaches out and each of the Ninja's fingers bend back.

As soon as she's released, Mum's eyes snap open and she kicks the Ninja's hand back through the hole in the van's floor. There's a thud from below. I wobble over to Mum and look down. There's no sign of the Ninja. He can't possibly have survived that fall after being hit by a speeding van. Relief surges through me, followed closely by horror. A man just died.

Mum grabs me to steady me as we race round another corner. 'That was a thing.' She's having trouble getting her words out. 'That wasn't a person. I helped make it, but after that ... Betrayed ... Re ... Re ... Re ... Smoothed over.'

'We've got a problem!' Femi yells. 'I think the Ninja cut the brake line.'

'Can't you fix it?' Emily shouts.

'And he's done something to the steering! Hold on!' Femi cries.

Mum grabs my hands and moves them so we're both clutching the straps holding the hoverboards. Emily looks back at us. She raises her hands and holds one towards us and one out the window. 'Feck!' she yells as the van hurtles off the road and flies into a wall.

Metal and brick smash together, filling the air with sound and—

Everything stops.

Mum gasps next to me. 'Are you OK?'

Am I OK? It felt like I should have been flung across the van, but I stayed exactly where I was.

'I'm OK,' Femi calls from the front.

'I'm OK,' I mumble. 'Emily?'

It was Emily. She saved me and Mum. She's still in the front. Her head is down on the dashboard.

'Emily!' Mum cries.

I follow as she leaps out of the back doors and runs across the concrete to Emily's door. The front of the van must have already been damaged by the Ninja, but now it looks like a crumpled crisp packet.

We wrench Emily's door open.

A thin line of red runs down past her closed eyes. My heart twists. Emily is too powerful and too annoying to die.

'She's alive,' Femi calls across. 'Knocked out. She tried to absorb the impact and—' Femi gasps. 'Also, I'm trapped, and my ribs … I … I'm not going anywhere fast. First thing to do is kill Jenna's tracker.'

I step back – it's too late. The HPA will already be on their way here. Emily is out, Femi is trapped, Mum's power is reading objects, which is awesome, but not hugely helpful in a fight. They're sitting ducks.

I take another step away from the crash, away from Mum.

'Go round to Femi, we need to get your tracker disabled,' she says.

The van crashed in an industrial area – no one will have seen us and it doesn't sound like any alarms have been triggered. If I give Mum, Femi and Emily some time, they'll be able to escape. I take another step away.

'Jenna!' Mum yells at me like I'm seven years old again. 'Get here, now!'

'I'll distract them. I'm good at that.' I shrug at her. 'Maybe that's my power.'

Adrenalin courses through me as I leap back into the van and grab a hoverboard.

'Jenna!' Mum's scream bounces off the warehouses as I sprint away.

My helmet joggles on my hair, but I don't have time to stop and take it off. From above I must look ridiculous; a girl in a wobbly helmet struggling to carry a hoverboard that she has no idea how to use. Megan was right; I shouldn't make the plans.

'How do you work?' The board is smooth, with no helpful on switch.

'Activate hoverboard?' a small voice says in my ear.

'What? I mean yes! Yes! Activate hoverboard.'

'Activating.'

The board vibrates and I skid to a halt as it flies from my hands to in front of my feet. I step gingerly on to it. What am I doing? I can't even surf. My Villain boots make several clicking sounds and connect to the board, holding me securely in place.

I allow myself a small smile. My mum makes pretty incredible tech.

'*Set a course?*' the voice asks as my board rises off the ground.

'Er, yeah?'

A map appears on the visor in front of me. I'm still close to the museum. Femi must have circled back after we left the car park. The Safe Road is off to the left or, almost directly in front of me, is the Wild Road.

'*HPA vehicles incoming.*'

I try to spin and look and almost fall over. There's no sign of cars yet, but I can't stay here much longer. 'Set course for Nine Trees,' I say hurriedly.

'*Route A?*' A yellow dotted line appears on the map, showing me the way home along the Safe Road. '*Or Route B?*' The line shifts to head on to the Wild Road, the last place I want to be.

There's a screech of wheels in the distance. The longer I can stay out of sight, the longer the HPA are going to think I'm in a van full of Villains. The Wild Road is the closest, darkest option. 'Route B!' I yell.

The board shoots up and into the air and I crouch to keep my balance, even though I don't think the boots will let me fall off. I zip through the deserted city streets, past the orange street lamps and above seagulls fighting over rubbish, and I figure out how my board works.

'Left is left.' I lean left and shoot round a corner. 'Right is right.' I straighten up. Lifting the top of my front foot takes me higher. Pressing down, lower. 'Nailed it,' I mutter, and settle into my route down the middle of the empty road. The broken white line zips under my board like I'm on a track.

I'm not going to think about what will happen when I get caught. This was the right thing to do. If I give them a chance, the Villains can stop Ron. They can save all those people. My life is over, but maybe my life has been over since the moment I ran back into the fire. I lean into the corner and enjoy the rush of skimming over someone's expensive-looking car. If this is my last night of freedom, I might as well enjoy the ride.

This thing is fast, but the first glimmer of headlights appears behind me as I shoot past the illuminated signs of the Wild Road:

EV THREAT LEVEL: SEVERE

HPA WARNING: DANGER OF DEATH ON THE WILD ROAD

And

CAUTION: UNEVEN SURFACES

The enormous black trees of the Wild Road loom ahead, looking even more terrifying in the dark night. I breathe out, *two, three, four,* and crouch a little lower. Flying on to the Wild Road on a hoverboard is not something I ever felt I needed to do.

'Let's go,' I whisper, trying to channel my inner Emily.

As I race under the twisting branches, the inside of my helmet fills with the mangled scents of old puddles and rotting leaves. There are no lines to follow on the Wild Road, just a black river of broken tarmac. Something rustles in a branch above me and I dip my weight to fly as close to the ruptured road as I dare.

The vehicle behind me is closer now, and its bright headlamps flash off the dark trunks in front of me. I breathe out, *two, three, four.* The longer I lead them along here, the more time Mum and the others will have to escape.

The blast of a horn from directly behind me almost makes my heart stop. The sound ricochets off the trees and a flock of birds takes flight above us. I swing to the left and a jeep roars past and swerves in front of me. The glare of its headlamps is immediately replaced by another behind me. I am sandwiched between two HPA vehicles.

A flash of light from in front of me makes me swing to the left instinctively and something zips past my helmet.

'Incoming projectiles,' the voice in my ear mentions.

'Thanks,' I mutter.

There's another flash from in front and something thuds into my board.

'Incominggggg ...' The display in my helmet flickers and dies.

I push down on the board, trying to send it lower, but my foot slips. Mother Earth, the boots are no longer connected. I fall to my knees, managing to stay on the board as it loses altitude. There's a screech of brakes ahead. The jeep in front has stopped, directly in my path.

'Skies!' I fling myself off sideways and roll to a stop as my board crashes into their bumper and snaps cleanly in half.

'How do you like our targeted EMP, eh? Electromagnetic pulse trumps technopath!' A ring of black boots surrounds me. I sit shakily up in the pink pool of light created by the mix of headlamps and rear lights. I don't think I'm injured, thanks to the sturdy boiler suit and helmet, but there's nowhere left to run.

'Hands in the air, Controller,' a soldier snaps, swinging his gun up to point at me.

I put my hands up. They think that I'm Femi.

'You're going to tell us where the rest of your little gang are.'

Boots scuff off the dark road and I blink the pink light out of my eyes as someone lifts my helmet off. This is bad. I am well and truly caught, but the sharp intake of breath from the soldiers is strangely satisfying.

'But that's Jenna Ray,' one of them says.

'Argh!' The scream comes from behind me.

'Stay where you are!' the soldier with the gun snaps as I twist to look.

'Skies!'

'Private! What's happening? Report!'

'It's the squirrels, sir! Argh!'

More shrill screams of pain fill the air and, a second later, the branches that surround us are filled with small, blinking pairs of electric-blue eyes.

CHAPTER 29

'Ev creatures! Fire at will!'

The soldiers fire wildly up into the trees. The blue-eyed squirrels have scattered across the dark branches. Their grey bodies scamper from tree to tree almost too fast to track. There's another scream of pain from behind me and I whip round to see a soldier trying desperately to keep a squirrel off his face. It slashes towards him with claws that glow pink in the jeeps' lights. Another soldier knocks it off and it scurries back up a tree.

The blood is roaring in my ears. I'm sitting at the centre of this storm of bullets and squirrels. I need to move before I get hit.

'You're not going anywhere, Love Interest.' The soldier pointing his gun at me shifts his weight. I see the squirrel before he does. It hangs off the branch directly above him and for a moment I almost stay quiet and let it get him.

'Look out!' I point up as the squirrel drops. My guard manages to roll out of the way, but he doesn't get a chance to call for help. The squirrel has apparently decided to target him and it launches itself at the soldier as he gets to his feet.

A gun rattles and shots fly over my head. I flatten myself. Feck.

Feck! Feck! Feck!

It's chaos, but no one fires a gun or aims their claws in my direction. The soldiers and the squirrels are targeting each other. I'm not stupid enough to think that I'm being saved, but maybe I've got a chance to save myself. The front jeep is a few steps up the road with its doors open. I crawl towards it through the mayhem.

A soldier screams as a squirrel drops on him and, as the others rush to help, I duck behind the driver's door. I can't drive, but this seems like an excellent time to try. 'Feck.' There's no key in the ignition.

'Come on.' My breath catches as I slide my hands round the seats and open the glovebox. There's no key, but there is a phone. My phone is still in a metal drawer in the Villains' van, so I grab the HPA one and slip it into a pocket.

'Retreat!' The shout cuts through the strangled screams and bursts of gunfire.

I throw myself out of the jeep and half run, half crawl behind it. The soldiers are still fighting off the squirrels and struggling to lift their injured colleagues.

'Get to the jeeps!'

Maybe I should give myself up and let them take me back to the base. That might be better than taking my chances on the Wild Road.

'Jenna Ray!' A soldier points his gun at me. My heart stops.

324

He could fire now and tell them I was caught in the crossfire. Love Interest problem solved. A squirrel drops on the gun and scrambles up the barrel towards his face. 'Argh!'

I don't wait to see what my furry little saviour will do next. I leap off the road and slip through the enormous, tangled roots into a gap under a tree. The road isn't visible from here, but it doesn't matter where I hide if I still have a tracker on me. My fingers grope desperately at my shoulder until they close around a small metal disc. 'Feck,' I breathe, and there's a rip as I yank the tracker off my boiler suit. Feeling like I'm moving in slow motion, I peek back into the pink-lit chaos and toss the tracker into the mix.

Retreating into the earthy darkness, I try and calm my breathing. If the soldiers didn't see me jump in here, and if I don't alert them to my presence with my deafening heartbeat, perhaps I can hide until they've gone, or the squirrels have murdered them all. If I stay quiet, maybe I'll be safe.

A squirrel's upside-down head appears in front of my face and I clench my lips shut to stop myself from screaming. Its head tilts and it blinks its luminous eyes.

'I come in peace,' I whisper. 'Don't kill me.'

Another scream, followed by gunfire, comes from the road above. The squirrel whips its head round and launches itself back into the battle. I slide further under the roots and cover my head.

'Retreat!'

'Where did the Love Interest go?'

'Grab the sergeant.'

'Squirrel five o'clock!'

'Get the motor running!'

'Squirrel nine o'clock!'

'Should we find Jenna Ray?'

'No! The squirrels have her now!'

'SQUIRREL TWELVE O'CLOCK!'

'Get in the vehicle! Go! Go! Go!'

The screech of wheels disappears down the road, leaving nothing but the rustle of leaves. Have all the soldiers gone? The squirrels probably didn't give them the chance to set a trap. My fingers curl around a knobbly root and I shuffle up to peer out. There's nothing but the dust settling from the tyres and the last of the squirrels disappearing into the distance.

After all the screams, gunfire and chaos, it is now uncomfortably quiet. I climb out on to the black tarmac and freeze as something hoots above me. A huge moth with electric-blue markings drifts past and I jam my hand in my mouth to stop myself from squeaking. When I was pumped full of adrenalin and leading the HPA on a wild goose chase to save the Villains, I could deal with this. But now I am alone. On the Wild Road. In the dark. With a broken hoverboard and no plan.

I breathe out, *two, three, four*, and my hand closes around the phone in my pocket.

'Please don't be locked.' I turn on the screen. 'Ha!' The branches creak above me and I almost drop the phone, but there's nothing up there. 'I'm just going to be really, really quiet from now on,' I whisper, and sit on the edge of the road to see what the phone can do.

There's no access to maps.

There's no internet.

The battery has eight per cent charge.

There are a couple of saved numbers that I could call with my one bar of signal. One is BASE and the other is COUNCIL.

Who can I call for help? What phone numbers do I know?

Calling 778 and saying 'Jenna for Blaze …' is probably a bad idea, but there's another number that I know. 455398 on the only network that works in Nine Trees … She's not going to answer a call from an unknown number at 5 a.m., but she might see a text.

It's Jenna, can you call me?

The phone vibrates almost immediately. 'You're lucky I've got a tiny bladder.'

'Joy,' I whisper.

'Ray.' She yawns. 'Is this the only time you have for talking to your best friend now? Do I need to schedule in daily, predawn calls with you? Your line is terrible.'

'Joy—' The phone's battery is already down to six per cent.

'So what's been happening?' The sheets rustle like she's stretching. 'Everyone was asking about you after that whole bonfire thing. Nick is planning a storm party later. He said he wanted to celebrate failing A-level maths. You know his house has a great view of the sea? We're going to watch the lightning.'

She pauses for breath.

'I'm in trouble,' I blurt out.

'What?'

'I rescued my mum and there was a chase and a crash and squirrels. So many squirrels.' I manage to keep my voice quiet. 'They're gone, but I'm still out here. I'm on the Wild Road, Joy!'

327

The line goes silent for a long moment.

'They found out you were helping the Villains?' she finally asks.

'This phone has four per cent battery left.'

'Feck!' Joy lowers her voice. 'Feck. You're on your own?'

'Yes.'

'On the Wild Road?'

'Yes.'

Joy sucks in a breath. 'On your own?'

'Three per cent!'

'I'm sorry, it's just, feck. You can't call Blaze, I guess, or the Villains?'

'No.' My chuckle is humourless. 'You're my one call. It was sort of a reflex, but I don't even know what you can do. Maybe you can go to the police? Tell them that Ron is planning something bad, at the Culture Complex when the storm hits.'

'The storm that is forecast for midday?'

'That one. We've got just over seven hours until Ron tries something that could destroy Nine Trees.'

She goes silent again, but there's rustling in the background. Like she's putting her shoes on.

'What are you doing?' I ask.

'I'm coming to get you.'

'No!' I whisper. 'You can't drive on to the Wild Road. I won't let you. I'll find my way back and if I don't, tell Dad and Megan—'

'That I left my best friend to die on the Wild Road. Got it,' Joy cuts in.

'*Joy, are you OK?*' Joy's mum is just audible above the rustle of Joy's coat.

'Yes, Mum, I'm borrowing the car.'

'You can't drive!' I raise my voice as high as I dare.

'*Joy! You can't drive!*' Joy's mum yells in the background.

A door slams. 'I've had lessons. Just stay put.'

The phone dies.

'No, no, no.' I shake it, trying to magically recharge it. I need to call her back and tell her that driving out here is suicide, but it won't switch on. 'Feck.' I leap up and jog towards Nine Trees. The further I can get, the less time Joy will have to spend on this road.

The first hints of grey dawn light seep through the dark leaves, but it somehow makes the Wild Road even more terrifying. It lights up the bulbous, blue-veined roots that split the surface of the road and throws even more shadows into the undergrowth. I run down the middle of the road, trying to keep a steady pace, and there are flashes of blue from either side.

'Just keep running,' I huff. Nothing seems interested in a running girl, but who knows how long that will last?

I run along the Wild Road.

Past a patch of electric-blue flowers and through their thick scent of cinnamon.

Past flickers of tiny blue wings heading to a hive that buzzes louder than a lawn mower.

Past something rustling. Something big. I slow down and try to pinpoint the sound. There's an animal out there, maybe the size of a dog, and it's getting closer.

Beep!

329

The Jusics' tiny red car tears towards me. Its pale headlamps make it look as scared as I feel. I step out of the way as Joy brakes and then stalls. Watching her swearing at the ignition might be the most beautiful thing I've ever seen.

She leans over to open the passenger door. 'Come on then!' I jump into the car.

'Hi!' She's gripping the steering wheel so tight her knuckles are white.

'Oh, Joy!' I lean across to hug her; she's as tense as a statue, but she relaxes a tiny bit in my arms.

'OK, get off. We need to move.' Joy tries the ignition again and the car thrums into life. 'Now I have to do a U-turn on the Wild Road. It's fine. I've done one before in the Culture Complex car park. Look how lovely and wide this bit of road is because the trees haven't eaten it yet.'

'You can do it.' I hope I sound more confident than I feel. If we end up in a ditch now, we're both screwed.

I've never been in a car with one of my friends before. I stay quiet as Joy performs a very slow, very careful sixteen-point turn. When we're facing the right way, I give her a round of applause.

'Start talking, Ray.'

The sun is rising ahead of us and the shafts of light coming through the leaves have turned golden. We set off and I take a deep breath. Where do I start? Since the last time I saw Joy, I've broken into an HPA base, rescued my mum, discovered Ron's horrifying plan, been in a van crash, flown a hoverboard, been held at gunpoint, betrayed Blaze and been betrayed by Blaze.

'I kissed Blaze,' I say.

'I knew it.' Joy hits the steering wheel and the car wobbles, making us both gasp. 'You're in love with him.' She straightens the car.

'He's not who I thought he was.' I rest my knees against the dashboard and the whole story tumbles out of me.

Joy is quiet for a long moment after I finish, then she tilts her head at me. 'And you ran to Blaze when the Villains' darts shot him?'

I throw my hands up. 'I told you he stole someone's powers and that Ron is going to do a major power grab today which will leave hundreds of people empty and probably spark an EV catastrophe in Nine Trees, *another* EV catastrophe in Nine Trees, and *that's* what you focus in on?'

'I'm a details woman.'

A dog wanders out into the road in front of us.

'Feck!' Joy performs the perfect emergency stop.

'Oh no! Do you think it's lost?' She looks at me wide-eyed. 'Should we put it in the back?'

'I don't know. There was something big rustling out there before you rescued me. It could have followed us.' My voice slows. 'But that would make it faster than the car—'

The dog swings its head up to gaze at us with shining blue eyes.

'That's not a dog,' I whisper.

'But we don't have wolves here,' Joy squeaks.

'Tell her that!' The wolf tilts its head. 'Can you reverse?'

Joy nods and the car rolls slowly backwards. The wolf trots after us.

'Jenna?' Joy is looking over her shoulder. 'Did it get bored and go away?'

The wolf's electric-blue eyes light up the windscreen. 'Nope.'

Joy risks a look. 'Feck. We need to get round it.'

She brakes and changes gears just as the wolf decides to gallop and take a powerful leap. We both scream as the car lurches forward and the wolf sails over us. Joy puts her foot down.

'Is it coming?' she yells. 'IS IT COMING?!'

I twist round in my seat. The wolf is standing in the middle of the road, getting slowly smaller as it watches us drive away. Did it just want to scare us? 'No, it's—' I settle back into my seat. 'ROOT!'

Joy screams as she wrenches the car to the right to avoid a huge black root that has broken through the road.

'ANOTHER ONE!'

We both scream as the car screeches to the left.

By the time we reach the end of the Wild Road we're both exhausted. Joy giggles hysterically as we drive past all the warning signs and on to the sunny road to town. 'Do you know what, the Wild Road *is* dangerous.'

'Oh really?' A laugh bursts out of me.

Joy's phone buzzes underneath the handbrake.

'Could you check that?' she says. 'It's probably my mum.'

I enter Joy's passcode and the message pops up, but it's not from Joy's mum.

It's from Blaze.

King Ron steps up his search for the next Diviner

Tuesday, 28th May 2024
By Ian Collins
Hero Columnist

Ron King is a powerhouse in every sense of the word. With his illustrious past as a hero and successful governance of the British branch of the HPA, we should not be surprised that he is using every tool in his arsenal to find the Diviner, but yesterday's appearance in Westminster still came as a shock to many.

King used his visit to announce an unprecedented world-wide alliance to find the next Diviner. The governments of fifty-two countries, including the USA, Japan and Russia, have signed a pact to collaborate with their national Heroic and Power Authorities, and with each other. They have pledged to search for the woman and to share the priceless power when the next Diviner emerges.

'The Diviner is our main weapon against the EV,' King told reporters from the steps of the Houses of Parliament. 'This force threatens everything humanity has built, and the heroes are the one thing that can stand in its way. The previous Diviner predicted her successor this year. *2024. The Diviner does not love. She does not judge. She does not lie. Her role is to see.* There is a woman out there destined to serve the world and she needs to come forward. The British HPA and our fellow heroes across the planet will do anything to keep this world safe. We will do anything to find the next Diviner.'

Helplines, social media chats and even postal addresses have been set up so the entire world can help find this woman. And, with spikes in the EV becoming a regular occurrence, we can't find her soon enough.

CHAPTER 30

'This is a message for Jenna,' I read. 'If she contacts you, please tell her that we need to talk. Just the two of us. I can meet her where she accepted my proposal.'

Joy looks over. 'Is that from Blaze?'

All I can do is nod as my mind tries to switch back from survival mode. The Jusics' little car makes it to the top of a hill and Nine Trees is there, spread out in front of us: thousands of lives hidden under roofs and between roads. The sun is just above the horizon and the water flowing through the town and out to sea is molten gold. My town. The flaking science block, our overgrown garden, all the lighthouses. If I do nothing, it could be destroyed and the heroes who are supposed to be saving the day will be the ones responsible.

'Well, you're not going anywhere near him.' Joy frowns at the road. 'You're coming back to my house and we're going to figure all this out.'

'If Ron tries the power grab, the EV could destroy Nine Trees,' I say.

'And that's bad, yes.' Joy pulls into her estate. 'But we've got time to make a plan that doesn't end up with you captured or dead.'

I breathe out, *two, three, four.* 'The Villains are still injured in the city and the police are no match for Ron.' My finger hovers over Joy's smudged screen and everything falls into place. 'Blaze is the answer. He's the hero that's supposed to save Nine Trees, however he got his powers. I just need to talk to him.' My heart squeezes as I picture him. Blaze with his nose bleeding, Blaze making me laugh at the museum, a ten-year-old Blaze standing alone in an empty training room. 'I can do this. I can get through to him.'

Blaze and I are the only ones who could know where I accepted his proposal. The place where I agreed to go on his one date, the East Breakwater Lighthouse. I type my response.

8 a.m.

'Did you just text him back?!' Joy reaches out and grabs my shoulder, before hastily returning her hand to the wheel. 'What did you say?'

'To meet me at the East Breakwater Lighthouse at eight.'

'Mother Earth,' she mutters. 'What if it's a trap?'

'He's given me a meeting place that only we would know.' I stop myself from rubbing my hands. 'It's the right thing to do, I know it.'

'Skies!' Joy shouts at the windscreen. 'Why now? We've been friends forever, why do you have to start believing in romance now?'

'It's not romance,' I mumble.

The car rolls to a gentle stop outside her block of flats. 'I want this to be the right move, Ray, I really do.' Joy yanks the keys out of the ignition. 'I want Blaze to look into your eyes and repent and help you save the world. But this is exactly why your family held that intervention.' She twists to face me. 'You always pick the option that means you get to see him. BLAZECON, the wedding, even now when he could be about to arrest you or worse.'

A chill runs through me, but I shake it off; Blaze has saved me so many times, he would never hurt me.

Joy's voice is gentle. 'Is going to see him now the smart thing to do?'

'It's the only thing I can do.' I take her hands. 'I can't take down Ron on my own. It has to be him. He might have stolen his power, but he'll never let Nine Trees get destroyed. He's a hero.'

'You're betting your life on that.'

A dad walks past pushing a double buggy. One of the kids is asleep; the other is holding a croissant and looking very pleased with himself.

'There's more at stake here than my life.' I can feel Joy's eyes on me, so I watch the dad with a pram until he turns a corner.

'In the last two weeks you've run back into a fire to save someone,' she finally says. 'You took on a Villain and raided a HPA base. Now you're putting yourself on the line again for our town. There's a word for people like you.'

I exhale and look over at her. Her eyes are shining in the morning light.

'Is it idiot?' I ask.

336

She snorts. 'No. Give me my phone back. If you're doing this, we're going to make an insurance policy. Grab a pen, paper and some lip gloss from the glove compartment ...'

Grey clouds are rolling in by the time I reach the East Pier. The air feels thick and slightly damp. The smooth walkway atop the jagged sea wall is as deserted as usual, even the section before the hazard tape and UNSAFE signs only has one solitary pigeon pecking at the concrete. A wave crashes up against the sea wall and I lick a drop of salt water off my lip.

'This is going to work,' I tell myself as I approach the lighthouse. This has to work. The arms of the boiler suit flap around my legs in the breeze. I've undone the top half to show the black vest I had underneath, in the hope that it makes me look less like Blaze's enemy. Although my bracelet of betrayal is glittering in the sunlight.

There's no sign of him as I approach, but the door to the lighthouse is open, which must have been Blaze. I duck inside. The air in the museum is cool and smells of driftwood. I pass the donation bucket in the entrance and step down into a round room full of glass cases of flotsam, and boards memorialising shipwrecks.

'Blaze?' My voice echoes off the curved white walls.

When I see him, I'm going to say that Nine Trees is in trouble. That's how I'll open. *Blaze, Nine Trees is in trouble. We can figure everything else out later.* He won't want to kiss me. Not after I got him darted at the museum. And I don't want to kiss him again, not after everything I've learned, not after everything that's happened. I don't know why I'm even thinking about that.

My fingers walk over the cool glass of a case containing a telescope.

We held each other tight but the kiss had been so gentle.

I could have kissed Blaze forever.

'Miss Ray.'

I spin to find Ron silhouetted in the doorway of the lighthouse. My heart clenches.

Trap.

This is a trap.

Joy was right. I chose to trust Blaze and now I am cornered in this lighthouse. I need to keep breathing. Keep calm. I don't know how I can get past Ron. Adrenalin might be coursing through me, but I feel like I've been awake for weeks and he looks as collected as usual in a dark purple three-piece suit.

He motions to my boiler suit. 'You really are a Villain.'

'Where is Blaze?' My heart is racing, but my voice comes out clear and strong.

'At the base.'

'But, his message …' Idiot. Blaze called me an idiot before and that's the way Ron is looking at me right now.

'Did you really think he would betray me? The HPA? We're his family – and I thought we were yours.' Ron steps slowly into the room. 'There's still a way to make this right, Miss Ray. You've been led astray. We didn't look after you as well as we should have and I'm sorry.' A small flicker of hope ignites in my core. If Ron cares about me, maybe he'll listen.

'Ron—' I start, but he holds up a hand.

'If you tell us where the other Villains are, and what they're

338

planning, you can come back. You can come home.' His smile is at twenty per cent. It's paternal, encouraging. 'It's what I want, and I know that's what Blaze wants.'

Ron has been kind to me. He saved me at BLAZECON; first from my mum, then from Sydney Jones. He winked at me after I punched Trevor Donaldson. He tried to teach me how to become part of the hero world. I can make him listen to me now.

'Ron. Today, when you try and fill those batteries, the EV will react. It will be catastrophic. It could destroy Nine Trees.'

His eyebrows lower. 'I see you've been talking to Femi.'

'I know you're trying to do the right thing, to save us all from the EV, but you're going to make it worse.'

His face darkens. I've never seen Ron angry before; he looks like a different person. The charm is gone and his steel-grey eyes look cruel. 'And you're an expert on the EV now, are you, Miss Ray? After less than a week at the HPA?'

'Femi had no reason to lie,' I say.

'Except that when I draw in power today it will include his.' His mouth is set in a hard line. 'That EV apologist. I'll make one of my men the hero that he could have been.'

In the midst of a van chase, I took Femi at his word, but what he said felt right. I've been face to face with EV creatures and they only attacked when Blaze shocked them, or when soldiers shot at their forest, or when Joy drove a car through their home. The EV isn't evil, it's a defence system and it's where the powers come from.

'I know he's right. I can feel it.' I rub a hand across my gut.

339

That's where it lives, this knowledge. It's like Mum said, everything is connected.

'Ah, women's intuition, wonderful!' Ron throws his hands up and his eyes close in exasperation. I use the opportunity to step round him.

'You're not going to steal those powers. I won't let you.' I am between King Ron and the open door. I want to look strong, but I don't know what to do with my arms. Maybe this is why heroes put their hands on their hips.

Ron's lip curls. 'Well, it's quite clear whose side you're on, Miss Ray. I thought maybe you'd come back to the HPA, but there's another outcome that will be equally beneficial for our cause.'

There's a hand on my back. I twist my head and see the Secret Ninja out of the corner of my eye before he shoves me back into the lighthouse. I land on my hands and knees on the rough wooden floor. Ron steps over me and I scramble up to see him join the Ninja in the doorway.

How can the Ninja still be standing after his night being hit by vans and dragged along the city streets? He should be dead, or at least wearing several casts, but his outfit is pristine. There is a strange-looking glint of silver shining through the gap for his eyes, but he looks indestructible. I don't know what to do. I can't get past both of them.

Ron's paternal smile is back, with a tinge of sadness. 'Jenna Ray, beloved Love Interest, was kidnapped and murdered by Villains. The country will mourn, Blaze will be devastated, but he'll get over the loss of his Love Interest. I did.' He pulls a small metal box out of his pocket and draws a glowing power from it up into his hand. 'Goodbye, Miss Ray.'

He stretches out his arm and his fingertips glow white as they point towards me. The thought that King Ron is about to kill me is so surreal I could laugh, or cry. I did this. My choices led to this. I should have listened to Joy, to my family. I should have understood what I was capable of.

Ron draws in a sharp breath and I use the last of my energy to fling myself behind one of the glass cases. The energy bolt hits the floor where I'd been standing and screeches down through the foundations of the lighthouse and the sea wall below.

The floor is still juddering as the Ninja taps Ron on the shoulder and whispers something in his ear.

'Well, that will do,' Ron replies, before catching my eye. 'You really did remind me of Kate.' He shakes his head and they leave the lighthouse.

A crack races up the wall beside me.

Is that it?

Are they letting me go?

Is it over?

I take a step towards the door and the lighthouse rocks so violently I am flung back on to the floor. The wooden floor is breaking and more cracks spiderweb across the curved walls. My arms wobble as I try and push myself up. The door is right there, it's so close, but the lighthouse is jerking and juddering. I can't get my balance.

'Come on, Jenna.' I manage to get myself up. The lighthouse is breaking apart. I need to get out of here. This is the point where Blaze would normally blur in and scoop me up so we could watch this building crumble from the pier. Or Emily would nonchalantly save me with a flick of her fingers. Or Joy would risk her life to pull me to safety. I've almost died so many times, but there's always been someone there to save me. 'Help!' There's an enormous crack behind me and I scrabble towards the door as the floor tips.

'Help.' The cry dies on my lips as the pier falls away and the bright blue sky fills the doorway. The doorway is tilting. No, it's falling. And I'm falling too. I thud into the wall as the lighthouse crashes into the sea.

CHAPTER 31

'We're going swimming in the sea!' Megan ran ahead whilst Dad gave me a piggyback down the rocky path to Hidden Beach, with Mum following behind. The sea stretched out below us like a twinkling carpet that went on forever and I was terrified.

I was terrified as Dad pushed pink armbands up to just below my shoulders.

I was terrified as my family waded in and waited for me to join them.

I was terrified right up to the moment Megan shouted, 'She's too scared to go in the sea because she's a baby! You're a baby, Jenna!'

I clenched my fists and ran in, splashing through the foamy waves up to Mum, and held out my arms.

'You're OK,' she said, with her arms crossed. 'Try swimming, like you do in the pool.'

The sea was completely different to the small blue pool where

I played with my friends. All I wanted was to be picked up, and I was about to cry when the water swelled around my waist and lifted me off my feet. I laughed, which made everyone else laugh. After bobbing about for a bit, I lay back to float and look at the sky. The sea held me tight, and I knew that even though the water was salty and rough and endless, I was home.

Since that moment, so long ago, I haven't been scared in the water.

I'm scared now.

No.

I'm terrified.

The lighthouse smashes into the waves and the sea bursts in through the windows in explosions of glass. A grey torrent floods in through the door above me as I scrabble, trying to push myself up. I take a last, panicked breath before I'm submerged in dark water and debris. Everything spins as the building tumbles. The door is gone, replaced by grey bubbles rushing past my face. My arms raise instinctively to protect my head and I clench my eyes shut.

Something jabs my leg. Something else thuds into my shoulder. My stomach lurches and my body is cut and battered as the debris shoots past. I never close my eyes under water when I swim. The sea feels different in the dark. Cold. Sharp. Terrible. Something heavy bashes into my stomach and my air vanishes. My heart is thundering, drowning out the thuds of the furniture hitting the walls.

In all this craziness I can still feel my chest tightening. It feels like I'm having an attack.

Maybe it is an attack.

Maybe that's all the attacks ever were, practise for drowning.

But when I had an attack, it was the sea that I craved.

It was the water that I needed.

Because I know, maybe I've always known, that if I'm in the water, I'll be OK.

It's the place where I am most myself.

It's my home.

My eyes fly open. The lighthouse is still sinking but the water has stopped spinning. Broken furniture and jagged pieces of concrete hang around me, lit by a turquoise shimmer. This dark death trap has turned the colour of the shallows on a sunny day.

A bubble escapes from my shocked mouth, but it doesn't shoot off in search of the surface. It hangs in front of me and glimmers. My air is gone, my head is spinning, and the lighthouse is still sinking. There's no way I'm making it back to the surface. I don't know what this alien bubble is, but I've got nothing to lose. My fingers float up and touch it.

The bubble attaches itself to my skin and grows across my body. I don't have the energy to bat it away, all I can do is watch. The bubble layer prickles as it covers my face and sparkles in front of my eyes like I'm wearing iridescent goggles. There's air touching my face; the bubble is somehow keeping the water at bay. My vision is going dark around the edges, so without letting myself acknowledge how unreal this all is, I open my mouth and take a breath.

Cool air fills up my lungs.

I breathe out, *two, three, four.*

How is this happening?

Is there a hero here who can control water?

A shard of glass bounces off the bubble covering my hands. I'm still trapped and about to get crushed; I need to get out of this lighthouse. The water shifts around me, and, beyond a faded life ring, the door appears. I launch myself up and grab the gritty doorway with my shining fingers. A moment later I am through and floating in the clear water.

The lighthouse rolls into the deep. It crashes off the sea wall with a thud that vibrates through the water, and chunks of the building tumble into a dark channel below. That was almost me. I should be crushed and sinking, but instead I am floating far beneath the churning surface, breathing deep, clean breaths.

The water judders and the white trail of a motorboat shoots by above me. Was that Ron and the Ninja, waiting to make sure I didn't make it out? My head is still spinning as I replace my oxygen, but my heartbeat is normal, and the gut-twisting terror is gone. Perhaps I'm in shock; I should be dead right now. Is this bubble thing something Emily can do with her telekinesis? I float closer to the surface to look through the waves. She's not there. It's just me.

It can't be—

There's no way that it's—

I'm not the one with powers? Am I?

I hold my hand up. 'Make a bubble.' As if by magic a shimmering silver sphere detaches itself from the

346

suit and floats up in front of my face.

'Mother Earth,' I mutter.

I'm like Mum.

From the moment that the lighthouse fell to now must have been less than a minute. It took less than a minute for me to realise that I have powers. Or perhaps it took me my whole life up to this moment. I can control water. I must have been doing it when I shared my air with Blaze. Maybe I've been using this power every time I stayed under the waves for longer than is technically possible. I'm already a fugitive who Ron wants dead, now I'm an unregistered powered person. If Joy was here, she'd call this a mess.

The bubble hugs each of my fingers and the silvery layer covers every inch of me, even the trailing arms of my boiler suit. It looks awesome, but if I do have powers now, I don't know how to use them. I don't know how I did this, and I've got no idea how long it will last. It would be a shame to drown at this point, so I swim up to the surface and tentatively poke my head out of the water.

There are cracks running along the sea wall, but, apart from that, my town is OK. And my town has noticed that one of our lighthouses just collapsed. Ron's speedboat roars into the harbour as the wail of sirens drifts across the waves and blobs of colour rush towards the pier.

If they see me, it'll be headlines within minutes.

Love Interest Pulled Out of Lighthouse Disaster by Brave Man

Or

Jenna Ray Main Suspect in Lighthouse Destruction

The waves roll past as I tread water. Ron wants me dead and next time his energy bolt might not miss. I don't know if the Villains are back in the game yet, so perhaps, for now, it's better to stay off the radar.

The sirens and shouts from the harbour cut out as I dip back under the surface. I don't try and access my powers again. I need to feel the coolness of the sea on my skin. The stress of the last few days disappears into the wavering blue and the sea turns darker as I slowly sink. Maybe I should just stay down here. It's easy underneath the waves. It's safe.

Megan. The last time I saw my sister she was sick in bed.

Dad. He'll be at work. He's always at work. Maybe an internal announcement about the death of a Love Interest will go round the council before I end up on the news again.

Joy. Joy will try and take down the HPA all on her own.

I need to tell them that I'm not dead.

Bubble, I think, and my silvery suit races across my body. I need a plan and maybe my bracelet from the Villains will do something helpful if I am on dry land. Hidden Beach. That's where I'll go. A current flows past my knees.

'Am I doing this?' The current gets stronger, pushing against my stomach and then my chest. It's going in the direction of Hidden Beach, so I let it take me and hurtle off around the shore.

348

Every so often I look up at the sun-dappled surface and expect to see a hero up there controlling the water for me. But there's only me and the sea.

The bubble evaporates as my head pops up into the warm air of Hidden Beach. I stand, weighed down by my wet boiler suit, and the distant sirens drift past on the breeze. I'm not ready to leave the water yet, I want to try and do something else with my power. Can I lift water out of the sea? I hold my hands above the surface and mutter, 'Pull.' A swirling ball of water rises and rotates slowly in front of me.

'This is amazing!' I wonder what else I can do?

'Hi, Jen-bear.'

Megan is standing on the beach holding a rucksack. I let the water go with a gasp. All the tension I left under the waves is back and my mind goes into free fall.

How is Megan here?

Did she see what I can do?

Did she see my power?

What is she going to think of me?

Will she stop loving me?

Or has that already happened?

'I brought you a towel.' She drops the bag.

'Did – did you see?' I stammer.

She nods. 'I also brought a pasty.' She opens the rucksack and pulls out a small brown bag. 'And three cookies.'

'Megan.' I run out of the water and into her arms. She crushes the air out of me as she hugs me back. My body almost sings with relief. She's my sister and she's here and she still loves me, I think.

'I'm not dead,' I say, into her shoulder.

'I'm so glad you're OK.' She sways in my arms.

'Are you all right?' I pull back, still holding her, and my heart sinks. Up close she's pale and the circles under her eyes are as dark as bruises.

'Ha.' There's no humour in her laugh. Now that she's seen me, all her energy seems to have gone. She wobbles again and I help her to sit in the sand.

'Have a cookie. Did you bring any water?' I rifle through the bag. Megan has packed a towel, a blanket and a thermos of tea with two cups. 'How did you get down here so fast?' I hand her a steaming cup of tea. 'Am I already on the news?'

'I packed this last night.' Tendrils of steam curl in front of her exhausted eyes. 'I went to the bakery first thing this morning. I didn't know the time, just that it was today.'

'What do you mean?' I sit as close to her as I can get without making her spill her tea and reach for the pasty.

'I, um …' Megan trails off.

My stomach gurgles. The pasty is heavy in my hand and the smell of spices is drifting up from the bag. I should give Megan the time she needs to find the right words, that's the kind thing to do. I pull the golden pastry out and take a bite. 'Mother Earth.'

'What?' Megan asks, alarmed.

'It's potato curry! This is their best flavour.'

She snorts. 'Of course. I try to tell you that I have visions and you get distracted by food.'

'You have visions?' I repeat through a mouthful of potato. 'What kind of visions?'

'The kind where you see a lighthouse falling before it happens.'

I swallow. 'You can see the future?!'

'And you can control water.'

I slowly lift the pasty and take another bite. My sister can see the future. I can control water. Mum can read objects. They do say that powers run in families. This is incredible. In less than a day everything has changed.

'Megan, I've got so much to tell you.' Her head drops. 'Megan! Wake up!'

'I don't think I've ever been this tired. I just want to sleep. The visions, they won't let me sleep. It was visions of the lighthouse or the storm above the destroyed the Culture Complex.' She sounds like she's holding back tears, but Megan never cries. My own eyes ache for her. I've never seen her broken before. 'Why do you look so good after using your powers?' she asks quietly.

I hadn't stopped to think about how good my body feels, especially now that I've eaten. I haven't slept and was just trapped in a broken building tumbling into the sea, but I barely feel bruised. My senses are alert and I am ready to swim, fight, save the world. It's like I've levelled up. Why am I so different to Megan? Is it because my powers come from something I love? 'Have you been fighting the visions?'

'Of course I have.' Her hand shakes as she places her cup in the sand. 'It showed you trapped and drowning, over and over, until last night when I finally caught a glimpse of what came next.'

I scramble round to kneel in front of her. 'Do you know what else is going to happen today?'

'I saw you underwater, surrounded by a glowing blue light. I saw myself meeting you here, and me on the sand under a blanket. Then I woke myself up so I could get here.'

'Megan, if you're fighting your power, you're fighting who you are. What if you let the visions in?'

'That's not who I want to be,' she whispers. 'I won't do it. I won't be the next one.'

The next one. The words hit me like a block of concrete.

Megan can see the future.

Megan is the next Diviner, the one the HPA are so desperate to find.

But none of it matters if I can't stop Ron and it will matter even less if she fades away on this beach.

'Mum has powers.'

I expect her to gasp or swear, but she just nods, like that's all she's got the energy to do.

'You're the bravest person I know.' I take her hands. 'Please, try and use your power, I think that might be the only thing that will help you.'

She shakes her head, and a tear slips down her face. Fear grips my insides. What if fighting this power could kill her?

'Will you do it for me?'

She holds my eye.

'I don't know what to do, Megan. The HPA are going to destroy our town, today, and I need to find a way to stop them.' Somehow, she looks even more tired. 'Will you look, for me?

352

Maybe you'll see me staying out of everything and it all turning out fine. I promise, I won't breathe a word about your powers until you want me to. I swear it, Megan.'

'OK,' she mumbles. 'OK.'

Megan breathes out and the change is immediate. Her face relaxes as the battle in her mind stops and her eyes cloud over and slowly turn white. She can't see in our world any more. She's looking further.

'What do you see?' Her hands go limp in mine. 'How do I stop Ron?'

'I see.' Megan's voice has an echo. It's like there are two of her speaking slightly out of time. 'I see you and Blaze fighting. I see lightning striking the Culture Complex. I see Sydney Jones. I see the Secret Ninja frozen. I see that blonde smiling at me. I see King Ron connected to us all. I see the planet reacting. I see the waves. I see the lighthouse. I see.' Her voice relaxes and her eyes turn back to their soft brown. 'I see.'

'Megan,' I whisper. My heart is racing. Me and Blaze fighting. King Ron sucking in power. Emily. Is all of this going to happen today? Or is she seeing things that have already happened too, like the lightning?

Megan rubs her eyes. She still looks exhausted but breathes a long sigh of relief. 'That's better. I understand now. She was clever, that Diviner. The prophecy, our prophecy, it wasn't about Blaze.' She smiles at me and collapses back into the sand.

'Megan!' I scramble over to her. She's snoring softly, with a peaceful look on her face. She'd seen this too. My sister. The Diviner. The tide won't come this high, so I grab the blanket and tuck her in. Dark clouds are gathering on the horizon. The rain will wake her soon enough.

King Ron connected to us all.

The storm is coming. I need to get to the Culture Complex.

CHAPTER 32

The Culture Complex is a half-hour walk up a cliff and across a town where the HPA are on high alert for the Villains. They'll spot me the moment I go near a CCTV camera. My best chance is staying in the water for as long as possible; I can slip back into the milk-grey sea, head around the coast, up through the harbour and sneak out by the council, then it's a short walk to the ruins of the Culture Complex. No one is going to expect a dead, traitorous Love Interest to swim up to, and then stroll round, a HPA base, are they?

The wind picks up as I stride into the waves, away from the safety of Hidden Beach and my snoring sister.

'Let's go.' I sink into the water to find my bubble already around me, and the current sucks me back out to sea. As I hurtle round the coast I roll to look at the black clouds above the surface. I'm doing it again. Rushing straight back into danger. The only reason I survived my last encounter with Ron is because I magically manifested superpowers. Going up against him again is idiotic. But what choice do I have? Joy was right, there's a word for someone like me.

The water is still murky where the East Breakwater Lighthouse tumbled into the sea and the drifting silt offers some protection as I swim alongside the sea wall. Flashes of high-vis and blue lights are visible from above, so I go deeper as I enter the harbour. If anyone looks down, hopefully I'll look like a seal.

The boats clack above me as I look for a way up to the harbourside. The grime on the surface is almost impossible to see through, but I do know where one ladder is. The wooden tourist boat, that me and Blaze almost crashed into, bobs by the harbour wall. I breathe out, *two, three, four* and the bubble around my head gently expands and contracts as I approach it.

Am I making the right call? The boat might be full of tourists with cameras and questions. It might be directly under a CCTV camera. A low rumble of thunder shakes the water and I clench my fists. I'll just have to hope no one cares about a girl climbing out of the harbour. I need to get to the Culture Complex, and fast.

Water streams off me as I grab the first rung and pull myself up the bobbing boat. The wooden deck is empty except for the tour guide, still dressed as a pirate, who drops his stack of leaflets as I climb over the side.

'Jenna Ray?!'

'No, I just look like her.' I rush past and leap on to the harbour path.

It's hard to act casual when you've got harbour water

dripping off you. People are securing their boats against the storm and ropes litter the harbourside. My foot snags in a coil and I almost trip as I pick my way through a gaggle of tourists leaning over the rail, pointing at the place the lighthouse used to be.

The air is growing heavier, but there are no CCTV cameras as I make my way along the harbourside towards the steps that will take me up past the council and towards the Culture Complex. Perhaps this route will work. My ears prick up at the word 'Blaze', but none of the people moseying around the harbour are talking about his dead Love Interest.

Perhaps Ron hasn't told the world yet. Hope fizzes through me; perhaps Megan can tell Dad I'm OK before he hears on the news that I died. All I need to do is survive this next encounter with Ron and my family won't have to mourn me at all.

There's a small white camera focused on the stairs up from the harbour to the council. I jog past and into the car park as fast as I can.

'Jenna?'

Everything clenches and I keep walking through the car park. Like that's not my name. Like someone I love isn't saying it.

'Jenna.' A gust of wind passes me and then Blaze is there, standing in front of me in his hero outfit. A car pulls out of a bay further up the road and people wander into the council. The world is still happening around us, but I am trapped in this moment, with Blaze. The sight of him breaks my heart.

His hair is a mess.

His eyes are red.

He's looking at me like I'm a ghost. His face is awash with terror and sadness.

We lock eyes and everything that has happened melts away. All I want is to kiss him.

'Jenna.' He's closer. His hand comes up to stroke my cheek. 'I thought you were dead.'

'No,' I murmur, leaning closer to him and breathing him in. 'Almost, but no.'

His fingers trail down my neck and round to my back, making my body tingle. 'None of it mattered.' His voice is almost a whisper. 'That's all I could think when Ron told me you had died. I just kept seeing your face and thinking that none of it mattered. I should have helped you. I would have helped you.' He looks into my eyes. 'Jenna, I love you.'

I kiss him. There is no way not to kiss him. I'm drawn to him like the waves to the shore. It is inevitable.

He stole his powers.

He let me walk into a trap.

He loves me.

There's a low rumble of thunder and it starts to rain.

The same delicious pink glow that I felt last time spreads through my body, but it's deeper this time. Attraction. Desperation. Lust. Guilt. Love. Too many emotions are swirling inside me. His lips move down to my neck and he kisses me like he needs me to survive. Like I'm water.

'I thought you were dead.' His soft lips are back on mine and his fingers tangle in my hair. My hands run down his back and circle his waist to pull him closer. This is wrong. I need to stop and get back to my mission, but I can't get enough of him. I return his passion like I've just cheated death and am about to try my luck again. He moans softly as the kiss deepens. My fingertips flit up to his face and come away wet.

I pull away. Tears are running down his cheeks, mixing with the fat drops falling from the sky. My body screams *don't stop kissing him!* But my brain knows that this is my chance to save Blaze too.

'I thought they'd be able to bring you in, to keep you safe.' Blaze wipes his face. 'Ron got me to send that message, but then he told me staying here was the right thing to do, that it was the only way to save you. I should have argued. I should have been there. I would have protected you.'

I grip his arm. 'They collapsed a lighthouse with me inside. They tried to murder me.'

His eyes shine. 'And they won't get away with it. I'll hunt down every last Villain. I'll make them pay for trying to hurt you!'

My mouth drops open. 'What?'

'You're safe now.' He pulls me into a hug. 'We'll get out of this rain. We'll go and tell Ron that you made it back to the base.'

I lean back so I can see his face. 'Blaze, it wasn't the Villains that tried to kill me. It was Ron.'

He studies my face for a moment and then draws me back in. 'You poor thing.' His head nestles next to mine. 'It must have been terrifying. Ron said it was a huge fight, a big mess and you got caught in the crossfire. It was Ron that tried to save you.'

A laugh bursts out of me before I can stop it. Ron always has to be the hero, even when he's lying to his protégé about the death of his Love Interest. 'There was no fight.' My voice is partially muffled by his shoulder. 'Ron lured me in and tried to kill me, whilst the Secret Ninja watched.'

Blaze's arms go rigid around me. 'No. That's not right.'

I wriggle free. 'You weren't there because they didn't want you to see them kill your Love Interest.'

'No.' Blaze shakes his head. 'You're confused. The Villains, they confused you.' He reaches for me again and lays a gentle hand on my shoulder. 'But you can come back to the right side.'

My heart gives a painful thud. Ron is Blaze's family, and I am the Love Interest who betrayed him. He's not going to believe me, but I have to try.

I shrug him off. 'Ron is planning to draw in powers from miles around. He's going to steal them from innocent, unsuspecting powered people.'

'Who are wasting them or misusing them, like the Villains. Registered, law-abiding powered people's chip – their tag – will protect them.' Blaze's voice is still sympathetic. 'If we go and talk to Ron, he'll explain, you'll understand.'

'It's theft.' I wipe the rainwater from my eyes. 'No, it's closer to murder. Have you seen how the people who have their power stolen end up?'

'But that's just temporary,' Blaze replies quickly. 'Ron is going to give the powers to men who have been trained to be heroes. Good men who will do everything they can to be worthy of them.'

'Temporary?' How can he be OK with this? He's talking about stealing powers like it's the noble duty of the HPA. 'There's nothing temporary about it. The people who have their powers stolen are left empty. They are like zombies.' Blaze blinks at me, confused. 'How did you get your powers?' The words of the Villains slip from my mouth, shocking us both. This is a race against time that I need Blaze's help to win. Confronting him about his powers wasn't in my plan, but it might be the only way to get through to him. 'Tell me how you got your powers.' The rain hammers down as he stares at me, his mouth slightly open. 'Do you even know her name?' I ask quietly.

Perhaps there's still a part of me that believes Blaze could say, *'This is all a big misunderstanding, my powers are natural and Pari, the Villain, whose name I do know, is actually fine …'* but that hope fades as he shakes his head. 'I never asked,' he whispers. 'She's still— She's still like that?'

'Empty?' He winces at the word, so I say it again, louder. 'She's still empty. The other Villains found her under a bridge.'

'I didn't want to, but my powers … Ron said I was a sure thing. I left my family, I trained for years, but my powers never came …' Blaze looks desperately at my face. 'The prophecy was coming and there was no hero. People would have died. You would have died, Jenna.' He grabs my hands. 'It was the right thing to do.'

Rain runs off our entwined fingers. The rage surges through me, but I don't push him away. From the age of ten, Blaze was told he would be a hero and save people. Ron brainwashed him, moulded him into the perfect hero, stuffed him full of someone else's power and left him with that burden to carry.

The pressure on my fingers increases. 'It was the right thing to do,' Blaze repeats, but he doesn't sound as certain. Maybe he is finally starting to understand what he's done and what Ron has done to him.

'Ron gave Trevor Donaldson stolen powers. How was that the right thing to do?'

Blaze swallows. 'We needed to do that. Trevor was a demonstration for the private buyers. Most of the powers will go to future heroes, but we need enough money to make this all work so some will have to go to people who are … Some will have to go to other people. They'll be able to buy the weaker powers. It's a minor concession to the bigger picture.'

'A minor concession?' More of Ron's words coming out of Blaze's mouth. I shake my head. 'This is wrong. I know you want to do the right thing, but you're getting it wrong.'

The confusion in Blaze's eyes is painful to see.

'There's more,' I push on. 'If Ron does this, if he tries this power grab, the EV will react. It could tear Nine Trees apart.'

'You're lying.' Blaze's voice is like a dart to the chest, but I can't give up on him.

'This storm will give him the perfect opportunity to try.'

As if on cue a rumble of thunder shakes the air and the rain intensifies.

'Ron is going to destroy Nine Trees.' I draw his hands up to my heart. 'You have to help me.' He looks at me blankly. I don't know if he's hearing me. 'Blaze, we're friends, we're more than friends. You said you loved me.'

'But you were just pretending.' His voice is almost too quiet to hear.

'I wasn't.' I tighten my grip as he tries to pull his fingers away. 'I never wanted to like you; you know that. I never wanted to be your Love Interest, but the Villains came to me after BLAZECON. They told me the HPA were holding my mum captive and that I had to get on to the base to find her in time. Becoming your Love Interest was the only way to save her. I didn't want to lie to you and I really, really didn't want to like you. I just wanted to help my mum.'

The rain is falling in thick blobs, creating a sheen of water over the car park. The rest of the world has run inside. Just me and Blaze are left out in the storm.

He blinks the rain out of his eyes. 'You used me.' He's furious and hurt, but so am I.

'And you're on the wrong side.' I drop his hands. 'I'm going to go and save my town.'

'I'm not on the wrong side.' He chases after me as I head towards the car park's exit. Any minute now, Ron will activate those batteries. He'll suck away my power, Mum's power, Megan's power. He'll leave us empty.

'Jenna!' Blaze grabs my arm. His voice is desperate. 'We do the right thing; that's what the HPA do.'

I spin to face him one last time. 'One side in this fight is stealing powers, the other is trying to save a town. You're supposed to be a hero. Figure out which is the right one.'

I wrench my arm free and run through the puddles towards the exit.

Blaze blurs in front of me. 'I can't let you go.' His eyes are shining with guilt and confusion, but he's still choosing the wrong side.

'I don't want to hurt you,' I say. 'You got those powers the wrong way, but you can still use them to do the right thing.'

Blaze places a hand on my arm. 'I won't let them hurt you again.'

The frustration raging through me makes calling the water easier. 'Neither will I.'

Acting purely on instinct, I raise my hands and the ground water rises to form a shifting sphere behind Blaze. It wraps itself around him before he knows what's happening. His eyes lock on mine and there's a flash of panic in them before he squeezes them shut. I'd almost forgotten that he doesn't like the water.

'I'm so sorry.' The water swirls around him and I remember him losing huge bubbles of air when we were waiting out the pigeons. 'Don't die.' It's breaking my heart, but I keep the water up until Blaze falls to his knees and gently slumps to the side. I release the water immediately and rush to him. My hand shakes as I place it on his chest. Mother Earth, he's breathing. I could cry, but I don't have time. I won't let Blaze stop me from saving Nine Trees. I won't let anyone. I turn and run.

The look on his face as the water surrounded him has seared itself into my brain. I've had my power for a few hours and I've already used it to hurt someone that I love. Is this what it means to be a hero?

My Villain boots rub as I sprint out of the council car park and towards the high street. My stomach clenches as I replay my last thoughts.

I've had my power for a few hours and I've already used it to hurt someone that I love.

364

Someone that I love.

Love.

Blaze is on the wrong side. He's made terrible decisions. I just used my power on him, but I love him. The rain hitting my face helps me process. I'm in love with the hero who saved my life. It was what everyone else wanted and it happened too late to cause anything but pain, but it's my heart and I love him. I love Blaze. It's not the world's feeling or the HPA's, it's mine.

But it's painful and pointless. There's no way he'll still love me after what I just did to him. Whatever happens next, me and Blaze are finished.

A car rolls up beside me and the window slides down.

'Jenna.' It's my dad. 'Get in.'

CHAPTER 33

'Dad?!' In the turmoil of love, betrayal and brand-new superpowers, my dad pulling up alongside me like he's giving me a lift home from the pool is almost too surreal to handle.

Our car splashes to a stop and he leans out of the window. The rain soaks the top of his work shirt, but he doesn't seem to care. He hasn't been crying. He didn't think I was dead. He has the same look on his face as when he needs to get us all out of the door on time. Complete focus.

'Your mum told me what happened. Get in, I'm going to take you to safety.'

I freeze. 'What?'

'I didn't know how to find you and then I saw you from my office window talking with the hero. I thought he'd arrest you.' He shakes his head and raindrops spray off him. 'It doesn't matter. Get in. We'll get away from the HPA and figure it out from there.'

He talked to Mum.

He doesn't even sound surprised. Has he been in contact with her this whole time?

'You knew Mum was with the Villains.' There's a flash from somewhere over the sea. The storm is intensifying, but right now all I can focus on is Dad.

'There's a lot we need to talk about. Get in the car, Jenna, and I can take you to safety, just like her.'

'You took her away.' My voice sounds like it's coming from far away, or long ago. 'You knew where she was. What she was doing. All this time.'

'Jenna, please—'

'No!'

Somehow the rain is falling harder. I step back into a puddle as Dad swings his door open. 'You need to get in. I'll look after you now. You've done enough.'

'I'm not coming with you.' Ten years of hurt pour into my words. I breathe out, *two, three, four,* and try to get a grip on myself. 'I need to go.'

'Jenna.' Dad's voice is strangled. 'We did our best. We wanted to protect you and your sister.'

A decade of heartache threatens to tear me down and I can't let it. Don't think about the morning that you woke to find Mum gone. Don't think about the evenings you spent waiting for her to come back. Don't think about the questions that you were afraid to ask your dad. Think about Nine Trees. Another, louder, rumble of thunder cracks above us.

'Get in the car, Jen-bear, please.'

'No.' My voice is calm again. The rain is dampening my rage and bringing clarity with it. This might be the last time I see my dad. When the lighthouse crashed into the sea I thought of him, carrying me on his shoulders, taking me into the sea for the first time. Now, I'm going to face Ron again, and I might not survive.

A relieved smile illuminates Dad's face as I take a step towards the car and my heart sings to see him happy. It turns out, at the end of everything, love is stronger than anger.

'I'm not going to get in the car, but I forgive you, Dad, and Mum, and I love you. I left Megan on Hidden Beach. She might need a lift.'

For the second time in a matter of minutes, I sprint away from someone I love. The car starts behind me, but I turn up an alley that's too slim for Dad to follow. The cobbles are slick with rain, but I manage to keep my balance as I cross the high street and come straight out the other side.

It's so dark that the street lamps have come on, even though it's only midday. The short road, that leads to what remains of the Culture Complex, glistens under the orange lights. The fast-approaching jagged black struts of the collapsed glass building are illuminated by white flashes. Ron is already there, but so is someone else and it looks like they're fighting him. I need to help them. I push myself to run harder, but as I approach the signs my heart almost stops.

The HPA have put a fence up around the Culture Complex's car park.

'No,' I mutter. Through the driving rain I can see it's the flimsy stainless-steel type with a jagged top that will make it almost impossible to climb over. Maybe, if I run hard enough, I can push it over? If it's well secured, I could break my arm, but I don't have time to find another way round. There's someone fighting Ron and I need to reach them before he overpowers them.

My feet pound on the wet concrete, sending shudders up my tired legs. I grit my teeth and increase my speed and ... the impact disappears. I'm still moving forward but my feet are hitting something soft and I'm getting higher.

'Don't look down,' I huff. I don't need to look down to know that my feet are connecting with glistening platforms of rainwater. 'Don't think about it.' Don't even acknowledge how awesome it is. Don't do anything that might switch it off. How can my body know so much more about my power than my brain? I push myself higher through the driving rain that continuously lifts me, up and over the fence, before sinking back to the ground on the other side.

Glass crunches under my feet as I move as quietly as I can to the jutting ruins of the Culture Complex. The safest-looking entrance is the fire exit that I ran back through when the first storm hit. The door itself is on the ground now, but somehow the frame is still standing. I gaze at the blackened wood for a long moment. Am I ready to run back into the inferno?

The action is just out of sight, but the sound of blows and yells echo around the broken building. A flash lights up the ruin; the broken struts, the scattered chairs and tables from the restaurant, and the fallen portion of balcony blocking my view of the action. There were ferns on this twisted hunk of metal once. Ferns and books under a clear glass sky. The rain is stopping; the torrent is now little more than a drizzle. Does that mean I'm losing my advantage?

A high-pitched whistle pierces the air and a figure on a hoverboard crashes to the ground on the other side of the fire exit. I leap over a pile of rubble and rush through the door frame to find a Villain curled up on the ground.

'Femi?' I crouch next to them. I need to get them up. We're still out of sight of Ron, but maybe he's coming. The Villain groans under their helmet. It's not Femi, it's Mum. My heart freezes.

'Mum!' I get her on to her back and wiggle off her helmet. 'Mum! Are you OK?'

'Jenna?' She's struggling to speak. 'No. No, what are you doing here?'

'I'm going to help. Tell me what I can do.' There's no blood, but her eyes aren't able to focus.

'No.' She pushes me weakly away. 'No. Go.'

Her head drops back.

'Mum!' Is she dead? 'Mum ...' I place a shaking hand on her chest, and she groans and mutters something that might be *go back to bed*.

'Sima!' Femi's voice floats up from the helmet.

I place it over my head. 'Femi?'

'Jenna?! What are you doing there?!'

'Mum's been knocked out. Tell me what I should do.'

'Feck.' There's a bang and then a groan. 'Feck.' His voice is full of pain. 'I should be there. I could control him, but my ribs, the crash—'

370

'Femi! Tell me what the plan is.'

'Right. Wait. I'm sending the orb to your mum.' A silver orb, with a central green light, zips over. 'Sima was trying to put that on the Ninja.'

I grab the orb and it pulses in my hand. 'What does it do?'

He takes a sharp intake of breath. 'She wouldn't want you going in there.'

My fingers tighten around the glowing ball. 'The only thing you can control is whether I go in there knowing what this orb does or not. And you've got three seconds to make up your mind.'

Femi's exhale hisses in my ear. 'It's for the Secret Ninja. You need to put it on him. Anywhere will do, it just needs to make contact.'

'Thanks.' I wrench the helmet off and place it back by Mum, ignoring Femi's shouts. The orb needs to go on the Ninja. OK, at least I now have an objective. Another crash echoes through the complex and I grit my teeth. It's time for me to face Ron again. At least this time I know he won't hesitate to kill me. With a last glance at Mum, I rise and creep around the fallen balcony to peer at the foyer of the Culture Complex.

My eyes go straight to the metal strut that has fallen to run diagonally from the destroyed ceiling to the floor. A vein of blue runs down it and where the strut touches the ground there is a pool of electric-blue EV light the size of a large puddle. I didn't think EV energy would collect like water, but blue still dribbles down the metal strut, ready for Ron to use.

In front of the EV energy, spreading across the foyer, Ron has set up a circle of battery stacks. He crouches to connect the final stack to a web of cables that leads to a waist-height metal rod in the centre. What was it Mum said? He'll activate the batteries, use them to pull in powers from miles around and then store them, ready to sell or create his army of obedient heroes.

'Would you just stop?!' Emily staggers past, her attention focused on the Secret Ninja. Her helmet is gone. She's fighting him, but he's not giving her a chance to use her power. A kick sends her flying, and she rolls to a stop on the blackened floor looking at me. A split second later the Ninja is on her, wrenching her arms back and snapping cuffs on her.

'*I'm coming,*' I mouth.

Emily motions frantically across with her head and I look over to see Ron standing in the centre of the circle of batteries, staring at me. Thunder cracks directly above us as he shakes his head and shoots a white energy bolt at me. I dive out of the way and scramble behind the melted ticket machines.

'Miss Ray?'

These machines won't offer any protection from King Ron, the Conduit, when he has an EV power source right there. I need to find a way to get to the Ninja and free Emily. I breathe out, *two, three, four.*

'Wait!' I pocket the orb and stand with my hands up. 'Wait, Ron, I need to talk to you.'

'How exactly are you still alive?' Ron tilts his head at me.

I step out from behind the machines. Emily and the Ninja are a few metres ahead, between me and Ron. I walk slowly towards them. 'That's why I need you. Something has happened and I don't know what to do. I need your help.' Emily's eyes are wide, but she thankfully keeps her mouth shut as I edge closer to them.

Ron's face creases. Maybe a Love Interest asking for a hero's help has activated one of his core principles and he'll stop all this madness to help me.

His eyebrows rise. 'You have powers?' His arm swings up to point at me, fingertips already glowing. 'I can feel them. How did I miss this?'

Maybe not.

I cross the last couple of steps to the Ninja, reach into my pocket and shove the green orb at him. The Ninja is normally impossibly fast, but perhaps he's not expecting a Love Interest to throw herself at him. I manage to make contact and the orb attaches itself to his chest.

'No!' Ron cries as the Ninja staggers back. The green lines of light travelling across his body are visible under his black uniform. The Ninja takes one step back, then another, and freezes as the green light reaches his eyes.

'Activate.' Ron marches over to the Ninja. 'Restart code five-two-three.'

'D-d-d-d—' The synthetic sound comes from under the Ninja's hood before morphing into a smooth voice. 'Restart code five-two-three. Denied.'

My mouth drops open. Nick was right! The Secret Ninja actually is a robot! This must be how he survived the collision with the Villain's van and why Mum could read him. He had no Love Interest, no sidekick, no story and he was just a weapon for the HPA to control.

The Ninja slowly turns his head towards Ron.

'Restrain her.' Ron points at me. The panic is clear in his voice.

The Ninja looks at me with his sparkling green eyes and then back at Ron.

'Prince #2, I gave you an order!' Ron marches over. 'Restrain her!'

'The Secret Ninja is Prince #2?!' I sound like Joy in the cinema. What the feck is wrong with this man? Ron told me that Prince #2 was the friend he needed after Kate. He told me, no, he told the world, that the tragic fate of his incredible AI sidekick had been almost too much for him to recover from. He must have staged it all, like the confetti at BLAZECON. The world stopped looking at the selfless robot and refocused on Ron. And Prince #2's tragic fate was that Ron decided to reprogram him? It's as bad as brainwashing Blaze.

'Wild, right?' Emily says from the floor. 'A brilliant way to strengthen your position as the head of the HPA and an utter dick move.'

'I will not restrain her.' The Ninja's voice is gentle. He turns to me. 'Thank you for releasing my heart.'

I don't understand what that means, but at least the Ninja is no longer on Ron's side. 'Help us,' I say.

He shakes his head. 'I can't.' The Ninja leaps over the ticket machines, through the fire exit and away.

'Ingrate!' Emily yells after him. 'Think it was easy to program that orb?!'

'You!' Ron swings round and grabs me. 'You released my

sidekick. You've got no idea what you've done.' He lifts his free hand above my head. 'What is your power?'

His fingers dig into my arm as I struggle. I can't pull myself free. The water is floating up off the ground behind him, but it's slow, so slow.

'Never mind. It can be a mystery purchase. You women are getting powerful these days, someone will pay good money to find out exactly what you can do. Thank you for bringing it to me.' Ron's fingers glow above my face and I feel something shift inside me. A tiny, buried part of me is rising to the surface, travelling through my gut and into my chest. He's going to steal my power.

'Stop!' shouts Emily.

The water falls uselessly to the ground behind him. My heart thuds painfully and my breath vanishes. He's going to steal my power and leave me broken and empty and there's nothing I can do. That part of me, my power, rises up through my throat. I clench my mouth shut, but it's choking me. I can't breathe. My head is spinning. I can't open my mouth. I can't let it go, but it's killing me.

'Leave her alone!' I crash on to the floor as Ron disappears in a blur. I hurriedly swallow my power back down and feel it settle and sink back in just below my belly button.

Blaze is on the other side of the complex, standing over a floored Ron. My arms wobble as I try to push myself up and I end up back on the floor.

Everything is blurred, but I can still make out Blaze. In his hero outfit. Choosing me. Saving me.

My heart is racing. It's doing the opposite of breaking. It's mending. It's glowing.

'Woo! Plot twist!' Emily yells from the floor.

'Blaze, son, what are you doing?' Ron gets to his feet and Blaze lets him.

I want to yell at him to cuff Ron, but my tongue isn't working. My head is still whirling, and the image of Ron and Blaze facing off judders and flicks from side to side.

'You were trying to murder Jenna, again, just like the lighthouse.' Blaze's voice is choked with anger and confusion.

'Knock him out, Blaze,' Emily calls.

'Jenna Ray is the enemy.' Ron's gentle, paternal voice is back.

'She said that if you do this, if we do this –' Blaze motions to the batteries and for a moment they seem to swirl around him – 'it will destroy Nine Trees.'

'I'm sure she said a lot of things.' Ron places a hand on Blaze's shoulder. 'Who are you going to trust, the person who made you who you are today, or some girl you pulled out of a fire?'

'I—' Blaze is faltering. He's hesitating and my voice won't work. I can't help him.

'Everything I've done has been for your own good, son.'

'That may be, but you need to stand down.' Blaze straightens up and joy shoots through my unsteady mind. Blaze is good. He's finally choosing the right side. It's OK that I love him. His voice comes out strong and heroic. 'What you're doing here is wrong.'

Ron sighs. 'We'll straighten this out later.' The hand on Blaze's shoulder pulses white and Blaze crumples to the ground.

'No,' I gasp. I try to get up, to get to him, but the ground is still wobbling for me, like the lighthouse before it fell into the sea.

Ron glances over as he moves to the centre of the ring of batteries and grasps the rod with one hand.

'Don't do this!' Emily struggles against her cuffs.

'You'll destroy the town.' My voice comes out slurred.

'Or I'll finally have the heroes that I need to save the world,' he says calmly. A spark flicks down the rod and the circle of batteries switch on. Their red blinking lights flash up at Ron like tiny patches of fire. He stretches his hand towards the EV pool and flexes his fingers.

Blaze is down. Emily is out too. I'm the only person left in this fight.

But I don't have anything left. My head is spinning. My chest is aching. My heart is thudding. The rain is getting harder again, but it's not helping.

There's a crack of thunder and lightning flashes above the complex, illuminating the broken cinema sign behind Ron as he stands with his eyes closed and his arms outstretched. Will my whole town end up like this, a burned-out shell?

I need to get up.

For Nine Trees.

For my family.

For Joy.

For Blaze.

For me.

A bolt of pain splinters through my head as I push myself up and stagger towards the shining blue EV pool.

With a gasp, Ron draws power from the pool from one hand and sends it flowing down the rod with his other. A stream of white pours down the rod and splits across the floor into the batteries, leaving Ron at the centre of a clockface. The lights of the batteries flick from red to green and they snap open to reveal white light ready to rocket out in every direction and drain the powered.

Ron senses me by the EV pool and prises his eyes open. 'You can't stop this now.'

My voice echoes around the broken complex. 'I can try.' I step into the EV pool. It's odd. I thought it was light, but it's thicker than air and thinner than water. It's—

My head jerks back and my body goes rigid.

Power.

So much power.

Fresh.

Sharp.

Blue.

Mine.

'They're blue.' Emily's shocked voice is on the edge of my hearing. 'Jenna, your eyes, they're—'

My eyes are on Ron. His power is white hot, electric, flowing into those batteries ready to race across the country. It will find people. Emily, Mum, Megan, it will find them and suck them dry. Ron was right, I can't stop his power, but with the EV flowing through me, maybe I can redirect it.

With a cry, Ron sends a surge of energy into the batteries and white light shoots out of them in all directions. I fall to my knees as I call the water. Drops from the ground join the rain to form a watery barrier, hanging from the sky, circling the batteries. A sob tears itself from my throat as the power from the batteries blasts straight through the water barrier and out into the world. Behind me, Emily cries out.

It's not working. I'm kneeling in pure EV power. I need to use—

The change in the water feels like a jab to my chest. It's the EV energy. It's found its way through me and into the water. The circular wall of the glistening water barrier turns blue and Ron's power changes direction. It is drawn in by the water and it burns as it races up the wall to join the streams of rain and flow unfettered into the stormy sky. The clouds crack and thunder with the weight of it. There's a sound. I think I might be screaming, but I keep the water in place.

The last of the white-hot power is swallowed into the clouds. I break the connection and let the barrier of water turn back into rain and fall around us.

'What have you done?' Ron sags to the floor.

I am on my hands and knees too. The pool of EV energy is gone. My lungs burn like I've just swum a marathon, but there are hairs standing up on my arms. This isn't over. The rain stutters and stops as the air around us grows thicker and crackles.

'Get away from the batteries!' Emily struggles up, her hands still cuffed behind her back. 'Now!'

As my brain tries to make sense of her words, fingers grip the back of my vest and pull me back. I skid to a halt on the glass-strewn ground across the foyer as a figure blurs into the middle of the circle of batteries.

CRACK

The sound is like every window in Nine Trees breaking simultaneously. I'm on the floor, curled in a ball with my hands covering my head, but I'm still blinded by the white flash that accompanies it.

The lightning that hit the Culture Complex on the night of the prophecy had been a fast flash, a split second of fury, but this lightning feels like it might last forever. The intense white heat becomes my entire world. It has struck the middle of the circle. Where Ron had been. Where Blaze just blurred to.

'Don't be dead,' I whisper. 'Blaze, don't be dead.' My eyes are screwed shut. All I can do is stay motionless as the lightning returns all the energy I just sent up into the clouds.

The white eventually fades and my ears hum as I slowly lift my head, terrified of what I'll find.

'Feck,' Emily mutters.

The rod and stacks of batteries are gone, disintegrated into new heaps of black ash, and in the middle of the circle is a new, glowing pool of blue EV power.

'Blaze?' I stagger up, blinking the bright spots from my eyes. Ron is lying by the box office, unconscious but uninjured. 'Blaze?' I say louder. Did the lightning get him? Did he manage to push Ron out of the way but not save himself? 'Blaze!' My voice is thick with anger. He can't be dead. Not after everything we've been through. Not after everything I've endured. 'Please,' I mumble.

'Jenna.'

'Blaze!' He gets to his feet behind a broken piece of box office. I run round the shining blue pool and loop my arm around him to help him up. Touching him sends those same pink sparks running through me, but I try to ignore them. I can't kiss him now; one of his eyes has swollen shut. 'You saved me,' I say.

He wobbles and I hold his waist to keep him steady. 'And you saved everyone. I'm starting to think the Diviner's prophecy was never about me,' he murmurs, but before I can process that, he softly touches the ends of my Afro and says, 'I like your hair.'

I reach up and run my fingers along hair that's even bigger than usual. 'Is it standing on end?'

'Yeah. It looks badass.'

I snort.

'Jenna.' Blaze's hand moves down to my face. 'Where do we go from here?'

He stole his powers. He worked with the HPA. He saved my life. He chose my side. He has a good heart. I shrug. 'I like you.'

'I like you too.'

'Will it be enough?' I ask. The world is now even more uncertain. Blaze is on my side. We've defeated Ron, but what happens next?

'I don't know.' He holds my gaze and I see a decision light up his eyes. He leans in and whispers in my ear, 'Laurie.'

'Laurie?' I draw back to look at him.

'That's my name. Laurie Lin.' He grins and puts out his hand. 'It's nice to meet you.'

The boy behind the hero has a name and, after everything, he's chosen to share it with me. My heart glows. He trusts me. He's with me. 'Pleased to meet you, Laurie Lin, I'm Jenna Ray.' I take his hand, but instead of shaking it, I pull him towards me. My lips find his, and the uncertainty melts away. I love him and this is going to be complicated. But right now, all there is for us is this kiss, and it is perfect.

'Jenna,' Emily calls from the floor. We both ignore her. 'Jenna!'

'What?!' I pull away from Blaze. Can't she give me a minute to enjoy the start of my love story?

She glares at me. 'Ron's gone.'

'Feck.' I run over to her. 'Blaze, can you release her?'

He blurs over and a moment later Emily is on her feet, massaging her wrists. 'He went out through the front.'

Blaze's eyes darken and he blurs out through the fire exit too.

'Are you OK?' I help Emily towards the door.

'Peachy,' she replies.

'I thought the EV was going to react to all of that.' Blue and red lights flash on the other side of the fallen balcony.

'I think it did.' She gives me an odd look and strides off to the exit.

'Mum?' There's no sign of her or her hoverboard, so I follow Emily around the fallen balcony, take one look at the chaos in front of me, and immediately run back into the ruined Culture Complex and out of sight.

The complex is surrounded. Someone has pulled down the fence and the police are trying to control a growing crowd trampling over the signs in the car park. I can't go out there. My heart hammers against my ribcage. All those people. Whatever happens next happens in front of all those people. I lean my head back against the concrete and close my eyes. I can't do it. If I go out there, I'll have an attack.

'I'm starting to think the Diviner's prophecy was never about me.'

Blaze said that before we kissed. Megan told me the prophecy wasn't about Blaze before she passed out. They can't mean the prophecy was about me, can they? The thought makes me want to vomit, but maybe I'm not done saving my town. Mum thought that *the sharp blue heat of truth* line was the Diviner telling us it's our chance to expose Ron. Was it a message, from the Diviner to me, across hundreds of years? Am I supposed to be the one to expose Ron and the HPA? I rub my hands. Is that what happens next?

My eyes flick open as I picture myself striding out to address the crowd, and I squeeze them shut again. How can the prophecy be about me when I'm too afraid to go out there? What happens if I just stay hidden in here? I take a deep, shuddering breath. I don't think I've ever been this tired, but if I can control water, I must be able to stop myself from crying.

'Blaze has betrayed us all,' Ron cries. I wriggle round so I can see him, just past the balcony. He's standing above the crowd on a pile of rubble, a helpless old man pointing back at Blaze. Can he really pin this all on Blaze? My heart thuds even faster. Maybe he can. Maybe he'll get out of this. Maybe King Ron is untouchable and all of this was for nothing. 'Blaze has joined forces with the Villains,' Ron continues. 'He's trying to destroy Nine Trees. He's—'

'YOU KILLED MY BEST FRIEND!'

Joy?

Glass crunches as I spring up. I can't let Joy think that I'm dead. I rush out and almost run straight into the back of Blaze, who turns to help me on to the pile of rubble that he and Emily are standing on. My stomach clenches as I stand on this makeshift stage, but I can't turn and run, not whilst Joy is trying to single-handedly bring down King Ron.

'You killed Jenna Ray and I have evidence!' Joy pushes her way through the crowd.

I can hear a video playing on her phone, my tiny voice saying, *'My name is Jenna Ray and I'm not a Love Interest ...'*

Ron knocks the phone out of her hand, and it smashes to the ground. 'This girl is working with them!'

Behind the police, members of the crowd hold up their phones, all of them showing the same video of me.

'My name is Jenna Ray and I'm not a Love Interest ...'
'My name is Jenna Ray and I'm not a Love Interest ...'
'My name is Jenna Ray and I'm not a Love Interest ...'

'There's more, sir.' A police officer steps forward. 'This young woman also has a film of Jenna Ray going into a lighthouse, which you, and the Secret Ninja, step out of and watch crumble into the sea. Ron King, you're under arrest.'

'Wait!' Ron holds up his hands. 'You don't have the full story.'

'Arrest him.' The police officer and two others step forward.

'Jenna Ray is a Villain.' As he backs away, a flicker of white jumps between his outstretched fingers. 'I'm sorry, officers, but everything I do is for the greater good.'

'No—' I gasp.

'He's going to do the eliminator!' someone in the crowd cries.

385

The entire crowd holds their breath as Ron claps his hands together above his head, but instead of a spiderweb of brilliant white energy, there's a small spark and a sad sizzle. Ron's face freezes and I manage to stop myself from laughing. He's finally out of power. He shakes his head slowly, an old man accepting his defeat, and then leaps off his pile of rubble to sprint through the car park.

Blaze blurs after him and a moment later Ron is in hand-cuffs, being marched back towards the police. He leans back to whisper something to Blaze before locking eyes with me, a look of pure hatred on his face. For a moment I forget the crowd and I give him my ten per cent smile. It is the best it's ever felt.

'Jenna!' Joy yells. She scrambles up the rubble to get to me. 'Jenna. You're OK.' She squeezes me so tight that my back clicks.

Even as she hugs me, I can feel every single person looking at me.

I breathe out, *two, three, four.*

'This is Sydney Jones, on the scene, with none other than Jenna Ray, who is apparently not dead!' Sydney Jones appears from nowhere with a camera poking over her shoulder. 'Jenna, in your video you make a lot of outlandish claims about Ron and the HPA. What's the truth here and how did you survive?'

Joy steps away but I can feel her next to me. Blaze is beside me as well. I drop my Mia-approved smile. I don't need it any more.

'Every word of that video is true, Sydney.' My voice is clear and surprisingly calm. 'We just stopped Ron from stealing the powers of every unregistered powered person in the country.

He was going to give them to men like him, to create his own super-powered army and sell what was left to the highest bidder. It didn't matter to him that his actions could have destroyed Nine Trees. This has always been about power. About control. There are too many powered people who don't fit his definition of a hero and who won't bend to his will.'

'Like the women with powers stronger than men'?' Sydney looks at me with challenge in her eyes and damp hair sticking to her face. 'We're just supposed to take your word for that, are we?'

The crowd mutters and my eyes sweep over them. Mum is there, leaning on Dad, together for the first time in ten years. Dad looks shell-shocked, but Mum smiles at me, glowing with pride. Next to them is Megan, sand still in her hair, looking at Emily with the strangest expression on her face. There must be so many people with powers hiding from the HPA. They'll have never seen someone just like them standing where I am now. I am representing them, and I am ready to tell the truth. The world needs a new type of hero; the Diviner knew it then and I know it now.

'No, Sydney, I can prove it.' I look out at the damp car park and the myriad puddles glinting under the flashing blue lights. 'Here you go.' Mum's bracelet slides up my arm as I thrust out my hand. All the water I can find surges together to create a giant plume of water that shoots up into the sky.

People scream and on the edge of my hearing is the video that Joy and I made in her car. She kept telling me there was a word for someone like me, someone who would run back into a burning building, someone who would risk everything to

387

save the ones they love and fight for what they believe in. That word means even more now that I'm the girl with powers who saved Nine Trees.

'My name is Jenna Ray and I'm not a Love Interest. I'm a hero.'

Sometime later ...

Ron King reclined on the leather Chesterfield sofa he'd had brought to his cell. After another farcical day of show trials, he was exhausted.

'They can't find anyone that you allegedly drained.' His lawyer perched on the desk in the corner of the room. 'Which is good. But the evidence gathered from the night of the Culture Complex, um, events are going to be hard to fight.' The lawyer's suit was still uncreased. Whilst Ron could land a forward flip in a tuxedo, he hadn't been able to keep his suit trousers uncrumpled through the never-ending day in court. He should ask the lawyer how he did it.

'I recommend we take the plea deal,' the lawyer said.

Perhaps it was unfair to leave the lawyer to suffer through this legal quagmire, but there were more important things to ruminate on, and for some reason the legal jargon helped Ron to think. The HPA was in a state. The EV was becoming more destructive by the day. His protégé, Blaze, was floundering.

The Diviner's last prophecy was on a folded piece of paper in the chest pocket of his shirt. He took it out and reread it for the tenth time that day.

2024.
The Diviner does not love.
She does not judge.
She does not lie.
Her role is to see.
Until the one who comes after me.

Ron grazed his finger over the last line, *Until the one who comes after me.* The HPA had never released the end of the prophecy to the public – it would have caused hysteria – but it was the reason he kept the prophecy close to his heart. Reading that line was like a shot of coffee; it was his reminder that he was fighting to protect the world he helped create.

'Mr King, we really need to discuss this deal.'

'You do what you think is best, my old son.' Ron gave him a reassuring smile. The legalese didn't matter. He'd sign whatever they wanted and he would be back running the HPA again before the ink was dry. He had to be.

The Diviner.

The EV.

Prince #2 out in the world.

Deluded girls playing at being a hero.

The prophecy crumpled as it disappeared into his fist.

He was the only man who could save the world from what came next.

Mental health charities for young people

Jenna struggles with her anxiety throughout the story and I wanted to include a few UK-wide organisations where you can find advice and support for your mental health. For a more extensive list, visit mind.org.uk.

Anxiety UK

Anxiety UK is a user-led organisation that supports anyone with anxiety, phobias, panic attacks or other anxiety-related disorders. **03444 775 774** or text **07537 416 905**
anxietyuk.org.uk

CALM

CALM (Campaign Against Living Miserably) is a helpline for young males aged 16 to 35 years suffering from depression and low self-esteem. It offers counselling, advice and information. **0800 58 58 58**
thecalmzone.net

Mind

Mind provide advice and support to empower anyone experiencing a mental health issue. They campaign to improve services, raise awareness and promote understanding. **0300 123 3393**

mind.org.uk

The Mix

The Mix is the UK's free, confidential helpline service for young people under 25 who need help but don't know where to turn. **0808 808 4994**

themix.org.uk/mental-health

Nightline

Nightline is a student listening service which is open at night and run by students for students. Every night of term, trained student volunteers answer calls, emails, instant messages, texts and talk in person to their fellow university students about anything that's troubling them.

nightline.ac.uk

Young Minds

Young Minds provides information, advice and training for young people, parents, carers and professionals.

youngminds.org.uk

Acknowledgements

Grab yourself a cup of tea, it's the acknowledgements page of a debut author …

First, thank you to my own personal hero, my agent, Christabel McKinley. She opened the door to the publishing world for me, Jenna Ray, and my other stories, and then worked tirelessly to make them shine. Christabel also got my book into the hands of the brilliant Carla Hutchinson, my editor at Bloomsbury, who has been in equal parts exacting and encouraging. Thank you, Christabel and Carla! What a squad!

Thank you, too, to the wider Bloomsbury team, Bea Cross, Sophie Rosewell and Danielle Rippengill – what a dream it has been to work with you all. Thank you to editor Catherine Coe for your invaluable early feedback and thank you to genius illustrator Sarah Madden; my cover is the most beautiful thing I've ever seen.

I have had so many people help shape the writer that I am. From CJ Skuse, my mentor who got this story off the start line, to Lucy Christopher, Steve Voake and Jo Nadin, our teachers on the Bath Spa MA in Writing for Young People. They taught me the power of writing authentically and generously for the next generations – and insisted I sort out my commas (thanks, Steve).

If you're a writer, make writer friends. My writing buddies have been constructive, kind and invaluable. Natalie Harrison, Megan Small, Rosie Brown, Dev Kothari, Leigh-Ann Hewer, Jay Joseph, and my writing wife, Ash Bond. Thank you all, and thank you to all the friends and family who have read drafts of this story and the stories that came before; I would have given up a long time ago without your support. (Especially Dad, who is still helping me with the whole commas thing.)

When I'm not writing I'll normally be found working in and around the theatre. This has shaped my work so significantly I need to say thank you to my theatre family, especially Emma Rice and everyone at Wise Children Theatre Company, who showed me both the value of creating joyful work and (hopefully) how to be a pleasant creative to work with. Truly, you can never overestimate the power of simply being kind.

Thank you to everyone who asked, 'How's the writing going?' even if they'd had to put up with my previous rambles about writing, especially Mum (my first fan), Ginny and Alice, who heard it ALL over lockdown, and *especially* my partner, Gareth, and our dog, Cocoa, who have been unwaveringly enthusiastic.

This is my love letter to the superhero genre. Thank you to all the writers of superhero stories, graphic novels, movies and TV shows for the joy and the inspiration.

And then there's you, dear reader. Thank you for picking up my story and thank you for making it to the end. Know your power.

Helen x

JENNA RAY

WILL

RETURN

JUNE 2025

Helen Comerford writes funny and fantastical tales, with diverse casts of characters, for children and young adults. She is fuelled by a love of all things super-powered, feminism and chocolate raisins. When she's not writing, you can find Helen hiking around the Welsh countryside with her dog, Cocoa. *The Love Interest* is her debut novel.

helencomerfordauthor.com